WORSE than WICKED

SELENA

Worse Than Wicked

Willow Heights Prep Academy: The Enemy

Book 2

Selena

SELENA

Worse Than Wicked
Copyright © 2025 Selena
Unabridged First Edition

All rights reserved. No part of this book may be reproduced or transmitted in any form or by any means, electronic or mechanical, including photocopying, recording, or by any information storage and retrieval system, without the express written permission of the publisher, except in cases of a reviewer quoting brief passages in a review.

This book is a work of fiction. Names, characters, places, and incidents are used fictitiously. Any resemblance to actual persons, living or dead, business establishments, and events are entirely coincidental. Use of any copyrighted, trademarked, or brand names in this work of fiction does not imply endorsement of that brand.

Published in the United States by Selena and Speak Now.

ISBN-13: 979-8-89237-084-4
Cover © Black Widow Designs

WORSE THAN WICKED

*For every reader who begged for the twins' story.
Be careful what you wish for.*

SELENA

WORSE THAN WICKED

author's note

This book is not a romance. It is a PITCH BLACK story of 3 villains playing a deadly game.
Along with the triggers you've seen throughout the series, mental health struggles feature prominently in this storyline, including addiction, drug use, and depression, with its accompanying horrors.
Not recommended for readers with ANY triggers.

SELENA

one

Duke Dolce

When people say, 'the world is your oyster,' does that mean that any day, we can find a pearl? I never quite got that expression. Maybe it means everyone is their own pearl. But for me, pearls aren't rare. The world is full of pearls.

They slide down the chute in a great, rattling, bouncing rush, a blue wave coming in like a tide, adding to the ocean below. The bin is almost full. I hold my hand under the waterfall of them, sink my fingers into the new, warm batch and down below, into the cold, smooth beads.

Even when I go home, they stay with me—the smell of them in my clothes, the buzz of them in my bloodstream. When I close my eyes, their iridescent shimmer coats my eyelids. When I lay down for another sleepless night, I can hear their rush like hungry flames, can feel the exact pressure it takes to turn the crank when they're done. I see the swirling liquid, bubbling and fuming, before it forms into the drug that has become my whole life.

SELENA

"Hey, Duke," says a voice behind me. Her small hand snakes onto my shoulder, and I turn and smile down at my girlfriend.

"Hey, yourself, Duchess," I say, gripping her waist and pulling her in for a kiss.

She stands on tiptoes, pressing her soft lips to mine.

For one moment, everything is perfect.

Then she pulls back with a grimace. "I thought I told you to wear your mask when you're doing this," she says, pulling the covering up over the bottom of my face. "I can taste it on you."

"It's not bad once you get used to it," I say. "I don't even smell it anymore."

"That's probably not a good thing," she says. "Neither is breathing it in all day. Hence, the mask."

I don't tell her that I breathed in the smoke when they burned once. That I watched the flames shoot up while my father lay facedown in a tray of pearls, and instead of rushing to save him, I turned and walked out.

Sometimes, I wonder if he woke up before he died. If he tried to get out, to crawl across the floor and out of the room before the flames consumed him, writhing in agony. Sometimes, I see him standing there, silently watching, ready to pounce on me for the slightest infraction, but when I blink, he's gone. Sometimes, I wake up to the sound of him screaming as we burned him alive.

Baron says it's not real because we never heard him scream, but he doesn't know. I hear it all the time, whether or not my ears ever did. He doesn't understand. He would have saved Dad. He believes what Dad always told us.

Dolce blood is thicker than chocolate, more toxic than the Lady Alice.

He didn't say the second part, but it's the truth. After all, he's just one of the dead we've left in our wake.

Dawson.

Dad.

The man who fucked Mabel.

Jane.

Less than five, still only a handful. I tell myself that to console myself, just like I only call her Jane, never her real name.

Blue.

Blue, like the blue pearls, the pearl lady, Lady Alice, Alice in Wonderland.

Mabel smiles, sensing my mood, and gestures to the machines. "Everything off?"

I hit the button to turn off the lights. "It is now, Duchess."

Her smile turns secretive, the one she keeps just for me. "Okay, Duke."

On the way out, I snag her hand, and she lets me.

She lets me hold it all the way to the car, where Baron is waiting.

Does she wish they were his fingers between hers, though? Does she pretend they are?

SELENA

She climbs into the passenger seat, and I slide into the back of Baron's Audi e-tron next to their two school bags. They spend all day together at college, and even though they don't have any classes together—Mabel is a junior now, Baron a freshman; Mabel is a forensic science major while Baron is focusing on neuroscience—they go to the same school and drive in together every day. Sometimes I wonder about the best part of Mabel's day. Is it the moment I get out of the car in the morning, when she knows her time alone with Baron begins? Or does she dread the moment they drop me off and she's at his mercy?

"How'd your final go?" Baron asks Mabel as we pull away from the unobtrusive building that houses our operation.

"Good," she says. "I'm pretty sure I got everything right except maybe two questions. I knew almost everything on it."

"You should," I mutter. "You sure studied enough."

Baron glances at me in the rearview. "Everything good in Wonderland?"

It's ironic that he named the location after the pearls people call Alice in Wonderland, a Baron Original Recipe that has half the college students in the country getting fucked up and fucking their brains out at parties. The building where he set it up is the furthest thing from a fairytale—a drab, nondescript red brick square with barred windows that looks abandoned but is owned by some non-existent shell company he set up online, so the city never bothers about it.

"Every day's a thrilling adventure filled with new delights," I say sarcastically.

"You know we couldn't do any of this without you, right?" he says, watching me in the mirror. "You're the backbone of the whole operation."

"A monkey could do my job," I point out.

"That's not true," Mabel says, twisting around in her seat. "Besides, if you weren't there, what would you be doing?"

She's right. I'd probably be passed out in a ditch somewhere. That's the best case scenario. There's no way I'd have gotten into a good school like she and Baron did. I have no skills, no prospects. Cooking drugs is probably the best place for me. At least then I get the product for free.

"Alice pays for all of this," Baron says as we pull up at our posh townhouse in the trendiest neighborhood in the city. "If you didn't work there, we wouldn't live here. You're paying for us to go to school, vacations, everything."

"You're our sugar daddy," Mabel says, squeezing my knee before turning to undo her seatbelt.

Baron gestures around at the place we chose for the three of us, a perfect fit for each of our needs. We can walk to local breweries, coffee roasteries, and cafés; record stores, art studios, bookstores, and vintage shops. Even Mabel could walk alone at night around here.

Not that we'd let her.

The neighborhood is safe, it's thriving, and it's pricey as fuck. Baron loves it.

I can't tell if Mabel does or if she just appeases him by agreeing.

We climb out of the car and head inside. Unlike Baron's last place, there's no padded basement with torture devices and a starving girl. The place is light and airy, modern and elegantly decorated. The only girl here is Mabel.

I watch her hang her backpack and slip off her shoes. Since the day Baron made her break her toes, she's only run once. Of course it was when I was supposed to be watching her, so Baron got pissed at me. Since then, I've watched her more carefully. I don't like letting her out of my sight, not even when she's with him. She's slippery, unpredictable. Every time I wake up and she's not in the bed, I start to panic, worrying that she's out with another man again, that Baron will kill him again. That this time, we'll be caught.

Maybe she wants that. Now that she knows what he'll do, she could set him up.

"Are you excited about our trip?" she asks when she sees me watching her.

"No," I say, scowling. "Why would I want to go somewhere cold as fuck and not see anyone for the holidays?"

"It's not much colder than New York," Baron points out.

"New York had parties and fun shit to do."

"And Havoc Harbor has us," Mabel says, coming over to wrap her arms around my neck. "It'll be fun. Just the three of us. No homework, no studying, no school or work."

"I still don't see why we can't go home," I say. "Your family knows where you are. Our family knows where you are. You're not hiding anymore."

"Because I tried to kill Royal's girlfriend," Baron says from the table, where he's set down his bag and is petting Seeley Boots, who isn't supposed to get on the table but likes to lie there when we're not around.

"You went back for graduation," I point out.

He exchanges a look with Mabel, and I wonder if they've talked about this, and if it's me they're worried about returning to Faulkner, not Baron.

"What?" I demand.

"I'll talk to Royal," Baron promises.

"I'm going to take a shower," I say, and I stomp off to the pretty, tiled bathroom with the skylight and the fancy soaps that Mabel likes. I thought once we got Mabel, everything would be fixed, that it would all be good again, but it's not. I'm not even sure when it stopped being good. I thought it was when she left, but maybe it wasn't her at all.

Sometimes I wonder if I even know her at all. Or Baron.

SELENA

Or myself.

The problem of her being gone is gone, but there are new problems now. Like how I'm never quite sure if she slipped away while I was watching her just because it was easier, or because she knew Baron would be pissed at me, and she wanted that. Maybe she even wanted him to kill me. I don't think he would. But maybe someday I'll fuck up enough that he realizes he doesn't need me.

That *they* don't need me.

Before I drop my jeans, I remove my wallet, then slide a hand in the front pocket. I finger the smooth little bead, debating whether to take another one before bed. It will keep me up all night, but then, I never sleep well anyway. Too many monsters lurk there.

I already took one today, watched porn on my phone between batches, jerked off until my dick was sore. I have one here, though, and I'm already itching for it, so I swallow it dry, letting that bitter chemical burn spread from the back of my throat, seeping over my tongue as I shower.

I jerk off again, using plenty of cream rinse so I don't chafe. I picture Mabel, tied to the bed when Baron hunted her down, about what we did to her. I think about Harper, tied to the tree, what we did to her. I think about Mabel tied to the bed another time, what we all did to her, my brothers and me, one after another, one-two-three-four, the train we ran, and how we left her there, and Dad found her.

When I'm done, I get out of the shower and towel off. I hear Baron and Mabel talking in the other room. They're probably talking about me. That's if they even remember I'm here, if they care. They could be plotting, though I'm not sure what. It's a dumb thought anyway. I've been spending too much time in Wonderland—both the place where it's made and the place it takes me—and it's making me paranoid.

They're not plotting. They're not trying to get rid of me. I'm part of the family, equally important to both of them, just like they always say. Besides, the killings here have stopped since we all moved in together, so I know they're not luring some man to his death. If one of them was the Black Widow Killer, they've stopped now. That has to mean something. If I'm not contributing to our relationship, at least I'm contributing to society. I'm saving lives by being here, making sure they don't take any more.

Hell, I'm practically a superhero.

The thought knocks me back to that night in the woods, and I stumble against the counter, catching it so I don't fall. I'm too high to feel any pain, but I don't want to draw their attention. When I leave the bathroom, they've fallen silent, but that's not unusual. Baron and Mabel don't make much small talk. They'd rather talk to exchange information. I'm the one Mabel talks to about the little things. Baron thinks they don't matter, but they do.

SELENA

In the bedroom, I fall facedown onto the bed, then roll over and stare at the ceiling. I want a cigarette, but I told them I quit. They don't know what I do after they drop me off in the morning and go off together. That I get the first batch started, and then I go out back and sit on one of the cinderblocks grown over with grass, and light the day's first cigarette, and think about him.

About what I would say if I saw him again, how I'd make fun of his failure to launch—not only did he have to repeat his senior year, but now he's kicking around the same town, with no job, no plans, probably still going to high school parties like some creep.

I could text him, taunt him, but I never do.

If I did, he might make fun of me too, point out all my failures, all the things I already know and think about way too fucking often.

I pick up my phone and scroll for a minute, checking to see if Harper or Royal have posted. They haven't. No one in my family is big on social media, but I was hoping maybe there would be an update. I'm too much of a pussy to text and ask. She'll probably tell me to fuck off, that I don't deserve to know about Olive after I bashed her head in. And she's right.

Baron's not the only reason we're not going home for Christmas.

I hear Mabel murmuring in the kitchen. I toss my phone aside, consider telling her to come suck me off, but I don't have it in me to sweet talk her, so I just jerk it for a few minutes. Even that's too much effort though.

WORSE THAN WICKED

The Alice is coursing through me, and I'm horny as hell, but I'm already wrung out.

I pick up my phone again, meaning to find some porn, but I see a message from my sister on the screen.

UnsweetDolce: I can't believe you're not coming home for Christmas!
DukeOfBeavertown: I cant believe u call Arkansas home now
DukeOfBeavertown: or that u hvnt changed ur name
UnsweetDolce: I changed my name just not on here. All my msgs are here.
DukeOfBeavertown: so wsp? Pop out any new kids lately?
UnsweetDolce: haha
DukeOfBeavertown: srsly have u?
UnsweetDolce: no asshole
DukeOfBeavertown: babies actually come out of a different hole
DukeOfBeavertown: I kno dad thot u were his sweet little girl so he never had the talk w u but in case you don't know about the birds n the bees...
UnsweetDolce: v funny
DukeOfBeavertown: ig u discovered a lil thing called birth control then. Can't believe u made it a whole yr w-o making another bby. Must b some kind of record.
UnsweetDolce: on 2nd thot, glad ur not coming home
DukeOfBeavertown: r royal n them there?
UnsweetDolce: just got here yesterday. U left yet?

SELENA

DukeOfBeavertown: 2mro
DukeOfBeavertown: Olive ok?

I sit there, my heart hammering, feeling like such an NPC for being worried what Crystal will think. But she doesn't hate me like Harper does. She's the one I talk to the most, the only person I really talk to besides Baron and Mabel.

UnsweetDolce: yeah she's funny. I can c y u liked her sm
DukeOfBeavertown: wdym
UnsweetDolce: she told some kid at school she knows santa isn't real bc he never gives her what she wants. The kid told her that's bc she wasn't good. Olive punched her in the nose lol
DukeOfBeavertown: hell yeah gd 4 her
UnsweetDolce: Royal told her u cant ask Santa 4 ppl bc they have free will, n she said free stuff is lame, good stuff costs a lot like a Bugatti lmfao
DukeOfBeavertown: she has a point
UnsweetDolce: yeah she said u cant even get a car for free if its broke down and not running. Now Harper's trying to explain the concept of free will to her
DukeOfBeavertown: lmk how it goes
UnsweetDolce: I will. I wish u were coming home i miss u
DukeOfBeavertown: me too kid
UnsweetDolce: bruhhh I'm ur big sister

WORSE THAN WICKED

DukeOfBeavertown: gg but tell her I said sloths r still cuter
UnsweetDolce: ???
DukeOfBeavertown: she'll know
UnsweetDolce: kk drive safe 2m

I throw my phone off the bed and roll over, pressing my face into the pillow. I didn't have to go. I have no one here to talk to. I just couldn't bear it another minute, thinking about them there, picturing them all together in the living room with the fireplace and the gigantic tree, sitting on the couches and the thick rugs, casual and comfortable and cozy, laughing at Olive's antics and being a family. I want that.

"Mabel!" I yell. I have to call a few more times before she appears in the doorway.

She hovers there, watching me warily, her gaze moving from my dick standing up to my face and back. "Why are you hiding in here?"

"Why haven't you gotten pregnant yet?" I ask. "It's been six months."

"Maybe because I need to finish school first?"

"Are you on birth control?" I demand, sitting up.

"No," she protests.

I jump up and grab her by the shoulders. "Do you have an IUD?"

"No," she says, trying to twist away. I drag her to the bed and wrestle her clothes open, shoving my fingers into her as deep as I can reach, feeling for it. She winces, but she doesn't protest. She knows her purpose.

"Then why haven't you given us a baby?" I ask, spitting on my hand and slicking it over my cock as I loom over her. "My sister pops one out every time she even sees your brother's dick."

"Stop," Mabel protests, trying to push me off. "I can't."

"You can, and you fucking will," I say, jamming my dick into her. "You said we'd be a family. Why don't you want to? Are you trying to have Baron's baby instead? There's no difference. Our DNA is identical. A baby of mine is as much him as it's me."

"Duke…" She struggles, but I finish anyway. When I'm done, I roll us over on the bed, keeping myself buried inside her.

That's when I see Baron standing in the doorway, watching.

"Join, if you want to," I say. "She was probably thinking about you the whole time anyway."

Baron strides across the room, grabs the back of Mabel's neck, and pulls her up. She blinks at me from behind the strands of blonde hair sticking to her tearstained cheeks.

"Tell him that's not true," Baron says.

"It's not," she whispers.

"Tell him you love him," Baron orders.

She stares at me a long second. "I hate you."

"Wrong fucking answer," he says, shoving her head away. It smacks into my chest, and she whimpers, but he doesn't care. He's already undone his belt, and he crawls onto the bed, straddling my legs, and shoves into her ass. She lets out a squeal of pain. He rams in deeper, ignoring her cries of pain.

"You knew what would happen," Baron growls at her, stabbing into her ass. "You wanted this punishment."

She doesn't protest, just lets out a shuddering sigh. I can feel him moving inside her, his cock tearing into her, filling her. It makes me hard all over again, and I push her shoulders down, impaling her deeper onto him.

"Let me up," I say. "I want to make her cum."

Baron grabs her hair and drags her up until she's kneeling on the bed in front of him, her face a twisted mask of pain. He grips her hair in his fist, holding it near his shoulder while he thrusts into her. Her little tits bounce, and I kneel up, sucking one nipple into my mouth and then the other, burying my fingers in her cunt. She's hot and flooded with my release, and I fuck it into her for a minute with two fingers before I slide down the bed, between her legs and Barons, until I can grip her thighs and lift my mouth to her dripping cunt. I lick from her salty hole to her clit, circling the little nub with the tip of my tongue.

Her body shudders against me, and Baron thrusts harder, cramming her against my mouth. I suck, and she bucks, her thighs quaking. I close my eyes and drink her in, the taste of her like nothing else, like the home I no longer have. It's here, in her, in Baron, in the smell and taste of us together, the feel of him driving her cunt against my mouth, her smooth skin against my lips, her choked sobs and hot tears.

I slide my fingers into her again, and Baron pumps harder, and she cries out in torment, but I feel her walls clench when we both pump into her at once, my mouth sealed to her clit, my brother's cock wrecking her until she gasps with pain, begs for relief. Baron shows no mercy, and neither do I. I lick and suck and thrust until she shatters in my mouth, against her will, the orgasm dragged unwillingly from her body that always admits what her mouth can't.

When Baron's done, he drops her forward onto the bed, tucks himself away, and leaves the room, leaving us alone together. Mabel is shaking with quiet tremors and soft, moaning sobs. I slide out from under her and crawl over her back, laying myself like a blanket over her. I kiss her salty cheek while I ease inside her stretched hole to add my seed to Baron's. She's already loose and dripping with his cum, so I know it doesn't hurt too much, even though she cries and pretends that it does.

two

Mabel Darling

"Happy six months, Duchess," Duke says, holding up his glass of champagne. Baron lifts his, and I follow suit. I don't like drinking, though I've done it with them before. Sometimes I still think about the first time, in that magical cave Baron made for me when he was courting me, before I knew his intentions, when I told him my darkest secret.

Or maybe it wasn't my darkest secret, but my grandfather's. Maybe my deepest secret was the one I never told him.

Dahlia.

"Our little monster," Baron says, smiling at me, his eyes warm behind his glasses. "Who would have guessed we'd end up like this?"

"It's impossible to know that without knowing the predictions of everyone who's ever seen us together," I point out. "And most made those predictions without conscious thought."

"How right you are." Baron lays his hand over mine, and I force myself not to flinch.

SELENA

I've trained myself not to react to their touch the same way they trained me to tolerate it against my will. That doesn't mean I enjoy it. It means I don't want to give them the satisfaction of seeing my discomfort. Baron likes it too much, and Duke finds it too amusing. It is fuel to both, like the gasoline we poured along Devlin's back wall before we lit the match, watching it all go up in flame. We danced on the lawn until the firetrucks came, Duke spinning me around until I laughed, something that surprised us both.

He's the only one who's ever done that. Even Baron only engages my intellect. Duke brings me to a higher level, reminding me that my body is not simply a container for my brain, but a thing with its own sizzling sparks. Sometimes I regret that he'll pay for his crimes just like Baron will.

Then I remind myself that he committed those crimes willingly, gleefully.

"What's your favorite thing we've done so far?" Duke asks me, draining his glass.

Baron frowns at him.

Duke ignores it and refills his glass from the bottle.

"Mine was all the fucking," he says, offering me a grin and reaching over to squeeze my knee under the table. "Oh, and eating your pussy."

"Speaking of," I say. "Should we get an order of caviar for Seeley?"

"Anything you want," Baron says. "Now answer his question."

I think it over while the white-gloved waiter brings our food and sets it before us, China plates with tiny sprigs of watercress and a pinch of tender leaves and delicately shaved vegetables curling up from the center, a drizzle of dressing spiraling outwards from it.

"You can be honest," Duke says. "No one will overhear. Baron rented the whole room, so we don't have to worry about being disturbed."

He wiggles his brows and drains his glass again before picking up his salad fork. The waiter has disappeared, leaving us alone on the top floor of the restaurant, under the rafters wound with vines, the room lit only by the flickering candles in the center of each tablecloth. It's simple and minimal and elegant, like the food. Like Baron.

"I liked decorating our house with you," I say, searching for the answers that will please both men. "And I like our weekly date nights."

"But which one was your favorite?" Duke presses. "Sailing? The Halloween party? Painting with a Twist?"

I shake my head, finishing the bite of salad before answering. "I was better at trivia night."

"I didn't ask what you were best at."

"I like doing things that play to my strengths."

"Understandable," Baron says, and I can tell he approves of my answer, even if Duke doesn't. I hope that later, Duke will remember that the first thing I mentioned was something we did together, just the two of us. Baron had no interest in making our house feel like home or look beautiful—like me, he likes doing what highlights his brilliance, not his weak points.

Duke eats a few bites of salad and then pushes his plate away. "We need more champagne."

"I think we're okay," I say, touching his hand. "It's dinner, Duke. Not a party."

"I know that," he snaps, then drags his plate back and shoves the entire last forkful of salad into his mouth, making a big show of cramming it all in at once and chewing with his mouth open like the rude boy he pretends to be. I know better, though. He grew up like me, eating meals where the presentation was more important than the food itself, where knowing which utensil to use was as essential as waiting to be excused or answering the obligatory questions guests lobbed our way, though they had no actual interest in the answers. Embarrassing our parents was not an option.

Duke makes up for it now, but I know he's faking. That he's the fakest of us all.

Maybe he's the one playing both me and Baron. Or maybe he and Baron are still playing me, playing the long game, and they'll flip a switch as quickly as they did the last time.

But they don't know that I'm playing the long game too. That I don't care which boy is which. It doesn't matter. That's why I didn't care that, when we moved in together, they burned the same scar into Baron that Duke has. They had some excuses that made it seem like it was for us, even for me, but I know it was so that they'd be indistinguishable to me once again. That's when I knew they were still trying to outmaneuver me, and when I decided that despite his superior ability to elicit sympathy, Duke truly is just as cruel as Baron.

"Happy now?" Duke asks, snagging my glass and downing my champagne before offering me a cheeky grin.

I don't have a chance to answer, because the waiter is there to clear our plates and replace them with larger ones, our bite-sized entrees plated in the center of each, careful not to smear the elegant swirls of sauce that ring the very edge.

"Bring us another bottle," Duke says, lifting the empty one.

The waiter nods and whisks it away with our salad plates.

"Are you excited to be going back to Maine?" Baron asks.

I'm touched by his attempt at small talk, obligatory as it may be.

"No," I say. "It's just a place."

"Then why aren't we going back to Faulkner?" Duke asks. "Our families are there."

Baron sighs. "You know why."

"I'd think you'd want to go," Duke says to me. "You've been gone for years. Your family is probably dying to see you."

"I talk to them online," I say lightly. "My brother's back in rehab, and my stepmother doesn't know who I am."

"Colt's in rehab?" Duke asks, snorting with laughter. "What a pussy."

I eye the bottle of champagne the waiter brings, but I would no more embarrass Duke in front of him than I'd embarrass my parents by mispronouncing *foie gras* in front of the mayor.

"Do you feel bad about leaving your dad alone on Christmas?" Baron asks.

I know he's gauging my level of coldness more than casting judgment.

"No," I say. "He's having dinner with the family."

"I'm sure that'll be fun," Duke says. "Hanging out with the ex-wife he cheated on and his brother who married her. Hey, maybe they'll both bang her at once. Just like us."

He holds up a hand to high-five Baron, but Baron only frowns at him.

Duke laughs again, too loud, intentionally obnoxious. He knows I hate that I will never know if the rumors were true. That I only have their word, and they like to goad me to get a reaction. They probably never touched my mother. But there were rumors that they didn't just target the Darling men. That they tormented them by going after their wives too. I've seen it with my own eyes, when they attacked my aunt. But I like to believe that if anyone hurt my mother, it was their brothers, not them.

"You don't miss them?" Baron presses me.

"I see my aunt every summer," I say. "And my cousins, when they come to visit her."

Baron just shakes his head. I know he's impressed, though. He thinks I'm heartless, but he likes it.

"You don't miss Colt, though," Duke says. "Too fucking funny. Can't blame you there."

"Why's that funny?" I ask.

"Because you always acted like you liked him," he reminds me. "Now you don't give a fuck. Savage. I love it."

"I care," I protest, even though it will lose points with Baron. "I just wouldn't see him if I went home. I wasn't going to endanger either of us by contacting him before you found me."

"Before you knew we'd found you," Baron corrects. "We knew where you were for a long time."

I nod and pop a slice of duck into my mouth, chewing as I absorb his words. I knew that already, though I'm not sure how long he was watching. Some part of me always thought he was, from the very beginning. I was waiting for them all along, always knowing they'd come, long before they showed up in New England.

"When you disappeared," Baron says, slicing his meat while he speaks. "Why'd you choose that name?"

"What name?"

SELENA

My heart stops, and I try to swallow. I can't explain to Baron, but I can't avoid the question, either. If I try, he'll immediately see it, and he'll know that it's something I'm trying to hide. Once he gets suspicious, he'll start digging. I don't want that. I don't want to tell him how simple it is, either. He'll be disappointed. He won't understand that at the time, it was an easy choice. If I was going to be someone else, I wanted to be Dahlia. She was the only secret I kept from him, the only one I had left. And now, I have to give her up.

Baron arches a brow at me like I'm being intentionally obtuse instead of stalling for time. "Dahlia Suskind."

"The last name is from a book I like," I say. "The first name was... An imaginary friend."

We are sorry to inform you, we have no record of a student by that name...

"An imaginary friend?" Baron asks incredulously, his brows rising even higher. He shares a glance with Duke, who's not laughing, to my surprise.

I'm not crazy, I remind myself.

"Yes," I say, picking up my glass and taking a gulp of water to wash down the sawdust in my throat. "But then, you already know that, don't you?"

He exchanges another look with Duke.

I only ever mentioned her to him once, in passing, when I was talking about the founding families in our town. I didn't tell him we were friends. He had no reason to think she was any different than DeShaun Rose or

Cotton Montgomery or any other founding heir. She didn't want to be shared, so I never told him or Duke or anyone outside my family. My family that worried and threatened and hid her away until I knew not to speak her name ever again. But I spoke it inside my mind, whispered it like a prayer in my darkest moments.

"If you're talking about Dahlia Delacroix, I don't know much about her at all," Baron says.

I narrow my eyes at him. "Wasn't that part of your plot to make me crazy?"

He frowns. "No."

"It didn't work, anyway," I say. "I'm not crazy, and I'll never let you make me think I am again."

"We're not trying to."

I don't believe him, but when he asks about her again, I know he won't let it go.

So I shrug like it means nothing, like it's not a betrayal.

"We were friends when I was a kid," I say. "I thought she was real, but I guess I made it up. I don't really know. It was a long time ago, and I don't have a memory like yours. I remember us being friends, but we weren't."

"Why do you think that?" Baron asks, cocking his head.

"I used to write letters to her, at the boarding school where she went," I say. "But my parents didn't like it. They'd always act concerned, I think because she didn't exist, or our friendship didn't. They'd never talk about her, and when I did, they acted all weird. They told me it was best to leave her behind. They sent me to therapy when I kept bringing her up. And when I was older, I sent her a letter, and the boarding school wrote back saying she didn't exist. Unless you wrote that letter."

My heart hammers as I wait for a response.

Duke shakes his head. "We didn't write any letter. We don't even know about this chick. Right?"

He looks at his brother. Baron nods in agreement.

They may not know much about her, but she knew, far before I'd so much as guessed, that Baron would destroy me. She remained hidden in the dark forest of my subconscious like intuition, whispering from the shadows for me to be careful, that we can't trust anyone. She wrapped her chubby child-fist around my spine and tugged, filling me with unease, planting the tiniest seed of caution, like the poison mushroom she slipped between the priest's lips, silencing him forever.

"Okay, so she left that school, or the Delacroixs didn't tell you where they really sent her," Baron says. "That doesn't mean you imagined her. She's in their family tree."

"Is she?" I ask, my throat suddenly tight. "Did you check, or did you just believe me when I told you she was one of their kids?"

"Of course I checked," he says, his dark eyes earnest behind his glasses. "Mabel, you didn't make up a person. I did extensive research on every founding family in Faulkner. She's one of our lawyer's kids. She's not imaginary."

She's real.

My heart pounds erratically. They made me think I was crazy, but it was the other things, the things they didn't do, that solidified it. If it hadn't been for that letter, for the way my family acted when I told them I wanted to contact her again, I might have held onto the thread of my sanity. I would have known the Dolces were trying to destroy me. When all of their torture caught up with me, I would have had a lifeline to reality. When I lost Dahlia, that's when I realized it wasn't just these boys trying to drive me mad. It was my own mind slipping away, already lost.

I spent three years thinking it was all in my head, that she was.

Is this real? Or one more ploy, one more building block in their next, elaborate scheme?

"Were we really friends?" I whisper. "Or did I make that up?"

"I'm not sure about that," Baron says. "Obviously, it's harder to find anything on little kids. No social media, not many school or hospital records. The regular extracurriculars for that age, music and dance and gymnastics and swim. A couple of those pageants that southerners still do."

"Oh yeah," I say, smiling at the memory. "Another Delacroix tradition that ended with her."

Baron takes in this information without the judgment most show for the child pageant scene, his eyes serene behind his glasses. "She moved away, so I didn't think she was important. But I'm sure we can find out."

I shake my head. "I don't know. Maybe it's not a good idea."

"Why?" Duke asks.

I shrug, avoiding his eyes. "If she wasn't real, then I could be her. I could use her name because she wasn't using it."

"She doesn't own that name."

"But she does."

They both stare at me, and for once, I find myself wanting to talk. I don't know if it's the glass of champagne I drank, or the dim candlelight that makes it seem unreal, like the fairytale in that cave when Baron gave me wine the first time, and we tangled our legs together and he told me his secrets too—that he thought he was a sociopath, and maybe he knew what made him one.

Or maybe it's the way Duke is looking at me, his dark eyes filled with sympathy, the gold flecks like fireflies on a summer night; sparks spiraling into the black velvet blanket of sky that time we burned Devlin's house, when I learned what *fun* felt like for the first time.

Or maybe it's just the way Baron's face betrays the slightest shade of skepticism, like he thinks I'm the one making it up to play them.

"She wasn't like the other women in our families," I say. "The ones who did what they were supposed to do, who were quiet and obedient and soft. That's what Darling girls are supposed to be. And Delacroix girls too."

"I don't think girls in your family are any of those things," Duke points out. "Have you met your cousins? Or yourself?"

"It's what we're supposed to be," I say. "What people are supposed to think we are. But Dahlia wasn't like that. She wasn't afraid of anything. I remember the adults saying it was because of her mom, some outsider who worked her way in and captured a coveted Delacroix husband."

"You heard people talk about her, but you thought you made her up?" Duke asks.

"I guess... I thought I made that up too," I admit. "You don't know what it was like. You made me question everything. Not just you. Myself. Reality."

A tear slips down my cheek, and I angrily brush it away. They don't deserve to see my tears. Not when they caused them. Not when they're probably doing it again right now, telling me what I want to hear like they did at the start, making me believe because I want so desperately for it to be true—for someone to see all those same things that everyone always said made me a freak, and to think they make me special instead. To not scorn and shun me, or tolerate me for a time before realizing I'm not worth it and leaving me behind. To love me.

And when I've let my guard down, when I love them so completely, so stupidly, that I don't listen to the few people who want to help, then they'll take it all away.

Their love. Their lies.

My delusions that I could be loved, that I could be part of something, that I could be a normal girl with a family, with a career and a husband and kids and all the things I never knew I wanted because I never thought they were an option.

I will never fall for it again. I know those things are not options for me.

If they were before, they're not anymore.

The Dolces took that away like they took my sanity. I got that back on my own, and I won't let them destroy it again. I won't believe a word that comes out of their mouths, no matter how much I want to. What does it matter if Dahlia is real, anyway?

She's real to me. Maybe she was a part of me, the part that dared to fight back, to do things that sweet, quiet, bland Mabel Darling was never allowed to do. And when I took her name, I did those things too. For a while, I was Dahlia, and I made men pay.

Not anymore.

The Dolces took that away too.

It was too risky, they said. The FBI might connect it to me, after that man in Maine disappeared. The FBI might connect it to them, and then they'd discover the Alice in Wonderland operation, and we couldn't have that. I risked it all every time I met a man online, but they risk nothing. They let me risk nothing. They keep me safe, like Baron always says. They are here to protect me, like Duke always says.

Because sweet, bland, quiet Mabel Darling needs protection. She needs safety. She is a treasure, one who adorns their arms like a jewel, admired by all. She remembers her manners and doesn't make scenes.

Dahlia made scenes.

Dahlia didn't walk demurely to the restroom in a fancy French restaurant and let a man defile her because that's what he wants and it's his anniversary too. Dahlia didn't tolerate it without complaint, then walk back to the table like nothing happened.

They didn't want Dahlia, though, so that's not who I am anymore. I'm Mabel Darling. Just like they wanted.

They are men, after all, and Mabel Darling was always good at being exactly what men wanted her to be.

So why, after they took Dahlia away from me, are they trying to give her back?

SELENA

three

Baron Dolce

"This is hella nice," Duke says, looking around as we set our stuff down inside the Cape Cod style house. "It looks small from the outside, but you didn't skimp on materials, did you?"

"Why would I?" Mabel asks, unlocking the cat carrier and opening the door. "Just because I couldn't have insurance cover it, that doesn't mean I want it to be cheap."

Boots stalks out, waving his tail in irritation, ignores Mabel, and jumps down to walk away. He stops in the doorway to the hall, ears flicking, and looks up and down.

"The builders didn't clean up very well," Duke says, picking up an empty, clear plastic cup from the sink. Half a dozen more are cluttered there, takeout iced-coffee cups with the local coffee shop's logo printed on the side.

"I guess I forgot to have them buy a trash can," Mabel says, going to the cabinet under the sink. She opens a box of trash bags and shakes one out, holding it open while Duke drops the cups in.

"Wait."

Duke stops, the last cup hovering in midair, waiting for my inspection.

"There's lipstick on the straw," I point out.

"So?" Mabel asks.

I narrow my eyes at her. "Was your aunt here?"

"I had someone come in and furnish the place," she says. "They left their cups, that's all."

"Who?" I ask, scowling at her.

She shrugs, looking into the bag when Duke drops the last cup. She ties it without looking at me, then starts for the front door.

"It was that pink-haired bitch from the ice cream shop," I say. "Wasn't it?"

"I don't know that many people around here," she says, letting the screen door bang shut behind her. I don't know why it irritates me, that she's still in contact with the coworker we met last summer. I could go through her phone and see all their correspondences if I wanted. I check her phone sometimes. I like to know what she's looking at, who she's talking to. And sometimes I do it just because I can.

"Who cares?" Duke says. "It's a chick. She's not fucking her, and even if she did before, so what? She fucked those men too. It's in the past. Let's go check out the rest of the house."

He goes to the French doors, sliding them open to step out onto the deck. Icy December air barrels into the room, and he steps back in quickly. "Damn. That's brutal."

None of us have seen the new house she had built while we were in Tennessee, so we go to explore the other rooms. After Duke burned down her aunt's house, Mabel couldn't file an insurance claim without the risk of them finding out it was arson, or worse, going through it and finding evidence of the murder I committed there.

My first kill.

The first one that was entirely on my hands. I let myself savor the moment in my mind often—the sensation of the knife sawing through his throat, the gush of warm blood. I only wish I'd seen his face when I did it. Still, the power I took from him remains. It's faded now, but the dissatisfaction of not seeing the light disappear from his eyes lingers. I want to try again, but I haven't let myself indulge. The risk is too great.

Who would I kill, anyway?

"Looks like she made herself at home in here too," Duke says, gesturing to the California king in the master bedroom. It's made up and ready for us—or someone else. The two guest rooms have furniture, but the beds haven't been made. Mabel didn't have her set up everything or decorate. It's supposed to be furnished, nothing more.

SELENA

I decide to look into the girl more after all. I didn't bother with her after we left last summer. It didn't affect us anymore. We were back in Tennessee, and everything that happened here was behind us, including a random coworker with no social media to speak of.

Or so I thought.

Maybe I can finally see the light fade from someone's eyes after all. Once I satisfy the craving, exactly as I want it, it'll go away. The thrill will last me a lifetime. It won't be like the man I killed in the house that used to stand here, or the one who stepped off a bridge. I still remember the way the wooden beams underfoot shuddered when he hit the end of the rope. The look of terror and surrender in his eyes when Royal ordered him to jump. That brought me higher than if I'd pushed him. But I shared that kill with my brothers.

Jane was mine alone. The closest I've come to the kill I wanted. In the dark, though, I couldn't see her eyes as the light faded, as she struggled to draw her last breath before it gave out. I left her in her shallow grave before I had time to really savor my victory, my triumph, because I saw that Mabel wasn't at home, that her location wasn't where it should have been, where I told her to stay.

Next time, I'll get it right, do it perfectly, with more precision and leisure. I want time to revel in my kill, not to do it in a moment of passion, without a plan to dispose of the body or enjoy it while it's happening. Each kill was purposeful, intentional, and none were mistakes. But they were practice for the next one, the one I crave, the perfect crime.

Ingrid Wells.

She could be exactly what I need.

Later, after dinner, I hook up my computer and set up everything I need. While Mabel and Duke go to the store to stock up on supplies for the week, I start digging. By the time I hear them return, it's later than I expected. I lost track of time, and I'm impatient to talk to Mabel. I head into the kitchen to meet them.

"What took you so long?" I demand, my gaze moving from one to the other.

"We took a little drive up the coast," Duke says with a shrug, like I wasn't here waiting for them.

"To where?" I ask, narrowing my eyes at him.

"Nowhere special," he says. "Just to see the moon on the water."

"I got you those breakfast drinks you like, just in case," Mabel says, holding up a 4-pack. "I wasn't sure if you'd want real food over the break."

"Those are real food," I point out. "It's complete nutrition in a can."

"I'm sure that's what they tell all the old men in the nursing home," Duke says, holding up a box of cereal that's completely devoid of all nutrition. "But lucky for you, I also snagged this, so you can eat solid food like a big boy."

"That's for kids," I point out. "And it's nothing but sugar and dye."

"You forgot about the artificial flavor," he says, grinning. "That's the best part."

"I got eggs and toast," Mabel says. "I'll make everyone a real breakfast in the morning. Or we can eat in town. The coffee shop has a bakery."

"The one where those cups came from," I say, studying Mabel for a reaction.

"It's the only one in town," she says. "Havoc Harbor's not big enough for a Dunkin."

"Does Ingrid work there?" I ask.

"No, I don't think so," Mabel says, turning away after putting up a box of cereal bars. "Why?"

"How much do you know about her?" I ask, leaning back against the counter and crossing my arms.

"I don't know," Mabel says. "A little?"

I narrow my eyes. "How much?"

She sighs. "Not that much, okay? We worked together in the summers. Then I go back to Tennessee. The ice cream shop closes in the winter. I don't know what she does then."

"Does she live here all year?"

"As far as I know," she says. "Why?"

I think about telling her what I found, but I want to research a little further, and I'm not sure if she's lying to me. Mabel didn't used to lie, so one might think she'd be a bad liar, but the opposite is true. She's learned deceit, but I haven't learned her tells, which irritates me. I should know everything about her by now, but I still can't find anything to indicate when she's not being truthful. I need to find out more about Ingrid before I confront her with what I know.

"There's not much online about her," I say, opting for my own partial truth. "I'm just trying to fill in the gaps."

"I don't know why it's important, but okay," Mabel says. "If she lives around here, she might just do odd jobs in the off-season, like furnishing the house."

"We'll see," I say, turning and going back to the room I set up to work from.

It's too cold for them to hang out on the balcony, so they settle in together in the den. I like being able to overhear, even if I don't join them. They make popcorn and watch *Dexter,* and then I hear the glass door of the shower slide open and shut. They fuck, their bodies bumping and sliding against the wall, squeaking on the shower floor. I think about joining, but Duke needs more one-on-one attention than I do, so I let them have their time together. It's important that we all get what we need, not just what we want.

When they're done, I hear Mabel calling for Seeley Boots to show him where she put his litter box and food. A few minutes later, she comes in wearing a fluffy new bathrobe and slippers.

"Where are you going?" she asks when she sees me in my coat.

I lean in to plant a kiss on her damp, warm forehead. "I'll be back by morning."

"Where are you going?" she asks again.

"Out for a drive," I say. "Like you."

She hesitates like she might offer further explanation than they did earlier, but then she nods, her lips tightening. "Be careful," she says. "Goodnight."

A minute later, I'm sliding into Duke's new Lexus LX. Like Mabel, he gets attached to things, and he didn't want to give up the old Hummer he'd been driving for years, even when I pointed out that Mabel had gotten a new car and I'd upgraded every year since then. Finally I bought him this for Christmas so he couldn't drag his feet and make excuses anymore. Of course, the moment he got in and turned it on, he had to admit it's a huge upgrade.

He deserves it, operating Wonderland the way he does. He deserves more than all the luxuries money can buy, even if he won't get them for himself. I wanted him to know that, to believe the words I always tell him, that he's indispensable. The comfort and status of this car are only small indicators of how much we value him. As the head of our little family, it's my job to make him feel important, even when I don't understand why he doesn't.

I think about that as I drive up the coast, following the road along the edge of the cliffs. When I see the little pull-off where we parked the night I killed Jane, I turn into it and cut the engine. My heart is beating slow and steady, but it feels heavy in my chest, each beat like the thud of an approaching footfall. At last, I climb out and stand in the biting wind, listening for the sound of an engine over the shriek.

Nothing.

I hurry across the road and into the woods, not slowing until I've made my way deep enough into the pines that if a car passes, they won't see me, even if they're looking. In the dark, I blend with the trunks. The deciduous trees are bare this time of year, but the pine boughs cast shadows on the carpeted floor beneath, helping conceal me. I don't need a tracker to remember where I left Jane. I removed it before I left her, anyway, cutting it quickly from her arm when I pulled Duke's shirt off her and checked her slowing pulse before I walked away.

I knew I wouldn't need any help finding her. My memory is impeccable. And even though I'd ensured that her tracking device paired only with my phone, I couldn't be sure that it wouldn't malfunction when I was far away, unable to intervene if something went wrong. Even if her tracker did become discoverable, though, no one would find her because no one would look. No one ever filed a missing persons report. She has no family to wonder where she went. There is only Olive, and she doesn't know what happened to her sister, and she never will.

Jane is lucky I kept her so long, paid her all that attention girls want so much. If it weren't for me, no one would have even known she existed all those months. She would have lived on the street, selling her body and becoming a junkie until one day, she died in some alley and was tossed into the nearest dumpster like the trash she was. A girl like her has no future. She would have contributed nothing of value to the world, left no mark when she was gone.

I gave her a purpose. One might even say she taught me things about human endurance that I wouldn't have otherwise learned—at least not with firsthand experience and observation. I let her die with a legacy: informing one of the world's most brilliant minds. When I leave my mark on the world, in some small way I've let her be part of it, even long after she's gone.

As I make my way to the place where I left her, I try to picture what she'll look like now, what's left of her. Though I like studying the human body, I haven't studied it in advanced stages of decomposition, so I can only guess. It's freezing now, but after months of being out here, I won't find her frozen corpse intact.

I want to increase my pace, but tonight is much darker than the night we left her, with only a sliver of moon to light my way. I move methodically, and at last, I reach the spot. My eyes have adjusted, but even so, under the canopy of trees, I can't see much. I can't make out even a glimpse of white on the ground that could be bones. The wind wails mournfully overhead, and in the distance, I can hear the crash of the surf, but no other sounds reach me in the night. Finally, I reluctantly switch on the flashlight on my phone and shine it around the area.

Maybe I didn't remember as well as I thought, because not only do I not see a skeleton lying there, but I don't see the small trench I kicked in the dirt before I covered her. I search for a few minutes before I find what I think marks the place, a long indentation that's now filled with pine needles. I crouch and sweep away the debris with a gloved hand, examining the ground where she lay.

I move out from the grave in a slow circle, searching for a bone, a scrap of cloth, any sign of her. The area is remote, so it's not impossible that an animal dragged her off—a bear or fox or some kind of wildcat. Still, it's more likely they would have torn her apart here. I should have taken my time, dug a real grave for her. But I'm far enough from the road that no one can see my light, let alone a person. Even the stench of her rotting corpse wouldn't reach the lookout, since that's a good half mile up the hill.

For the first time since I left her body, I regret taking the tracker from her. At the time, I was more concerned with Mabel's disobedience than ever finding Jane again. Leaving the tracker in her body didn't make sense, since she wouldn't be going anywhere, and I had no interest in revisiting her. Worse, it could have drawn suspicion if anyone found it, possibly even lead to me if someone was better at uncovering digital connections than I was at erasing them.

It doesn't make sense, though. If someone found her, I would know. It would have been on the news, if only a line in the local paper about unidentified remains found in the woods. I may not have wanted to see Jane again, but I monitored the local Havoc Harbor news even back in Tennessee. It was important to know if the body was found, so I would know if I needed to be careful.

It was never found.

So where the fuck is it?

I expand my search, studying the ground for signs that don't exist. She's gone like a ghost, like the fog that blows up from the ocean.

Like Mabel.

It doesn't make sense. I felt her pulse slowing.

But I didn't wait for it to stop, did I?

I felt her windpipe cave in my hands.

But that's not always fatal, is it?

She has to be here...

But she's not.

At last, I'm forced to admit it. I make my way back to the place I left her, then back up the hill to the car, retracing my footsteps until I reach the road. Low clouds have covered the sky, and the wind off the ocean is biting enough to steal my breath. I listen for a minute to make sure no traffic approaches, then hurry across the road and into Duke's car. My fingers are numb, but I get the car started, and once the steam clears from my glasses, I drive back the way I came, obeying the speed limit, careful to stay within my lane around the curves. The last thing I need is a policeman pulling me over, questioning my whereabouts this evening, wondering why I'm out so late, why there's dirt on my shoes and gloves.

I pull into the driveway of Mabel's house and shut off the engine. Sitting there, I take a deep breath. I'm shaking with cold, but also, with rage.

Inside, I find them curled together in sleep, Mabel in Duke's arms. I drag her from the bed and slam her against the wall before she can blink the sleep from her eyes. She cries out in shock, and I slam my hand around her throat. "Where is she?" I demand.

This feeling coursing through me is unfamiliar—consuming and... Reckless.

I do not lose control.

I loosen my grip enough to allow Mabel to answer. Her wide, blue eyes skate back and forth, as if looking for a way out. I drag her forward and slam her back against the wall again.

"Where did you take her?" I snarl.

"Who?" she manages.

Her pulse is racing like a scared little bunny under my fingers, and it makes my cock harden feeling it, seeing her terror, her helplessness.

But Mabel Darling has never been a harmless little bunny.

"You know who," I growl. "You avoided the question when we brought it up, and we stopped asking because you stopped killing, but it was always you. Wasn't it?"

"What are you talking about?" she croaks, clawing at my fingers helplessly.

I squeeze tighter, watching her face darken, blood pooling under her skin.

"Dude, let her go," Duke says from behind me. "You're not making any sense."

"Are you the fucking Black Widow Killer?" I demand of Mabel.

She winces, prying at my fingers, unable to speak. Her mouth opens and closes as she mouths a denial.

"Then where the fuck is Jane?" I demand.

She can't answer, though. Her face is purple now. This is how I wanted my kill, looking right into her eyes, watching the realization dawn, the life slip away.

"What does that have to do with the Black Widow Killer?" Duke asks, scrambling up from the bed. He grabs my shoulder and wrenches me back. My fingers stay locked around Mabel's throat, but when Duke drags me back a step, she comes with me, and she manages to drag in a wheezing breath through my grip.

"Let her go," my brother barks, slamming his elbow down inside mine. Mine buckles at the force, and Mabel is jerked forward, her head colliding with Duke's forearm. The three of us wrestle for control for a minute before they free Mabel. She stumbles back and slides down the wall, her hand at her throat, the other bracing against the floor for balance.

She looks defeated, beaten, but I know it's all an act. She's not the helpless little princess she wants us to believe she is. She's a silent predator, sleek and deadly, a ruthless killer waiting motionless in her web, planning her attack.

"What the fuck," Duke says, shoving me aside and kneeling beside her. "You could have killed her."

I look down at my hands. I could have. I was thinking about it. Wanting it.

Planning it?

I'm not sure. I don't lose control like that, but something about this, about her fucking with *my* kill, when she's racked up dozens... Sneaking around behind my back when I'm supposed to know where she is at all times... Managing to evade the question each time I ask if she's behind the killings... It got to me. I spend every fucking day running myself ragged trying to stay on top of everything—maintaining my rigorous courseload at school, monitoring the news to make sure nothing incriminating surfaces, growing the operation that funds our lives, giving her the life she deserves, balancing Duke and his moods at every turn, so she doesn't feel like we're ganging up on her again.

And now this.

"You okay, Duchess?" Duke asks her, his voice gentle, that fucking nickname he gave her grating over my frayed nerves.

Her breath hitches, and tears pool in her eyes as she stares up at me, though she swipes them away each time they spring back, refusing to let them fall. At last, she nods.

"It was you, wasn't it?" I ask, narrowing my eyes at my brother.

"What?" he asks, blinking up at me with apparent bewilderment.

"You went back for her," I say. "For Jane. You took her, didn't you? I saw you in the woods with her. You didn't have the stomach for it, so I got rid of her. But you stayed, didn't you? You came back and got her once I was done with her."

"What are you talking about?" he asks. "I was with Mabel that night when you got back." He wraps an arm around her shoulders, pulling her into a protective embrace and scowling up at me with a wounded look, as if I hurt him too.

He's done this before, trying to make it into a competition, to make Mabel take "his side," even though we're all on the same side—the side of making it work. The three of us against everyone else. I thought he understood that, but maybe he still can't quite grasp the concept of us all needing each other, providing for each other.

"Are you lying to me right now?" I grit out. "Because if you are…"

"I'm not," he says, scowling. "We don't lie to each other. Neither of us did shit to Jane. You did. And if she wasn't there, it's not our fault. You just don't want to admit that you fucked up."

I stare down at him a long moment, wanting to turn it back on him, to deny what he said. But I can't. Not without lying, and we promised we wouldn't do that, no matter how easy it is.

So instead, I do something I only ever do for Duke.

"You're right," I say. "I'm sorry."

Then I turn my attention to Mabel. "But I'm going to need a straight answer here. Are you the Black Widow Killer?"

SELENA

four

Baron Dolce

"Really?" Mabel asks. "He gets an apology, and I get an interrogation? Where's my apology?"

"Maybe you can get one when you stop fucking lying," I say.

"I'm not lying," she says. "I already told you, I'm not. All I ever did was set the men up. I thought *you* were killing them."

"Pretty convenient, isn't it?" I ask. "Every man you went out with ended up dead, and as soon as someone's watching you, the killing stops."

"I told you all this last summer," she says. "Why are you bringing it up again?"

"It was always a little too convenient," I say. "But it wasn't putting us in danger once you stopped, so I left it alone and focused on our new life together."

"I don't believe that for a minute," she says, crossing her arms. "You'd never have just taken my word for it. You know it's not me."

Her face is still splotchy, and angry red handprints ring her neck, already starting to turn purple. Still, she manages to look fierce, regal somehow, like the queen she is.

"Fine," I say. "I knew you weren't with the men when they died. At least some of them."

"How?"

"I know where your phone is," I say. "I have a trace in it."

Her brow arches. "Just my phone?"

"I don't have one in your body, if that's what you're asking."

"And that's supposed to make me trust you?"

"I respected your autonomy," I point out.

"Maybe I left my phone at home."

"I had cameras in your apartment too."

She nods, no trace of surprise discernible in her features. At least not to me. Duke is expert on reading people.

"I didn't kill them," she says again. "And, if I believe you didn't, then neither of us are the killer. I guess we can move on and focus on our new life together after all."

I narrow my eyes at her, trying to puzzle what she's not telling me. "You're just going to ignore the fact that someone has been following you around, killing every man you fuck?"

"Why would that bother me?" she asks, cocking her head. "They deserved to die."

"Uh, maybe because *we're* fucking you?" Duke asks.

"And you're still alive," Mabel points out. "Which would lead anyone to believe one of you is the killer."

"But we're not," he says, then looks up at me. "Right?"

"I told you that," I snap.

"You did kill that one guy," he points out. "And then Mabel stopped fucking around, and guys stopped dying."

"Exactly," Mabel says. "Obviously, if she was going to get you, she would have."

"Who the fuck is 'she'?" I demand, resisting the urge to grab her again.

"I don't know," she says. "The police think it's a woman. You don't call a male a black widow. That would be a widower. Besides, men don't kill with poison."

Duke and I stare at her for a long minute.

"What the fuck?" he asks at last, pushing away from her and standing. "It is you, isn't it?"

"Stop accusing me," she protests. "I told you the truth. You can choose to trust me or not. I'm not answering again."

"It's that Ingrid bitch, isn't it?" I demand. "That's why you're so familiar with her."

"I'm familiar with her because we worked together a couple summers," she says.

"She has an hourglass tattoo on her thigh," I point out.

"Like a black widow," Duke says, nodding.

"I think she was part of that motorcycle gang," Mabel says, pushing up from where she sat against the wall at last. "They all have hourglass tattoos."

"Did she tell you that?"

"No," she says. "She'd just freak out and hide whenever they came into the shop. I think she left the gang or something, maybe ratted them out. Pretty sure she'd just gotten out of prison two summers ago when we both started there. We trained together."

"You never hung out outside of work?" I ask.

She shrugs. "We went to the bakery a few times. She liked looking at my pictures of Seeley, and she thought it was funny that I'd get tea instead of coffee. She said I was an old soul. No one ever called me that before."

"You liked her," I say. "You never asked what she did on the off-season? You didn't want to visit her at Christmas?"

"Not really," she says, slumping onto the edge of the bed. "I mean, I do like her. She's…"

She trails off, touching her neck and wincing.

"What?" I press.

"She kept to herself," she says, wrapping her hands around her knees. "She didn't ask about my past, so I didn't ask about hers. I don't care if she did time, or what it was for, or what she did when I wasn't around. She was nice to me, and she didn't make me feel like a freak. She's my friend."

"She's a ghost."

Mabel's eyes widen, and her voice comes out faint. "She's dead? Did you...?"

I shake my head. "She was always a ghost. She died a hundred years ago."

They both stare, dumbfounded.

Finally Duke speaks. "I don't think they had pink hair dye a hundred years ago."

"Not an actual ghost, you idiot," I say. "Lay off the Alice. It's frying your brain."

"You made it for me."

"*We* made it," I remind him, not letting him downplay his contribution. "So we could double-team girls in high school. Not so you could spend your whole life high."

"Better than low," he mutters.

I turn back to Mabel, who sits silent, digesting the information.

"So she used a fake name," she says at last. "Maybe she wanted a fresh start when she got out, like me."

"She's not your friend," I say, not caring if it's harsh. "You don't even know who she is."

"I know who she is," Mabel insists. "A name is just a name. She knew me as Dahlia. She still knew me."

"Then you know she could be a serial killer," I say. "She could have followed you to Tennessee every fall when you left."

"That's highly improbable."

"Is it?" I ask. "You don't even know what she did time for. I can tell you a few things about her you probably didn't know. Like she has no prison record. I found a marriage record, though. Some kids. No death certificate, which is probably why she stole her identity."

"It's not illegal to change your name."

"It's illegal to steal someone's social security number," I point out. "Even if they're dead."

"So she probably killed someone and went to prison," Duke says. "Then she got out, and now she's the Black Widow Killer."

"And she's stalking *our* girlfriend."

"She's not—"

I cut Mabel off. "Did you know she never picked up her last check at the ice cream place? Didn't leave a forwarding address for it either. They were pretty pissed, though. Apparently she just never showed up to work one day. Funny how that happened not too long after we left. You know what else is funny? There's no record of her getting a new job anywhere, either. No bank accounts, credit cards..."

"She didn't believe in credit cards," Mabel mutters. "She was anti-establishment."

"She didn't rent an apartment anywhere," I go on, ignoring her excuses. "Or enroll in school. She just disappeared into thin air, like she couldn't live without you, Mabel."

"Are you saying I made her up?" she demands, covering her ears and rocking forward and back. "That you pretended you saw her too, and made this whole line of questioning, and now you're going to tell me you faked the whole thing, and I created a whole person in my head just so I could have a friend? I'm not crazy. You can't make me think I am. I'm not. I'm not!"

"Whoa, calm down," Duke says, drawing her hand down. "No one's saying you're crazy." He gives me a significant look. "Are we, Baron?"

"Of course not," I say, scowling. "You didn't make up anyone. What I want to know is, why are you protecting her?"

"She's my friend," Mabel says, like she's trying to convince herself more than us.

"Your friend, who you worked with for a few months, had coffee with a few times, and who didn't even tell you what she was in prison for. But she probably followed you halfway across the country and killed every man you so much as went on a date with," I say. "You don't see a problem with that?"

"She didn't hurt *me*," Mabel points out.

"Yeah, well, I have a huge fucking problem with it," I say.

"Why?" Mabel asks. "She didn't hurt you, either. We've been together for months. If she was going to get rid of you, she would have. She must know I want to be with you, so she's leaving you alone."

"She has a point," Duke says. "She knows we're not some weirdos trying to get with little girls. We love Mabel. We're good for her. If she wants what's best for Mabel, that's us. Kinda cool, when you think about it. We got the Black Widow Killer's stamp of approval."

"It's not cool," I growl.

"Why?" Mabel asks, narrowing her eyes at me. "Are you planning to do something terrible to me again, and you're afraid she'll come after you then? If you're right about her, which I still don't think you are, but if you are… If you're not planning to hurt me, why do you object to someone protecting me?"

"Because that's *our* job," I snap, turning to pace the room.

I can't decide which one irritates me more—the thought that someone else is watching over Mabel, and might see us as the enemy, or that I can't tell if she's lying. If someone is really watching over her, they'd have struck already. We may love Mabel, but we don't show it in a way that most people would recognize. Mabel recognizes it and understands it, but an outsider wouldn't. They'd have seen what we do to her, and they'd have killed us already.

It makes more sense that Mabel is the killer. She stopped because we've been there, preventing her from going through with the schemes she was doing before. It's too fucking convenient to believe that she was innocently dating these men, and they just happened to all die within weeks of their date with her, no matter that she chose a different alias each time, a different VPN from which to contact them. If she's not doing the killing, she's definitely coordinating with the person who is.

So how did I miss their communications?

I don't like the thought of someone else watching over our girl, protecting her like she's theirs, not ours. I like the thought of her and her accomplice outsmarting me even less. Was someone else watching through their own cameras, or did they hack into mine? And now that we got Mabel, has someone been watching all of us? Someone invisible not just to Mabel, but to me, a panther slinking through the night like a whisper, a shadow shrouded by darkness.

"Who took the body?" I demand at last, wheeling on my heel toward her bed. "The one in your aunt's house. That one wasn't the Black Widow Killer. Why would she clean up after someone else?"

"I don't know," Mabel says. "I guess... To protect me?"

"But you didn't kill him," I point out. "So who was she protecting?"

"Maybe she's protecting all of us," Duke says. "Our own twisted guardian angel. She must want us together."

"Or she's Mabel," I say. "Because that makes a hell of a lot more sense."

"I'm not answering that question again," Mabel says, standing from the bed. "I'm going to take a shower. It's getting light already."

"I'm going back to bed," Duke says, flopping down on the mattress. "Hit the light on your way out."

A minute later, I hear the shower running. I can't stop my brain from working overtime, thinking about what Mabel must be thinking. Is she triumphing that she outsmarted me? Does she have some secret device I don't know about, one she communicates from when she's outside her house, so I never got my hands on it or saw it through the cameras? If she did, that means she knew I was watching. She was one step ahead of me all along.

The idea both pisses me off beyond reason and makes me mad with lust. I turn and head into the bathroom, sliding back the door to the glass shower to reveal Mabel's wet, naked body.

"What are you doing?" she demands, wrapping her arms around herself as if she can hide her body from me—a body that's already mine. It's her mind I can't conquer. That's why I can never forget her, never move on. No one else can make me doubt everything, even myself, the way Mabel Darling can.

"Let me see you," I say, my voice low.

She swallows hard, then drops her arms. She's not a brat, one of those girls who are mouthy and stupid to think they could ever win. And she's not weak and trembling, begging for mercy, despite all the times I've hurt her. She knows it's not personal, that I need the pain. She understands, and she gives me exactly what I need—not a fight, but unwilling participation. She will never want me, never want pleasure. That makes me want her more, makes me harder than seeing her knotted rosebud nipples and scarred skin swept with gooseflesh.

I undress quickly, set my glasses on the counter, and step into the shower. She cowers back against the wall, but she doesn't try to escape. She knows she can't.

She sobs when I force myself inside with no prep, but she doesn't fight me. I lift her legs around me, gripping her ass and slamming her down onto me, watching the tears spurt from her eyes, her face twisted in pain, her cunt offering friction that's nearly painful, a tightness that drives me wild with need. I pin her to the wall and pump into her, driving to the hilt while she chokes on the pain. I'm quick, not out of mercy, but because I know her body will adjust and get looser and wetter if I last too long, and she'll start seeking pleasure, and that will ruin it for me.

I cum inside her, holding her pinned to the wall, my hands protecting her from the hard tile. I want my cock to cause her pain, nothing else, so all her focus is there—on how deep I am, how much of her I've claimed, ravaged, destroyed. How helpless she is to stop me. I enjoy the power, the violation, as much as her physical pain.

When she whispers a tiny plea, I punish her by drawing back and slamming in deep again, past her depths, into her resistant core. I grip her chin, holding her head back against the wall, and press a kiss to her wet, trembling lips. They taste like salt and surrender.

"It doesn't matter if you're the killer," I murmur into her mouth. "I hope you are. I don't want you any less for it. But know this, my little monster. No matter what you do, you belong to us. If you put me six feet in the ground, I'll crawl out of the grave and come back for you. Nothing can stop me, not even death. You are mine. Now and forever."

She shudders against me, trying to lift off my punishing length impaling her. I grip her hip and hold her pinned, my cock throbbing inside her.

"If you try to meet another man again, I'll take him with us," I say. "I'll kill every man you touch, one by one, until there's not a man alive on earth but me."

"What about Duke?"

"Duke is part of me," I say. "The best part. He's yours too."

"What if I left you anyway?" she asks. "What if it wasn't for a man?"

"I'd kill every woman on earth too."

"What if I just wanted to be left alone?"

"You can be alone with us."

"I could kill myself," she said. "What then?"

"I'd put myself in the ground with you," I say. "There's no escaping me, little monster. As much as you are mine, I am yours. We will be together. The three of us. Always."

"That sounds like a threat."

"If you want it to be," I say. "A promise, a threat, our fate... It's all of those things. You've always been mine, even before you existed. If you try to take yourself away from me, I'll follow you down. If you try to get rid of me, I'll take you to the grave with me. I'll follow you to the end of the world, through space and time, through death and every lifetime, through all eternity. No matter what you do, I will never let you go. I promise you that, my monster."

"Promise you won't make me think I'm crazy again," she says, her breathing rapid, her bare belly pressing to mine with each inhale.

I run my knuckles along her jawline, tipping her chin up before wrapping my fingers around her bruised throat just to watch her flinch. I smirk down at her, loving how she just revealed her greatest fear, her deepest insecurity to me, making herself vulnerable in a way that usually only her body is. Leaning in, I graze my nose against hers, watching her nostrils flare when she feels my cock throb inside her, stiffening again just when she thought I'd take mercy on her.

"I promise."

Then I fuck her again because I can and because I want her to know it, to never forget that she's mine as much as I'm hers. She ensnared me, trapped me like the spider she is, and this is the consequence. She wanted me, so she got me. She shouldn't have woven me into her web if she didn't want every part of this—the hand around her throat, allowing her to breathe; the cock inside her deeper than anything is meant to go, then in her ass when her cunt's too wet; the smile on my face when she finally cracks and begs me to stop. I do, but only after I've gotten rough enough to draw the sweet scream that rises out of her like a siren's call, making my orgasm erupt inside her.

I step out of the shower, letting her crumple to the floor, sobbing and shaking. I leave her there, the water beating down on her, mingling with the blood trailing toward the drain in rivulets. She asked for it. She wanted to the love of a monster, and she got it.

five

Duke Dolce

I squeeze my eyes shut and pull the pillow over my head, trying to block out the sound of her screams. I can't save her, so I don't try. That probably makes me a pussy, or just as bad as him. That's what I always did, ever since I figured out that my brothers were more ruthless than I'd ever be. I never had the stomach for it, not since we were five years old and we saw my uncle kill a man. They had to cover for me, make our dad think I was tough like them. That's when I started to learn. I'm not quick like Baron, so it took a while, but eventually I figured it out. How to fake it. How to look tough, act tough, so everyone thought I was. The only thing I never figured out was how to *be* tough.

Substances help with that. Alcohol, molly, pills, and then, finally, the pearl lady. With enough of anything in me, it didn't feel like I was walking around flayed while everyone else had a skin suit to protect them. I was always raw, every grain of sand stinging, every word or look or rejection, a hot match to an exposed nerve.

I sit up, reaching for my jeans. I need one now, need Lady Alice to take me by the hand and lead me to Wonderland.

The door swings open, and Baron strolls in, dick swinging, water droplets still shimmering on his shoulders in the light from the hallway behind him. He stops when he sees me sitting up.

"I thought you went back to sleep," he says, lifting the blankets and sliding in on his side.

"Kinda hard when it sounds like you're killing her," I mutter.

"I wasn't killing her," Baron says, turning away and setting his glasses on the bedside table, which gives me a chance to swallow the pearls. "I was fucking her."

"You tried to kill her like an hour ago," I say. "You can see how I'd be on alert."

"She's fine," he says, adjusting his pillow. "You can hear her crying, can't you?"

He's right. Mabel's soft sobs echo in the bathroom, which means she's alive.

"You can't go off on her like that," I say quietly. "What if I hadn't been here?"

"I know," he says, serious now. "I shouldn't have done that. It won't happen again."

"What if it does?"

"It won't," he says firmly.

I turn to face him, resting my face on my hand and gazing into the mirror of my twin, visible in the dim light coming through the open bedroom door.

"Was it because it was her?" I ask.

"No," Baron says, scowling. "You think I care about that dumb runaway?"

"I guess not." I don't correct him, tell him that she's not a runaway. Maybe she is. Just because she has a sister, that doesn't mean she didn't run away.

"No one cares about her," he says. "She was garbage, so we threw her out."

He's wrong about that. Olive loves her. Olive is waiting for her, even now.

"Did you really kill her?" I ask. "After I left. You didn't let her go?"

"Of course I fucking killed her," he snaps. "I tried, anyway."

"Did you?" I ask. "I wouldn't think any less of you if you let her go. If maybe you didn't really want to kill her, subconsciously. Maybe, whatever you did, you didn't do it as much or as hard as you thought. If you hit her with a rock, maybe some part of you made you hold back. Maybe that's why she wasn't there."

"Or maybe you and Mabel are fucking with me," he says. "I don't do shit halfway, and no part of me wanted to spare her. I'm not you, Duke. I don't have some misplaced savior complex."

"No lies?" I ask. "Promise?"

"I promise," he grits out. "I killed her. If I didn't, you can be damn sure it was a mistake. Now you. Did you fuck with her?"

"No," I say. "No lies. I went back to get Mabel, and then we left the next morning. She was never out of our sight, either."

"Yeah, you're right," he says, lifting his head and dropping it back onto the pillow, like he can't get comfortable. But I recognize the gesture of frustration. I know all his tells, like he knows mine. "Maybe an animal got her. That's what I'm hoping. Even if they couldn't identify her, a body discovered in the woods would have made the news. If not... I fucked up, Duke."

"I'm sure you're right," I say. "I'm sure something got her. A bear or a moose or something."

"Moose are herbivores."

"Okay, Olive," I mutter.

She always knew random animal facts. Thinking about her annoys me, and I get up to go check on Mabel. I wish I could get the kid out of my head, stop worrying that one day, I'll have to tell her that her sister's not coming home. Of course I won't, though. Even if I went home, she'd never want to see me again. I bashed her head in on a chunk of cement last time I saw her.

In the bathroom, I find Mabel cleaning herself up, wincing and biting her lip so as not to cry out, her legs shaking and her eyes swimming with tears. I pick her up and carry her to bed, grabbing the ice pack on the way. She huddles against me, like she can't bear to be near Baron right now.

"You want me to kiss it better?" I whisper, pressing my forehead to her damp, warm skin.

She shakes her head, a shudder rolling through her. "No."

I would roll her over, but Baron likes her to be in the middle, between us. Since that day she tried to run, I've liked it too. He'll wake up if she gets up and tries to slip out again.

But now, he's satisfied, and after a few minutes, he stops moving, and I know from the rhythm of his breathing, as familiar as my own, that he's asleep.

"I could make you feel better," I tell Mabel, pushing my cock against her belly. She can feel that I'm hard. It's impossible not to be with the girl I love lying naked in my arms.

"I'm too sore," she murmurs.

"I could just lick you a little," I say. "The way you taste... God, just feeling you cum on my tongue gets me off too."

"Baron just came inside me."

"Even better," I say, pulling her leg over me and rocking against her. "I love it when I can taste my brother in your cunt."

"You don't have to always clean up his messes."

"I'm not," I protest. "I like it. And you're not a mess. You're my duchess."

"And a mess," she says, looking away.

I rumble a groan when I feel what she means—she's getting wet, coating my shaft with her slickness.

"You're my mess," I say. "All juicy and full of cum. I love it."

"And blood," she mutters, hiding her face against my chest.

"You think a little blood bothers me? I fuck after Baron all the time, and if you aren't dry enough for him to make you bleed, he doesn't get off."

"Don't make excuses for him."

"It's not an excuse if it's the truth," I say, lifting her chin and leaning in, giving her a second to pull back if she wants. When she doesn't, I press my lips to hers, and the calm that only she brings settles over me, a feeling like going home. Like I can stop striving for one goddamn minute and just breathe, just *be.*

I know I give her the same, and that's why I'm here. Not because I match her brain like Baron does, but because I match her body.

"Wait," she whispers, a tremor going through her. "You're going to hurt me."

"It's okay," I say, stroking the side of her bruised throat, where her pulse flutters under my fingertips. "I have something that'll relax you. It won't hurt at all."

I give her a pill, and even though she doesn't like them the way I do, she takes it. "What is it?"

"Don't worry, baby," I say. "Just swallow it. You won't feel a thing."

She hesitates only a moment, then takes the glass of water I offer and washes it down. She's out in minutes, the sedative doing its job. I lay still until I can't bear it a moment longer, feeling her warm, bare body against mine. When she's asleep, she doesn't tighten up and cause herself more pain, and she doesn't cum either. She hates when I make her do that.

I roll her over and fuck her as long as the Alice in my blood tells me to keep going. I know she'll be sore when she wakes up, but she'll probably think it's mostly from Baron's roughness. She doesn't know I'm in Wonderland, and that I'll be here for hours. Even if I tell her, she won't make a big deal out of it. She's given me permission before. She knows what she's here for, and she'll probably be grateful that I spared her the ordeal of being awake for it. That's the difference between me and Baron. He gets off on her pain. I get off on her.

A few hours later, I'm sweating my way through the comedown when Baron gets up and goes out for his run. Mabel's still knocked out, so I slip from the bed and dress, considering whether to leave her like that. I decide it's too risky—Baron will be pissed to find her alone even if she's asleep. Instead, I cuff her and tie her to the bed. Baron will like that. She'll be all ready for him when he gets back.

Or maybe that Black Widow chick will find her like this. Maybe I'll come back and find her eating Mabel out, sucking my cum out of her, and she'll be fingering herself and all wet and needy, and I'll fuck her from the back, and Mabel will wake up and be pissed to see my dick in someone else, but she won't be able to get away, and the Black Widow will force her to squirt while she cums all over my cock, screaming my name into Mabel's wet pussy.

Or maybe I've been watching too much porn at work.

In the kitchen, Boots watches me warily, then lets out an evil hiss when I come near.

I hiss back at him, and he draws up, his eyes as round as saucers, looking gravely offended.

"Oh, get over it," I mutter to him. "Your girl loves me."

He arches his back, his orange fur standing on end when I walk past.

"Sucks to suck," I tell him, opening the pantry.

I search for some gum to keep from grinding my teeth, but we must not have gotten any, and the thought of eating makes me retch. I toss a few treats on the counter for Boots, not bothering to set him on the floor since he's not supposed to get up on stuff. I figure we should let the little guy live his life in peace, not try to teach him rules. Humans already have way too many of those.

Then I grab the keys and head out. It's bitter cold outside, and the sun is sharp as knives, the light more silver than gold this time of year. I almost hit a car going around one of the turns on the way up the hill and realize I'm doing about forty over the speed limit, way over the line. I wrestle the car under control, then keep going. The other guy ends up in the ditch, but they didn't hit anything, so they'll be fine, and I really don't want to be cussed at. I go slower now, watching the speedometer, since I can't really tell how fast I'm going when I'm fucked up.

I park at the lookout, then cross the road. I figure I'll be able to see Baron's tracks and follow them to where he was last night. He'll remember where he left the body. That's not something Baron would forget, and since I wasn't there when he killed her, I'm not sure exactly where she ended up after I gave her the light and the gun and told her to run.

I picture her huddled against a tree, waiting for me. Baron took the gun, so she can't hurt me. She won't want to, anyway. She'll be so happy to see me, so grateful, she'll forget that I didn't save her before. I'll be her savior now. I'll bring her home, and when Olive sees her, she'll forgive me for bashing her head in. She'll show Blue all the sloth stuff I got her, and Blue will see how much I love her sister, and she'll fall in love with me. Baron won't even care. He has Mabel, and when he sees how happy they make me, he'll let me have Blue, and we'll raise Olive together as our daughter. No kid on earth will ever be more spoiled than we spoil her. She deserves it, after everything she's had to go through already.

Of course that's not possible, though.

It's just a drug-dream, a wisp of Wonderland clinging to me even now that I'm back up the rabbit hole, on solid ground. In reality, she'd probably file a restraining order and tell me never to come near her little sister again. In reality, it's been six months, and she's not going to be waiting like it's the next day after I left her. And it turns out that it's a lot harder to track someone than I thought. I can't find any footprints at all in the leaves and pine needles. Finally, I find a partial one in the sand, and I head down the hill. I have the shakes, and my stomach feels fucked up, but I'm hyper focused. I need to find her. For Olive, I'll find her. Even if I can never see her again, never tell her I'm sorry, it would be my way of making amends.

But I don't see another footprint, and for all I know, I could be ten yards, a hundred yards, from where Baron went. Maybe I already passed it. I can't seem to keep track of time. I wander around in the woods until I'm pretty sure I'm lost. I hear a twig snap and spin around, but there's nothing. I keep seeing flashes in the corners of my eyes. Whatever animal ate Blue, maybe it's out here. Stalking me.

Maybe it's the Black Widow, ready to claim one more victim. Maybe Blue has been living out here in the woods, surviving on acorns, waiting for me to return to the scene of the crime, the betrayal, so she can jump out of the trees like a superhero and blow my brains out. If Baron spared her, she could have spared him in return. He might have bargained for his life by telling her he'd send me instead. It would be such a tidy way to be rid of me, so he could have Mabel to himself.

I hear a car and consider running out and hitchhiking. Even if it's the wrong road, it'll lead me somewhere. I think about walking along the road like she did the night Baron picked her up, on his way out of Faulkner. But look what happened to her when she hitchhiked. If that's not a cautionary tale, I don't know what is. I'd probably get someone even more psycho than Baron. At least he loves the people he loves. Some psychos don't love anyone. If karma's real, I'd get one of those.

It was winter then too, just about one year ago, but it feels like a lifetime has come and gone since then, and I don't think it's just the drugs fucking with my sense of time. I think about what I was doing that night—not being a hero. Not saving my father.

Is that his ghost between the trees, watching? I walk towards it, not daring to blink. He's standing there, a dark shadow, a frown of disapproval on his face. But when I'm close, he melts away, and it's nothing but the shadow of a tree trunk.

Dad isn't here to save me from myself. That's all he wanted to do.

I think about him burning to death. Screaming for help.

I was sitting on Lo's car, smoking a cigarette with Colt while he died.

Maybe, if I hadn't been itching for that closeness, to prove something to him—that I was good enough for his sister, cool enough for him—I would have gone back in.

I might have saved Dad.

I step into a low spot and pitch forward, almost falling before I stumble back upright, catching myself on the trunk of a pine. The big sections of bark are smooth, their edges rough against my fingertips. I stare for a second, sure if I lift my hand, I'll see blood. That it will bubble from the cracks, running down the trunk in thick, sticky rivulets.

I yank my hand back and stare at my clean palm.

Then I turn back to the ditch I tripped on. My heart is beating all crazy and fucked up, and I'm not sure if the shakes are still from coming down. I'm suddenly so empty, so ravenous, and so fucking tired I don't think I can stumble back to the car.

That's when I notice the disturbance in the surface of the ground at my feet. All the pine needles and sticks and leaves have been swept back, leaving a stretch of bare dirt. It's an indentation, about five or six feet long, too deep for an animal path, too short and shallow for a natural gulley or even a dry streambed. The way it's been cleared tells me all I need to know.

I fall to my knees, forgetting the weakness in my limbs, and dig. The ground is hard packed and unforgiving, and I feel my nails peeling back, breaking and tearing, but I don't stop. It seems impossible it could have been packed down this hard in six months, but that's all I can think. It has to be her grave.

I have to stop after a while. I sit back, my head swimming, my stomach churning. I step away to get sick, only then noticing my fingers are black with dirt and blood, my nailbeds caked with it. I stumble back to the ditch, now about twice as deep as it was, which is only maybe a foot deep. There's no way Baron dug into this. He didn't even have a shovel.

If this is her grave, she's not in it anymore.

I sink slowly down, down, onto my knees, my hands, and then onto my side. The scent of dirt and pine invades my nostrils, stings until my eyes burn and blur, until hot tears trickle from the cold corner and drip into the dirt.

I wish I'd found her, even if it meant she was dead.

I wish I'd saved her, even if it meant Baron hated me for it.

I wish I could take her place, even if it meant I'd be the one who never made it home.

I didn't do it then, but maybe I can now. Maybe I can finally make everyone happy. That's what I'm always trying to do, but it's impossible when everyone wants something different, so I always fail. I'm tired of failing, tired of being a loser, tired of being wrong and not realizing it until it's too late to make it right. This time, I can make it right. No one can blame me anymore if I'm not there to blame. No one can hate me if I don't exist.

Not Harper and Royal, who might forgive me but never forget.

Not Mabel and Colt, who can't forgive me or escape me.

Not Olive and Blue, from whom I could never ask forgiveness.

Most important of all, I couldn't hate myself anymore.

SELENA

six

Mabel Darling

"Do I need to cuff you to the bed again?" Baron asks. "I'm going out."

I scowl at him, cuddling Seeley to my chest like a shield. "How are we 'equal partners' if I have to be tied up every time you leave the house?"

"How are we partners if you try to escape when we leave the house?"

"I'm not going to escape," I grumble.

"Good," he says, coming over to the table where I sit. "Because you'll never be able to. Run to the end of the earth, and I'll be waiting when you get there."

He grips my hair and tugs my head back, planting a kiss on my forehead that's more possessive than any forehead kiss has the right to be.

"I'll be back soon."

And then he's gone, phone still in hand, door banging shut behind him.

Seeley slinks from my arms and strolls over to lie directly in front of the refrigerator, like he's trying to place himself in the most inconvenient spot in the house.

I shake my head and watch the door for a minute, considering whether to follow Baron.

He's acting strange. He wouldn't tell me where he was going last night, and he didn't explain at all just now. He never goes out for a run more than once a day.

I woke up when he got home from his run earlier, only to find that Duke had tied me to the bed. That was upsetting, though not wholly unexpected. After my one half-hearted attempt to leave from school in October, they rarely let me out of their sight, and they've tied me up every time they've had to leave me alone at home. That was my punishment, right up until now.

Of course Baron wanted sex when he saw me like that, and it was worse than usual, since I'm already so torn up, and Duke wasn't there to soothe me in the aftermath of his brother's torment. In light of his strange behavior since we got here, though, the fact that he still wanted sex is a normalcy that offers a small comfort as I sit here alone, untethered for the first time in months. It sets me on edge, that he just took my word so easily, believed I wouldn't leave. What is he planning?

He might want me to leave, having come up with a particularly gruesome torture as punishment if I do. If I leave, he'll have an excuse to employ it. If I don't, he'll have proof for Duke that I stay because I want to, that I could have left, but I chose not to.

Or maybe he was simply distracted, as he seemed. That's so unlike Baron, though, it makes me even more ill at ease.

He could be toying with me, trying to make me question everything like he did before. If that's the case, he's succeeding.

But where is Duke?

Is that part of the plan, or did he run away this time? He's been subdued lately, so unhappy that even Baron noticed. And he wanted to go back to Faulkner so badly. Maybe he used the opportunity, cuffed me to the bed and left while Baron was away. I debate whether Baron would tie his brother up if he tried to run, or if he'd try to fix things. Is he a captive too?

I pace the hallway, and after a minute, Seeley joins me, looking as distraught as I feel. When he reaches the wooden staircase at the end of the hall on our fourth pass, he perches on the bottom step, watching me. I join him, and he bounds up the stairs, so I follow.

We all slept in the master bedroom downstairs, but there are two more bedrooms up here, a bath, an office. The house is nice, and set up well, with almost everything to make it a home. I use the restroom and wash my hands, then open the medicine cabinet. A generic assortment stares back at me—rubbing alcohol, bandages, antacids, painkillers, antibiotic ointment. A small perfume bottle is wedged into the corner, dark smoky glass in the shape of an angel with a polished, round golden head as the lid. With shaking fingers, I move aside the box of aspirin and take it out. When I turn it over, the back of the lid features a tiny black spider, its legs thin as threads of silk, the hourglass like a dot of blood in its center.

Men don't kill with poison.

I tear open the other drawers, the cabinets, rifling through them recklessly, searching for something, anything, though I can't say what I'm looking for. A sign she was here, that it wasn't Baron or Duke who placed the perfume there, that I'm not crazy. I stop when I find a black tube of lipstick with gold trim in one of the drawers. I take it out and pull off the cap, rolling up the stick of hot pink wax, the end blunted and smeared from where it was used.

I stare at it a long moment, then pocket it and go back downstairs. I sit at the kitchen table with my phone and dial.

For a minute, it only rings, and I don't think she'll answer. At last, the call connects.

"Cecily," I say, sinking back in my chair in relief. "You picked up."

There's a long silence, long enough that I have to tap my screen and check that the call is still going.

"Are you still with those two monsters?" she asks at last.

"Yes, but—"

"Do you need help?" she asks. "Are you trying to get away from them?"

"No, but—"

"Then I have nothing to say to you."

"Please," I blurt. "I just need to know."

"I told you, I don't know anything about it," she says. "It was there the last time I checked. I don't know how long it was before you came over. I didn't want to see it, so I didn't look at it again. If it was gone, one of those... *Boys* took it."

"But you just left."

She sighs. "I'm sorry, Mabel. Maggie was coming for the summer, and I couldn't have her in a house where those monsters had access. God knows what they'd do to her. I couldn't live with myself if they got to her the way they did you."

She doesn't say the other part: the way they did *her*.

"I'm sorry," I say, dropping my forehead into my palm. "I know you don't understand, but—"

"No, I don't understand," Cecily says. "After everything they've done to our family... To be honest, I understand your mother more than I understand you."

"Aurora is not my mother," I say stiffly.

No, my mother wouldn't swallow a bottle of pills rather than face another day of seeing her daughter destroyed by the Dolces.

My mother fled with her husband in the dead of night, leaving me to fend for myself.

Don't worry, Mom. I always did.

"Yes, well, I am Magnolia's," my aunt says. "It was my responsibility to protect her, so I did that. It wasn't my responsibility to take care of that mess you brought to my house."

"You're right," I say, straightening and picking up the lipstick. I wrap my fingers in a fist around it. "I'm sorry they hurt you. I never imagined they'd do that. I shouldn't have led them here."

She's quiet a long moment. Finally, she says, "Thank you for your apology."

She doesn't offer forgiveness, and I neither expect it nor ask for it. I have a different request.

"Can you tell her something for me?" I ask. "I know this was your house before it burned, which means it's really her and Sullivan's house more than mine. But tell her not to come here. Not ever. Even when I'm not here, it's not safe."

"I will," she says. "I'll tell them both."

"Can I ask you one more question?" I say, then go ahead before she can refuse. "Do you remember Dahlia?"

"The Delacroix girl?"

"Yes, her," I say, relieved. "Were we friends? When I was a kid, was I friends with her?"

She's quiet a moment. "I remember your mother saying that."

"What happened to her?" I ask. "They sent her to boarding school, and she never came back. Why?"

"That's something I don't know," she says.

"Okay. Thanks anyway. I'm sorry, Aunt C."

"I know. Goodbye, Mabel."

She hangs up, and I sit there staring off for a while. I could find her if I wanted, find where she went. Baron could, anyway.

But if I told him to find her, he'd want to know why, and I can't put her in more danger. There's no reason I need to know, anyway. She was a lifeline for me for a long time, but that line has been severed. When I left Cedar Crest, the hospital where I had to go when I had my mental breakdown, I couldn't go back home, and I couldn't go to college yet because it was summer. I didn't have the strength to find somewhere else to go, but I knew I had an aunt in Maine, so I drove all the way there without stopping. I showed up on her doorstep with nothing but Seeley Boots and my Prius, and she welcomed me in without question.

She must have known from my mom what was happening to me back here, but she never pushed me for answers, for rent money, for anything. She just opened the door. She said that's what family does. So, when campus closed again the next summer, I packed up everything and came back. I couldn't go home. They were there. So I came here, and I kept coming, and she kept a room for me.

And I led them straight to her.

That's the worst part. I should have run again after they came to the ice cream shop. I should have never toyed with them. I just never thought they'd hurt her. I thought they'd come for me, that they wanted me and only me. So I don't blame Aunt Cecily for her coldness.

She's not my mom. She's not responsible for me, and she wasn't even before I turned eighteen. I'm on my own, just like I always was.

I slip my hand into my pocket, wrapping my fingers around the dark angel. I imagine spraying it in a man's face, watching him choke and gasp for air, fall to the floor. His face turns red and then blue as he convulses, spittle flying from his lips, his eyes begging for mercy as his hands claw at his throat. At last he goes still, his tongue protruding, the tip just starting to turn black. I smile.

Then I get up and go outside and bury the lipstick in the trash.

A while later, I hear tires on gravel, and I know Duke is home.

Seeley comes trotting in, tail up, and stares at the door expectantly.

The twins come through it together—Duke staggering, arm over Baron's shoulder, barely on his feet; Baron half carrying him, gripping his arm to keep it in place.

I stand from the table, my heart stuttering in my chest.

"Go upstairs," Baron orders. "Start a bath. Warm, not hot."

"Is he—"

"Go," he snaps.

I do. The upstairs bathroom is lovely, just what I wanted, with huge windows facing east, overlooking the ocean. A vintage clawfoot tub sits in the middle of the room, so you can soak in the bath and watch the sunrise. It has no curtain to block the view.

I don't like shower curtains.

Sinking onto the edge of the tub, I press my hand to my belly and swallow down the wave of horror that rises inside me every time I remember what they did that day. The day I lost it all and ended up at the hospital where I went before Cedar Crest, because Royal Dolce wouldn't let me lose my life too.

You don't get to take the easy way out. You get to suffer, just like the rest of us.

I shake the thought away and turn the water higher, then leave the bathroom, hurrying back downstairs. I don't like bathrooms in general. Most of them remind me too much of the bathroom in my nightmares, so I tried to make this as far from that as possible, as welcoming, a place I would want to take a shower without having to recite the mantra they gave me to get me to bathe once I left Cedar Crest. The first summer, I could only use the outdoor shower on the back of Cecily's house, the one meant to wash off sand from the beach.

I step into the kitchen to find Baron standing over Duke, coaxing him to drink something from a mug. When he sees me, though, he steps between us, blocking my view of his brother.

"Go to our room," he says. "Don't come out."

"Let me help," I say, not sure what's going on, what's wrong.

"He doesn't want you to see him like this," Baron says, hoisting Duke from the chair and dragging him out of the room. I hear them making their way up the stairs slowly, knocking into the wall a few times, Baron ordering him to take steps. Then I hear the bathroom door slam upstairs.

I swallow hard, trying not to think about what I saw—his hands black with dirt and blood, nails torn away, olive skin now an almost colorless grey-green; his eyes sunken and hollow, lips blue. I pick up Seeley and hold him to my chest, pressing my face into his fur. He purrs and rubs his head against my face.

Colt found him first, out behind the house in the woods, crying for his mother. He was just a kitten. My parents wanted to take him to a shelter, but I knew what they did to unwanted cats there. I hid him in my room and wouldn't bring him out when they said it was time to go. I didn't even care when he had an accident under my bed. Finally Aurora said I could have a cat if I wanted one so badly, but wouldn't I rather have a Russian Blue or a serval or even a Maine Coon? But I didn't want a purebred or a designer cat. I wanted the little orange tabby with his white paws and chest. He needed someone to look out for him, and I knew he was special, even if they couldn't see it.

I sit with my back against the bathroom door for a long time, Seeley cradled in my arms, purring. Inside the room, I can hear Baron's low murmurs, soft splashes of water, the faucet going on again a few times. After a while, Duke answers. I can't make out their words, and I want to know what happened, but they don't want me in there. There is always a line between them and me. I'm not sure if they put it there or if I did. Maybe it's a twin thing, and I'll never be able to cross it. They have their own relationship, independent of me, and I never minded, except when they used it against me.

But maybe once, I'd like to come first to someone. To not be an outsider looking in, a loner figuring out the shape of the other puzzle pieces so I can sneak into the box and pretend I belong. I'd like to be loved the most, not because I look a certain way or carry a certain name or keep the secrets of dangerous men. That's where Baron got me. He made me feel like I was truly special, not for what he could get from me—he could get any beautiful girl, had his own name, and learned all my secrets, and he still wanted me. He made me think he saw what I was and valued it.

And then he destroyed it.

I should be happy that he's upset right now. I should be glad that he's suffering, that he's feeling something he rarely gets to feel. But I can't be, because Duke is suffering, and his hurting brings less satisfaction than it should. At first, it did. I thought he deserved it, that he was paying for what he did to me. But I think it's like Royal said—living is paying. For someone like Duke, his conscience is his punishment. He's done his brothers' bidding, his father's, but it's taken a toll. He may try to blot it out with alcohol and drugs and sex, but he carries the weight of guilt that neither Baron nor I feel.

I can't say I've forgiven him, but I can say that he's paid.

When I can't bear the thought of him not wanting to see me any longer, I set Seeley down, scoot up the wall and grip the knob. To my surprise, it's not locked. I turn it and swing open the door.

Duke's in the bath, his head resting back on the edge, eyes closed. The color has come back into his face, and his arms lay along the porcelain sides of the clawfoot tub. One of his hands is clean, and Baron's holding the other one, painstakingly cleaning it with the kind of expert precision that he'll need as a surgeon. One of Duke's lids twitches, probably when Baron hits a sore spot. The fingers have more nerve endings than anywhere else in the body, and Duke's are in bad shape, his skin shredded, his nails broken and torn.

I try to imagine how it happened, Duke in a closed coffin, scratching at the lid and screaming while dirt rained down on it. Trying to slow his breathing and not panic so he can conserve oxygen in the small box until Baron got there. Does he know to do that? Is that a thing normal people know?

And if he was buried alive, who held the shovel?

"Can I come in?" I ask.

"Refresh the water," Baron orders. "Then you can wash his hair."

I step into the room. Baron kneels on one side of the tub. Water has sloshed out, creating puddles on the tile floor, but for once, he doesn't seem to notice that everything is not neat and orderly. His knees are soaked, the water creeping up the legs of his pants, splashed down one side of his shirt. His glasses are folded neatly a few feet away, the lenses fogged over. It's disconcerting how much they look alike when Baron's a little unkempt. Even the DOLL scar on Duke's chest doesn't set him apart anymore.

I move to the other side of the tub carefully. If I slip on the water, that could be the end. My feet will slide out from under me, my head hit the side of the tub just so. My neck snaps, and my body seizes, convulsions wracking it, my head flopping limply on my broken neck. My spinal cord is severed, and my body goes still on the floor in a lifeless heap. Baron buries my body in the grave that he dug for Jane, the one she buried Duke alive inside. But not before he finds the angel of death in my pocket.

Baron hands me the shampoo, and I sit on the step stool at the head of the tub. The film in my head rewinds, the dark puddles of blood turning clear again, changing back to water. I pick a few pine needle shards from Duke's thick hair before massaging the foam into his scalp.

"Are you okay?" I ask finally.

"Would you care?" he asks.

SELENA

"I would," I say, my fingers sliding under the back of his neck, where his skin is gritty with dirt. "I do."

Baron said Jane was gone when he went back for her.

I examine my feelings around that. I don't like that he still feels enough connection to her that he had to go see her. I don't like that he went to kill her at all. I told him to have Duke do it, if not directly, then to plant the seeds of the idea. That was Duke's punishment, but it was also her best shot at escape, especially when I told her what to say to him, how to get to him the way I got to Baron. I had to try, after what I saw. After what she told me. I hadn't anticipated Baron following his brother, though, finishing the job.

My throat tightens at the thought. My only solace is that maybe she somehow survived them both, and that's why Baron couldn't find her. Maybe she found Duke instead, when it was his time to go back and see her, and she got her revenge. She doesn't know him like I do. She doesn't know that life itself is painful for him, that he's paid for his part in her fate every day since we left her here. And if she did, maybe it still wouldn't be enough for her. Sometimes, it's not enough for me, when I remember all they did to me, that he's the reason I lost everything I never knew I wanted. He was there. He didn't just witness. He participated. He reveled in the chaos, the madness, the pain. He caused it as much as Baron did.

I tighten my fingers on the back of his neck.

Wrapping my fingers around his head, I twist, snapping his neck in one swift crack.

I tip his head back, pull the bottle from my pocket, and dump the contents down his throat.

I lift his head and slam it down on the side of the tub again and again until his skull caves, blood swirling through the water, transforming it into a bathtub full of strawberry syrup.

But if I did that, I'd still have Baron... For a moment.

Even if Baron walked out, and then I struck, once Duke was gone, I'd be left alone with him and his depraved punishments. He'll never let me go. Duke is my guard dog, the only thing standing between me and his brother, the attack dog. The best I can do is to survive them both, appeal to Duke's humanity, and direct Baron's dark impulses towards those who deserve it. And when I can't do that, aim them at the one person who can survive them—me.

SELENA

seven

Duke Dolce

They put me to bed between them. That place is usually carefully reserved for Mabel, both because we can protect her and because we can guard her there. Baron's also very aware of touching me, even when we're with Mabel. He always scoots away, adjusts positions, moves his hands. I think he knows, even though I've never told him. He always knows everything.

Just like tonight, he knows that I need this, even though I hate it as much as I love it beyond reason, without reason. Mabel scoots close and wraps her arms around me like we're dancing, threading her fingers in my hair and resting her cheek against my chest.

I hold back from returning the gesture, even though I crave the comfort, the intimacy. For once, she can know what it's like to give more, and I'll make sure she knows it, even if it keeps me from getting what I need. So I let my arms hang at my sides instead of wrapping her into a mutual embrace. Neither of us deserve that, anyway.

"You going to tell me what happened?" she whispers in the dark.

"I just…" I say, turning my face toward the ceiling. "Stopped. That's all."

"Well, I'm glad you restarted."

She wraps her arms tighter around me, like she doesn't even need me to hold her back.

Tonight, she's the first to fall asleep. Usually it's Baron if we've brutalized her enough to satisfy him, or me, if I resisted an evening pearl and drank myself stupid instead.

I lay there, annoyed that my cold shoulder didn't work on her. After a while, I hear Baron shifting in the sheets.

"I think we should go back tomorrow," he says.

"We just got here," I point out, absently scratching at my arms. Inside me, under my skin, the itch for more has sprung up. I can't remember the last time I went a whole day without visiting Wonderland.

"This place isn't good for any of us."

I know he's just saying that so he doesn't single me out. He and Mabel are too rational to let a place get to them.

Then again, he's the one who snapped first. He choked her out. I didn't hurt anyone.

"Don't you want to find her?" I ask, giving in at last and wrapping my arms around Mabel. She nestles closer in her sleep, as if I've ever protected her.

"I'm not a bounty hunter," Baron says behind me. "I can work from anywhere."

"What about that Ingrid chick?"

"I'd rather put distance between her and Mabel," he says. "If she's even the one who was here."

"You think it was Jane?" I ask, a little shiver racing up my spine.

"I don't know," Baron admits quietly. "If she's alive, and she wanted to find me, she would have gone back to the rental we had last summer."

"She could have asked around," I point out, turning onto my back. "Even if no one in Havoc Harbor knows us, we're pretty noticeable, even in a place that sees a lot of tourists in the summer."

"True," Baron muses. "They could have found out that we had a connection with Mabel and where she lived, especially if her aunt is still around here somewhere. Which is all the more reason to leave."

"So if Jane was staying here before we came back..." I trail off, cold dread racing like spiders over my skin.

"Where is she now?" Baron finishes.

"Don't you want to know why she waited for us here?"

"There's only one thing she'd want."

Revenge.

I roll back toward Mabel and cradle her close, suddenly sure we're being watched, even at this very moment. Selfishly, I'm glad I'm in the middle, that no one can creep up behind me from either side.

SELENA

"What if she's here now?" I ask into Mabel's hair. I don't want to see my brother's face, to see his disappointment or scorn. He's not afraid of Jane. Nothing scares him, not even death.

"We'll leave in the morning," he says, resting a hand on my shoulder. "I'll stay up tonight. I want to look into some things."

"You don't have to," I say, but I'm relieved.

"I can't sleep anyway." Baron stands and grabs a pair of sweats. "Besides, I have a connection to establish on the way home."

When he's gone, I lie in bed, unable to sleep even after the long, fucked up day. I think about going back. I think about my family, what's left of it, back in Faulkner sitting around the tree, laughing and talking, telling the kids about Santa. I can't stop wishing I was there, even though it wasn't that great last year. Baron was gone and Dad was dead and Ma didn't come home because she had some charity gala to go to the day before and she was too hungover to fly the next day. Besides, she said, we were all grown up now and we wouldn't want to spend time with her anyway.

She was wrong, but no one argued. It's impossible to argue with her.

At least I had Olive. This year, I won't be able to hang out with her. Harper and Royal wouldn't let me near her after what I did, and it's probably for the best. With all the Alice I take, I probably would get hard if she climbed in my lap this time.

I told myself I'd slow down over our time away, and the thought of not getting that break fills me with dread. At the same time, the craving intensifies at the thought of how close we are to going back, to being around all those shiny blue pearls all day long, able to pop them at will, any time, without anyone knowing. I can still slow down, though. I can limit myself to one pearl per day. It'll be good for me to clear my head a little.

Mabel stirs against me, her lashes fluttering against my neck. "Duke?" she whispers sleepily.

"It's me," I say, relieved that it was my name on her lips when she woke. I wrap my arms around her, pulling her tight to me.

"Where's Baron?"

All the good feelings sour. Of course she asks for him.

"I don't know," I say, rolling away from her. "Why don't you go find him if you're so worried about him?"

She's quiet a long moment, and I think she fell back asleep. But then her fingers brush my side. "I'm worried about you," she says quietly.

Some mean, selfish part of me is vindicated. It likes that she's worried, that she noticed, that she cares. I think it's my demon, but I can't be sure anymore. Colt broke the barrier between us when he said what he did, that there's no demon, there's just me. Now we bleed into each other more and more often, so I can't tell where he ends and I begin.

"You shouldn't be," I say. "I'm not a good person."

She lets out a soft snort of breath. "None of us are good people, Duke."

"You were," I point out. "Before we ruined you."

"I was ruined long before you came along," she says quietly, her tone bitter.

"But we made you a monster like us."

"That may be true," she says. "But if I'm a monster of your making, that doesn't make me less monstrous than you."

It's my turn to think that over, and then I say the thing that's been tormenting me since last summer, the thought I try to drown with pills and booze, try to escape in Wonderland.

"I might be the kind of monster the Black Widow takes out." My words come out flat, but suddenly I'm shaking, sick at having said the words aloud.

"Why do you think that?" Mabel says, her voice careful.

"I—I have a friend who's a kid," I say. "Isn't that the kind of man you kill?"

She thinks about it, and even though I wish she would jump in and reassure me right away, her thoughtfulness reassures me more than any denial could. She's considering it before she gives me an honest answer, something I can't rely on most people to give. That's why I told her first, before even Baron.

But finally, I can't take her silence. My stomach is knotted and sour, and my heart is racing so hard I can't think straight. "Is that weird?" I manage. "Is it more than weird?"

"I wouldn't say it's normal," she says at last. "Why are you friends with her?"

"I don't know," I say miserably. "She's just... Fun, and simple, and I don't have to impress her or worry about what she thinks. It reminds me of how it was to be a kid, when I didn't care about all the shit I have to care about now." I cover my eyes with my arm, since looking at her when I ask this would be unbearable. "Do you think that means I'm a pedophile?"

"Are you attracted to her?"

"No," I say, horrified that she'd ask that.

"Have you done anything physical to her?"

"What? No! It makes me sick to think of it. We just hung out and ate cereal for dinner and, I don't know... She's easy to talk to."

"Then why would you think you it's wrong?"

"Because. Everyone said that. Or acted like it."

"Sounds like they're the ones who shouldn't be around children," she says. "Why else would their minds go there?"

"Probably because our dad was basically one," I say, wanting to fucking die. "And they think if I was raised by one, I'm suspect, and now I have a kid friend, so they've got to watch me and see if I'm as sick as him. What if I am?"

I'm quaking so hard Mabel can feel it, and she rests a steadying hand on my chest. "I don't think wanting to feel like a kid again makes you sick," she says. "Sounds like they're projecting, or else they're just sanctimonious cunts who would rather ruin someone's life than consider the many facets of being human."

I've never heard Mabel use that word before, but she says it so calmly, in such a straightforward manner, as if it's an indisputable fact. Maybe it is.

"You really think so?" I ask, rolling back to face her. I tuck a pillow between my head and my arm, watching her. "Are you just saying that to make me feel better?"

"That's not something I do," she says, but I'm not so sure.

Maybe she doesn't mean to, or do it intentionally, but hearing her get defensive of me like that has already made me feel a thousand times better. Just as she needs me to get out of her head, I need her to get out of mine, to calm the raging storm inside it. In all the time I've spent with her, the pearl lady has never made me feel as good as Mabel has in these five minutes.

"Am I sick for wondering, though?" I ask. "Because they'd probably think so. They didn't even like her coming in my room."

She's quiet a minute, and then she answers slowly. "I think that's good," she says. "Not because of you, but because they're protecting her. More people should do that instead of assuming everyone has good intentions. But their caution doesn't mean you're doing something wrong. Just as being introspective and wondering if you're a monster because you were raised by a monster and everyone is telling you that you are one doesn't make you a monster. It makes you self-aware. Your actions make you a monster."

I swallow hard and force the next words out because I've come this far, and maybe I want her to finish what I couldn't today. "I thought about her once... when we were hooking up."

She stiffens in my arms. "You were fantasizing about her while you were fucking me?"

"No," I snap, a shudder going through me. "She popped into my head, like, I didn't want to think about her, but she came up."

"And then?"

"And then I pushed the thought away," I say. "It wasn't a sexual thought. It was... I didn't want to think it. I hate that it happened, that I can't control my mind, Mabel. What if it happens again?"

"That sounds like an intrusive thought," she says. "Not like you were getting off on it."

"I wasn't," I promise her, so miserable I want to die. "I hate that my mind does that. What's wrong with me?"

"You can't control intrusive thoughts," she says. "They intrude. You don't want them to. They're terrible."

"It was terrible," I agree, squeezing my eyes closed. "How do I make them go away?"

"You don't," she says, pressing her ear to my chest and wrapping her arms around me again. "You just know that you'll be okay anyway. They're not real. Just thoughts."

"How do you know?"

"Because I have them all the time," she says. "Mine are gruesome. Usually someone dies in a terrible way. Sometimes they're things I'd want to happen. Sometimes they're the worst things that could happen. But I don't get to choose which one comes."

"I love you so much," I blurt, diving into her. I press my face into her chest, my eyes burning, and squeeze her tight. I didn't know how scared I was that she'd say something different.

She wraps her arms around my head, holding me to her heart like that's where I belong. "You're allowed to have friends, Duke," she says. "And anyone who's never stopped and asked themselves if they're a bad person when someone told them they were, only proves that they're incapable of self-reflection and therefore, by most humans' definition, a bad person. Anyone who would question why you did is not only a bad person but a stupid one."

"You love me?" I ask, running my hands up her sides, pressing my ear to her chest to hear her heartbeat, as if I can hear a lie if she tells one.

"Yes," she says simply, threading her fingers through my hair.

"I won't let him hurt you," I tell her, my voice ragged but fierce. "I promise."

It's a promise we both know I can't keep, but I wish more than anything that I could find a way to protect this girl who understands me and lets me be my most vulnerable self without judgment. I wish I could find a way to make her trust me enough to do that with me. But I don't know how, and I don't know how to protect her from my twin the next time he comes for her. One of these times, I'm afraid it will be the last.

SELENA

eight

Duke Dolce

Time passes like a fever dream back in Wonderland. Nothing changes from hour to hour, day to day, month to month. Ingredients go in, pearls come out, sliding down the chutes in warm, loud rushes. I still hear them falling when I lay down in the silence at night, in the charming little place I decorated with Mabel. I smell them in my clothes, my nose. I taste them in the back of my mouth when I go to sleep, in the thirst in my throat in the morning. I see them cascading in shimmering waves when I close my eyes. All I see is blue.
Blue.
She doesn't come back, but she haunts me anyway. If she was okay, if she was alive, she would go back for Olive. I check in with Crystal, ask her about the kid more than I should. She probably thinks I'm a pedo, like everyone else.

But Mabel doesn't think so, and she knows about predators, so I tell myself it's okay if I ask, if I check to see if Blue came back for her. Maybe Baron damaged her brain and she forgot about Olive. Maybe he cracked her skull and she got amnesia like Colt did when Royal beat his head in. But how could anyone forget Olive?

She haunts me as much as her sister. Sometimes, when I'm sitting on the cinderblocks in the dead grass, smoking a cigarette and debating whether I can take one more trip with Alice before they come to get me, I see her instead of Dad. She's standing in the corner of the yard, in the corner of my eye, a little girl ghost who melts with the smoke tendrils curling from my mouth when I turn her way. Sometimes I think I'm imagining it, but sometimes I'm sure someone was there.

I know it's not Olive. I'm not stupid. But is it Blue?

Or the Black Widow Killer, finally come to collect?

Even if I don't like kids, I hurt people.

Mabel and Harper and Lo.

Dawson.

Dad.

I see him almost every day now, standing with hands on hips, disappointment on face.

I hear him say, "How long has this been going on?" and "The priest will take care of this."

I feel the impossibility of refusal, the helplessness, the shame—for what I do and can't stop doing, for allowing him to bring me back again and again, for not standing up to him or the priest. I let it happen, so why does it fuck with my head so much?

It's not Dad outside the barred windows of Wonderland or in the overgrown back lot, of course. It might be Mabel's stalker, though. Or the FBI. Maybe they know what we're doing here, what I do here all day every day. Maybe they're watching, like Baron watched Mabel. They want me to see them, to go to Baron and tell him. Then they can prove he's the mastermind, that I'm just a grunt. He always tries to give me credit, but all I did was test his first iterations. I was his subject before Jane.

He got rid of her once she served her purpose. He called her garbage. One day, he'll see that I've served mine.

The FBI doesn't think I've served my purpose yet though. That must be why they wait, why they duck away every time I blink, so I'm not sure if I'm seeing things or if they were really there. Maybe they don't care about Lady Alice at all, because they think they're onto the Black Widow Killer, and even busting a drug operation isn't worth blowing their cover.

Or maybe they were collecting information, and today is the day they'll make their move. I might even be their target. After all, I make the stuff, all day, every day. Maybe that's why Baron put me on this job. I make all the money, make it all possible, and I take all the risk. He knows I won't rat him out. And if we're caught, I'm the one who will take the fall. Maybe he's even tipped them off—him or Mabel. They needed the money, but now that Baron crossed the nine-figure mark, they might be ready to get rid of me and disappear off the map. They could start over anywhere with that kind of money, and Mabel already knows how to disappear.

SELENA

I try to imagine prison, but I can't. It's too similar to my life now, plodding through endless, monotonous days in a dark building, an hour in the yard here and there. If that was my future, I would find a way to cut it short. If I couldn't get a belt, I'd make the other inmates do it. It wouldn't be hard. Talk shit to the wrong guy, and if that didn't work, tell them what everyone thinks about me is true, turn a life sentence into a death sentence.

"Hey."

I look up. Someone is standing in the yard, grass seed stocks around her ankles. I squint into the bright, afternoon sun. My skin is damp with sweat, but a chill passes over me before she steps out of the sun, and she's more than a silhouette, more than a ghost of a girl who didn't stay in her grave.

"I thought you quit smoking," Mabel says, nodding to the circle of butts on the ground around my feet.

How long was I out here this time?

"I did," I say, pocketing the gold pack, the same ones her brother smoked in another life. "Mostly."

"We've been looking for you," she says. "Baron closed up shop."

"Damn," I say. "Sorry. Must have lost track of time."

"You really shouldn't take so many of those."

"Don't smoke, don't take Alice," I say. "You don't want me to have any fun."

I stomp past her, but she catches my elbow. "Duke," she says. "I don't mind if you have fun. I'm worried about you."

I look down at her, those blue eyes so convincing, and I melt. I cup her face in my hands and kiss her, and she lets me, even though I've been smoking and she hates that.

"I'm okay, Duchess," I say, drawing back and sweeping a strand of hair back from her cheek. "I don't take that many. It's just something to pass the time. It gets boring being in there all day."

"Promise?" she asks, searching my eyes.

"I promise."

We're not supposed to lie to each other, but how can I know she's holding up her end of the bargain? And if she's not, then I don't have to, either.

"Good," she says, stepping in and wrapping her arms around me, pressing her ear to my chest. "Because I don't think I could live without you."

She doesn't think Baron would let her live. That's what she means. That I'm the only thing keeping him from going too far, like he almost did that day he found out about Blue. I like knowing her survival depends on me. That's the only thing either of them really need me for.

"I have a surprise for you," Baron says when we slide into the car.

I don't answer because I think he's talking to Mabel, but then they're both looking at me in the back seat.

"What?" I ask.

"We're going back to Faulkner for the summer," Baron says.

I wanted that so much at Christmas, but it's not Christmas anymore. It's the last day of classes for the students, which means Baron and Mabel are done with the school year.

"But... What about the operation?" I ask, gesturing back toward Wonderland as Baron pulls away.

"I found someone to run it," he says. "A couple people, in fact. It's past time you were out of there, anyway. You shouldn't be making the product. We're too big for that now."

"I don't mind," I say, trying not to panic at the thought of leaving without grabbing a handful. If I'd known we'd be leaving, I would have taken more than that. A handful won't last me all summer. I need a whole bag. I have some at home, but I would have been stockpiling if I knew he was going to pull me out.

"I know you don't," Baron says. "But you should be in a higher-level position. You're joint owner. You shouldn't be in the trenches with the stuff. Besides, it's not good for you to be around that all day."

Fuck. I try to calculate how many I have at home against how many I'll need, how many I take per day, and how many days of summer I'll need to make them last.

Did they plan this, make sure I wouldn't go back in and grab some on the way out? Is that why Baron closed up, and why Mabel didn't tell me we weren't coming back tomorrow?

"Aren't you happy to be going home?" Mabel presses, turning around in her seat to look at me. "You haven't seen your family in a year."

"I thought Royal wouldn't let you come back," I say to my brother.

"We worked it out," he says, like it's all inconsequential, though I know it's not. Family matters to Baron more than anything else.

"How?" I ask, narrowing my eyes at him.

"I made a deal with Harper."

"What kind of deal?"

He pulls up at our place and turns off the car before meeting my eyes in the mirror. "I told her I'd help her track down her missing friend."

"What friend?"

"You know which one," he says, holding my gaze. My heart lurches, and I wonder how long he's known. We never talked about it. I hoped he didn't know, hadn't put it together, connected her with Olive. I didn't until I was about to kill her. But of course Baron's always three steps ahead. Maybe he knew the whole time. Probably he did.

"She's dead," I say, because she has to be. She would have gone back for Olive if she were alive.

"She doesn't know that," Baron says, swinging open his door. "And for that matter, neither do we. I'd like to find out what happened to her too. So we all win."

Inside, we pack our things. I scour the apartment for pearls, searching every nook and cranny, every spot I've taped them in case I need a boost when the others aren't looking. By the time I'm done, the stash I've put together is pathetic. Despair thrums inside me, and I resist the urge to pop one right now.

Maybe this will be a good thing. Time to dry out a little, so when we come back in the fall, I won't need so many to reach Wonderland. Besides, I won't be sitting around all day in a dark warehouse going out of my mind. I'll have lots of other stuff to do, so I probably won't even need them.

We take my Lexus because it's the biggest and most comfortable. Baron drives, and I sit in the back, thinking it's funny, because in high school when Royal drove, Baron always sat in the back. But he never felt less important like I do. I'm sure of that.

"I thought you'd be more excited to be going home," Mabel says to me as we cross the bridge into Arkansas.

Only a few hours left. My stomach tightens, and I lay my head back, refusing the nagging urge to reach in my pocket and take one of the pearls. I don't want to be high when I get home.

I don't want to see disappointment on Crystal's face. Judgment on Royal's. He was always too strong to get addicted to anything. He'd never let a substance control him. And I don't either. I'm the one in control.

I'm not a junkie like fucking Colt Darling, who's been in and out of rehab since graduation last summer.

Suddenly I'm back there, outside the Slaughterpen, the last time I saw him. His fist around my cock, his fingers in my mouth, the taste of my own cum on my tongue. I shove the image away. That was the night I hurt Olive. That's why I let him do that, to punish myself. That's all it was. That, and being fucked up. And he was probably as fucked up as me, if not more. He probably won't even remember. And if he does, he'd never say it aloud. Hopefully he's back in rehab and I won't have to see him at all, and we can both pretend it never happened, that none of it happened.

I wanted to go home so badly at Christmas, but maybe that's because I couldn't. Now that it's not only an option but a reality, everything comes crashing in. Not just Colt, but Olive. What I did to her. What will she do when she sees me? Will she run away scared? Will Harper even let me see her? And then there's Harper, who I got used to, but it was always there, the guilt of what I did following me like a dark cloud over my head, always lurking, waiting to drop reminders like acid rain when I forgot for a moment and laughed with her or noticed how hot she was. Then it would dump onto me, burning away my skin, eating away at me like fire.

Crystal wasn't there for that, so at least she can look at me without seeing a monster. But even she was there the night we left Dad to die. She left him too, and that shared knowledge doesn't just bind us together, it weighs us down. The more of us who are in a room together, the heavier it gets, the burden magnified by the weight of each person's guilt. We are all murderers, not just me. We all made the decision together.

Getting away from that, being with only Mabel and Baron, who weren't there that night, has let me put it out of my mind for hours, sometimes days at a time. When I'm back in Faulkner, it will be all around me—not just Dad's vengeful ghost, but the people who helped create it.

Crystal, Devlin, Royal, Harper. Even my old friends from high school, who I never talk to anymore. That's probably why. None of us want to remember, to go back to that night.

Suddenly I can't remember why I ever wanted to go back to Faulkner.

But we're already passing the city limit sign, and it's too late to turn back.

nine

Mabel Darling

The minute we open the doors and climb out of Duke's SUV, a gangly child with her hair swinging around her shoulders comes bounding out of the house, across the gravel, and flings herself at Duke. He catches her, stumbling back, and she wraps her arms and legs around him like a monkey and clings on tight.

"Dukey," she screams. "You're back!"

"Olive," he says, his face buried in her shoulder. "You're not mad at me?"

"Why would I be mad?" she asks, pulling back and frowning up at him.

He tries to pry her off, and I'm sure he's thinking about what he asked me. It makes me mad that someone let their own inappropriate thoughts color his opinion of himself, though I don't blame him for asking. If someone told me I was a pedophile, I'd be self-conscious around children too, and I've never even wanted to be around them. They're messy and unpredictable.

I hate to be the bearer of bad news, Miss Darling...

"You look different," Duke says, finally untangling himself and setting her down. "You're all tall, and your hair..."

"I know," she says, grabbing his hand for balance and swishing her hair dramatically back and forth. "Royal took me to a place called a *salon* when he found out only my sister had ever cut my hair. It cost *more than a hundred dollars* to cut it!"

"Okay, you don't have to tell everyone how much it cost," says an older girl with a dark complexion and dark hair who just emerged from the house. She pulls the girl little girl away from Duke. She's probably the one looking after her, and even though I hate that it's made Duke so insecure, it makes me like her a little more for being the kind of girl who protects kids.

"It's not everyone," Olive says, pouting. "It's Dukey boy!"

"And all his haircuts cost that much too," the older girl says.

"That's crazy," Olive bursts out, laughing and pointing to Duke's head. "You hardly have any hair."

"I'm Harper," the older girl says to me, tipping her chin.

"Hi, I'm Mabel," I say, reciting the words my parents taught me to say, so I didn't embarrass them at parties and around strangers. "I don't like to shake hands, but it's nice to meet you, Harper."

I smile, and she gives me an odd look, so I know I didn't get it right despite my best efforts.

"Damn, it's weird that we've never met," she says. "I feel like I already know you."

"Even if we'd met, it's unlikely that you'd know me."

The corner of her mouth twitches up. "Too true."

I'm mystified, since she smiled instead of staring at me like a freak when I said something that most people probably don't say when they meet someone, and when I said the proper words, she looked uneasy.

After an awkward pause, she says, "Let's get your bags inside."

"Thank you, but we're staying at Summer House."

I watch her momentary surprise melt behind a mask of indifference. This is Royal's girlfriend. I've heard a lot about her too, but she's as foreign to me as a single hair of unidentifiable origin at a crime scene. I wonder what he's told her to make her feel like she knows me.

I wonder if she knows that once, her boyfriend was tied to a chair and bleeding, and he begged me to help him, and I walked away. I shiver at the memory, but I no longer feel ashamed. If there's one thing the Dolces are experts at, it's payback. Royal did far worse to me.

"What's a summer house?" Olive asks, interrupting my spiraling thoughts.

"It's a house where you stay just for the summer," Duke says. "Like a beach house."

"Summer House is the name of my grandfather's house in town," I say. "It's not a summer house."

"Do you have a winter house?"

"Yes."

"Is it named Winter House?"

"No."

"Does it have a name?"

"Yes."

"Why do you name your houses?"

I stare at her a long second, trying to figure out what developmental stage her brain is in and how to explain it in a way she'd understand. This is why I never wanted children. I didn't understand them, even when I was a child.

Except one.

A prick of pain, a soft gasp, a drop of blood. Dimpled knuckles, small fingers interlacing, palms meeting. "Now we're sisters forever."

Olive is still waiting, so I answer after a long pause. "So that, when the family is talking about property, we know which house we're talking about."

"How many do you have?" she asks, gaping at me.

"I don't have any," I say. "But one day, Summer House will be mine."

I don't tell her how impressive that is, that hundreds of years of tradition were broken when our grandfather put me in the will. Only sons inherited before that. I don't tell her, because I never tell.

"Then how do you mix them up?" she asks.

"My family has ten or twelve houses," I explain. "But that's between six men."

She turns to Duke, her eyes so wide we can see white all around her irises. "She's even richer than you?" she asks, clearly awestruck.

"Tons," he says, smiling at me over her head. "In fact, she used to own this house."

He nods to the house they emerged from, the house where I grew up with Colt, with Devlin across the lawn where parents passed like strangers in the night, ducking behind lilacs and azaleas, their footprints in the silvery dew the only evidence of their treachery.

"That's right," I say. "I lived here when I was your age. If you look inside one of the closets, you might still find my name scratched into the wall."

"You're Ma-bel?" she asks, pronouncing it like two words: *May Bell.*

"Mabel," Duke corrects her, putting an arm around me and smiling down at Olive. "She's my girlfriend now."

Olive looks from Duke to me and back. "Do you have sex?" she demands.

"Only when she wants to," Duke says, squeezing me against him.

"What about when you want to?"

"I always want to," he says. "I love her, and she's sexy as fuck."

"Okay, let's go inside," Harper says, putting an arm around Olive's shoulders and steering her that way.

"Was that inappropriate?" Duke mutters to me as Harper leads Olive inside, Baron on her heels.

"A little, judging by her reaction."

SELENA

"So you dropped your stuff off already?" Harper asks.

"We went by Summer House and got settled first," Baron tells Harper. "Mabel had to get her cat situated."

"You have a cat?" Olive asks, twisting free of Harper and coming back to us.

"Yes," I say. "Seeley Boots."

"Is he named after a seal?"

"No."

"Good, because seals are scary. They eat penguins. Did you know that the ones that balance balls on their noses at the circus aren't seals, they're sea lions?"

"No."

"What's he named after?"

"A character on a TV show."

"My favorite TV show is *Pimp My Ride*. Have you watched that?"

"No."

"It's not on TV anymore, but Royal found all the episodes online, so I get to watch one every night before bed. Sometimes I watch more, if they forget to lock my laptop before they leave."

"I heard that," Harper calls back.

Olive giggles and lowers her voice. "I know they won't catch me watching extra if they're making noise together because that means they're having sex. They have sex *a lot.*"

I try to imagine the man she's describing, a father figure limiting a kid's screen time, but I can't fit it with the pictures of Royal in my mind—a boy with dry, cracked lips begging for freedom; one with only hatred burning in his eyes when he looked down and saw the blood, and instead of letting the river wash me away with it, he told me I didn't get to take the easy way out, that I had to suffer like everyone else.

And then we're stepping into the living room, and he stands from one of the chairs, and my mind loops in on itself. He's even bigger than I remember, too big—*make it fit*—and he takes up all the air in the room, and I can't breathe.

Baron is snuggled against me, "he hasn't been with anyone since that night..."

He's smiling, pleading, and I want to make him happy, and Royal is over me, inside me, and I'm tearing in two, and he spits on my face.

Darling whore.

Now Duke is pounding him on the back with his arms around him, and Royal skips the back-pounding and just wrenches Duke into his arms and wraps around him like he's some sort of amoeba absorbing its food. He closes his eyes when he hugs his little brother, and I think it's such a strangely personal thing to hug someone, your whole bodies pressed together, eyes shut tight so you don't see anything, all you do is feel.

And then Baron's greeting him, and they embrace too, and I watch with a detached fascination as they stand there with their chests pressed together, arms circling each other, neither of them slapping each other's shoulders the way males typically do to assert dominance, establish comradery, or avoid giving the impression of intimacy. It's like they're aliens engaged in some inhuman form of communication, a portal in their chests plugged in to each other, information passing at light speed along the connection.

And then Royal's lids lift, and he's staring directly back at me with those inky black eyes, and I'm sure he knows, he knows everything, even though I never told.

Duke sits and pulls me onto his lap, and I can't breathe, I can't—I can't—

"Hey." Duke's fingers wrap gently around my chin, and he brings my face around. His eyes stare into mine, the warmest chocolate with tiny flecks of caramel, sweet and comforting. "You okay?"

I nod mutely, trying to breathe. I'm not crazy.

You said you'd let him. Why are you acting like you didn't want to?

I'm not crazy.

You're lucky someone brought you in when they did... With this amount of internal bleeding, you could have died.

Lucky. I'm lucky. Not crazy.

Would you like to tell us what really happened, Miss Darling?

This is a normal reaction. I'm a normal girl, and this is a normal feeling, and I'm not crazy.

"I'm right here," Duke murmurs, touching his forehead to mine. "Nothing's going to hurt you, Duchess. You're okay."

"Okay."

I'm okay. I'm lucky. I'm alive.

"Look what I can do," Olive says, bracing her hands on the arm of our chair and bouncing up and down. "I can run with the same arm and the same leg at the same time. Want to see?"

"Sure, kid," Duke says. "Let's see. That sounds complicated."

Olive starts galloping around the room, swinging her arm forward on the same side as whichever leg is moving forward.

"Thank you," I whisper to Duke.

"I'm doing it, I'm doing it," yells Olive.

"Yeah, you are," Duke says, encouraging her. *"Brava!"*

Then to me. "What do you think we should name our kid?"

"Duke," I say, my heart twisting and my throat thickening.

"I know," he says. "You want to finish school, but what about when you're done?"

"I don't think that's in the cards," I whisper through the pain in my throat.

He squeezes me and kisses my temple. "Okay, but one day, I bet you'll change your mind. If you had a kid, what would you name it?"

SELENA

"I don't know," I manage. "What would you?"

Duke's face lights up, and he starts rattling off a list, and he's too excited to notice me wiping away a tear. And even though he took everything from me, I can't bring myself to take this from him, so I let him go on.

ten

Baron Dolce

"I'm going for a walk," Mabel says, stepping into the doorway to the study, where I'm working.

I finish up what I'm doing before I spin the chair to face her. "Are you asking permission?"

"No," she says, scowling. "I'm telling you, so you know that I'm not running away."

I take in her appearance—white tennis shoes, navy shorts, a white T-shirt, a ponytail. She looks like the classic American girl-next-door, the exact type that a serial killer would target. Not for the first time, I consider that the Black Widow Killer was stalking her, waiting for the perfect victim. Is he one of her dates, one that got away?

I push myself up from my chair. "I'll go with you."

"Don't you like to run?" she asks. "I'll slow you down."

I know I made the right call, since she wouldn't argue unless she had something to hide. I'm beginning to think I'll never know the new Mabel. Even more unsettling, I wonder if I ever knew the old Mabel. I'm still not convinced that she's not the killer herself.

"I ran this morning," I say, stepping over her cat, who likes to sleep under my feet while I'm working. "I don't mind keeping you company."

I know this will bother her, since we think alike, and it would bother me for someone to erroneously assume I wanted company when I notified them of my plans. Goading her is usually Duke's specialty, but I'm particularly frustrated at the moment, and susceptible to more petty urges than usual.

"Should we get Duke?" she asks as she waits for me to lace up my shoes.

"He's over at the other house."

"Hickory House."

"What?"

"That's the name of your house," she says. "The house I grew up in. Hickory House."

"What about Devlin's house?"

"Lilac Place."

"Preston's?"

"That's just Preston's house," she says. "It wasn't in the family before they bought it, so it doesn't have a name. Same with my father's house. He had that built when he left Hickory House, so it wasn't a Darling family home."

Summer House is inside city limits, but it's on the north side of town in a nice area. Behind each house sprawls a large lawn, and beyond that, a section of woods. Mabel heads for that, and I follow, since she seems confident in her direction. It's a sweltering afternoon, and we're both sweating by the time we reach the shade of the trees.

"You could get a treadmill," I tell her. "That way you wouldn't have to leave the house."

"I like leaving the house."

"I remember that," I say, catching her hand. "From when we were dating."

"You could run on a treadmill too."

"I did last year," I say. "I didn't like to leave Jane alone more than necessary."

I watch her from the corner of my eye, searching for signs of jealousy or guilt.

Mabel is quiet for a minute. "Did you love her?" she asks at last.

"Of course not."

"Not even in the way you're able?"

"No," I say, scowling at her. "Why would you ask that?"

"Because you didn't kill her."

I bristle, but she doesn't notice. "I tried to kill her."

"I don't think so," Mabel says, never breaking stride as she steps over rocks and fallen branches. "I don't think you'd make a mistake like that."

"I wouldn't have, if you hadn't run," I grit out, stopping to help her over a log. "I saw your location, and I had to hurry back to get you. Was that your plan all along? Is that why you ran, knowing I'd come after you, and it might save her?"

She shrugs. "I don't see why you chose her. She didn't deserve what you did to her."

"You told me to get rid of her," I remind her.

"Death seemed preferable to torture."

I remember the night Royal came home and told us he'd taken her to the hospital after dragging her out of the river. "I think she jumped," he said. "That, or she walked in and tried to drown herself."

I was pleased with myself, knowing we'd pushed her to it. That we had won, making her life so unbearable she craved death.

I turn to Mabel now. "If death is preferably, why are you upset that I tried to kill her?"

"Not at all," she says. "I'm curious why you spared her."

"I didn't intentionally spare her," I say slowly, forcing my voice not to betray my irritation. "And I don't think you're in any position to cast judgment, seeing as how you led a half dozen men to their deaths. If you didn't kill them outright."

"Those men deserved it."

"Why?" I ask. "For talking to a girl who they thought was underage? You weren't, so did they even do anything wrong?"

"They had a sickness that can't be cured," she says. "They were removed from society before they could do further harm. What harm was Jane doing?"

"She was contributing by being my subject," I say. "Until you wanted her removed."

We walk in silence for a few minutes, Mabel having pulled her hand away and taken the lead again. "Maybe I made a mistake," she admits. "I let my sympathy get the better of me."

"That's unlike you."

"I'm not heartless," she says, and there's that defensiveness in her tone, just under the surface, the same one that creeps in when she says she's not crazy.

"You think I am."

It's not a question, and it doesn't bother me, but I enjoy turning the thought over in my mind, considering its implications.

"No," she says after a minute. "Duke is your heart."

The woods have grown thicker, the canopy so dense the sun barely shines through. Where it does, bright patches spot the leaves underfoot like blood left by a wounded animal.

"Are you bringing me out here to kill me?"

It's my attempt at a joke, but my gaze sweeps over her, searching for a gun. She couldn't have hidden even a small one in the scant clothing she's wearing, though.

"You wanted to come," she reminds me. "I would have come out here whether or not you joined me."

"Or maybe you knew I'd want to come if you told me you were walking alone. Especially if there's as killer still out there, stalking you."

Stalking her better than I can. That thought keeps me up at night far more than Jane.

"We're on Delacroix land now," she says, stepping over a pile of rocks on the invisible footpath she seems to be following through the woods. "Arkansas is a stand-your-ground state, so technically, they could shoot us if they saw us trespassing. They would never harm a Darling. Do they have a reason to want you dead?"

"No," I say, scowling at her. "I fit into society better than you do. The Delacroixs like me."

"All of them?"

I remember publicly humiliating Walker Delacroix in the café at Willow Heights, but he's only a teacher. We made Gideon fuck Gloria, and he left school afterwards, but that was his choice.

"The important ones like me," I say, annoyed by Mabel's perceptiveness.

She smiles, that secretive smile that makes me question everything, that makes me love and hate her in equal measure.

"What?" I demand.

"Who decides which ones are important?"

"Society," I say flatly. "Robert Delacroix is our lawyer. He's important."

"And Dr. Delacroix?"

I swat a mosquito on my arm. "You know I don't believe in psychology."

"Did you find anything about Dahlia?"

"No," I say. "If she's still alive, she's invisible. Probably going by another name."

"Another ghost," Mabel says, sounding vaguely pleased.

"She's not Ingrid, is she?" I ask.

Mabel would know that, but I wouldn't. Ingrid doesn't resemble the photos I found of the kid Mabel was friends with, but I can't be certain she hasn't had work done to disguise herself or simply changed dramatically since childhood.

"No," Mabel says. "But I was thinking I might go see my parents and ask them about her. They don't like me bringing it up, but... I remember once after I started asking about her again, my stepmom was talking on the phone to Grandpa, saying, 'I don't know what we're going to do with her.' When I walked in, she shoved an envelope in a drawer and pushed it closed like she was trying to hide it. She looked guilty. Maybe she was hiding her letters back to me."

"This seems like a distraction," I say, watching her closely. "We have a missing girl who has a lot of incriminating evidence about me on her body, and a ghost who might be following you and killing people for you."

"And Duke."

"And Duke."

We walk in silence for a few minutes. "I need to know," she says at last. "You can focus on the other girls. I don't find them important."

"And Duke?"

"He's important," she says quietly. "Do you know what's wrong with him?"

There are too many answers to that, and too many of them he wouldn't want me saying to Mabel. At last, I choose the one that covers all of them. "He's too sensitive."

"What can we do about him?"

"We'll figure it out."

We come out to a slight clearing that's not much more than a gap in the canopy. To our right, a series of two-by-four sections were nailed to a tree in the distant past, though they're greying and rotted away on the ends, covered over with a skim of green moss and splotches of flat, blue lichen. At the top of the rudimentary ladder, an equally decrepit platform spans the space between two branches of the old oak.

"Oh," Mabel says, her voice faint, her fingers going to her mouth.

"What is it?" I ask, frowning at her reaction.

In answer, she rushes toward the tree, grasping the highest board she can reach and bracing her foot on a lower one. It twists when she puts weight on it, and her shoe scrapes down the trunk.

"Mabel," I call, hurrying to her. "That doesn't look safe."

"You can stay down here," she says, lifting her foot to the next rung up from the one that caved. "I just want to see."

"See what?" I ask, but she's already climbing, not even testing each step with her weight.

"Careful," I order when a piece of wood comes off in her hand and tumbles to the ground.

She reaches the top without an answer and folds her body over the edge of the platform, boosting herself with her hands and scrambling over.

"This better be worth it," I mutter as I start up after her, going much more slowly. I'm not used to this side of Mabel. She's never reckless, never overcome by emotional urges.

When I reach the platform and climb on, she's sitting with her back to the trunk of the tree.

"You made it," she says. "I didn't know if the ladder would hold your weight."

"So it was a trap," I say, brushing off my hands. "Care to explain yourself?"

She shakes her head and uses her foot to push off some of the leaves wedged under a branch that's grown against the platform. "This is where I'd meet her."

"I don't think my nanny would have hiked all the way out here," I say, looking around at the decaying boards under us, some of them barely intact, all covered with a scummy layer of accumulated pollen, dirt, and patches of moss.

"Oh, she didn't," Mabel says. "And I wasn't allowed to go into the woods alone because there are coyotes and bears and snakes. But whenever my cousins came over to play with Colt, she had her hands full, so she didn't miss me. Or I'd tell the adults I was going to nap or read in my room, and then I'd sneak out."

She smiles at the memory, and I watch her, captivated by this tender side of her I haven't seen since I was courting her the first time. I thought it was gone.

"So even then, you only pretended to be a good girl?"

"Sometimes we read," she says with a smug little smile. "I'd bring a backpack with a picnic and books, and we'd sit on the blanket and eat pastries and read all day."

"Why?" I ask, cocking my head. "Your room would be more comfortable, and you have a bathroom. You could have your cook make whatever you wanted to eat, your drinks would be cold, and you could get online if you got bored."

She stares at me for a second. "The boredom was the point."

I shake my head. "I don't understand."

"If we finished our books or got tired of reading, we had to think of other things to do. I wasn't good at that, so if it was my turn, we just told stories. She knew all these Armenian fairytales from her grandma, and I knew the original versions of the ones she'd only seen on Disney—the evil queen who had to dance in the burning shoes until she died, the stepsisters who cut off their own toes to fit into the slipper, the Sleeping Beauty who was used by the king for years and only woke up after giving birth to his baby, when it sucked the splinter from her finger trying to nurse."

"That doesn't surprise me."

She smiles a little. "Dahlia liked to play pretend. She played in the woods without me, but I didn't like to get dirty, so when it was just us, we stayed up here. We could be pirates, and the deck was our ship, or it would be the desert island we were stranded on. Sometimes we'd braid our hair and hang it over the edge and pretend to be Rapunzel."

"Who would the other one pretend to be?"

"What?"

"There were two of you," I point out. "So who was Rapunzel?"

"We were both Rapunzel," she says, like that makes sense.

Like they were one person.

I remember her asking if she made it all up, and I start to wonder if she did. Dahlia existed, but there's no evidence they were friends. Mabel said we made her think she was crazy and that she'd made it all up, but we never did that. Her parents did. I have no love for any Darling except the one in front of me, but her parents aren't that sort of cruel. If they made her think Dahlia was an imaginary friend, then in all likelihood, she was.

Or maybe Mabel's playing an angle even now, though I'm not sure what she hopes to gain from it. The fact that I don't know irritates me, but I won't give her the satisfaction of knowing that. There's only one reason she'd want me to think Dahlia was imaginary, and that's to protect her. But that doesn't make sense, since she's already asked me to look into her. I decide to watch Mabel even more closely. She was born sneaky, and she hasn't changed.

"I don't get it, but okay," I say, shrugging like I don't care about her childhood memories.

She peels up a circle of lichen with her thumbnail. "You had your brothers to play with. You like them. I didn't like my family, especially when we were staying here. That meant I was with my grandpa."

I nod, finally making some sense of the picture she painted.

"Did you get in trouble?" I ask.

"Sometimes," she says, straightening her legs on the floor and staring at her knees. "If I stayed out too long and they realized I was gone. Dahlia would lose track of time, but I never did. I just didn't want to go home."

We sit in silence for a while, each of us dwelling in our own thoughts. Then we climb down and go back to the house she avoided so much that she'd risk getting punished by her grandfather for it.

After our walk and a shower, we drive over to the Dolce house. Devlin and Crystal live there now, right next door to the new house his parents built on the foundation of the one Duke burned down. Our house—Hickory House, according to Mabel—is big enough that Royal and Harper can move in for the summer. We could have moved back in too, but since Summer House stands empty, it made more sense for us to stay there.

Royal still hasn't completely forgiven me, and I thought it would be better not to be under the same roof as Harper.

We find Duke sitting on the living room floor surrounded by a handful of kids. Crystal is lying on the couch with a towel over her eyes, one hand on her distended belly.

"What's with her?" I ask Duke, nodding to our sister.

"Migraine," he says. "Who knew teen pregnancy could be so hard?"

Crystal holds up one hand, middle finger raised. "I'm not a teenager anymore, asshole."

"What your mouth, woman," he says. "This asshole is watching your hoard of children."

"Thank you," she says, putting her hand back on her belly.

"Maybe if you spent more time with the kids you already have and less time making more, you wouldn't be in this situation," he says, but he smiles at Knight, who's frowning at the brightly colored contraption they're assembling.

Olive is coloring at the coffee table with Diamond, who's just scribbling on her page, while Prince is hiding underneath, munching on a crayon.

"Who's that?" I ask, pointing to a fat, generic-looking baby sitting in a swing. "Did you have another one that I missed?"

"Nah, that's Preston's spawn," Duke says. "Good thing it came out with two eyes, right?"

He winks at Olive, who grins and goes back to coloring an intricate koala bear page.

"That's not hereditary," Mabel points out. "Baron took out his eye."

"I'm joking, babe," Duke says, snapping the next piece into place.

"Really?" Olive asks me with childish, demented delight. "You scooped out Preston's eyeball?"

"No," I say, frowning at her. "I burned it out."

"Cool," she whispers, gazing up at me with obvious awe. I bet she'd think all the things I did to her sister were cool too, if she didn't let emotions cloud her judgment.

"We're going to visit my stepmom," Mabel says to Duke. "Do you want to come with us?"

"Will Colt be there?" he asks. "Or is he in rehab again?"

"He's not in rehab," Mabel says. "I'm not sure if he'll be in or not."

He laughs quietly and mutters under his breath, "What a pussy."

"We're not going to talk to Colt," I point out. "She wants to talk to her parents. Why do you always bring him up?"

"I don't," he says, scowling at me. "I don't give a fuck about him. I just think it's funny."

"Are you coming?" I ask.

"Why would I come?" he asks, his tone belligerent now. "I don't care who's there. I don't need to see one more fucking Darling. They're crawling all over this place already. Why do you think I'm not out back with Royal and Devlin and Preston?"

I have one of those moments of stark clarity where I'm reminded how much I missed when I left town. Then, it would've been unthinkable for Royal to willingly hang out with the Darling cousins. Apparently he can forgive them more easily than his own brother.

After a beat of silence, Prince's voice rings out from under the coffee table. "Fucking Darling."

"Great," Crystal says. "Now he probably thinks that's the name of his new sibling."

Duke starts laughing louder than warranted. He doesn't look up when Mabel and I excuse ourselves and leave. I can tell something is bothering him, but I won't ask in front of the others and risk his fragile ego.

SELENA

eleven

Mabel Darling

"Are you nervous?" Baron asks, glancing at me from the corner of his eye as we turn onto the long, dirt drive to my father's house.

"No," I say. "Why would I be nervous?"

"You haven't seen your family in three years," he points out.

"But they're still my family," I say. "And I've been talking to them for the past year."

He nods and pulls Duke's SUV into the shade of the oaks that hang over the parking area in front of the house. I don't recognize any of the handful of cars parked there, and I think Baron was trying to remind me how much things have changed, little things that I might not have talked to them about over text or video chat but that add up when taken together.

When we reach the front door, I'm not sure if tradition dictates I knock. Since my family buys into that sort of thing, and I don't live here, I decide to be on the safe side and wait to be invited in.

SELENA

Dad opens the door, holding a cane in one hand and the knob in the other. He takes one look at me and pulls me into a bear hug, saying all the customary things, that it's good to see me, he's so glad I'm home, that he missed me. I can't imagine that he did. It must have been a relief to have the danger gone from the house, the constant worrying that he'd get a call from the hospital or police.

At last, he releases me and grabs into the edge of the door again for balance. Baron hands him the cane that he dropped when he hugged me, and he nods, his lips tight. I notice the new wrinkles around his eyes, that his hair is streaked with more white than is evident over video.

"Come in," he says, and he steps back.

Baron and I follow him as he makes his slow way to the living room, holding up our progress. The hallway is silent except for the scuff of his shoe that drags a little with each lurching step and the thump of the cane on the hardwood. When we reach the living room, Colt jumps up and comes to meet us, then stops.

"I know you don't like hugs," he says. "But fuck, it's good to see you in one piece."

He looks me up and down as if searching for missing parts, but Baron doesn't do permanent damage to his own property. He likes me to look perfect on the outside, an unbroken doll.

"Thanks," I say. "You look... A little different."

One corner of Colt's mouth quirks in a wry smile, and he points to his face. "Reconstructive surgery."

"Right," I say. "I knew that."

Again, I knew he looked different over video, and not just because he's twenty instead of seventeen, but the slight alteration in his appearance is more apparent in person.

"I'm still the same old asshole," he assures me, then steps back and gestures to the three remaining people in the room. "Mom's still Mom, and this is her caretaker, Mildred. Really, she's a caretaker for all of us. She comes every day and takes care of stuff around the house when Mom's sleeping."

I swallow hard, my eyes drawn to Aurora, who sits staring out the window with vacant eyes, as still as a statue.

The last person, a strange man, stands and holds out a hand. A weird sense of *déjà vous* sweeps over me, because I know I've never met this man in my life, and yet, there's no mistaking his familiarity. He's fortyish, with expensively cut, dark blond hair with golden streaks from the sun and a tan to match, blue eyes behind thin bifocal lenses, a square jaw, and broad shoulders clad in a fitted, Ralph Lauren polo shirt.

"Hi, Mabel," he says. "Your dad's told me a lot about you. I'm your uncle James."

"Oh," I say, glancing at his hand and then back to his face. "Hi. I'd rather not shake, if you don't mind."

He smiles only a little, but his eyes crinkle at the corners. "No problem," he says, dropping his hand. "Should I take that as a rejection of my reunion with the family, or just good hygiene?"

"More of a personal space issue," Baron says, extending a hand. "Mabel doesn't like touching strangers. I'm her boyfriend, Baron."

They shake, and any sense of awkwardness brought on by my refusal to shake hands melts away as we take our seats around the room. Baron smoothly and easily answers my estranged uncle's obligatory questions—we met in high school, we've been together a year, we go to college together. I marvel at him, how completely at ease he is, how seamlessly he fits in when he wants to. While I struggle to understand the norms that seem to come naturally to others and still manage to make people uncomfortable without even trying, he's a social chameleon, saying just the right things, smiling at the appropriate times, asking polite questions in return. I know he finds small talk tedious, but an outsider would never guess.

While they chat, I turn to my brother, who's taken a seat next to Aurora.

"Why is he here?" I whisper.

"Don't worry, I'm sure your inheritance is intact," he says, but he can't be sure of that at all. He should have gotten Summer House, and he would have if Grandpa Darling wasn't so angry that our father didn't stay married to the woman he chose for him. I'm the only offspring from the sanctioned union, so I inherit a property instead of Colt. Grandpa's pettiness took precedent over tradition that time.

But if one more of my uncles is added to the will, maybe he'll inherit the house, or his son after him, if he has one. Grandpa disowned two sons before I was born, and I've never met either of them. Colt already told me Preston's been trying to find our relatives around town, both legitimate and illegitimate children that the Darling patriarch fathered through the years. What he hopes to gain from the endeavor, I don't know. Maybe I should have gone outside to talk to him and Devlin when we went by our old house on the way here.

"How can you be sure?" I ask.

"Be sure of what?" Dad asks, sitting on my other side from Baron.

Mildred comes in with a tray bearing sweating glasses of sweet tea and hands them around.

"She's just curious about our uncle," Colt says to Dad.

"You don't have to worry, I'm not here to disrupt your lives," James says. "I'm not a Darling and haven't been for a few decades now. I have no interest in anything our father has to offer, and I've done well for myself without him."

I realize he must have overheard my whispered conversation with Colt, and I try to smooth things over, since I know it's tacky to talk about money. "What do you do?" I ask.

"I work for an indie music label," he says.

"James is being modest," Dad says. "He founded one of Europe's biggest labels."

"Co-founded," James says mildly.

I glance at Baron, knowing he'll like my dad talking up his brother. I try to imagine him and Duke like this someday, as easy as if no time has passed. It strikes me that maybe he was right about this being a big deal. I'm not nervous about seeing my family after all this time. They're still my family. But I'm on edge, knowing that Baron will be judging me based on them, and they'll judge me based on him. More than that, they're judging me for bringing him here, for being with him. They don't know him, though, and they don't know my reasons. They could never understand.

But he did. He understood this was an important meeting, even if I didn't. Even without knowing that one of my grandfather's disowned sons would be here.

I try to think of what a normal person would ask, what small talk an uncle I've never met might enjoy. It's a ludicrous idea, but I know that's what they're all expecting. A girl like my cousin Lindsey, a mild girl, unobtrusive, a reflection of her aristocratic upbringing.

"You live in Europe?" I ask, sipping my sweet tea like a lady, the way my mother taught me.

"At the time, putting an ocean between myself and the rest of the family seemed like a good idea," James says with a wry smile towards my dad.

"Then what are you doing here?" I ask.

Colt rolls his eyes, and Dad frowns, and I know I said something wrong, though I'm not sure what.

Baron smiles and picks up his tea. "What she means is, what brings you back to the States?"

"That's what I said," I mutter under my breath.

"My son," James says. "But when Preston contacted me, I thought it might be nice to meet all of you. Even though I'm not a Darling by name, I do appreciate being asked to weigh in on the decision." He smiles at my father.

"What decision?" I ask, glancing from one of them to the next, aware that I'm missing some pivotal piece of information.

"What to do with Grandpa Darling," Colt says.

My heart does a sick little dive into my stomach, and I take a sip of sweet tea to wet my mouth that's gone suddenly dry. "What do you mean?"

"As you know, he's been living at the manor house with Preston," Dad says. "Now that he and Dolly have the baby, though, they've decided they don't have the bandwidth for him too."

Baron picks up his glass, takes a drink, and then sets it back before putting a hand on my knee. Some little part inside me tears, that he made that gesture look natural, subtle, by taking a drink first, so no one would notice that he's comforting me in a moment of torment. No one else knows me like he does. Even though my face, my mannerisms, give nothing away, Baron knows. He knows, and he's grounding me with a touch, forcing me into my body so I can't spiral in my mind. I have to focus on enduring a touch, so I can't retreat to my head.

Usually that's where I go for safety, but sometimes, it's the most dangerous place of all.

My heart is hammering, but I concentrate on Baron's hand and not the panic that Preston knows. That somehow, he found out, and that's why he wants to get his baby away from Grandpa Darling. But I'd rather him know about me than have him find out another way, if something happened to the baby to bring his suspicions to light.

I think I'll be sick.

"So, the family has been discussing options for him," Dad says. "Would you like to have some input, Mabel?"

He looks at me, but I can't speak. They're all staring. If Preston found out, did he tell them? Do they all know?

Numbly, I shake my head.

"I can think of something we could do with him," Baron says.

Colt turns to him, and my breath catches. They've been civil for me, because they know that I'm with Baron, but none of them will ever forgive him for the things he did to this family. Not just to me, but to Colt, Dad, Aurora.

"Why are you even here?" Colt demands. "This is a family matter. James didn't bring—"

"Colt," Dad barks, cutting off my brother.

"James brought himself," Baron says to Colt, cool as anything. "He admits he's not part of the family."

"He didn't try to destroy our family."

"Oh, so you're only pissed because we didn't lay down and take it?"

"He didn't do that," Dad says. "He took his freedom and ran with it."

I think I hear a trace of wistfulness in his voice, and I wonder if he's wishing he'd done the same. His wife would have been spared, like James. Even Mom was spared the worst of it. The Dolces didn't bother with anyone as long as they left town and left me alone.

"So you're pissed because when we fought back against your family, we were successful," Baron says.

Colt shakes his head. "That's what you call success? We're still here, and your family is more fucked than ours."

"Maybe I should go," James says.

Baron gestures to him. "Or, if you're saying only blood gets a seat at the table, why is your mom here?"

We all turn to Aurora, who's gone a little pale and shrunk down, clutching the arms of her chair like she knows there's conflict happening around her, even if she's not cognizant of what it is.

Colt's nostrils flare with anger, and his voice is icy when he speaks. "You want to talk about my mom? Let's start with why she's like that."

"She's like that because she did a sloppy job," Baron says. "Like everyone in your family always did. Just look at Mabel."

Everyone stares for a second, and I'm sure they're thinking about how I jumped off that bridge, how I failed to complete the act just like my stepmother. But I know. I know what Baron means, that he won't come out and say it because he knows that it's not his secret to tell, but he's furious about what Grandpa did to me. He hates them for not protecting me. That's why they hit my family hardest, while Preston's and Magnolia's and even Devlin's were hardly touched.

"I think you need to leave," Dad says, his voice deadly calm.

Colt gives a curt nod, and I see the same rage shimmering under his surface, but he's trying to keep things under control in front of guests, just like Dad. They're so much alike.

"That would be wise," Colt grits out. "In fact, I'm not sure why you're in Faulkner at all. Didn't Gloria tell you it was hunting season when you came back to town?"

"And yet, she's nowhere to be found," Baron says. "Oh, that's right, she's locked up in the nuthouse because like your family, she can't get the job done. Guess she'll fit right in."

"Maybe you should ask Dixie if you don't think she's capable of hurting someone," Colt says with a little smirk.

"Dixie is off living her best life with no repercussions for what she did to Lo, or you, or Mabel," Baron counters. "My point stands."

Colt looks at me. "What'd she do to you?"

"She put that video on her blog," Baron says.

"Because you told her to," Colt grits out.

"It was her choice," Baron says with a shrug. "She did it because she wanted you to stop protecting Mabel."

Colt grits his teeth and doesn't say anything. I know he hates that he was manipulated for so long as much as I hate that I was.

"We'll go," I say, turning to my father. "But not before I get what I came for. I want to know what happened to Dahlia."

His brows rise in an expression of surprise. "Dahlia Delacroix?"

He glances at Aurora, but she remains motionless in her chair, face devoid of expression. I know there's something, though. He looked to her because they hid something together. Anger lashes inside me, but I keep myself as placid as his wife.

"Yes, Dad," I say. "Where is she?"

"I don't know," he says. "No one knows."

"I wrote her letters," I say. "I remember seeing Aurora hiding something. An envelope. Did you intercept my mail?"

"No," he says, his shoulders slumping. "We contacted the school when you asked about her, and we got a concerning letter back. We thought it would be best, considering your state at the time, if you didn't get the news that she was gone."

"You made me think I was crazy," I say, my voice carefully even. "That I made it all up. That she wasn't real."

He frowns. "That was never our intention."

"But you did," I say. "You didn't want me to contact her. You didn't want to give me the name of her school. And when I wrote her, I got a letter back from her school saying she was never there. Did you lie to me?"

Dad rakes his hand through his thinning hair. "We were trying to protect you, Mabel. That's all we ever wanted. We may not have always done the best job of it, but we did try."

"By lying to me?" I ask, rising to my feet. "That's never protected anyone, except maybe yourselves." I turn to my stepmother. "I came for answers, and maybe revenge, but I see you took care of it yourself. You got what you deserve."

"Mabel," Dad barks.

Of course Aurora doesn't answer. She doesn't even look at me. If there's something going on in her head, I can't reach it.

I turn to my father. "And so did you."

"You need to leave," he says again, standing as well.

"We were already on our way out," Baron says, standing and taking my hand. He leads me toward the front door. I hear footsteps behind us, and I turn to see Colt escorting us out.

When our eyes meet, he shakes his head, his expression filled with disappointment.

But Aurora's not my mother. She's his.

"That was unnecessary," he says when we reach the door.

To my surprise, Baron stops and turns back after stepping outside. "Now that we're alone, I need to ask you something."

Colt just stares out at us, his eyes guarded. "I don't owe you shit."

"What do you have on Duke?" Baron asks. "He gets cagey and belligerent whenever your name comes up."

"Why don't you ask him?"

"Please?" I implore, knowing Baron won't beg. He won't escalate things to violence like Duke would to get answers either. Baron has more self-control, and he doesn't get angry. He fought with the kind of detached precision he'll use as a surgeon, that will make him the best, not out of emotion. But I know how much this means to him. He wouldn't ask my brother at all unless he was desperate.

Colt's expression doesn't change. I read men well, but I can't read him. Not anymore. He's changed, and not just his face. He glares at Baron, his eyes filled with nothing but cold loathing.

"He's not doing well," I say. "We just want to understand why, what might have happened that last semester that he hasn't told us. You were here. We weren't. We don't know unless someone tells us, and he won't talk about it."

"You're right," Colt says, his gaze moving to me. "You weren't here."

"I'm sorry," I say, because I know what it's like to be left at their mercy. I left Colt just like my mother left me. I failed him like they all failed me.

He must be thinking the same, but his eyes soften at last.

"I'm glad you weren't," he says, and then he turns his attention back to Baron. "I told you, I don't owe you anything. Not even answers. Now I'm going to do something I should have done the first time you came knocking."

Before we can answer, he swings the door closed in our faces. I hear the lock engage, and then I'm left standing on one side with Baron, and Colt's on the other with our family.

His family.

I may not have been officially disowned, but I chose a side, and it wasn't the Darlings'.

twelve

Duke Dolce

I turn over and check my phone. It's 2 AM but I still haven't fallen asleep. I keep thinking about them going over to Colt's house, and how I didn't go. I couldn't. Not after what Baron said.

But he was there.

They said so when they got home. They saw him.

I couldn't ask how he looked, how he was. It would have made Baron wonder why I asked, why I cared.

I don't care.

I have his sister right here. The girl I love. The girl I always loved. The girl who loves me, as far as she's able. I have the life we dreamed about for two years, that I never thought I'd have. Now I do. I have the life, the girl. The one who was supposed to make everything good again.

So why can't I be fucking happy?

I flop back on the pillows. Mabel and Baron are sleeping. She's nestled into his arms, both of them fitting together like halves of a whole.

That's my place, but she took it, and now I don't fit.

SELENA

I don't fit anywhere. Not with them, not with Royal and Harper.

I sit up and swing my legs off the side of the bed, then check over my shoulder. Without his glasses, Baron looks just like me. Another version, the mirror image, the one who fits. We should fit together. We're the two halves of the whole, after all. Literally one person divided in two.

We used to be. Mabel was the third wheel then, the outsider. It was me and Baron, Baron and me. We worked together to destroy her, laughing all the way. When we did, it was my victory too. When we realized we needed her, it was my epiphany too. When we decided to wait until graduation and then go get her, it was my plan too.

But Baron didn't wait.

He left, and I was here, and everything changed, and I don't know if it will ever be good again. He broke the whole, and it doesn't fit back together the way it used to.

That's the midnight thought, the 2AM thought, that keeps me awake. Not the dawning realization that everything is not good, not the frustration that it should be but it's not. It's the gnawing sense that it never will be.

I grab my glasses and slip out of the room, pad down the hall, down the creaking old wooden staircase. In the kitchen, before I hit the light, I see something hanging from the ceiling, swaying slowly in the dim light from the window—a body. I choke back a startled sound, not wanting to squeal like a pussy. I hit the light, and it bathes the kitchen. My heart is hammering erratically. It was just the light fixture.

I go to the fridge, take out a beer, and tip it back, downing the bottle in long, slow pulls. When the last of the cold bitterness gurgles down the neck of the bottle, down my throat, I toss it and get another one. Maybe they'll help me sleep. At the very least, they'll keep the ghosts at bay.

The ghosts are always with me now, even when I'm not high. The only difference is, when I'm high, they don't always disappear when I look directly at them. Sometimes they stay, whisper to me like my demon, tell me what to do.

I thought being here would help. That Mabel wasn't the thing that was missing after all. If I was here without her, I wasn't happy. And when I was somewhere else with her I wasn't happy. So it made sense to put the two things together. The last time I was happy, I was here with Mabel and Baron, and we were all together, and there were no ghosts.

But here we are, and I have everything, and I'm still moping around like a little bitch.

Even Olive wasn't mad at me. She was happy to see me, like I never hurt her at all. If anyone has something to be pissy about, it's her. But she's happier than ever, like she doesn't even remember. Like she doesn't miss her sister at all.

SELENA

I've been torturing myself over it for a year, and she doesn't even care.

I open another beer. Somehow I've gone through the whole six-pack already.

At first, it felt like a miracle that she wasn't mad. She didn't care at all that I could have killed her. But now it's starting to feel like a punishment. I know it's sick, but I want her to be mad. I don't deserve to get off the hook that easy. I wanted to show her how sorry I was, to earn her forgiveness, but she didn't even care, so there's no reason to. There's no reason to be here, to see her. She doesn't miss me. She was perfectly happy without me, off living her big New York life with Royal and Harper.

Maybe not everyone gets to be happy. At least Olive deserves her happiness. I don't deserve shit.

The ghosts creep in, whispering in my ears, reminding me of what I've done, why I will be forever seeking, chasing, never content until the day I die.

Dawson.

Dad.

The man who fucked Mabel.

Blue.

Olive wouldn't forgive me so easily if she knew.

This time, when I go to the refrigerator, I bring a whole six-pack back to the table with me. I'm smart enough to know this isn't going to make me happy either, but I keep going anyway. At least it can make me numb.

I don't know how the others deal with the guilt, the ghosts that visit in the night, that linger in every corner, whispering warnings. Harper and Royal seem fine. Happy, even. Crystal and Devlin were there when we left Dad in the burning building. They're fine. They're still making babies and raising more, kids who will never know that their parents are murderers. I don't know what happened to Gideon and his brother. If I wanted to find out, I could call their dad and ask, or go to church and see if they were there, but I don't want to see them. We were never friends, and I haven't talked to DeShaun or Cotton since we graduated.

I talk to Baron, but he doesn't understand. He can't because he never would have let that happen. Family is everything to Baron, even the bad ones like Dad.

Like me.

He forgives me, even when I can't forgive myself, even when I don't deserve it, even when he would never have done what I did.

Patricide.

That's the word for it. Killing your own father.

Baron would no more do that than he'd kill me. People think he's a psychopath, but he's better than all of us. There's no shades of grey to him. It's black and white. Simple. You don't kill family. He doesn't make excuses or exceptions. He knows it's wrong, so he wouldn't have done it.

I wish I had that kind of clarity. But I can't find the border between good and bad, between black and white. It's all blended into a dull grey fog, where nothing feels good and pure anymore. Even Olive, who was the last good thing I had, the one pure and simple part of my life after we killed Dad, when Baron was gone, has been perverted by what everyone's said to me. Even after Mabel told me that I was probably okay, I can't stop worrying. I can't hug her without wondering if someone is going to think I'm a sicko, can't hang out with her without wondering if they're right, because what kind of person wants to be friends with a kid?

The people I should be most comfortable with, who share that dark secret, that terrible bond, can't be trusted because they don't trust me. They poisoned my mind against myself, and I can't get the venom out. It's part of me now, the doubts, the fears, the questions that circle around and around in a never-ending, claustrophobic spiral.

I stumble from the table, needing to get out, to breathe, to leave my head that's closing in on me. The beer isn't enough. I need Alice.

I'm out, but I know where to get more. I grab some clothes from the hamper in the bathroom and stumble outside. A low, sluggish layer of clouds hangs over the town, trapping in the heat. The air hits me with its choking suffocation, oppressive and ominous. I hurry to the car, feeling the ghosts close behind. I don't dare look back.

In the car, I'm shivering but I turn the air on full blast, needing it to suck away the dread that curdles in the heat, the vapors. I don't know why I ever wanted to come back here. Faulkner is a curse, a scourge on the world. I want to burn it all to the ground, leave it obliterated, wipe it off the face of the earth like Chernobyl.

I take out my phone and thumb it on, correcting when my wheel goes into the ditch. I clip the mailbox, then jerk the car onto the road and give it some gas. In the rearview, I can see the post jutting from the ground at an odd angle, like a crooked headstone.

My phone connects to the speakers as I hit call. I have to try three more times before he answers, sounding annoyed.

"What do you want?"

"I need some shit," I say.

He sighs. "It's three in the fuckin' morning."

"I know," I say. "But you work for us, don't you?"

"No," he says, and I can hear the scowl in his voice.

I probably disrespected him, which might be cause for killing in his world. I decide it doesn't much matter. Even the people who would miss me would be better off without me.

"Okay, well, I need it," I say. "I'm on my way."

"I'm not getting out of bed for you, pretty boy."

"We make the shit you sell," I say. "You owe us."

"What's in it for me?"

"Money, dumbass," I say. "And you get to move some product. I'll buy enough to make it worth your while."

"I can do that in the morning, so unless you're going to eat my ass so good I see God, you're not worth losing sleep over, and if you're desperate enough to do that to get a fix, I don't trust where your mouth has been."

"Why?" I demand. "You got a girl there with you?"

"Because it's three in the fucking morning."

"You got a guy there?"

I throw in a slur for good measure, but he just laughs.

"Only you would think that's an insult."

The phone disconnects, and when I try him back, it goes straight to voicemail.

I curse and punch the steering wheel. The car swerves, and the light pole comes up fast, so fast I barely miss it. I drop down off the curb and keep driving, cursing Maverick, and Mabel, and Baron. He doesn't have to be so good. He doesn't have to have such strong morals, like he got them all when we were divided before birth, and I got none. I don't know what's right or wrong. Baron always knows. I have to look to him, or my brothers, or Dad. How do they just know, while I can't even figure it out when I watch other people?

Because when I do what they want, what they ask, half the time, it's wrong, but I don't know until after the fact. I never know until it's too late, until it's done and there's no taking it back. Baron has a code to live by. So does Royal. He doesn't believe in killing. He lets people live because he knows that's worse.

Except Dawson.

Except Dad.

He knew when to make exceptions to the rules, while I can't even figure out the rules to begin with.

I think about sitting outside Maverick's house all night, waiting for him to come out with whatever piece of ass he found to fuck him tonight, but I'm not sure I want to be alone with myself until then. So, I let Alice take me by the hand and lead the way.

Fifteen minutes later, I'm standing in the gravel lot of the familiar house, staring up at the dark windows. I remember the first time I came here, when I showed up to help Mabel get ready for her date with Baron. There were other times too, times when I was Baron, times when I was myself, times when I got so lost in pretending that I almost couldn't remember which one of us I was. If we drove her over the edge with our games, she took part of me with her.

I think about it now, how much easier it would be if I were Baron. If I didn't have to feel any guilt because I always did what I knew to be right, and since I was always certain, no one could ever change my mind. It must be paradise.

I pick up a pebble and throw it, but it bounces off the side of the house. It takes three or four tries before one of the pieces of gravel hits the window. After a few more, the curtain moves aside. I can't see him, only the sway of the white curtain. Aside, and then back.

I don't know if he's coming, so I throw a few more pieces.

After a minute, the window slides up, and he sticks his head out. "Baron? What are you doing here?"

"No, you asshole," I say. "It's Duke."

The window slams, and the curtain swings back. I stoop, scoop up a whole handful of gravel, and hurl it against the house. "Colt! I know you're awake. Come out, come out, wherever you are!" I sing the last words, cackling to myself as I grab another handful. I won't let him ignore me just because I'm not my brother. I'm important too.

Before I can throw more, the front door opens, and Colt stumbles out, still tying a thin robe around himself. "Are you out of your mind?"

"What the fuck are you wearing?" I ask, nodding to the robe, which ends just above his knees.

"What the fuck are you doing here?" he counters. "Throwing rocks at my window like a lovelorn puppy?"

"More like a dog lured by the scent of a bitch in heat."

He stops on the railing on the big wooden deck that wraps around their house. "You can't come here, Duke."

"Why?" I ask. "I thought our families were on good terms now. So we can be friends."

"We're not friends."

"Why not?"

"I'm not inviting you in," he says. "We have company."

"I don't want to come in."

He sighs and rakes his fingers through his hair, which is disheveled from sleep. Unlike Mabel's straight, silky strands, his is curly and chaotic. I imagine running my fingers through it, how they'd tangle in the strands, how it would make him moan.

"What do you want?" he asks, sounding weary and defeated, as if I've been here every night in more than my mind. Maybe I haunt him like he haunts me, and he's as sick of me as I am of him.

"I want a cigarette."

"Fuck, Duke," he says, smacking his palm down on the railing. "What are you doing?"

"I don't know," I admit. "I just can't get right, you know? You're the only person who understands."

"I don't think I do," he says, but he sounds so beaten that I know he's lying.

He might hate it, but he gets it.

"Let's go sit in the hot tub," I say, starting for the back.

Colt doesn't move from where he's standing. I stop at the corner of the porch and gesture for him to follow.

"You know I won't give you what you want," he says, his expression guarded.

"You don't know what I want."

"Oh, but I do."

He smirks at me, his hair blowing in the breeze like a lion's mane, looking all mussed and rumpled. I can almost smell him again, the masculine scent I used to know so well, tobacco and leather and smoke. I itch to move closer, to see if I can catch a hint of it on the wind.

"Fuck you," I say.

"Pass," he says, reaching into his robe pocket and pulling out a pack of smokes. "I've got Lo for that."

"And I've got your sister," I say. "If I wanted to fuck, I'd bust in one of her holes."

He tries to act like he doesn't care, tossing his hair back all cool and lighting a cigarette, but I see the tick in his jaw. I know Colt. I've watched him simmer for years. I always thought he'd erupt one day, but he never did.

"Then what do you need me for?" he asks, sucking casually on his cigarette.

"I just wanted someone to talk to."

"Sounds like something for your therapist."

"I'm not a pussy," I snap. "I don't go to therapy."

He arches a brow like a cocky bastard and drags on his cigarette. "Explains why you're at my house at four in the morning instead of at home in bed with your girlfriend."

"Fuck you," I say. "I'm not gay."

"I know."

"Give me one of those."

He hands me the pack. I slide one of the long, white sticks out. My fingers shake as I put it between my lips. Colt lights me, and I stare at the flame, hypnotized as it licks over the tip. When it flicks off, the ghost of it dances behind my eyelids.

"Got any Alice?" I ask.

He shakes his head. "I don't do any of that shit anymore. I don't even drink. Just these." He lifts his hand, gesturing to his cigarette.

"You're lucky," I say, dragging on mine. "I wish that's all in needed."

"Real fucking lucky." The corner of his mouth tugs up in a rueful little smile. "That's what everyone tells me."

"You are," I say. "I'd trade places with you in a heartbeat."

"But you got everything you ever wanted," he says. "Don't tell me it's not all you hoped for."

"It's not," I say, climbing the stairs to stand next to him. Every step feels like slogging through mud. "I think... You were right. I don't think Mabel can ever love me again."

"Shocking."

"I know it's dumb, okay? But I thought... I really thought she could. That she would, once she was with us. I thought she'd remember how it was before. I know you didn't understand it, but it was good between us. She loved us. She was exactly what we needed. It might seem weird to someone outside it, but inside, we all fit."

"If you say so."

"We did," I say. "I know you don't think I'm capable, but I loved her. I still love her. But we broke her, and now... Now she's broken. She's not the same, Colt."

SELENA

He snorts out a breath and taps his cigarette on the railing. "You broke her, but you expected her to... What? Fix herself, and then fix you?"

"She was supposed to fix everything."

"You mean to tell me your actions have consequences?" he says. "And not just for you, but for all the innocent victims you targeted?"

"Fuck you," I say, spitting the words at him like poison darts. "You're not innocent."

"I wasn't talking about me," he says coolly.

"Your sister isn't innocent either."

"Assuming you mean because she dared to carry Darling blood, I beg to differ," he says, like some snooty asshole. "But that aside, even you can't deny that Gloria and her sisters did nothing to deserve your wrath."

"It wasn't wrath," I say. "We weren't mad at them."

"Then why'd you destroy them too?"

"I don't know," I say, shaking my head and dragging smoke into my lungs, feeling it turn them black like the videos they made us watch in health class. Everything inside me is black as tar, heavy and cloying, smothering me slowly from the inside out.

"It was like a game," I say. "I don't know why I played. I got caught up in it, and it just never ended. My brothers knew the rules, they told me to play, so I did. That's how it was with your sister too. I'm not going to play innocent and say I didn't enjoy it. I did. I loved the game. But it didn't seem real. I loved her, but destroying her was part of the game, so I loved that too. Even when she left, when she almost died... I knew she didn't mean it. That she was waiting for us. It was just another move, a countermove to what we did. We had to play the long game after she disappeared, to wait and be patient, and then it was our move again. But now the game is over. We won. We got our prize. But it's not the prize I was playing for."

"So you broke your doll, and now you don't want her?"

"She doesn't want me," I correct, staring at the sky in misery. "She's different."

"Or maybe she's exactly what you made her," he says.

"If she was what we made her, she would have made everything good again, like she did before."

"Stop looking for someone to fix you," he says. "There's no easy fix, no magic ingredient to add that's going to make it all better. No one's coming to save you, Duke."

"So what, I'm supposed to just give up and jump off the bridge like she did? Swallow a bunch of pills like your mom?"

He sighs and rakes a hand through his hair again. "You're supposed to start pulling yourself out. Yeah, it sucks. It's a lot of fucking work. You have to face all the shit you've done and make peace with it."

I flick my cigarette butt into the gravel. "I don't know if I can do that."

"I know you can."

SELENA

I shake my head. "If you knew half the shit I've done, you wouldn't say that."

He knows about some of it, what we did to girls, not just his girlfriend and his sister, but all the others. Harper, the Walton twins, so many more I lost track. He can at least guess.

But he doesn't know about Dawson jumping off the same bridge as Mabel, the sound we heard and felt when his weight reached the end of the rope, the snap that still makes my stomach churn.

He doesn't know about the man on Mabel, the blood gushing onto her face, how I jumped on him and shoved his dick into her while his body flopped lifelessly on top of her.

He doesn't know about Blue, how I watched her suck soup off the table, how I curled the pillow around my head and pretended I didn't hear her screaming when Baron went to the basement. How he buried her in a grave so shallow the animals dug her up and dragged off every piece of her, not leaving even a single tooth.

He only knows about Dad.

"How can you make peace with it?" I ask, turning to him. "With what happened at the mall?"

He pockets the pack of cigarettes and leans back on the railing, hands tucked into his robe. "He deserved worse. Look at you, Duke. Do you really think you'd be that way if not for him? I know I wouldn't. The world is a better place without him in it."

"Easy for you to say," I mutter. "He wasn't your dad."

"That's true," he says, straightening. "All my dad did was cheat. Even knowing that sucks. I can't imagine having your dad's shadow over me. No wonder you're all so fucked up."

Something settles in me then. At last, someone said the words I needed to hear, that I've needed to hear for so long. That it's not my fault. That it's harder to be me than anyone knows.

That vindication spears into me, and for the first time in a long time, I want to laugh. I step towards him, grab his face in both hands, smash my lips to his.

He shoves me back. "What the fuck, Duke? You're with my sister."

"Maybe I'm not satisfied with half a heart."

"Then you won't be satisfied with none of one."

"So give me more than none."

He stares at me, and I grab the front of his robe this time, hauling him to me. He clamps a hand around the front of my throat, stopping me from leaning in again. His eyes narrow, and he works his jaw back and forth. Then he spits. The warm, wet blob lands on my lips, and his gaze drops to my mouth.

"That's as close as you'll ever come to kissing me again," he says coldly.

I swallow hard, staring back at him. I want to shove him away, but my fingers refuse to obey, and they stay clenched in his robe.

He smirks at me. "Go on," he croons. "Lick it off. I know you want to. Let me see you really enjoy it."

I open, letting my tongue trace over the seam of my lips. I want to close my eyes, to savor it, to coat my lips with him and keep him there as long as I can. But I won't give him the satisfaction of seeing me tremble at the taste of him on my tongue. So I stick out my tongue, making it as lewd as possible as I lick and suck his saliva off my fat lower lip.

Colt just shakes his head, smiling a little. "You're such a fuck boy."

"Come on," I say, opening my mouth wide. "Give me more."

"What is wrong with you?" He shoves me back in obvious disgust, but I know I turn him on too.

"What's the big deal?" I taunt. "You didn't mind spitting all over my dick when you sucked it."

"Because you forced me to."

"You must not have hated it too bad," I say, smirking at him, enjoying the upper hand for a moment. "You kept coming back for more."

"*You* kept coming back for more," he corrects.

"You were there too," I say. "In fact, if I recall correctly, you got more out of it than I did."

"Sure," he says. "I got something out of it. Watching you crawl in the dirt begging for my dick was the sweetest revenge."

"You got off on it too."

"Getting off doesn't mean anything," he says. "I'm human. I cum. Don't think for a second that means I ever wanted you."

His cruelty cuts through to the bone, but I relish the pain with something close to rapture. This is what I've been missing, what I crave even more than Alice. Wonderland is just an escape from this craving, from the hunger that only punishment sates.

"You're fucking heartless," I say, even though I'm halfway hard already.

"You act like you didn't know," he says, tipping his head back and watching me through hooded eyes.

"You're right," I say. "I must be a fucking masochist to come here."

"No shit," he says. "That was always why you came to me, wasn't it?"

It was, and he knew that even before I did. He knows me. He gets me. And he gives me everything I need, even when he doesn't mean to. He probably hates that he does every bit as much as I do.

So when he turns and walks away, I follow. He goes around the side of the house, not through the door, so I know it's not over. He has more pain to dish out, and I'll take it, eager as a puppy. I fucking hate that he makes me this way, but I can't stop myself from following like the dog I am.

SELENA

thirteen

Duke Dolce

"What's the big deal," I say again, following Colt to the back deck. "Mabel's fucking my brother. Why shouldn't I fuck hers?"

"Because I'm with Lo."

"She's been locked up for a year," I point out. "You expect me to believe you were sitting around celibate as a monk that whole time? Come on, Colt. I know you."

"We have an arrangement," he says, flipping open the cover on the hot tub. "We promised never to put limits on each other. We can hook up with other people if we want."

"Then what's the problem?" I press, peeling off my shirt before he's even slid the cover all the way off the tub.

"I don't want you."

His words lacerate my soul, but the more he hurts me, the more I crave. I stand there watching him through the curls of steam rising into the muggy morning. It's too warm out to sit in a hot tub, but I don't care. I undo the button and let my jeans fall, holding his gaze, daring him to look away.

"God, your cock is huge," he says, shaking his head.

"Thought you said you didn't want me," I say, wrapping my fingers around it while he watches.

He grimaces and turns away, hangs his robe on one of the four hooks on the wall. Their family probably sat out here in the tub together. It seems like something sick that the Darlings would do.

He climbs into the tub in his boxers, not waiting for me.

"Afraid to be naked with me?" I challenge, climbing into the hot water and sinking onto the bench opposite him.

"Not afraid," he says, setting his cigarettes on the edge of the tub. "Smart enough not to hang a juicy steak in front of a hungry dog."

"Fuck you," I say. "You know I don't bite."

"Yes, I do."

For a second, we smirk at each other across the rippling water.

Finally, I look away. I tip my chin at him. "Gimme another cigarette."

"Take off your glasses."

"Why?" I ask, leaning back and resting one arm along the rim of the tub while I stroke my cock with the other. "You don't want to pretend you're glazing Baron's dick instead of mine?"

"No," he says, making a face.

He didn't say he wasn't glazing my dick, though.

"You sure about that?" I ask, but I take off my glasses and fold them before setting them on the ledge. "Everyone knows Baron's the better brother. Don't you want to dom the best of the best?"

"No one with a working brain thinks Baron is better than you."

He takes his cigarette pack and flips it open with his thumb, then taps until a few slide out. He bites down gently on the end of one, sliding it free with his teeth so he doesn't have to touch it with his wet hands. He closes his lips around it, picks up his lighter, and flicks it open, sucking until the tip glows bright in the blue dawn. He inhales deeply and then drops his head back on the edge of the tub, exhaling smoke into the sky like a chimney.

"I hate you," I say.

"Atta boy."

I sink down in the water, laying back and staring up at the last few stars with him.

"If I hadn't done all that to you and your sister," I say. "Would the answer be different?"

"We can't undo the past," he says. "What's the point in wondering?"

"I just want to know."

"Why? You did what you did," he says. "You are what you are. That's your burden to bear. We all have our own. I can't absolve you of yours, no matter what answer I give."

He didn't say no.

SELENA

Somehow, that's worse. I thought I wanted him to say yes, it would all be different, and of course he'd want me. That maybe part of him does anyway. But it only makes me hate myself more. I lift my head and bang it down on the side of the tub hard enough to make pain blossom in the base of my skull. "I never see until it's too late. Why don't I see?"

He shakes his head. "No, Duke. There was never a chance for us. Not since the day you put me on my knees in the basement."

"That was years ago."

"Yeah."

"So it was over before it began."

"It was never over because there was never anything to end."

At last, he takes one more drag and hands the cigarette across the water.

"So, what now?" I ask.

"So, you go home," he says. "You sleep in the bed you made. As soon as Lo gets out, we're leaving town."

"Why would you leave?" I ask. "You're the king of Faulkner again."

The past year, I made fun of him for staying, but now I don't like the thought of him leaving. I like the thought of him here, rotting, doing nothing with his life and going nowhere.

"Nah," he says. "Devlin and Preston can have it. It's too full of memories."

He doesn't say the rest. He doesn't have to.

It's too full of memories of what we did to them, both him and Lo.

"It could have been worse," I say. "You may not see it because I had to hide it so well even my brothers wouldn't see it, let alone you. But I tried."

He lets out a quiet scoff. "Burning my arm until there was no skin left was your way of protecting me?"

I remember that moment, though. He's right. I loved doing it. I loved the softness of the skin on the inside of his forearm, how warm it was. I loved watching it bubble under the flame, ravaged by the beautiful spear of fire. If there's a god in this world, it's that. The pure, incinerating heart of a flame. I remember how he moaned and cursed and screamed. I loved that the most. The raw, carnal brutality of it, when it burned us all down to bone and hunger.

"If Baron had done it, he would have cooked your arm until the flesh fell off the bone," I point out, shaking the memory away. "You wouldn't have half your arm."

"Well, gosh," Colt drawls. "Let me run right down to the trophy store and get you a gold medal."

"And if I hadn't convinced him to take your finger, he would have chopped off your dick, just like they did your dad and your grandpa."

"That one doesn't surprise me," Colt drawls. "You always were obsessed with my dick."

"Fuck you."

"Yeah, you want to."

SELENA

I finish the cigarette in miserable silence. There's no point in denying it now.

"You know, it's hard to make it work with three people," I say at last. "I've done it. I know how."

"Good for you."

"I'm just saying. Maybe I need more than your sister can give me now."

"That sounds like a you problem."

"You have to admit, I give you something Lo can't."

"On the contrary," he says. "Lo gives me exactly what I need."

"What about me?"

"What about you?"

"What about what I need?"

"I'm not in your relationship, Duke. I can't help you with that."

"What if you were?"

"I'm not."

"Hypothetically," I insist. "It's not that unthinkable. You like guys and girls."

"Lo doesn't like to be shared."

"Could've fooled me."

"She did, didn't she? That was her job. To make you believe you weren't a bad guy because you didn't really mean it."

"I didn't," I growl, glaring at him.

He just shakes his head. "You forced her every bit as much as you did me."

"So, we've all fucked," I say. "That just makes it make even more sense. We've been together, so Lo wouldn't worry that you'd go find some other dude to give you what she can't. I've already been with her, so you wouldn't have to be jealous. I've fucked you both, you've fucked us both, and she's fucked us both. What difference does it make?"

"Fucking isn't love."

I stare at him through the steam, the smoke. My heart does a thud in my chest, a flop like a fish turning over on the boat when you first haul it up. "Is that what it would take? You want me to say it?"

"No," he says. "In fact, please don't."

"Good," I say. "Because I'm not a very good liar."

His brows jump. "With all that practice lying to yourself, I'd think you'd be an expert by now."

"No limits, huh," I say. "With you and Lo? If you really think that's going to work, it sounds like you're the one lying to yourself."

"I've had enough of controlling women to last a lifetime. And she's had... You."

"Exactly," I say, chuckling. "You really think she'll be happy with you after she got fucked by the biggest three cocks in Faulkner for three years in a row?"

"Haven't had any complaints yet."

He hands a new cigarette across the water. I take it, my damp fingers brushing his dry ones.

"She won't tell you and hurt your ego," I say, taking a puff. "But she'll want more. So will you."

"I don't."

"But you will," I say. "That's what marriage is for. To tame you, tie you down. It sounds bad, but it's a good thing. Otherwise... There are no limits for men like us."

"That's the goal."

"We need limits," I say through a mouthful of smoke, leaning in to hand the cigarette back. "It's human nature to always want more. When there's nothing you can't have, you have to want things you shouldn't have."

"Like what?" he asks, watching me from the corner of his eye while he draws on the damp filter.

"I started looking at porn at the regular time," I say, laying back again. The sky is getting lighter already, blue edging out the darkness. "You know, eleven or twelve. It didn't much matter to me what I was watching. It was all hot, because I wasn't allowed to watch it. But then Mom caught me, and she took me to Dad to explain why I was watching a video with no girls in it. You know what he did?"

Colt shakes his head and hands the smoke across the steaming, shimmering water around us.

"He told me it was okay to watch porn, but not to let Mom catch me again. And that I had to watch the right stuff. So he showed me what that was, and then he brought me a girl to fuck."

"That's... Unorthodox."

"Just wait, I have a point here." I hand the cigarette back to him, though it's not much more than a filter.

"The thing is, after that, I watched what Dad told me to, but it wasn't the same. Watching the shit he told me not to watch, that I wasn't allowed to watch, made it more exciting. So I snuck it."

"So, wanting what you're not supposed to want just means wanting to fuck a guy every now and then?" he asks, arching a brow as he draws a new cigarette from the pack.

"Not everyone has a family like yours," I say.

"Oh, you mean my staunchly Baptist, old-money, southern family? You think they're going to make matching PFLAG shirts and throw me a Pride parade?" He shakes his head. "Fuck them."

"Yeah, well, not everyone has the luxury of not giving a fuck about anything but themselves," I say, snatching his cigarette. "You know what my dad did when he caught me again?"

"Made you go cut your own switch from the tree out back?"

"No. He took me to this priest who pulled the wire out of a shock collar made for dogs, and he'd wrap it around my dick and make me watch gay porn, and then if I got hard, he'd hit the button to shock the fuck out of me. I should be glad he's dead."

Colt just stares at me a second, but the look in his eyes is worse than all the gloating and taunting, worse than his usual smug indifference. "Jesus Christ, Duke..."

"You know what, fuck you." I hurl the cigarette away as hard as I can and stand, water sluicing off my skin. "I don't need your pity. I'm an asshole, remember? I deserve all the bad shit that happens to me, right?"

Colt slouches down in the water, all cool, his tatted up arms lying along the edges of the tub on either side of him. "No one deserves that," he says, leveling me with those smoky blue eyes, the kind you could wander into and get lost there, never find your way out before it choked you to death.

"I don't need this shit," I mutter, turning away.

"Then why'd you come?"

When I don't answer, he stretches his hand above the water, fingers not quite extending fully because of the burned skin between them, a tight webbing between his knuckles. "You did this. I hate what happened to you, I do. But it doesn't justify the damage you caused."

"I'm sorry."

"Are you going to apologize to Lo too?"

"Yes, damn it," I say. "I'm sorry for all of it, Colt. I didn't mean to hurt anyone."

"We both know that's not true."

"I'm sorry," I say again. "I don't know what's wrong with me. I want to make it better, to be better, but I don't know how."

"You can start by being honest with yourself first, and then everyone else."

"I'm trying."

"How?"

"I don't know, okay? Honesty doesn't fix anything. Like you said, it doesn't undo all the damage I've done. How do I do that?"

"You can't."

"So I have to be punished forever?"

He levels me with a cool look, but there's still a little of that pity, even when his words offer no mercy. "If living with the knowledge of what you've done is punishment, then yeah, I guess you do."

I climb out of the tub and pick up my jeans, yanking them on without toweling off and then swiping my glasses. "Why are you such an asshole? You act like you want to help, but you won't tell me anything when I ask."

"What are you asking?"

"How can I make up for everything I did? To you, and your sister, and Lo, and everyone? How can I be forgiven?"

"That's something you'll have to figure out for yourself."

"That's what I'm trying to do," I grit out, glaring at him. "That's why I'm asking you. Why can't you understand that?"

He sighs and stands too. His nipple piercings glint, and all his tattoos stand out stark in the pale morning light, graceful lines curling around his body in patterns Maverick inked onto his skin, a hundred paths I'll never get to take. "If you need help, I can recommend a place," he says. "I can't do that for you. I'm sorry. I've got enough of my own shit to work through."

"What place?" I ask, scratching at the prickling skin of my arms, the itch clamoring inside me. "Do they have Alice?"

"No," he says, giving me a funny look. "It's Cedar Crest, Duke. They have a treatment program. It's nice. It helped me a lot. I think it could help you too."

"Fuck you," I say stumbling backwards, the heat going to my head. "I'm not going to rehab. I'm not a junkie like you."

"Everybody needs help sometimes," he says. "It's okay to ask for it when you need it."

"But when I ask for what I need from you, you tell me it's my problem, figure it out."

"I didn't say to figure it out alone," he says. "I said it's not my problem. I can't take that on, Duke."

"So, what if I get better? What if I'm not a problem anymore? Then am I good enough?"

"It's not about being good."

"Because you know I'm good," I say, looking him up and down as he stands there all wet, water clinging to the carved muscles of his torso. "You know how good we are together."

"Duke," he says. "We're toxic as fuck together. I give you one thing you need that Mabel doesn't. Don't you see that? She gives you everything else. Just be happy with it."

I shake my head. I don't want to be with him and Lo. I just want him to tell me he wants it. He has to say it.

"If I went to Cedar Crest, even if I don't need it, just to prove to you I'm sober, would you do it?"

"No."

"Then who do I have to run over for you to consider it?" I ask. "That's what Lo did, right? She ran over Dixie for you to get her out of the way. If I ran over Lo, you'd never forgive me. So what do I have to do?"

He shakes his head. "Listen to yourself. You sound deranged. Even my dick isn't that good."

"Fuck you," I say, because I can't say what I want to say, what I mean. That it's not his stupid pierced dick. It's everything—the way he hates me that brings me to my knees, the way he acknowledges what no one else does, that I'm not just some spoiled rich boy whining about my champagne problems. That he couldn't do any better in my shoes, that he couldn't survive what I have, and he doesn't see my falling apart as weakness. That he believes I'm strong enough to fix myself, even when I don't know how.

And maybe he's right. That's the one thing I can't get from Mabel. What he doesn't understand is that I can't just be happy without it. I've tried. But even if she forgave me like Olive did, it would never go away. What I did will never go away. Nothing makes it go away except him.

SELENA

I stumble back around the house and down the front steps. There's some guy sitting at the picnic table on the front deck, a Darling man I've never seen before. I don't expect to see anyone else when I look back, but Colt is standing there, frowning down at me.

His footprints glisten on the wood, incriminating evidence of his crime.

He followed me.

"You shouldn't drive, Duke. You're fucked up."

"What do you care?" I shoot back. "If I drove off the road and wrapped myself around a tree, would you even come to my funeral?"

"Yeah," he says quietly. "I wouldn't miss it for the world."

I stare up at him, a lump suddenly in my throat. I won't ask him what that means. "Would you cry?"

He shrugs. "Maybe."

"Pussy."

I turn around and walk away, and even though he said he cared, he doesn't stop me.

When I reach the car Baron bought me, he finally calls after me.

"Duke."

I stop and wait, but I don't look back.

"My sister's a good person," he says. "If you can't be happy with her, let her go."

fourteen

Baron Dolce

It's after five in the morning when the door finally opens and Duke comes stumbling in. He kicks the door shut behind him and doesn't bother resetting the alarm before heading for the stairs. When I see that he's going to ignore me entirely, I speak.

"Where have you been?"

He wheels on me, and I realize he wasn't ignoring me. He didn't notice me at all.

"What are you doing in the dark?" he demands.

"Waiting for you."

"I'm not Mabel," he says. "You don't have to keep tabs on me."

"Where were you?" I ask again.

"Driving around," he says, avoiding my gaze.

I know where he's been because I have his location too, but I want him to say it.

"No secrets," I remind him. "No lies."

"No lies," he mutters, still looking at the floor.

"So, one more time," I say slowly. "Where were you?"

"I told you," he says, scowling at me.

I just stare at him, waiting, still not quite believing it.

He's lying to me.

And if he lies now, about this, what else will he lie about? What else has he already lied about?

I've never felt betrayed before, but I think that must be the feeling that slides through me, clean as a scalpel.

My brother has never been sneaky, so I don't think he went to Mabel's old house for nefarious reasons like trying to win points with her, take her for himself. I know he's been having a harder time sharing than I am, but I thought he'd get used to our dynamic. Maybe I should have worked harder on it, done more than simply tell him that he is important, vital, to what we have.

But I've never been good at knowing when to stop. My boundaries are different from other people.

So are my handicaps.

It would have been enough to tell Mabel. She would understand and accept my words. Probably, Duke even accepts them. But he needs more, needs to feel them, and I'm not sure how to make someone else feel something I never have and never needed to.

Frustration slides along the seam cut by the scalpel, filling the cut, chasing the sting out and replacing it with the more familiar sensation.

After a long, long silence where he has every chance to come clean, I finally accept that he isn't going to.

"You're too drunk to be driving around," I say, but there's no harshness in my words.

"How do you know I'm drunk?"

"Alice is just as bad," I say. "Maybe worse. You're taking too much."

"I ran out," he says. "I haven't had any in days."

"Don't lie to me, Duke. We promised we'd never lie."

"I'm not lying!"

I want to believe him, but I'm not sure. That kills me a little. I could always, always trust my twin. There shouldn't even be a question. "Good," I say at last. "If you don't want to tell me, then don't. But promise you won't lie."

"I won't lie," he says, glowering at me.

"Is that where you went?" I ask. "To get more?"

"So what if I did? You made it for me," he reminds me.

"We made it together," I remind him.

I may have mixed the compounds, but he tested it, helped me know what he needed to get it just right. I'm beginning to think that was a mistake, but I don't tell him that. At least I know why he went over. I knew it must have been to see Colt, since Mabel's here, and there's nothing of hers that we'd want over there anymore. That must have been why he asked if Colt was home earlier. He makes fun of Colt's addiction, but he shares it. They must have used together while I was gone. That's the only explanation for their inexplicable tolerance of each other now.

"I'm sorry," I say at last. "I didn't know it would hook you like that."

"I'm not hooked," he says, his tone defensive. "I told you, I haven't had any in days, and I'm fine."

"When we get back home, you won't be on production. Not being around it so much should help."

"I told you, I'm fine," he snaps. "Let it go."

"You're not fine," I say quietly.

We stare at each other a long moment.

I don't understand why he doesn't understand, and that's the most frustrating part of all of it. Duke is the most important person in my world. There's never been any question in anyone's mind—not mine, not his, and not anyone else's. It's a fact as true as the earth turning and the sun rising. I never thought anyone would question it, that I'd have to find ways to prove something so unquestionably factual, not to mention obvious.

But now there's a question, and it's the one person who should never have to question it. I need to fix it, but I don't know how. That's the part that fucks with me. I could always fix anything, but I don't know how to fix this. I never felt the need to prove anything to anyone before, have never cared enough to try. But Duke should always, always know he's the best part of me, the best humanity has to offer, the best person in any room, no matter who else is there.

It seems impossible to show someone that, if they won't simply take the words as the truth that they are. The earth can't see the sunrise that shows that it's turning.

"Then give me some," Duke says at last. "If you think I'm not fine without it, I'll take some more. Is that what you want?"

"No," I say, scowling at him.

"Come on," he says. "You must have some with you. You made it."

"*We* made it," I correct. "And I don't have any."

I've taken it of course. I want to know how my creation affects people. But I don't enjoy it the way most people do, and I wouldn't carry it across state lines without a good reason.

"I'm sure you can get some," he says. "Anyone in town would give it to you."

"I'm not getting you Alice."

"Why?" he demands. "Don't you want me to be happy?"

"Of course I want you to be happy," I say. "But I don't think that's how you get there."

"Why not?" he asks, coming to sit down at last. "Who gets to say what makes other people happy, or what way is the right and wrong way to be happy?"

I shrug. "Maybe you're right. I'm not sure what that word means, what it entails, and why it's so important to people. Why do you need to be happy?"

"Because it feels good," he says, like I'm missing the obvious. "And if I'm happy when I'm high, isn't that better than never being happy at all? Why should I be miserable all the time just because society says that's not an acceptable way to be happy?"

"I don't want you to be miserable," I say. "But I also don't want you to OD and kill yourself."

"What do you want me to say?" he asks at last. "You want me to go to rehab like Colt?"

"No."

"Good. Because I can handle myself. I'm not a fucking pussy."

"I know that."

"Dad would never want me to do something like that," he says. "He'd say that all it takes is discipline and self-control."

"You can't know what he'd say," I point out. "He's not here. He didn't see you like this."

"He saw me fucked up plenty," he argues. "You know how he was. *Real men don't go to therapy, real men tough it out, real men take care of their own business.*"

"Therapy is bullshit," I say.

"I didn't say it wasn't."

"Then you'll slow down on your own?"

"Not like I have much choice," he mutters.

"Is that what you did with Dad on your outings?" I ask. "He taught you how to be a real man?"

"Something like that," Duke says with a little scoff. "I told you, I fucked a nun."

"Yeah," I say. "But how is that father-son time? Did he fuck her with you?"

"No," he says, scowling. "Mostly he watched and gave me pointers. Or he'd take me to see a priest so he could lecture me and toughen me up."

"Yeah, that sounds like dad."

Duke slouches in his chair and glares at me, a belligerent tilt to his chin. "Are you ever going to ask why I stood there and let him die?"

"Why did you?"

"I don't know," he says, bending forward and dropping his head into his hands. "Everyone else was going along with it, and I wanted to do the right thing, and if everyone said it was right, I figured it must be. I don't know what's right and wrong, Baron. How do people know that?"

"They don't," I say. "They learn by studying what other people say it is. Then you follow that."

"But you know," he insists. "You would have pulled Dad out, even if fifty people were there, ready to let him die. You would have stood up for him anyway."

"Maybe."

"You would have," he insists, raising his head.

"I would have done what was best for me in that moment," I say. "The same as you did. You can predict what other people will do afterwards, but not with any real accuracy. There are too many variables with humans, especially when they're free to interact with other humans in the world. In a lab, it would be easier to predict."

"Like Jane," he says glumly.

"Yes, like Jane," I say, disgust rising at her memory. "She was predictable. That's why I got rid of her. There was nothing more I could learn from her."

"I thought you got rid of her for Mabel."

I shrug. "I wouldn't have agreed to it if I weren't already bored of her."

"And you're happy with your decision?"

I pause, thinking over how to answer that. At last, I nod. "I'm glad we got rid of her, and that we have Mabel. I'm not happy that I couldn't find her, and that therefore, I can't be certain she's dead. I'm annoyed with myself for being sloppy that night and not trusting that you had Mabel under control. I knew you were capable of it."

"No, I wasn't," he says. "I made a mess of things. I burned down Mabel's house. I think that's partly why I let Dad die. If they'd chosen something besides fire… You know I can't think around it. The flames hypnotize me."

"I know."

He rubs the heel of his hand against his forehead. "But even if they hadn't burned him… Maybe I would have let them. I don't know when to do what will make me happy later. It's like nothing will. And I don't see it's going to make it worse until it's too late, and I've already done it. I don't know what will let me have a clear conscience. I don't think I've ever had one."

I've never had anything else, but I don't say that. It's not the time to brag.

He goes on anyway. "Everything I do to try and make it better just makes me feel worse. I want to make everyone happy, but the happier it makes them, the shittier it makes me feel. That's fucked up, right?"

"So, stop trying to make other people happy," I say. "Make yourself happy."

"I try," he says, throwing up his hands. "That's what's so fucked. I think if I make them happy, that'll make me happy. But it doesn't. It's like... There's only so much to go around. If I give them happiness, then I have less. If I do what I think people want, then they're all happy, and I'm fucking miserable."

"So next time, do what you want. Who cares if they're happy? You're the important one."

"That doesn't work either," he says. "I always did that, whatever's fun, whatever feels good in the moment. It just hurt more people, and I still feel like shit afterwards. So I do another thing to feel good, fuck another girl, take another pearl, and I feel good again. But when it's over, I feel even worse. I just keep getting lower and lower. It's like I don't have a rock bottom."

"Okay," I say. "What if you don't? If you know that, will you stop trying to reach it?"

"Is that what I'm doing?"

"Aren't you?"

"I don't know," he says, his voice a tortured groan. "Why can't I get over this, Baron? Everyone else moved on and is living their lives. They probably don't even think about it, and when they do, they just think they did the right thing, so it's okay. I'm the only one fucked up over it."

"How do you know that?"

"Because look at them," he says, gesturing around with one arm. "Royal and Harper are happy in New York. Devlin and Crystal are still fucking, making babies, living in his fucking house like they don't even remember they're the reason he's not in it. It's just another day in the line of work for King and Eliza. They kill people all the time."

"Has this been bothering you?" I ask. "Is that why you're acting different?"

"I don't know," he says morosely. "Probably."

"Let me see if I can make you something," I say. "When we go home in the fall, I'll get back in the lab for you. If I could make you a drug to cure your whiskey dick, surely I can make one to cure you of a conscience."

fifteen

Duke Dolce

"Are you happy?" I ask, glancing sideways at Mabel as I pull through the gate into our old neighborhood.

She thinks about that for a moment before she asks, "How can I tell?"

"You know," I say. "You feel happy with your life. Like good, in general. You like the way things are."

"I think so," she says. "I'm satisfied with our arrangement, if that's what you mean."

"Why?" I ask.

"Why what?"

"I mean, why would you be happy with that? Baron's a monster to you."

"And you're not."

I cruise along past Devlin's place, then turn into our drive. "But how can you be happy with us?" I press. "He hurts you. I hear you screaming."

"But you don't hear anyone else screaming."

"So you're happy with him because he doesn't fuck other girls?"

"Exactly."

SELENA

When I park, she picks up the basket from under her feet and climbs down from the car without waiting for me to go around.

I meet her at the front of the car. I catch her elbow, and she stops and looks up at me, waiting.

"Are you happy with me?"

"Of course."

"You're happy with both of us?"

"Yes."

"Who are you more happy with?" I insist.

She hesitates. "Why do you ask?"

"I just want to know," I say. "If you had to pick one of us, who would you choose?"

"I don't have to pick," she says. "That's the agreement."

"What if you did?"

"I wouldn't be happy."

I sigh. "You like us exactly the same amount?"

"If I had to," she says slowly. "I'd choose you. Of course I would."

"Why?" I ask, narrowing my eyes. She has to be lying. No one likes me more than Baron. He's the special one, even more special than Royal. He was always the favorite.

Mabel smiles and touches my arm. "Baron would be upset, but he'd be okay."

She turns and walks into the house before I can answer.

I pull out my smokes and light one.

Baron would be okay.

That means she'd only choose me because she doesn't think I would be. Because I need her, and she has to take care of me. That's what they both think. That I couldn't make it on my own.

After tossing my cigarette butt in the gravel, I stomp into the house, where I hear voices in the kitchen. When I step through the door, I find them in the breakfast nook.

"Where's Mabel?" I demand, looking around for her.

"She went up to look at the nursery with Devlin," Crystal says, scooting down to make room. "She said she wanted to talk to him about their grandpa. Have you eaten?"

Maybe she'll see the nursery and change her mind about kids, and I'll have something to look forward to.

"I'm not hungry," I mutter.

"It's my birthday," Olive says, picking up a glittery, plastic wand with streamers on the end. "That means it's Everything Day."

"Shit," I say. "Why didn't you tell me? I would have gotten you something."

Harper gives me a funny look. "I texted you last week."

Of course she did. But I was high when I read the text, and I didn't remember it until now, when she says it, and I have a vague memory of opening my phone and seeing her message.

SELENA

"Well, happy birthday," I say to Olive, trying to smile and look like everything is normal and I didn't fuck up as usual. "What's that thing? Are you a fairy or something?"

I meant it as a joke, but I hear my father's words echoing in mine, the accusatory tone. I'm sure he said those exact words to me a few times.

"A kid at the park gave it to me," she says, waving the wand around, so the silver streamers flutter and the baby on Crystal's lap reaches for it. "Isn't it dumb?"

She grins, so big I notice she's missing a molar, but I'm not sure if I've seen it before, so I don't comment. After my fuck-up with her birthday, I don't want her to think I don't care, that I don't listen to her when she's yapping or notice when she loses a tooth. I also don't want Harper or Royal to realize that I've been high around her. They probably wouldn't like that.

"Sit down, have a bagel," Royal says, nodding to the platter in the center of the table.

I sit.

"They're everything bagels," Olive says. "Because it's Everything Day. Crystal says parties should have themes, so that's our theme. Do you like it?"

"Who doesn't like everything?"

"Right?" she says, biting into her bagel and then squirming in her chair as she chews, trying to finish so she can talk more. She barely swallows before she goes on. "When we went to New York, Royal found out I'd never had a bagel before, so he drove us all the way into the city to get one. He said he knew the best bagel shop. We got all the bagels so I could try them."

"Let me guess," I say, picking one up. "Your favorite is the everything bagel."

"Yep," she says. "Have you ever had one before?"

"Sure," I say. "Lots of times."

"Royal says everything bagels are a lie, because they don't really have everything," she says, glancing at my brother. "Not even everything you can put in a bagel, like blueberries and cinnamon and asiago. That's a kind of cheese."

"I know."

"It's good, but not as good as American cheese."

"That crap you like isn't even cheese," Royal says.

"To us it is," Harper says, shooting Olive a conspiratorial look. "But it's cheap, and we don't have to eat it anymore."

"I like it," Olive declares. "And I think it's fancy. Each slice has its own wrapper."

Royal shakes his head like she's hopeless.

"Every single slice?" I ask. "No way. That *is* fancy."

Olive grins and shrinks down in her seat, biting into her bagel again before glancing at Royal to see his reaction to my amazement. She's clearly pleased to have impressed me with her poor-person food, which makes me feel about ten times better about forgetting her birthday.

"This one time, I asked why they don't make everything anything else. Like why don't they have everything pizza or everything cookies? So we went to a pizza place, and Royal had them put everything on one pizza. There was so much on it that it kept falling off."

"I bet."

"It wasn't that good, so we're not doing that for my birthday," she says. "But the next day, we went to the store and got everything you can put in a cookie, and we made everything cookies. Those were good. So we're having those tonight, and everything ice cream. And we're going to watch every kind of movie I like."

"How many is that?"

"A lot," she says. "We're starting out with *The Fast and the Furious*, if you want to watch."

"*The Fast and the Furious*?" I ask, glancing from her to Harper. "What happened to Tow Mater?"

"That's for babies," Olive says, wrinkling her nose.

All the good feeling melts away as I think about how much I've missed, how much she's grown up and changed in just a year. When she was talking about bagels, I kept thinking how nice that sounded, which meant I should have been happy for her. After all, she deserves all the best things, someone to spoil her. And now she has it.

But it doesn't make me happy because I'm a selfish bastard. All it does is make me wish I'd been there to take her to the bagel shop, that I'd thought to make her cookies when she lived with me. Not that I know how to make cookies. But I should have learned. For her, I should have.

I didn't, though, and now it's too late. One more time I didn't see what was important until it's gone, and I can't go back.

"And then we're going to watch a show about koalas," Olive rambles on. "Oh! Can I show him what we got?" She turns from Harper to Royal, bouncing up and down in her seat.

"Go," Royal says. "It'll give us a break from your yapping."

Olive ducks under the table and races off, and Harper swats Royal's arm. "Be nice," she says. "It's her birthday."

"You should be nice to her every day," I say, scowling. "She's been through a lot. She lost her sister."

"She didn't *lose* her," Harper says. "That makes it sound like she's dead."

Fuck.

"Don't you think she would have come back if she was alive?" I ask.

"Let's hope that's not true," she says. "I tried to find her, but obviously I'm not that good at stalking people online, and there were like a million Greens in Oregon, and most of them didn't answer when I reached out. But I'm sure Baron can find her."

The bite of bagel I was chewing lodges in my throat, and I start coughing so hard everyone makes a fuss. By the time I get myself under control, Olive is back.

"Look what I have," she says, holding up a fuzzy grey onesie with feet and a hood. "It's a koala!"

SELENA

I shrug and take a drink of orange juice. "A sloth would be cuter."

"No, it's not!" she howls in protest, picking up the other two huge piles of grey fluff she dropped beside her. "Here's Harper's, and we got one for Royal, but he refuses to wear it—" She pauses to stick her tongue out at my brother before finishing, "So Harper said we could bring it for you."

"Really?" I ask, turning to Harper. "You brought it for me?"

She shrugs. "I mean, we already bought it. Might as well get some use out of it, and I figured you don't mind looking like a dumbass."

I know I'm supposed to shoot back an insult, but my throat's all clogged again even though I haven't taken another bite, and I can't think of anything to say. I thought she hated me for bashing Olive's head in, but she doesn't care either. Maybe it's just because we share something now, the murder of my father, or maybe she just forgives me. It seems like she does. She even brought me a matching suit to include me in their movie night.

And all I can think about is that Baron's pretending to look for Blue, and I know what happened to her, and if I told them, they'd never speak to me again.

So don't tell them, whispers my demon.

We spend the day doing everything Olive wants while the party planner takes care of the setup at the house. Later that evening, everyone comes for the birthday party. When Baron walks in, all the ugly, churning, mixed-up feelings come rearing up—resentment, anger, hurt, frustration, helplessness. I hate that I can't hate him. After spending the day with Olive, I want to, but I can't. He's still my twin, still half of me, and I can't stop loving him any more than I can stop breathing.

When Olive blows out the candles on her cake, she grins around at all of us.

"I wished my sister would come home," she announces.

"You're not supposed to tell anyone your wish," I say, glancing at Baron.

He shows absolutely no sign that he knows her sister is Blue. But he does. He knows, and he knows that he killed her, and that she's never coming back.

"I always wish for that," Olive says.

"I bet this year, you'll get it," Harper says, smiling at Baron. "I have a good feeling about it this time."

"Me too," Olive says, plopping down in the chair and waving her sparkly wand. "Now, what does everyone else wish for?"

"It's your birthday," Crystal explains. "Only you make a wish."

"I know that," Olive says, rolling her eyes. "But I want everyone to get their wish. So you each get to say what you wish for. It's my birthday, so you have to do it."

She holds up her wand expectantly.

"Okay," Crystal says. "I wish for a healthy baby."

SELENA

Devlin wraps his arms around her from behind. "Me too. And a healthy delivery."

"Now you," Olive says, pointing her wand at Harper.

"Well, since it's your birthday, I'm going to wish your sister comes home too."

"I'll also wish for that," I say when Olive points at me. "Three's the magic number, right?"

I feel a pit in my stomach, but my demon is pleased. Or maybe it's just me, being shitty and smug that I got away with it, that she still loves me even though I let her sister die.

"You," Olive says, pointing at Mabel.

For a second, our eyes meet, and I'm sure she's going to say something. But then I remember that Mabel doesn't even know who Jane was.

At least, I don't think she does. She did go down in the basement and talk to her that day.

What did Blue say to her?

"I wish for justice," Mabel says. "For all who deserve it."

"Damn," Harper says. "That's a good one."

But a cold chill has wrapped around my spine. Mabel says she forgives us, but if she wants justice to come to those who deserve it, doesn't that mean justice in every sense of the word? Justice isn't just for victims to receive. It's also for villains to face.

sixteen

Mabel Darling

"Have you found anything about Dahlia?" I ask Baron, setting down my battered paperback copy of *Outbreak*.

"No," Baron says. "These things take time, and I have a lot on my plate. All your past dates are dead or seemingly normal, though. And I think I found your coworker."

"Devlin said some cousin of Preston's is a hacker. He might be able to track her down."

"I don't need Nate's help," Baron growls, glancing up from his laptop. He sits on the step, the computer balanced on his knees, while I lounge in the hammock. "At least we can rule out your coworker. She's a red herring, no one important. But I still haven't found Dahlia or Jane or your stalker."

"Jane?" I ask, sitting up. The hammock sways sickeningly. "You're looking for Jane?"

"Yes," he says, frowning. "Don't you want to know if they find her body and are looking for us?"

"I don't want to know *you're* looking for her," I say.

"You can't seriously be jealous of a dead girl."

SELENA

"Is she dead, though?" I ask. "You said you'd get rid of her, and then you let her go, and now you're looking for her. Are you hoping you'll find her alive?"

"Of course not," he says, sounding slightly annoyed. "That would be worse than if they find her body and search for her killer."

"Well, you can see why I'd be upset," I say. "I thought you gave her up for me, and a year later, you're still obsessing over her. What am I supposed to think?"

"You're supposed to think I made a mistake," he says. "And be grateful I admitted it, and that I'm trying to fix it. If she's alive, I'll find her and change that. Otherwise, she compromises everything we've built."

"She compromises *you*."

"Duke and I have the same DNA," he says, not looking up from his laptop this time. "Whatever evidence she could take to the police incriminates him equally."

I lay back and consider that. I think about the emaciated, disfigured girl in the basement of the twins' rental, how she grabbed my leg and begged like I was Baron while I stood on the wooden steps.

"He's going to kill me."
I couldn't tell her otherwise.
"I'm sorry," I said, and I thought she was the physical embodiment of the psychological toll they'd taken on me.
"Are you a captive too?" she asked.

"No," I said. "I'm something else entirely."

"You have to help me," she begged, clinging desperately to my khakis. "Please."

"They don't let me out of their sight," I told her. "Baron keeps the key to the basement close, and there's no windows. I'm not sure how I could get you out."

"You have to help me. I think...I think..." She started crying. "I think I might be pregnant."

My stomach dropped, and I squeezed my eyes shut, and I tried not to remember the day Royal dropped me off at the hospital after pulling me from the river. He said dying was the easy way out. But when I told Jane that, she didn't want the easy way out.

I'm not sure how to help her now. If she's out there, Baron will find her. The only thing that will stop him is death. I'm just not sure whose death it would take.

At least the deaths I've orchestrated were well-deserved.

"Would you do something for me?" I ask at last.

"I would do a lot of things for you, little monster."

"Would you take me to see my grandpa," I say, swinging my legs over the side of the hammock. There's one way to find out for sure if the Black Widow Killer is done. Maybe I can arrange for some more suitable targets than Jane. If she starts killing again, it will distract Baron from his project.

If nothing else, I can get closure before they send my grandfather away.

"What sort of visit are we paying?" Baron asks.

"A last farewell."

He raises his brows and makes a noncommittal sound. "Just say when."

A few days later, we're heading that way. "Should we stop over at the other place and get Duke on the way?" I ask. "I don't want him to feel left out."

"I don't think he wants to be involved," Baron says. "He's dealing with enough."

"What is he dealing with?" I ask, though I doubt he'll answer. If there's one thing Baron won't do, it's spill family secrets to someone outside the family. Even I don't get an exemption. Even here, in a relationship with both twins, I'm an outsider. They will always come first to each other. As long as we're all together, the most I can hope for is second place.

"A guilty conscience," Baron says, glancing over. "You should talk to him about it. A different perspective might help him."

"I don't have a guilty conscience," I say, watching the old neighborhood slide by outside the window as we continue along the winding two-lane road toward my grandpa's.

A few minutes later, we turn down the road towards his house, and then the bridge looms ahead. It's not a covered bridge, but one with exposed wooden beams rising above it, as if that were the plan at some point before they abandoned it. It's painted white now, rising stark above the river, the one-lane wooden planks underneath still weathered and uneven.

Baron glances at me as he eases the Lexus onto it.

"Brings back memories, doesn't it?" he asks, and though his tone is casual, the cruelty in his words reminds me who I'm dealing with. I can never let my guard down again, can never let myself love him the way I did before, even when he's being kind to me or protective of Duke.

"A few," I say, my tone equally casual, as if I'm not curled into a ball in the fetal position inside the blank cardboard box that is Mabel Darling to the world.

As if the worst memory I have is jumping off this bridge and trying to die, when that's nothing but a frustration to me, a failure. Baron only thinks about the bridge though, not the reasons that drove me here—them hanging me in the bathroom, standing there watching to see if I'd die or work myself free in time. And when I did, it was Baron who shoved the broken curtain rod inside me, Duke who kicked it. It was Royal who pulled me out of the river when I stumbled here after pulling it out, blood gushing down my thighs. It was Royal who didn't let me die, who drove me to the hospital.

It was a nurse who said, "We couldn't save the baby. I'm sorry."

It was me who said, "What baby?"

It was a doctor who told me I'd been pregnant, but I never would be again.

SELENA

I'd thought I didn't want kids until it wasn't an option.

From the corner of my eye, I watch Baron watching me from the corner of his. I wonder if he knows that. He probably does. He probably hacked my medical records at Cedar Crest. He wants me anyway, but I wonder if he wants me less. If he'd known what Jane told me, he might have wanted her instead. Or maybe he did know, and that's why he didn't kill her.

We pull up to my grandfather's estate in silence. He punches in the code without asking, but nothing happens. We have to buzz in. Even now that the Dolces are no longer targeting our family, Preston is still paranoid.

When I saw him at my childhood home, I told him I was surprised to see him at Royal's house. He always hated the Dolces the most out of all of us.

He said, "It's not Royal's house. It's Devlin's."

I said, "Royal and Harper live here too."

He said, "Only for the summer."

Then he went on to explain that he was on "uneasy good terms" with Royal. "But things can change in an instant," he added as a caveat. "This time, we'll be ready."

His paranoia lingers, an internal scar like mine. I don't have the external scars that he does, that almost everyone in my family does. Preston is missing an eye and his face is burned. Colt is missing a finger and his arm is burned. I'm outwardly intact, but I'm missing a uterus, and I'll be forever changed mentally. Dad is missing a penis and his leg was broken so badly he'll never walk without a cane. One of my uncle's was similarly dismembered. Another is dead. Preston's dad is in prison. Mom is nearly catatonic. Nearly every Darling who stayed in Faulkner is damaged irreparably in some way.

And yet, despite the staggering damage the Dolces did to our family, they haven't paid any tangible price. Preston hasn't taken any of their eyes. Colt hasn't chopped off their fingers and tortured them with a blowtorch until they passed out from pain. Everyone seems ready to move on, leaving only a single casualty on their side. Tony Dolce is gone, but his sons are all still here, beautiful and flawless, untouched by the Darlings they so thoroughly destroyed.

It doesn't seem fair.

Preston buzzes us in a few minutes later, and we pull up the drive and around the back of the garage to park. I left my Prius here, but of course Grandpa didn't keep it. He only keeps expensive, rare collectibles. Not a car that his favorite granddaughter dumped here after her stay at Cedar Crest, where I went directly from the hospital when they discharged me. After a month in the mental wing, they told me I was well enough to go home, but I never did. Not even to get my things. I dropped my car here, took Grandpa's McLaren, and drove to the bus station.

Preston's the one who met me there, who took the keys and handed me Seeley Boots in his carrier, my diploma from the graduation I missed, and an envelope full of cash.

He said, "I hope I never see you again," and I knew he meant it in the best way, that they never found me.

I said, "Me, too."

But I always knew they would.

Even when I bought a bus ticket with cash, when I went to Chicago and New York and Philadelphia and Boston; when I went to Milwaukee and Minneapolis and Montana; and to Seattle, San Francisco, Phoenix and Amarillo and Memphis. Finally, I was satisfied that no one could have followed that track, all paid in cash, on different bus lines and taxis and even a plane or two. Finally, I settled in and became Dahlia, and like Preston, I was ready.

"Ready?" Baron asks, and I realize he thinks I'm stalling because I don't want to face my grandfather.

"Yes," I say, unbuckling my seatbelt. I climb out of the car and smooth my daisy sundress down.

Preston meets us at the door. "Do you have any weapons?"

He's wearing a holster on his hip with a black pistol in it and a plain white mask that covers the side of his face that Baron ruined.

"No," I say, then turn to my companion.

He shakes his head no, then pulls up his shirt and does a full turn so Preston can see his waistband. When he's satisfied, my cousin steps back and lets us enter.

"My family is out," he says. "So there's no one to take hostage if you turn feral."

"We're here to see her grandfather," Baron says coolly. "That's all. I have no interest in your family."

But I'm glad Dolly isn't home. I don't like that she slept with Baron, even if it was before he ever spoke to me.

Preston leads us up the staircase to the left and unlocks the door to the west wing of the old brick mansion that sits creaking under its own weight in the midday sun. Then he looks at me.

"Do you want me to go in with you?"

"No," I say. "I want to talk to him alone."

He glances at Baron.

"He's coming with me," I say.

"Are you sure that's a good idea?" Preston asks.

"You think I can't protect my girl?" Baron growls, wrapping an arm around my waist.

I flinch, and Preston notices. His good eye locks on my face, but his expression never changes. "I think you're capable," he says to Baron. "I think you're equally capable of holding her down and letting our grandfather do what he wants to her."

"Anyone's capable of that," Baron says. "That doesn't mean I'd do it."

Preston's eye moves to me. "You trust him?"

SELENA

I swallow hard and nod, giving both men the answer they want.

"I'll be standing outside," Preston says, leading the way down the hall. "If I hear anything that tells me I need to interrupt, I will. And I won't hesitate to repay the favor you did last time you were here."

He stares Baron down with his mismatched eyes, one real and one prosthetic, as he unlocks one of the bedroom doors. Then he steps back and lets us in.

Inside, the room is spacious like all the rooms in the manor house, a suite with its own bathroom, a king bed, and a cozy living area with a coffee table and comfortable seating near the floor-to-ceiling windows that look out over his expansive estate. My grandfather sits in one of those chairs, surveying his domain. He rises when he sees us. He's aged more than the three years since I've seen him can account for.

"Mabel," he says, stepping toward me and holding out his arms like he thinks I'll run into them. "It's good to see you!"

"Grandpa," I say, nodding. "I'm not much of a hugger."

"And you brought a friend," he says, striding over and extending a hand to Baron. Even though he's in his seventies, he's still stout and solid and straight, without a tremor in his big hand when he holds it out to Baron or a curve in his spine. He looks like he has a good twenty years left in him. Darlings do tend to age well and live long—at least the men.

"If I take that hand, it won't be attached when you get it back," Baron says. "So I suggest you keep it far away from me. And Mabel."

"Oh—of course," Grandpa says, laughing like it's a joke. "Mabel, you sure I can't interest you in that hug? One for your papa, for old time's sake?"

Baron's hand drifts my way like he'll put it around my waist, but he must think better of it, knowing I can't handle the contact right now. So he just puffs up and stares down the older man. "Preston's outside, and if he hears any sounds of distress, he'll come in guns blazing," he says. "Otherwise, I'd gut you alive right now. The only thing stopping me is that Mabel wants to talk to you. The second she says the word, though, this meeting is over. And for you, that could be a permanent situation. So I'd tread carefully, old man."

Grandpa looks from me to Baron and back, and then he laughs. Not like he's mocking us, but like this is all fun and games, like Baron's teasing him the way his buddies would when they came by to shoot the shit with him on the dock of the catfish pond. More deals were made out there than anyone probably knows—he was the most powerful judge in the county, and alliances were made and lost out there by the water, with no witnesses and no one to overhear.

"To what do I owe the pleasure of your visit?" he asks heartily, like everything is under his control, like it always was. He'll never admit otherwise, even when he's locked away in his bedroom and can only come and go at Preston's discretion.

"I wanted to talk to you about some things," I say.

"Of course," he says. "Come right in and make yourself at home. It's been so long. Not that I get many visitors anymore, you know." He makes a half-hearted laugh. "I keep to myself these days."

"Is that because you're locked up where you belong?" Baron asks.

"He's not where he belongs," I say. "He belongs six feet under."

"Mabel," Grandpa scolds, but his tone is wheedling too, like he thinks I'm being too hard on him.

"Am I wrong?" I ask.

"Why don't you sit down and we can have a nice talk," he says. "I'll get the maid to bring up some iced tea. Unless you'd like something a little stronger."

He winks at us, smiling his big jovial smile that shows too many teeth, the one he gave while he shook hands with politicians and prosecutors that made them think he was friendly and clever—you scratch my back, I scratch yours, and we can all go home for dinner.

To me, it was always the smile of the big bad wolf in a fairytale, prowling and hungry for a little girl to gobble up. Too bad the girl he swallowed was more hemlock than honey.

"I think tea will be just fine," I say.

"You want to have a tea party?" Baron asks, raising a brow.

"Yes," I say. "I think we have some things to discuss. Don't you, Grandpa?"

"Certainly," he says, taking his seat in the easy chair again. He gestures for us to join him. "You've been gone what is it? Three years? Tell me about your schooling. How's university life treating you?"

"I'm not here to talk about school," I say, watching him put in the order on his tablet. He may not get to do all the terrible things he used to, but he's still living like a king up here.

"What is it you'd like to discuss, snowflake?" he asks, setting down the tablet.

I wince at the nickname. "Do you remember that time when I was little, and you took me to that burger place after it was closed, and there was a girl there with her baby?"

"No, I can't say that I do," he says, watching me expectantly, as if this is the first he's ever heard of the night in question.

"Who was she?" I ask.

"I'm afraid I don't know," he says. "Are you sure it wasn't your dad or one of your uncles that took you? I can't say I made a habit of going out for fast food, and I wouldn't have even known how to get into a place like that once it was closed."

"Baron already knows," I say. "And you got away with it. I never went to the police, and no one would believe me anyway. It's my word against yours, and just like you're doing now, they'd say I misunderstood because I was a kid. But I remember."

I remember the way I remember everything then, the facts laid out like a dusty card catalogue or a series of bones bleached by the sun, each one faded but still in its place. Back then, each thing that happened was simply catalogued, one event as meaningful and meaningless as the next. That night, I was a big girl. I helped by getting a bottle of water when he asked. I sat in my car seat on the way home, licking my ice cream cone.

"Well, you must be remembering wrong," he says, like it's the end of the discussion.

"You threw her baby in the vat of fryer oil," I say. "Does that ring any bells?"

"Now you're just being ridiculous," he says. "You always had quite an imagination, I'll give you that. I can't even imagine what else she's told you."

He looks at Baron for this, like he thinks Baron will believe him over me. For one sickening moment, I consider what will happen if he does. If he'll say I never told him this, and I made it all up, and Dahlia too, and all the dates we went on, everything we ever said and did. He'll say there's no Jane, there never was a Jane; there's no baby, there's no us. There's not even a Duke. There's only one of them, and he barely knows me. My heart starts skipping and I have to grip my chest at the stab of pain there.

But he's on his feet, hauling my grandfather up by the front of his shirt.

"Mabel doesn't lie," he growls, and then he shoves Grandpa back, hard.

Everything happens slow, and then fast.

His arms pinwheel. He stumbles backwards. He trips over a potted plant.

Glass shatters. And then he's gone.

He screams, but he doesn't even get to finish before there's a solid, gruesome thud.

Glass shards are still raining around us, cascading over the furniture.

The door flies open, and Preston is standing there, his gun drawn.

"What happened?" he demands, scanning the room. "Where's Grandpa?"

"He seems to have had a little accident," Baron says. "Stumbled right into the window."

Preston looks from me, to Baron, and back.

"Oops," I say with a shrug.

"You're not hurt?" Preston asks me. "You're okay?"

"Never better," I say. "But you might want to call down and tell the maid we only need two glasses of iced tea now."

"Better yet, tell her we'll come down and get it," Baron says. "We need a moment to grieve. But you might check on that body. If it's still breathing, I trust you'll take care of that."

Preston mutters a few curses and turns on his heel, disappearing out the door as suddenly as he came.

A hiccup of a laugh bubbles up inside me and bursts forth, high and slightly hysterical. Baron looks at me and grins, then picks me up and drops into the furthest armchair, pulling me astride his lap. His eyes blaze with a hunger I rarely see there.

"You sick little monster," he says, raking his hands up my thighs, pushing my dress to my hips, his fingers ghosting over scars. "Ride me while he's dead on the ground outside."

"Preston might hear," I point out, trying to squirm away. "He'll shoot you."

"Then save your screams until we get home," he says, undoing his pants and dragging his cock out. "I'll savor them even more after what we just did. But right now, I want that tight cunt showing me just how much it appreciates what I just did for you."

I swallow hard and nod, lifting up. Biting my lip, I fit him to my entrance, forcing myself down onto him. The sting of him entering me when I'm so completely unaroused has tears dripping down my cheeks, and he growls his approval, lifting his hips to force himself in further. His girth stretches me, and I choke on a cry as he starts dragging himself out and then tearing into my dry opening.

I hold in the sound, swallowing it like I did so many nights in this house, sealing the horror and pain and shame up tight inside the seamless blank of a doll. I let him play with me the way he likes, because I'm his doll now. I made a bargain with the devil, and these are the terms. He hurts me because that's what he needs, but he will make sure that no one else ever does. And because I give him this, he gives me his loyalty, and the promise that he won't hurt anyone else.

Just me. I'm his special little monster. And he is mine.

SELENA

seventeen

Duke Dolce

Baron and Mabel have been gone for hours. They don't even bother checking in, and they have my car, so I can't leave. After a while, I start to wonder if they're coming back. They could just leave me in Faulkner and go, say it's for my own good. After all, I don't have classes to return to, a degree to earn. They could ditch me and disappear. They wouldn't even have to give me a cut. What am I going to do, go to the police and tell them I got stiffed the money I'm owed for cooking drugs for a year?

I'd run out of money soon enough. Most of my inheritance was in Dolce Sweets stocks, and I signed all of mine over to Olive. Even if Mr. Delacroix could reverse that, I'd never ask him to. She deserves that money after what I did to her sister, and to her.

I'd blow it all on drugs anyway.

I'm probably just being paranoid. Just because Baron and Mabel don't need me, that doesn't mean they don't want me around. Just because I'm a liability doesn't mean they'll get rid of me. I'm not Jane.

SELENA

Except you were, my demon reminds me. *Before he found her, you were the one he experimented on, testing the early versions of Alice, before they took the user to Wonderland.*

I push that idea down. Like Baron says, we made Alice together. I was his assistant.

More like his guinea pig.

When he won't shut up, I leave Crys and the babies and wander downstairs. There must be ten kids in the living room, all sitting around Olive. She's holding her hair back with one hand, separating it with the other to show the scar that runs along her forehead and back onto her scalp.

"That's where he cut my head open."

A few of the other kids make faces and turn away, but most of them lean closer, their eyes wide.

"Whoa," says a boy who looks about ten, obvious awe in his voice.

"Told you," Olive says, beaming. "It's the same guy who took out Preston Darling's eye. He keeps it in a jar in his lab. One time, he let me hold it."

"Whoa," says a whole chorus of voices this time.

"Mad scientists aren't real," says a girl, looking skeptical.

"Well, he's not totally mad," Olive says. "But he said he wanted to open up my skull and look at my brain because it's so interesting. So I think that makes him pretty mad."

"Why is he mad?" asks an Asian boy who looks a few years younger. "Did you do something to him first?"

"Not mad like that," Olive says, running her finger along the scar. "Mad like, crazy."

"Like the Mad Hatter in *Alice and Wonderland*," says the older boy.

"Exactly," Olive says, then widens her eyes so you can see the whites all around and whispers, *"We're all mad here."*

"Okay, Olive, stop scaring your guests," Royal says, stepping into the doorway with Harper, both of them carrying big bowls of popcorn. "Next thing, I'll be getting calls from angry parents, and I'm not dealing with that shit today."

A couple girls look shocked and then giggle, like they've never heard a swear word before.

"Yeah, let's keep it light," Harper agrees. "This is a birthday party, not Halloween. And you want them to come back, don't you?"

"If any of them don't want to be my friends, I'll just have Royal kick their dad's ass," Olive says smugly.

"My dad's in jail, so he can't get him," says another girl.

"Then Harper will beat up your mom," Olive says, like it's the simplest solution.

"I don't know," the girl says, eyeing Harper. "My mom's a lot bigger."

SELENA

"She's small but mighty," Royal says, setting down a bowl of caramel popcorn on one end of the coffee table and a bowl of buttered popcorn on the other.

"No one's beating up anyone," Harper says, handing out two more bowls to the girls. Then she turns to me. "Are you staying? I think they're going to watch *Back to the Future* after this. None of them have seen it, and Olive wants to prove to them that there's a car that goes back in time. I'm not sure if she actually believes it's a time machine, but telling her it's not seems like telling a kid there's no Santa, so we're tiptoeing around that until we know for sure."

I look at Olive to see if she wants me to stay, but she's busy fighting over the caramel popcorn with two other kids. She didn't even notice I was here. She's with her friends—the ones her own age. She doesn't need me.

No one needs me.

"No," I say. "I'll go."

I'm outside before I remember I don't have a fucking car. I go back in, but Harper and Royal are busy with the kids, and Crystal is napping with the baby.

I find Devlin out back, putting up a tree swing.

"Hey," I say. "Let me borrow your car."

He straightens and squints at me. "You been drinking?"

"No," I say, scowling at him.

"You smell like you've been drinking."

"Fuck off," I say. "And stop knocking up my sister. She needs a break."

I turn and head around the other side of the house. I sit on one of the curving staircases out front and call Maverick.

"Hey," I say. "I need something."

"Yeah?" he says. "Pull up. I'm at the shop."

"I don't have a car," I say. "Come get me."

"Needy little bitch, aren't you?"

"Fuck you."

"Been trying for years, pretty boy."

"I'll make it worth your time," I say.

"Oh yeah?"

"I'll pay you double what you'll make at the tattoo parlor."

"I don't make house calls."

"Bullshit," I say. "You make them for Colt."

"Colt's my friend."

"I'm your friend."

"You're barely a client."

"Pick me up," I say. "I gotta get out of here, and it's not two in the morning this time."

"Where you at?"

"My house. And bring some bitches. I wanna fuck."

"I fuck."

"You can fuck them too."

He laughs quietly. "You owe me."

I go inside and grab a couple beers, then peek into the living room. The kids are all piled onto sofas and chairs and pillows on the floor, watching Olive kick some kid's ass in a car racing video game. He spins out and crashes, and the game ends.

Olive throws down her controller and jumps up and starts doing a victory dance, which is really just twerking. "Oh yeah!" she yells, bouncing her non-existent ass up and down. "Suck my clit, loser!"

I duck outside again, my head spinning. Where did she learn to talk like that? Or move like that? It's disconcerting, but then, maybe all kids talk like that. I was only a couple years older than her when Dad brought home two girls from our class and showed us how to fuck them. Thinking about Olive doing that shit in only two more years makes me think maybe her sexy dancing and language aren't so premature. It's not like I know anything about kids.

I sit on the front steps again. It's the exact place I was sitting when Olive came bopping up the driveway the first time with her skinny ankles showing and her uncombed hair. She sat here and drank a beer with me, and that was a year and a half ago, so I guess she's always been pretty mature for her age. But I haven't noticed anyone giving Harper and Royal shit about how she talks or acts like she's already a teenager. I'm sure Crystal and Devlin wouldn't allow any of that shit around here, but Harper said she made a promise to Blue and she wasn't going to break it, so they took Olive to New York with them.

Maverick pulls up in his sick, restored El Camino, interrupting my bitter thoughts. Colt said I didn't know anything about cars, but that's just because I didn't spontaneously ejaculate at the sight of his shitty old truck. I can appreciate an old car when it's actually cool, like Maverick's.

I climb onto the passenger side of the bench seat.

"You have little sisters, right?" I ask when Maverick starts to back down the drive.

He stomps the brake. "Yeah, and they're way too fucking good for you, so if you're going to even speak of them, you better get the fuck out of my car before I make your throat smile from ear to ear."

"Whoa, I'm not saying shit," I say, holding up both hands. "I just wondered how old kids are when they start twerking and talking about sex stuff."

"Eighteen, unless they want to get sent to a convent," Maverick says. "But my family's a little traditional. The girls aren't gang-bangers like us. Our dad's protective."

"Yeah, same," I say, then realize a second too late that I spoke about Dad like he's still here.

Suddenly, my throat hurts so bad I can hardly swallow.

"You got the pearls?" I rasp, sliding him an envelope.

Maverick leans back and digs around in the pocket of his jeans. I watch him, remembering how Colt always did that, taking his time to drag out his lighter, loving the way I watched him. That crease in his jeans at the hips that made me want to fucking kill the guy.

"Twenty dances with the devil," Maverick says, handing me a baggie of little blue pearls. "Or the Pearl Lady, if that's what you call her."

Twenty. It looks like barely anything. I count them discretely so as not to offend him.

"You counting?" he asks, shaking his head.

"No," I say, shoving the baggie in my pocket. "I know you wouldn't short me."

"I'd do the same thing," he says. "It's all good."

I tell him where to go, and a few minutes later, he pulls up.

"You want to take a couple?" I ask, pulling out the baggie again.

"Nah," he says. "I got to get back to the shop."

He has his seat tipped back and his wrist resting lazily on top of the wheel, tattoos swirling over his light brown skin from the backs of his fingers to the sleeve of his black tee stretched around his muscular bicep. He reminds me of Colt, all tatted up like that. His skin is smooth, though, not all fucked up from burn scars, and he's got all ten fingers.

"You sure about that?" I ask, wetting my lips.

He just shakes his head, a little smirk playing on his lips. "You and me and Alice? That sounds like a dangerous threesome."

"I thought you were a big bad gangster," I taunt. "Since when do you run from danger?"

"Since it started looking like you, pretty boy."

"So it was all talk all along," I say. "Pussy."

He shrugs. "Someone finally made an honest man of me. Should've climbed the ladder while you had the chance."

I climb out of the car and slam the door as hard as I can. I stomp up the steps and into the house. Mabel's house. She should have made an honest man out of me. She's my girlfriend, and I love her. But where the fuck is she when I need her?

Off with Baron, that's where.

Seeley Boots meows at me like a demand, so I go and fill his bowl. He crouches over it and starts eating. I try to pet him, but he gives me a dirty look and growls, so I back off. Even the fucking cat hates me.

I grab the box of beer from the fridge and slog upstairs to our room, ignoring the voice whispering behind me. I could lie in the bed and chain smoke to piss them off. I consider it, but it doesn't bring any real joy. So I step out the sliding glass door onto the small balcony. Each of the bedrooms has its own little private deck, three in a row. From here, there's not much of a view, just the big backyard and the woods beyond.

I'm glad I can't see Maverick leaving. I don't even like him. He's a dick with an ego the size of Manhattan, so I shouldn't care that he didn't want to hang out. I'm not even sure I wanted to hang out with him. I just didn't want to be alone.

SELENA

Popping the top off a beer, I wash down a handful of pearls.

I hear the crunch of his tires on gravel, and then the growl and roar of his engine as he accelerates. When the noise dies away, the sawing sound of summer insects fills the silence.

I open another beer.

The cap bounces across the balcony and tumbles through the railing, over the edge. It seems to float down, but finally, it clinks musically into the gravel below.

I wonder how it would feel to float like that.

But of course I'd fall faster, probably land with a disgusting crunch. I wonder if the drop would kill me. Probably not. It's only twenty or twenty-five feet. It would break a lot of bones, though. I wonder how long I'd lie there before they came home. Maybe they wouldn't even notice I was gone. They wouldn't think anything about it until tonight, when I don't come home from Royal's house. By then, I would have died from internal bleeding or some other slow death.

They'd get home and shower and fuck and make dinner. They wouldn't even miss me. They'd be happy to have the house to themselves.

And all the while, I'd be lying right outside the door, slowly succumbing to my injuries.

Maybe they'd finally feel bad then.

Or maybe they'd be happy I was out of the way for good, without them even having to get their hands dirty and make it happen. No one else would care. I saw that with Dad.

Oh, they'll make a big spectacle, have a funeral and play sad for a few days. But then they'll go on with their lives, just happy it's over. One less Dolce in Faulkner. And in a few years, someone will remember to ask about me, and they'll say what Colt said about Dad.

The world is a better place without him in it.

The Alice finally takes hold, and I put on some music and vibe, and then jerk off for a while. Finally, the door closes downstairs. I hear Mabel greeting her cat. I lie on the bed, staring at the ceiling.

"Duke?"

I look up and there's a girl in the shadows of the hallway. "Blue?"

She steps into the doorway, and it's not Blue. It's Mabel, with her hair in two pigtails, each dyed a different color. She has a long, butcher knife in one hand. She lifts it and grins, her tongue flicking over the end. Her mouth is full of blood, and it pours out, down the knife blade, but she just laughs. "Duke's fucking a dead girl," she sings, her words a twisted mockery of what I said when I pushed the dead guy into her. The blood gushes faster from her mouth, and she chokes on it, spraying it from her grinning mouth.

"Duke?" It's Baron's voice, more demanding now.

I try to blink the vision away.

Heavy footsteps ascend the creaky old steps, and then Baron is standing in the doorway. I blink a few times to make sure it's really him, that the Harley Quinn Mabel is gone.

"Why didn't you answer?" he demands, stepping into the room and flipping on the light.

"I don't know," I mumble. Even high, I know it would sound dumb to say I was waiting to see if he'd come find me, and even worse to tell him what I saw.

He studies me from behind his glasses, like I'm a specimen, just like Jane.

"You're drunk?"

"I had a few beers."

Mabel appears in the doorway next to Baron, holding Seeley Boots. She's smiling, happy. Her teeth are white, without a trace of blood. Despite what she says, she's clearly fine after being alone with Baron all day.

"What took you so long?" I ask.

"We had to talk to the police," she says, checking Baron from the corner of her eye.

She looks positively giddy.

"The police?" I ask, sitting up, my heart pounding erratically. "What for? Are they coming here?"

I just got the fucking pearls after days without. If I have to flush them, I'm going to be pissed.

Or maybe they knew.

Baron might have contacted Maverick ahead of time, knowing that's who I'd call. He might have told him to call if I asked for drugs, might have told the cops to come here so they can bust me and teach me a lesson.

"They're not coming here," Baron says, watching me with a frown.

He knows, my demon whispers. *He's going to turn you in. That's why he made them in the first place. He knew you'd get hooked. He knows you're weak.*

"Grandpa Darling had an unfortunate accident," Mabel says, beaming up at Baron.

"What kind of accident?" I ask, my heart still galloping at a concerning rate.

"He fell out a window," Baron says.

Mabel giggles. "It really was quite unexpected."

"I'm guessing you had something to do with that?" I ask, scowling at my brother.

He shrugs. "The police ruled it an accident. Mabel and I were the only witnesses, but Preston attested to the fact that he's been unusually clumsy lately."

"And you didn't think you should run that by me first?"

"Would you have wanted to be there?" Baron asks.

"No," I grumble. "But still."

How can I tell him that I want to be part of everything they do, that I want to be included, even when they do shit I want no part of? I had my share of killing already—more than my share. Even if he is an evil bastard, I don't want to kill anyone.

"It just happened," Mabel says, coming over to the bed. "We didn't plan it."

Boots squirms free and drops to the floor, stalking off with his tail flicking back and forth like even being close to me is an annoyance. I don't know what his problem is. I'm always nice to him.

"Whatever," I say.

"You can be there for the next one," Mabel offers.

"The next one?"

"Yeah, I'm not sure that's a good idea," Baron says. "In a town this small, if random people start showing up dead, they're going to know it's not an accident."

"I didn't mean for you to push Grandpa," Mabel says. "I thought we'd lead the Black Widow Killer to him. Now he's already dead, so we can't test her and see if she's still watching."

Baron frowns. "Why didn't you tell me that?"

"I didn't think you'd just kill someone like that," she says, looking absolutely starstruck.

"Why not?" he asks. "You saw what happened to the last guy who fucked you."

She blanches, her smile fading.

Blood gushes over her face, into her eyes, her mouth, bubbling in her nostrils.

Blood gushes out her mouth, and she cackles, ponytails swinging.

Baron doesn't seem to notice.

Still, he's the one who impressed her, which isn't easy to do. He's the one who defended her against her creepy abuser. He's the one who killed for her.

I can't compete with that, so I do the thing I know he never does.

"Come over here and sit on my face until your thighs quake."

"Can I shower off first?" she asks, biting her bottom lip.

"No," I say. "I want to taste how much murder turns you on."

She approaches hesitantly, but when she reaches the bed, I lift her onto me in one swift motion. I shove her skirt up, pull her panties aside, and bury my tongue in her cunt. It tastes like blood and cum, and I realize someone else got here first.

"You fucked Baron?" I ask, looking up at her from between her thighs. But when I check the door, my brother's gone.

Mabel nods, searching my eyes uncertainly.

"Then I guess we already know how much murder turns you on."

I drag my tongue lazily through her slit from her hole to her clit, and she whimpers.

"Did you fuck on the body, like last time?" I ask.

She shakes her head. Her pigtails bob. Her teeth are sharp as glass, dripping blood.

I blink up at her, and she's just Mabel again. "Or maybe thinking about doing this with the old creep turned you on," I say. "Did he eat your pussy as good as me?"

"Let me go."

"Or maybe the old guy just fucked you," I say, swirling my tongue around her clit. "Does thinking about it get you wet, you little freak?"

I grin up at her, but she's pale and frozen, unsmiling.

"I won't judge," I say. "Think about him while I'm eating you out if that's what makes you cum."

She tries to climb off, but I clamp my hands down on her thighs, dragging her down and plunging my tongue inside her.

"Please," she whimpers, but I thrust my tongue deeper, harder, curling it inside her and making her quiver. I hold her pinned, making her sit and endure until she gives me what I want. When she's climaxed, I finally pull her down on top of me after dragging off her panties and tossing them off the bed. I notice she's crying, though I'm not sure if it's just because I made her cum or because of what I said to her.

She tries to roll away, but I keep her pinned on top of me, refusing to let her go.

"Baron?" she whispers against my chest, her fingers brushing the scar through my shirt.

"What?"

"Are you really Baron?" she asks.

"Does Baron eat your pussy like that?"

"I thought only he could be that cruel."

"You thought wrong," I say, adjusting myself between her legs and pushing up into her. "Now sit up and ride me like you did for your grandpa all those years."

eighteen

Mabel Darling

"What's that?" I ask, peering over Baron's shoulder at the derelict little ranch-style on his laptop screen. I set down a glass of sweet tea beside him on the picnic table, one of the four sitting out back around the ancient oak sprawling over the back porch and a swath of the yard.

"This is Jane's house," he says.

My heart flips, and I resist the urge to reach for Seeley, who's twining between my feet. "You found her?"

"No, over on Mill Street," he says. "Where she lived before I picked her up."

"She's from Faulkner?"

"Yeah," he says, not looking up. "Her mom still lives there, though she doesn't seem to do much except run up credit card debt shopping online and apply for government aid. I can't find any evidence that they've been in contact at all."

I can't breathe. I grab one of the glasses of iced tea and carry it to Duke, who's lying in the hammock nearby, swaying gently in the hot summer breeze.

SELENA

I'm grateful to have an excuse to walk away for a minute, glad that Baron has such singular focus when he's working that he misses everything else around him unless it's spoken aloud. While I'm occupied, I examine the new information, turning it over in my mind, studying it like a crime scene fiber under a microscope. He took Jane from here. Maybe he even had her when they still lived here. I shouldn't be upset. I know they were with lots of women while I was away. But something about it bothers me.

I get the feeling I'm missing a piece of evidence that's right in front of me. That must be the missing friend of Harper's, the one Duke said was dead. The one he agreed to find, in exchange for being allowed to return to Faulkner. Like he was doing her a favor, one he had no connection to.

I shiver and hand Duke the sweating glass.

"Thanks, Duchess," he says, smiling up at me. "Can I get a kiss too?"

I lean down and plant a chaste kiss on his lips. "Any time, Duke."

He hasn't gotten dressed, and he's in athletic shorts and nothing else. With the *DOLL* scar on his chest and his glasses on his nose, he looks so much like Baron it's disconcerting. Only the sleepy smile and the warmth in his dark eyes gives away his identity.

That, and the fact that Seeley is rubbing against Baron's legs under the picnic table.

I return to them and slide in on the opposite bench. "If you think about it, you never really fulfilled your end of the bargain."

"Not this again," Baron says, sounding annoyed. "I got rid of Jane, like you asked."

"How do I really know that?" I ask. "You could have taken her into the woods and let her go for all I know."

"This isn't one of your childhood fairytales." He sighs and closes his laptop, and for the first time, I notice how tired he looks. He and Duke both have trouble sleeping, though I think it's for very different reasons. Behind his glasses, his eyes have dark circles, and I wonder if he's been up more nights than I know. I sleep pretty well, aside from the nightmares that wake me screaming in the dark, clutching for a way out.

"How did you prove what you'd do for me if she's still alive?" I ask. "I've been at your mercy for a year, and I got nothing out of it."

Baron glances around, but there's a reason I chose this location for the conversation, a reason I waited until his laptop was closed.

"I just got rid of your grandpa for you," he points out.

"I know," I say. "That was really special. But it wasn't a sacrifice for you. You already hated him. You would have done that for yourself. I only got you access to him."

"What do you want me to do?" he asks, narrowing his eyes at me.

"What are you willing to do?" I counter.

He watches me a second, his dark eyes inscrutable. "To make you happy?" he asks. "Almost anything, little monster."

"If someone hurt me," I say, watching Seeley pounce on something in the grass. "Would you avenge me?"

"I think I've proven to you what I'd do already."

"Who hurt you?" Duke asks, sitting up in the hammock to look at us.

"Mr. Harris."

"The science teacher?"

"Yes."

When Baron doesn't say anything, I peek up at him.

"How do you want us to avenge you?" he asks carefully, pushing up his glasses.

"You know how."

"You want me to kill him."

"What did he do to you?" Duke asks.

"You know what."

I look away from them both, up at the canopy of glossy oak leaves shading us, not able to bear their eyes on me when I know what they're thinking. They know what sort of thing he did to me.

"I think every man I set up deserved it," I say. "I don't regret a single one of them. But I *know* he deserves it, and he's still walking around free."

Baron makes a noncommittal noise, looking thoughtful. "And how would we go about that?"

"It was easy enough with my grandfather."

"That was an accident," Duke says.

I open my mouth to correct him, but Baron frowns at me, and I close it again. Duke needs to believe that the same way he needs to believe that if he can make my body respond, then I want it.

"I told you, we can't just leave dead bodies all over town," Baron says. "People will notice it happened when we came back, and the FBI will have a solid case when they realize that people also died in Tennessee when you were there, and a guy disappeared in Maine, even if they never found a body. His wife reported him missing."

"And Jane," Duke says.

"She's a variable too," Baron says, nodding. "Though there's no police reports that match the description of what we did to her, and no Jane Doe has been found in the area."

"So, Jane disappeared from here, but she wasn't reported missing, so that doesn't count," I say slowly. "And one old man died of a fall. I don't think it's enough for the town to get suspicious yet. I think we can afford one murder."

"One murder can put you away for life," Baron points out.

"Maybe we don't have to do the killing," I say. "Maybe the Black Widow Killer will do it for us."

"He's still following you?" Duke asks.

I shrug. "Only one way to find out."

Baron watches, eyes intense behind the lenses of his glasses. At last, he nods. "We can set up a trap. It should be easy enough, using your old methods. If they're still watching you, they'll see what you're doing and follow your teacher like they did your other victims."

"They weren't victims," I say. "They were predators."

Neither of them argue. They don't say, "We're predators too." They don't think of themselves that way. They don't consider that I've taken them off the streets as much as the other men. The only difference is, they're alive. But as long as they keep their promise to me, they won't harm anyone else.

Baron opens his laptop, and we set up my new profile. I've always simply gone into a male space and dangled myself like bait, and the creeps swarmed. This time, we're hunting with purpose. As if he can sense the shift, Seeley Boots comes trotting back across the lawn and hops up into my lap. I pet him while I watch Baron cast a line. To my surprise, he slides the laptop in front of me.

"You want me to lure him in?" I ask.

"You're the expert," he says, and I can tell by the way he's looking at me that he's impressed by my skill. He's probably the only man alive who would like to know his girlfriend possesses that ability, but that only makes me glow brighter than his praise did.

I take the laptop and start working while Baron watches with a mixture of curiosity and pride. Duke swings one foot back and forth lazily until Seeley takes notice and stalks over. He crouches low, watching the enticing motion. At last, he launches himself, pouncing on the moving object. Duke yelps when the cat sinks his teeth and claws in, scrabbling for purchase as Duke howls and tries to shake him loose.

I can't help but laugh.

Duke dumps out of the hammock, and Seeley shoots off across the yard while his victim hops around on one foots, cursing and casting me grievous glances.

"That cat's a menace," he says, stomping past us and through the back door. "It ought to be put down."

"One could say the same about you," I say lightly, still grinning as I type in all the things I know Mr. Harris will love to hear.

It was my senior year, after Dixies posted the video on her blog, after they'd started to torment me, that he got involved.

I was in the library one day at lunch, avoiding them and checking over the presentation I had to give in my next class a final time, when Duke's grinning face appeared around the end of one of the shelves.

"Found you," he said, leering at me.

I stood to bolt, but when I turned, Baron was behind me. "You can run, but you can't hide," he taunted.

Still, I tried. I ducked between the shelves, but Duke darted around the end and dragged me back. I thought about screaming. Even the deaf, grandmotherly librarian who had been there since the dawn of time could hear one of my screams. But when I thought of her heaving herself out of her chair and toddling through the stacks to where we were hidden at the back tables, when I thought of the look on her face if she saw us, I swallowed it down. I would endure in silence, just as I always had. I wouldn't scream. I wouldn't tell.

Duke shoved me into Baron's arms, and he bent me over the table, dragged up my khaki skirt, and ripped off my underwear. He shoved into me like it was his right, with no preparation, no words. Baron wasn't rough. He knew he was big enough to cause pain without it, especially when he went in dry. He fucked silently, methodically, at an unhurried pace. Each thrust was a new punishment.

Duke crouched next to the bookshelf, keeping a lookout, cackling quietly when a whimper escaped me. I lay over the table, gripping the edges in agony, silent tears dripping down my face, until Baron finished and tucked himself away. He pocketed my underwear and then nodded to me, giving Duke the go-ahead.

Duke dipped his fingers into me and groaned, unzipping with his other hand. "Fuck, you're so wet with his cum," he said, and then he was slapping his dick against my thighs, my butt. He teased the head over my entrance, then eased in slowly, another moan escaping him. His fingers bit into my hips as he held me pinned, rocking into my depths, the hot pool of liquid Baron had left so far inside.

"Don't get it on my skirt," I say, trying to tug it from between me and the table. The one thing worse than this was having people know.

Duke cackled and started moving, his thrusts erratic, slow and then fast, slamming into me hard, scooting the table across the floor. I pictured the grumpy librarian at her desk, probably annoyed with the noise but not enough to walk back here. She was always sour-faced and prim, with a pearl necklace topping a three-piece ensemble in varying shades of pastel that consisted of a matching skirt, shirt, and sweater with one button done at the top. She wore pantyhose to hide her varicose veins and orthopedic shoes, and she always groaned when she stood and huffed and puffed after walking one aisle. She did not take kindly to being roused from the half-slumber that occupied most of her day.

Duke finished just as the bell rang, and I quickly stood and pulled my skirt down, wiping my face dry with the back of my hand. I didn't want anyone to look at me in the hall more than they already did, to whisper that I had nothing to cry about. I could feel the slime of their cum sliding down my thighs as I walked to class. I sat there in silence, like I did every day.

I liked science, so I liked Mr. Harris. He was always nice to me, always praised my answers and looked impressed when I had unique viewpoints instead of making me feel like a freak, like some of my teachers. When he called me up to do my presentation, I heard people whispering. Snickering.

SELENA

I turned around, and I saw several people with phones out, aiming them at me. I turned back toward the front, ducked my head, and hurried up. Everyone was laughing by then.

I discretely ran my hand down the back of my skirt, and my heart sank. Wetness met my fingers.

Everyone was howling with laughter, shrieking, their mouths dark maws of cruelty. Their faces looked like something in a funhouse mirror, distorted with malicious glee.

I couldn't speak.

"Go ahead," Mr. Harris said.

But I couldn't. I just stood there in front of the class, the laughingstock of the school, the girl from the video. The slut. The whore. The disgraced Darling girl with cum on her skirt, sticky between her thighs, crusty on her legs.

Mr. Harris tried a few more times, but I just shook my head. Finally, I ran back to my seat.

Everyone laughed harder.

Mr. Harris told them to get quiet or he'd keep them all after class.

They got quiet. The next person presented. Then the next. I wondered if I'd get a bad grade for my failed presentation. I wondered what the people with phones had posted online, how bad it looked.

When the bell rang, Mr. Harris didn't keep the class. He kept me.

I didn't mind. I didn't want to walk the halls, to have the whole school staring at the stain on the back of my skirt where their cum leaked through.

The teacher asked what happened. His eyes were kind, sympathetic.

I didn't want to go out in the hall, so I had to say something that would convince him to let me stay a while. He said I could trust him. I knew better than to trust a man, but I didn't see many options. So I told him I had something on my skirt. I turned around so he could see. I asked how bad it was.

He asked me what it was from.

And suddenly, the months of hiding what was happening to me caught up. I started crying. He patted my hand. I was used to being touched by then, but I didn't like it. When I pulled away, he didn't act offended. He handed me tissues.

He said, "Lots of people get nervous speaking in front of the class."

I said, "That's not it."

He asked what it was again, and I finally told him. I whispered the words, sure they'd come back to haunt me, that the Dolces would kill me for being a rat. Part of me didn't care. I was tired of enduring in silence. I was tired of enduring at all. I felt ashamed when I was done, with Mr. Harris watching me. But I also felt relieved. Like it was finally over. The secret was out.

He was a teacher. A mandatory reporter. He had to tell the authorities if I was being hurt.

And then he said, "When did this last happen?"

I said, "At lunch."

"That's what's on your skirt?"

I nodded.

He said, "Show me."

My heart sank. I knew then that it would never be over. That no matter how nice a man acted, he wasn't nice. That no matter who he was, what position he held, he would never be on my side. Some men hid it well, some repressed it, some had the self-control to resist the urges society told them were wrong, but in their nature, they were all predators. They could no more help that than a wolf could help killing a rabbit.

But a rabbit wasn't forced to keep company with a pack of wolves every day.

I thought of them out there, prowling the halls, looking for me between classes.

Baron. Duke. Royal.

I thought about their brother, who was gone now. Their dad. My grandfather.

So many men, all wanting the same thing. All so simple. They looked at me, and they saw a girl who allowed things to happen to her. If she never told, then she couldn't tell on them. By telling Mr. Harris, I hadn't protected myself from the Dolces. I'd let him know I was easy prey.

"Go on," Mr. Harris said, licking his lips nervously and glancing at the door. "No one will see you but me. And you're safe with me."

I would have laughed, but I was still crying. I would have laughed, but nothing about it was funny except his own self-delusion and my complete and utter stupidity to think that he would help me. To think that any man would help me. But there was only one man here, and there were many out there, in the hall, in the classrooms, in the office. They prowled like hunters, ready to devour, and destroy, and deny. Ready to pretend they believed each other's lies, ready to defend each other because they are all liars.

So, when he told me again, I lifted my skirt and showed him.

That day, he only looked.

Later, he would touch.

Later, he would take.

This time, I will take.

This time, he's the prey.

SELENA

nineteen

Baron Dolce

"Are you sure you don't want me out here with you?" I ask.

"He'll be scared off the second he sees you," Mabel says. "Besides, I'm not going to fuck him. I just want to talk. I'll keep him long enough so the killer thinks we did, and then I'll leave him to his fate."

It makes sense. The killer probably sees her messages online, although I was watching and couldn't find even a trace of someone else spying on her connection. Then they follow her for the meeting, and after that, they have the victim in their sights. Sometimes they take a while to strike, a week or even a month. What she's doing is putting a target on his back. This time, though, I'll be watching too, waiting for her stalker to show themself.

If there is a stalker. I'm still not convinced it's not Mabel herself.

Maybe all those alter-identity games went to her head, and she does it in some kind of fugue state. She might not even be aware of it, so she's not exactly lying.

SELENA

Mabel Darling may not be the killer. Dahlia Suskind might be.

That explanation might be far-fetched, but it seems likely at this point. After what we put her through, it isn't inconceivable that she compartmentalized her trauma by creating a second identity that wasn't just on paper, but also in her mind. That explains why the killing stopped when we moved in, why they made an exception for us. Because try as she might, Mabel can't deny that she wants to be with us. She needs us the way we need her, maybe more.

Without us, she doesn't know who she is. She has no purpose. We broke her, and we made sure to take some of her pieces with us, so she could never be complete on her own. She could never fully heal, never put herself back together until we were there to help her. Now she needs us to survive, to stay sane, to be whole.

"He's here," Mabel says. "Go on, get in the bathroom."

"You sure you don't want to leave him waiting a few minutes?" I ask, taking her hand and pulling her in. "All this scheming has been an aphrodisiac."

I circle her slender body with one arm, drawing her against me. A soft, quick inhale is the only indication that she's uncomfortable. After all we've done, the thousand times we've fucked her, she's used to being touched, but she still doesn't like it. I smile down at her, proud of how far she's come.

"I don't want him to have time for second thoughts," she says. "It was harder than I expected to lure him here. He's paranoid about losing his job."

"He'll be losing a lot more than that soon enough," I say, giving the tip of her nose a quick kiss before I release her.

"I know," she says, her blue eyes bright in the dimly lit motel room. A little grin flashes across her face, but she quickly hides it. "Now go."

Reluctantly, I step into the bathroom and pull the door closed. She suggested the closet, but I couldn't bring myself to lurk in there. She really wanted me to stay outside, but there's no fucking way I'm leaving my girl with a predator. He could hurt her before I got inside. This is the compromise.

I lean against the counter and open my phone, pulling up the feed from the camera I placed in the room. Hiding is not in my nature. Dolces like to be known. But when a situation calls for stealth, I can perform it well enough.

I watch Mabel open the door. I can't have the sound on, in case the man hears the echo and gets suspicious, but the walls are thin, and I can hear them better than I expected.

"Wait," Mr. Harris says. "You're not—Hey!"

Mabel has grabbed him and dragged him a few steps into the room so she can slam the door before he backs out. She stands with her back against it and smiles at him. "I'm not what? Seventeen?"

"What is this?" he demands, looking around the room. The bottle of wine he promised hangs forgotten in his hand.

"It's the place you chose," Mabel reminds him. "Don't you like it?"

We offered to meet at the Hockington, but he said it was too conspicuous. When she suggested the seediest motel in town, he was more agreeable, but now he looks with distaste at the thin, polyester cover on the bed, the cheap wall art, the paneled walls, and dim lighting.

"Is this... Some kind of sting operation?" he asks. He pushes up his thick glasses—Duke called them 'serial killer style'—and licks his lips nervously. "Are you a cop?"

"No," Mabel says. "I'm a college student."

"Because you have to tell me if you are," he says. "You know that, right?"

"Actually, that's a myth," Mabel says. "But I'm not a cop, and I'm not working with any cops. I just wanted to talk to you."

"About what?" he asks.

"About us."

He doesn't speak for a long minute. Finally, he smooths his fingers over his short, neatly trimmed beard. "I'm not sure I know what you mean."

"Sure you do," she says, pushing off the door and moving past him. She snags the wine bottle from his hand as she goes.

He turns to watch her walk to the bed, checking her out behind her back.

My fingers clench around my phone, and I have to resist the urge to throw open the door and show him what happens when he messes with the wrong girl.

Our girl.

"I should leave," Mr. Harris says. "I think there's been some kind of misunderstanding."

"Right," she says. "You thought you were meeting an underage girl, but you got a whole adult. Don't you want to reminisce about the good old days with one of your favorite students, Mr. Harris? Or am I too old for you now?"

"I'm just going to go," he says, turning to the door.

"I wouldn't do that if I were you," Mabel calls, all the teasing gone from her voice.

He stops. "I thought you said you hadn't involved the police."

"I haven't," she says. "Yet."

He stands there another few seconds before turning back. "Are you going to?"

"That depends," she says. "Why don't you come have a drink with me and we'll talk about it."

She pats the bed, but he goes to the single chair in the room and pulls it out from the desk affixed to the wall. He sits stiffly facing her. If I hadn't seen him checking her out, I'd have a hard time picturing this guy as anything but a nerdy science teacher. He hides it well.

"What do you want?" he asks.

"Hmm, what a loaded question," she muses, twisting the top off the bottle of wine. The bastard didn't even bother to get one with a cork.

"If you're in some kind of trouble," he says. "If you need money—"

Mabel laughs, cutting him off. "You think I want your money? I don't care about money. I care about the fact that you—you took advantage of me."

She's sitting on the edge of the bed with her back toward the camera, and I can't help but think she must have done that on purpose. She watched me put it up in a spot where I could see the whole room, small as it is. But she could have sat in a way so I could read her expression to the best of my ability. Instead, I can only see her back, her shoulders that sink a little at her words. I want to know what she's thinking, want to unlock her skull and swing it open and see everything that's happening in her beautiful mind.

"That's not how I remember it," Mr. Harris says.

"It's not?" she asks. "You don't remember that I came to you in desperation, and instead of helping me, you became just another man who took what he wanted because he knew I'd never tell? What is it with you people? Do you have a sixth sense, or do you spend your days watching your students, sniffing out the vulnerable ones you can exploit?"

"That's not what happened," he says firmly.

She gets up and thrusts one of the hotel's plastic cups at him so hard he jumps back like he thinks she's going to dump it on him. When she doesn't, he takes it carefully and then quickly returns his gaze to her, watching her warily.

"You asked what I want," she says, turning and sloshing wine into another cup, not seeming to notice it splashing onto the bedside table around it. "I'll tell you what I want. I want you to have helped me when I finally, finally, finally worked up the strength to speak after seventeen years of silence. When I summoned the last of my strength after everything they'd done to me, and I went to someone I thought I could trust, I want that to have not been a mistake. I want you to have done what you were supposed to do, and called the police, or at least told the headmaster so that he could. Aren't you required to do that? You're a mandatory reporter. You should have reported it."

She stops and throws down her wine like a shot, then turns back to him and takes a breath. I can see her shaking on my screen, and I move toward the door, but she goes on speaking. I hesitate, not wanting to interrupt. She needs this, needs to say what she came to say.

"So, that's what I want," she says, pressing her hands to her thighs. "I want to never have let you touch me because I didn't have the strength to fight one more battle that year. I want to never have gone into your class freshman year, or junior year, or senior year, and thought that because you were nice to me all that time, it meant that I could trust you. I want to not have to wonder if all that time, every time you called on me in class or told me I did a good job on an assignment, you were watching me, biding your time, and waiting for an opportunity. And most of all, I want to know that you'll never use your position of power to gain someone's trust again. I want to know that you'll never do what you did to me to anyone else."

She's crying now. Mabel is not a crier, so I know this man did more to her than she told us, that it hurt her more than she let on.

I grip the doorknob in one hand, my phone in the other, and force myself to stay still and not intervene, not go to her. She needs me, but she needs this more. This is her moment, and I won't take it from her. I watch her shoulders shake as she stands at the nightstand, head bowed, gripping the neck of the wine bottle where it stands in a puddle of bloody red.

"How many more were there?" she asks, so quiet I can hardly hear her through the thin door.

Mr. Harris sets his wine cup aside. "There weren't any more."

Mabel is quiet for a moment, motionless. Then she spins around, raises the bottle above her head, and brings it down on his face.

"Liar," she screams, the sound more animal than human.

I'm out of the bathroom in a second, reaching for her, but she's already crumpled to the floor on her knees. I sink down and gather her into my arms. She feels so small, fragile as a bird with two broken wings. I pull her into my lap, cradling her head to my chest as she shakes with big, loud sobs that wrack her entire body. I've never seen her cry like that, in all the time I've known her, after all the ways we tortured her. I know it's a privilege and an honor to witness her in this state, so I treat it as such. I don't try to fix it, don't offer words at all. I just let her cry.

When she finishes, she's limp against me, warm and still, diminished somehow.

Wine is still trickling in a thread from the neck of the bottle, soaking the carpet. Mr. Harris's broken glasses lay in the burgundy pool. He's slumped over in his chair, head back, mouth open. He lets out a low moan, and Mabel shivers against me, burrowing closer.

Like I am her protector.

She has chosen me for that role despite our past, and I know the weight of that decision, what it must have cost her. I don't take that lightly.

I pick her up and lay her on the bed before bending to pick up the wine bottle. I grip it by the neck and smash it on his face—once, twice, three times. It shatters on the third blow, and I sink it into his neck to make sure the job is done. I'll never make the mistake I made with Jane again.

When I've sliced open his throat and the blood stops gushing and slows to a trickle, I wash my hands in the bathroom sink. I regret that I had to do it while he was barely conscious, that I've killed two more men, and each was as unsatisfactory as the last. I still haven't gotten my perfect kill, to watch the life drain from someone's eyes, to know that in their last seconds, I am what they see. Their executioner. *Their God.*

But this was for Mabel, not for me. So I pick her up, cradling her in my arms as I carry her out to the car to take her home. I gently place her in the passenger seat and buckle her in. Then I walk around the car, climb into the driver's seat, and start the engine.

Before I shift into gear, a voice comes from the back seat. "Did you leave another mess for me to clean up?"

twenty

Mabel Darling

Baron spins around in his seat to face the intruder. He has no weapon, though. The Dolces never carry weapons—they are weapons. I don't have a weapon either. I learned the hard way how easily they can be turned around on the person trying to defend herself. But I reach for the broken wine bottle wrapped in plastic that Baron carried out with us before turning in my seat. I don't hurry. I'm too wrung out to be surprised.

There's a girl sitting in the back seat—almost lounging. Her arms rest along the top of the seat on either side of her, and her knees are spread in a relaxed, arrogant pose, her combat boots kicked up against the bottom of each seat. She's dressed in black from head to toe—tight cargo pants with a knife holstered on her thigh, a v-neck tee, gloves, and a utility jacket, the pockets bulging. A small black pack sits beside her in the seat.

We may not have armed ourselves, but she certainly did.

Even after a decade, she's unmistakable, with the same raven waves tumbling around her shoulders, golden complexion, and full, bee-stung lips she got from her mother.

"Dahlia," I breathe.

"How the fuck did you get in our car?" Baron asks.

Dahlia smirks. "Wasn't much of a challenge."

That's the wrong thing to say to a Dolce, especially after she out-smarted him online for so long. I see the muscle tick in Baron's jaw, but he doesn't get out of the car and grab her, throw her to the ground and do something to her that will change her forever. Instead, he looks at me.

"Did you know she was coming?"

"No," I say. "No more than you did."

"Are you planning to hurt Mabel?" he asks her.

"No. Are you?"

He stares at her a second. "What are you doing here?"

"I thought you wanted me here," she says, her dark gaze sliding to me. "You were summoning me, weren't you? Here I am. The genie in your bottle."

She gives me a secretive smile, and with a jolt, I remember that bottle in the cabinet in Maine. Was that her?

Somehow, I know that she won't answer if I ask. At least not in front of Baron.

"You're the Black Widow Killer?" he asks carefully, like he's trying not to sound incredulous.

"I don't believe such a person exists," she says, taking her arms from the top of the seat. "I do like to check in on my old friend now and again, though. Keep tabs on her whereabouts. We make such a good team, don't we, Dahlia?"

Another jolt goes through me. She knows I took her name.

But of course she does. If she's hacked into my computer and left without leaving a trace, she surely knows everything about me there is to find, especially my borrowed identity.

"I think we do, Dahlia," I say, smiling at her.

Now that the shock is wearing off, I'm dying to know more about her—to know everything, even more than she knows about me.

"You planned this?" Baron asks, looking back and forth between us.

"Plans are overrated," she says, not taking her eyes from me.

Baron frowns. "Okay, well, what are you here for?"

She finally drags her gaze away from me, as if it's tiresome to look at him, as if he's not a work of art in human form. She must be immune to beauty. She shows nothing but slight annoyance when she looks at him. That comforts me for reasons I will examine later.

"Did you leave a mess?" she asks again.

Baron cuts his eyes towards me.

"Yes," I admit.

"Of course you did," she says, pulling a sleek object from her pocket. "Dead or alive, men are always so messy."

SELENA

I don't realize what she's doing until she twists her hand, sliding her fingers down and her thumb up at the same time, opening the object. It's some kind of high-tech flip phone made entirely of black glass with a futuristic, angled design.

Baron eyes it with fascination, and I know he's dying to get his hands on it.

"Cleanup on aisle five," Dahlia mutters to herself, tapping on the panels for a few seconds before closing and pocketing the device.

"I was going to go back and clean the room once I took Mabel home," Baron says.

"Of course you were."

"How do we know you're not going to take evidence from the scene that could incriminate us?"

"This is as close as I come to the scene," Dahlia says. "And I trust my team."

"I have no reason to," Baron points out.

"I didn't notice you filling out a complaint form last time," she says, smirking again.

"That was you?" I ask. "You took the body from my aunt's house in Maine?"

"*I* didn't go near it," she says.

"Damn," Baron says. "So you did that, and you're the one who's been following Mabel all this time? And I'm assuming you got rid of all those men she went out with?"

I realize then that the reason he's not being completely rude to her, like he was my coworker, is that he's impressed. It's not easy to impress Baron Dolce, but he's definitely being nicer to her than I expected, especially after she broke into his car and eluded him for so long. I should know, though, that Baron isn't threatened by competition. So few people can compete with him on any level that when he finds someone who can, he loves it.

"I don't kill men," she says. "I kill monsters."

"It's really you," he says. "I was halfway convinced it was Mabel, and halfway convinced one of her dates made it out alive and was stalking her to take his revenge."

"Men don't typically kill with poison," Dahlia says, adjusting the fingers of her glove. "Like I said, y'all are messy."

Baron's eyes narrow, and he turns to me. "That's what you said."

I shrug. "It's common knowledge. Off the top of my head, I can name a half dozen plants in the woods behind Summer House that could kill a man. Mistletoe, foxglove, pokeweed, nightshade, amanita... Want me to go on?"

"You've made your point."

"How many can you name?" I challenge.

"I'll count myself lucky that you don't cook," he says, but his eyes shine with admiration. "I couldn't name one."

Smiling, I turn to Dahlia. "So, what now? Are you back for good?"

She cracks a grin. "That's not how this works, babe. You need me, I'll be there in a heartbeat. But I'm a rolling stone. I don't gather moss."

"No," I say, smiling over my shoulder at her. "You prefer mushrooms."

"You got me there."

"Does your family know you're home?" Baron asks. "I'm sure they'd want to see you."

"They see me all the time," she says. "Even if they don't know it. You've probably seen me a few times yourself."

"I very much doubt that," Baron says. "You'd be hard to miss."

I don't like that, but Dahlia doesn't seem to notice he paid her a compliment.

"On the contrary," she says. "A moving target is very easy to miss."

"Can you stay for a while?" I ask. "Even just tonight? I have so many questions."

"I don't like questions."

"Then we'll just talk," I say. "Like we used to."

She's quiet a moment, frowning down at her glove. Then she darts a glance at Baron. "And him?"

"He'll keep a lookout," I say. "He won't be with us."

Baron frowns. "How do I know you'll be safe with her?"

"I'm safer with her than you," I point out. "She's never hurt me."

"I'm not used to playing errand boy," he grumbles, but he starts the car. I halfway expect Dahlia to slide out and disappear into the dark, but she doesn't look at all concerned to be in a moving vehicle with us. A few minutes later, we pull up at Summer House and climb out of the car.

"Is the other one in there?" she asks, nodding to the house.

"Duke," I say. "Yes, he's home."

"Tag, you're it," she says reaching out and brushing one knuckle against my shoulder. "I'll see you there."

She hoists her small backpack higher, turns, and cuts a diagonal across the lawn towards the woods.

"What was that about?" Baron asks.

"It means I have to bring snacks," I say, smiling after her. She still remembers. She probably never wondered if I was a figment of her imagination.

"I can see why she made a lasting impression on you as a kid," Baron says, watching her cross the section of the back lawn we can see from our vantage point before she disappears into the forest.

"Seems like she made an impression on you too," I mutter.

He grins. "Are you jealous?"

"Do I have a reason to be?"

"Mabel Darling," he says, stepping forward and brushing his fingers up the side of my neck. "I'm yours until they put me in the grave. And even when I'm buried in the ground, I'll still be yours. And you will be ours." He slides his hand behind my neck and draws me close. "Don't let that girl tell you otherwise. I'd hate to have to kill her. She's a rare one. But you... You are one of a kind."

"What kind am I?" I whisper, searching his eyes.

"Mine." He leans in and presses his lips to mine, firm and quick, like a stamp. His seal of ownership is on me like a brand I carry while I check in on Seeley and Duke—both sleeping—and pack a few snacks and a thermos of sweet tea.

At the back door, Baron grabs me by the throat and pulls me in, planting another kiss on my lips and pushing a flashlight into my hands. "Don't forget what I said," he tells me. "And if you hatch some plan to kill us, just know, it will fail. And things will be very unpleasant for you afterwards."

I shiver in his grip.

"For how long?" I ask.

"You saw Jane," he reminds me.

My stomach turns at the memory of what I saw, the emaciated skeleton of a girl. She probably manipulated me to get away, but I don't mind. I don't care if she was lying, if she was too thin to carry a pregnancy. I would have said anything to get out of that situation too. And I would have tried to get her out even if she hadn't said that. I just wish I could have foreseen that Baron would follow Duke and check up on her. I'm afraid I didn't do enough to save her, that she's dead anyway.

"I'd kill myself before I suffered through that," I whisper against Baron's lips.

His mouth twists up in a ghost of a smile. "You'd still be mine, little monster. Your corpse would be my puppet, and when your flesh rotted away, you'd be my bones."

He smashes his mouth down on mine again, this time with hunger, passion. I pull away, knowing if I let him get worked up, he'll want sex, and then I'll be bloody and need a shower, and I don't know how long Dahlia will wait. I'm not even sure she'll be there when I reach the treehouse if I leave now.

"I have to go."

"I'll be waiting," Baron growls against my lips, and it sounds more like a threat than a sexy promise. I shiver and pull away, and he chuckles at my discomfort.

But he lets me go.

It's more than I expected. I didn't think he'd leave me alone with her, and the fact that he did lets me know exactly how much she impressed him. Maybe he even wants her to come after him. Then, he can finally prove himself if he outsmarts her and lives. There's nothing that makes Baron Dolce feel more alive than a challenge, so a challenge that could end in death would be the highpoint of his existence.

What would be the low point?

I think about that as I hurry through the woods until I find the old stone boundary and step over it onto Delacroix property. Losing a contest of wills and intelligence against Dahlia wouldn't be Baron's nightmare. He considers her a worthy opponent, so to die at her hands would be honorable in his mind. He would fight his hardest to live, of course. Unlike Duke, he doesn't entertain notions of right and wrong, of self-sacrifice or atonement. But if she won, he would still be proud to have given her a good fight.

When I reach the tree, I still haven't figured it out completely, but I don't think death is the worst outcome for Baron. If it is, a death at the hands of someone he considers far beneath him, or a random accident, would be the ultimate insult. Someone like Jane, or back in high school, Dixie.

I climb, hand over hand, up the broken rungs nailed to the tree, tossing the snack bag up before I scramble over the lip and onto the platform. Dahlia is perched in a branch like a cat ready to descend on her prey.

"Did you bring the boy?" she asks.

"He stayed home to clean up."

"You've trained him well." She drops down onto the platform next to me.

I laugh quietly. If she's following me online, she definitely hasn't been spying with cameras in my apartment like Baron did. Otherwise, she would know it's the opposite.

But I don't correct her because I want her to think well of me. Her compliment gives me the same feeling of success that Baron's do, like I've earned something special.

"Sorry, but I gotta ask. Are you wearing a wire?"

"No," I say, pulling up my shirt, then unzipping and letting her see my waistband.

She pulls out a device and scans it over me before she steps back. "I know, that's rude," she says. "Can't be too careful, though. Anyone can double cross you."

"I get it," I assure her as she scans my picnic bag before putting up her equipment.

She sits cross-legged and begins tugging off her gloves one finger at a time. "No men, so I guess we don't get to feast preying mantis style," she says. "What have you got?"

"Sweet tea," I say, handing her the thermos while I spread the picnic blanket and lay out our haul. "Honey buns, cupcakes, strawberry shortcakes, crackers, cream cheese, strawberry preserves..."

When I'm done setting up, she smiles. "No sparkling grape juice?"

"Oh—no," I say. "We didn't have any. I'm sorry. Should I have gone to get some? I still can, if you'll wait here..."

"I'm kidding," she says, cracking a smile.

"Oh," I say faintly. I'm not usually one to get flustered, but I'm not usually one to care. This is Dahlia, though.

"You don't remember?" she asks. "We used to pretend it was champagne."

"I remember."

"Oh," she says, picking up a sleeve of crackers and tearing it open. "Cool. So, you really didn't know it was me?"

"No," I admit. "I thought it was Baron for a long time. He's the type, you know. Possessive. Doesn't like other men touching me."

"Ah," she says. "Explains the mess. Crimes of passion will do that."

"I'm not sure I'd call them that," I say. "Baron's not the passionate type."

"What type is he?" she asks, popping a cracker into her mouth.

"He's smart," I say. "Brilliant, even. And methodical. He's careful. I know you wouldn't think that after the motel, but he would have scrubbed every inch of it so clean no one would ever suspect a thing. I guess he's a monster. But he's my monster."

She nods. "Sounds like a good one to have on your side."

"I'm not sure he's on anyone's side but his own," I say. "But we'll see."

"He treats you okay?" she asks. "Because you said he's a monster, and I told you I kill monsters. Do you need me to take him out?"

"No," I say. "I've got it handled."

"And the other one?" she asks, like she's already forgotten his name. "The drug addict?"

"Don't call him that," I say, bristling. "He's mine too."

"Yikes," she says. "Do either of them suspect?"

"They both know," I say. "We're a family."

"Ah, okay," she says, nodding. "Look at you, being all trendy and progressive with your relationships. Wouldn't have predicted that."

"Why?" I ask, not sure if that was an insult.

She shrugs and tears open a honey bun with her teeth. "Oh, I just figured you'd grow up to be more… Traditional. But hey, I'm not judging. Good for you. You deserve as many partners as you want."

I'm still not sure if I should be offended, but I know she can't be monitoring any cameras, if she thinks all that. I'm not sure how she knows about Duke's drug habit, but the rest of it makes sense—why the killing stopped, why she didn't go after the twins.

"So, you found me online," I say slowly, picking at the food while she plows through it like she hasn't eaten in days. "You knew about my dates, and you got rid of them?"

"I thought you must have figured out it was me," she says. "But I guess I didn't know it was you until I saw you go in to meet one of them. Then you led me to more, so I thought you were working with me, leading me to them on purpose. You really weren't?"

"I was leading *someone* to them," I say, pleased that I could surprise her in some way. "I just thought it was someone else."

"Ah," she says, nodding. "I wondered why the Maine killing was so different. I thought you must have finally snapped and done one in before I got there. I didn't know about the boyfriend."

"Boyfriends."

"Are they both serial killers?"

"I wouldn't call either of them that."

"I don't know," she says. "The body count says otherwise."

"I mean... Don't serial killers have to have a technique? An M.O. that makes it a pattern?"

She shrugs. "I'm not sure, really. I can't say I'm an expert. I do have a favorite style. Even got a tattoo to prove it."

"That seems risky," I say. "Couldn't they use that as evidence?"

"I don't plan on being caught again."

"You were caught?" I ask, my heart lurching at the thought of what they'd do to her.

"Once," she says, opening a package of cheese. "Once was all it took. But you know that."

I don't know what to make of her. She's exactly the same, but she's a serial killer. In some way, I think she always was, even before she had the body count to prove it. There's something in her that's different from even Baron. He may have killed a few men, but the title doesn't seem to fit him like it does her. I don't know what it says about me, that the one person I chose to befriend as a child turned out to be a mass murderer. It probably explains why I was so drawn to Baron.

It also explains why my parents tried so hard to distance me from Dahlia once she was sent away, to cut me off from her. They were probably scared I'd turn out exactly the same.

In a way, I did.

I may not have dealt the killing blow to any of the victims, but I'm no less responsible for their deaths than she or Baron is. Maybe even more so. I put a mark on every single one of those men, chose them for execution. After the first few times, at least, I knew what I was doing, that I was sentencing them to death. I found the target and aimed the gun. All she did was pull the trigger.

"Your snack game has improved, by the way," she says. "This is dope."

"Thanks," I say, taking a cracker and nibbling the edge.

"You can keep working with us, you know," she says. "Even if we're not in the same place anymore."

"Who is us?" I ask. "You and your cleaning crew?"

"Like I said, I'm not the Black Widow Killer. *We're* the Black Widow Killer. There's a network, a system. You're the bait, I'm the venom, we've got a cleaner…"

"Wait, so I am the Black Widow Killer?" I ask, turning the information over. "At least… One of the legs of the spider."

She laughs quietly. "I like that. There are other legs. Other jobs. I don't even know all the members. But I know you, and you know me, so if you wanted to keep working together... I think we make a good team."

"Me too," I admit, feeling shy all of a sudden. I can't help but smile though. She wouldn't have asked me if she didn't trust me, despite the scan when we arrived. In truth, I wouldn't trust her as much if she hadn't done that. I like that she's careful, not sloppy. I like that she knows I never tell, and she let me in on all of this. And most of all, I like feeling like part of something important.

"So, what do you say?" she asks. "Want to help make the guilty pay?"

"I can't sleep with the men anymore," I tell her. "Baron would never allow it."

"And judging from the messes he's left, that would be a lot more work for us. I've already had to get an apprentice for my cleaner."

"You still want me?" I ask, peeking at her from under my lashes as I pick up the thermos.

"You're the best at what you do," she says. "We could definitely use you. And we can have your job end online. You never have to meet them in person. It'll make it easier, and safer for us, if we don't take all the men from one area."

"Okay," I say, smiling at her. "I'm in."

"Swear a blood oath?"

I swallow hard. "I mean... If we have to..."

She laughs. "I'm joking."

"No," I say. "I think we should. To show that we trust each other."

"You're serious?"

"We did it before."

"I know, but we were kids."

I hold out my hand. "Got a knife?"

She hesitates, then pulls a hunting knife from her pocket and hands it over. I pull it out of its sheath, then stare at it, wondering if she's killed with this knife.

"It's clean," she says, reading my hesitation.

"I guess it's no more risky than sex with a stranger," I say, putting the blade to my palm. I haven't cut in a long time, not since the last time my grandfather touched me.

One cut for each time.

I brush the thought away and press my lips together, take a breath, and slice open my skin for the first time in seven years.

"Damn," Dahlia says, looking impressed when I hand the knife back. "I didn't think you'd really do it."

I nod at her. "Your turn."

She makes a small cut in her hand, and my mind loops back on itself, to the day so long ago when we did this the first time. Knee to knee we sat, dappled sunlight dancing around us, the insects louder than the wind tossing the branches. Neither of us wanted to go first, so we both hesitated. That time, she was braver. I remember the sickness that swam up when I saw the scarlet beads rising in her palm. But I knew I couldn't back down once she'd already made the first cut.

Now she holds out her hand, and I take it. Her fingers are calloused, but her palm is warm and soft, and it strikes me how delicate her hand feels, almost dainty, not the hand of a killer at all, but a lady who belongs in the big house at the end of the trail that winds a mile through the woods, over the stream and past the low bluffs.

"Let the guilty pay," she says.

"Let the guilty pay," I agree.

Still gripping my hand, she leans forward and presses her lips to my cheek. Then she releases my hand and stands. "See you in another ten, Black Widow."

"You're leaving?" I ask, my anguish undisguised.

"We'll meet again," she says. "Our paths will cross when the time is right."

"In a decade?"

"I didn't mean that literally," she says.

"How do I contact you?"

"You don't," she says. "But if you need me, I'll be here." Then she gives me a conspiratorial smile, like we're in on this together. "And you never know. You might see me tomorrow."

She crouches, grips the side of the platform with both hands, and kicks off, dropping over the edge and into the darkness. I wait to hear her hit the ground, but I never do.

twenty-one

Duke Dolce

"Remind me again, why couldn't we go over to the other house for breakfast?" I ask, peering down into the bowl where my cereal bar is floating. I thought it was supposed to turn into cereal when you added milk, but it's just floating there like a soggy, bloated turd.

"We don't need a cook," Mabel says, setting a plate with an English muffin and two perfectly poached eggs next to my bowl on the picnic table out back. "It's really not that hard to put something in the toaster, and even a kid can scramble an egg."

"You had a cook growing up," I point out, deciding not to tell them what happened when I put some eggs in the microwave because I didn't want to cook them on the stove and risk starting a fire. I'd probably just stand there watching it burn the house down, dumbass that I am.

"I didn't like to bother her," Mabel says. "I had to eat dinner with the family, but otherwise, I made my own meals and ate them by myself unless I was required to attend a special breakfast or luncheon."

"Yeah, well, we can't all be robots who don't need anything from anyone," I say, dumping an egg onto the English muffin. "I like my family, and I like having a cook."

"You should know how to feed yourself," she says.

"I'm feeding myself now, aren't I?" I ask, stabbing my fork into the soggy cereal bar. I pick it up and start chewing on the end, letting milk dribble down my chin. Mabel makes a face and daintily breaks a yolk.

"We're having breakfast here because we wanted to talk," Baron says. "Make sure we're all on the same page. I think we should go back to Tennessee."

"What?" I ask, my fork clattering back into the bowl. The mushy bar plops into the milk, splashing it onto the weathered grey wood. I've lost my appetite, and all I want is to swallow a few blue pearls and reverse time, make this go away.

Baron hands me a napkin. "Next week would be ideal. I can get started on that new product we talked about."

"I don't care about that," I say.

"We don't want to leave too soon after the disappearance," Baron says. "That might draw attention. But two people have died in Faulkner this week, and I don't want any link between them to come up."

"That's unlikely," Mabel says. "One is a philandering teacher at a fleabag motel, the other is the richest man in Faulkner having a simple accident at his estate. He was old and infirm. Preston lives with him, and he said so himself. Nothing suspicious about his death."

"It's all over the local news," Baron points out. "Your grandfather was hugely influential in this town, but he had important ties all over the state."

"Which means Mr. Harris's death will be barely a blip," I point out. "No one cares about teachers."

"Maybe no one has to know," Mabel says. "They haven't found the body. Maybe we get rid of it. A disappearance instead of a death."

"I thought only girls disappeared from this town," I point out.

"What if it's never reported?" she says slowly. "What if we make it look like he left."

"How do you propose we do that?" Baron asks.

"Maybe he left a note for his wife," Mabel says. "Sent her an email telling her what he did, saying he can't live with the guilt anymore, and he can't go back to the school where it happened, so he's leaving."

"That's not something men like that do," Baron says. "They don't feel guilt."

"Never?" Mabel asks, and I'm sure she's disappointed to learn her grandpa never suffered, not even his own conscience.

Baron slices through the organic egg, letting the bright orange yolk spill out like blood. "They don't think they've done anything wrong, so no. If anything, once they're caught, they're the victims, unjustly persecuted for taking what they're entitled to."

"How do you know that?" Mabel asks, narrowing her eyes at him.

Baron slides a wedge of muffin around in the yolk on his plate, soaking it up. I see the blood on the floor of Mabel's house, spreading around the body of the man we killed.

"Because we lived with a man like that for eighteen years."

I frown at Baron, surprised he would say something like that. Out of all of us, Baron is the most loyal to our family. Even if he didn't show it, I assumed he was devastated about Dad. Devastated enough to leave us all behind and move to another state so he didn't have to deal with it, not even coming to the funeral, like Mom when Crystal disappeared. But I also know that he's the observer, and he wouldn't say that if he hadn't studied it long enough to come to that conclusion.

In his own way, Baron is the most accepting person there is. He takes everything in, but because he doesn't have a moral compass, he doesn't place expectations on them to meet any standard or share his values to be considered a good person. He accepts everyone and loves the ones that society tells him to as well as he is able, all along knowing exactly who they are.

Suddenly, I'm flooded with this swell of love for my brother, and I miss how it used to be so much that my ribs ache.

"You're probably right," I say. "But here's the thing. Most people aren't like that. The majority want to believe that even the most vile predators have some redeeming quality that makes them human, because that means we are too. Most everyone fears, deep down, that they aren't a good person. But if there's someone worse, and he can be worthy of sympathy, then so are we."

Baron's eyes light up, and I know in that moment that he feels exactly what I feel, that he misses me too, misses the way we'd play off each other, each playing to his own strengths, to challenge each other. Two parts that are made to go together, reflections of each other and therefore mirror opposites—the sun and moon, the faces of comedy and tragedy, Batman and the Joker.

"Go on," he says.

"That's why people believe in death bed confessions," I say. "That even the worst person can change, and if they truly change in their hearts, they're still deserving of heaven, no matter if they've committed the most heinous crimes. It's the same reason people watch documentaries about serial killers. They want to dig into their pasts, know about their abusive childhoods and say that's what made them that way. They have to make sense of it. They don't want to believe anyone can be simply evil with no reason. That's too scary to comprehend. That means anyone can be evil, even the people we love the most."

"Or ourselves," he says.

"Or ourselves," I say, smiling at him.

"Okay," he says. "It'll be risky. An email creates a trail, and a trail can be followed, or come back to us, no matter how well I hide it. A written letter can have forensic evidence on it, not to mention handwriting."

"Handwriting analysis isn't as conclusive as they make it look in the movies," Mabel says. "It's often not even admissible in court. But hold up a second." She looks back and forth between us, pointing her fork. "What just happened?"

A little smile tugs up the corner of Baron's mouth as his gaze holds mine. "We need a place to bury a body."

Reluctantly, I break eye contact and turn to Mabel. "Know anywhere? Maybe the woods over there?"

I nod to the forest beyond the yard, a curtain of green hiding dark secrets in its shadowy depths.

"I don't want his body on my land," Mabel says with a shiver. "Or the Delacroixs. Obviously Dahlia would be okay with that, but she doesn't live there, and if someone else found it, they'd turn it over to the cops. But I still don't understand."

"We don't want his disappearance to be cast as a tragedy, and we don't want a big manhunt," Baron explains. "If his wife thinks he's a predator, she'll be too ashamed to make a stink."

"But what if she doesn't tell the police that part?" Mabel asks. "Women cover for their husbands too. What if she just tells them he's missing?"

"Then we post something online from a throwaway account," Baron says. "Start a rumor at the school that he was inappropriate with students. People will spend a lot less time concerned about finding him if they think he's not worth looking for."

Mabel nods, chewing thoughtfully. "It's not a bad idea. I'm sure I wasn't the only one. If we posted something, maybe the others would start to come out. Some of the girls might feel safe to come forward now that he's gone."

"Exactly," I say. "If his wife is smart, she'll foresee something like that. She probably already has some inkling. She lives with him. Most creeps can't turn off the creepiness full time. Even if she's in denial now, I'm sure she's seen something that she can look back on once she knows. But she also wants to believe that if her husband is a pedo, at least he's good enough to be ashamed of it. So she'll believe he left on his own, out of guilt, because she wants to believe it."

"Okay. I might know somewhere we can get rid of the body."

"Where's that?" Baron asks.

"The less people who know, the better," she says.

My eyes narrow. "How do we know you're not going to go to the cops? You could be setting us up."

She just smiles that mysterious little smile of hers. "Haven't you ever heard someone say that Darlings can get away with murder in this town? That's not hyperbole. They can, and they have. Trust me, I can take care of it."

"Why not have Dahlia do it?" Baron asks. "She did a good job in Maine."

"I don't have any way to contact her except to go hunting online, and that just creates another body."

I shiver at her wording, how callously she says it. I'm beginning to think Baron's not the biggest psycho among us. After all, she's the one who had every single one of those men killed, including the ones Baron killed for her. I'm not sure I buy that she didn't know he'd do that. She must have.

"Why would we trust your family to do it?" I ask. "They've probably been waiting for a chance to take revenge on us."

"They won't know you had anything to do with it," she says. "I'll go to them and tell them I need help, and they'll help me. The Darlings always cover for their own. Look at what Preston just did for us. Unless you want to bury it at Hickory House."

"No," I say, picturing Olive coming out, nosing around, and finding us with a corpse. "There are too many kids there. Plus, there's only the backyard, so people would see the ground all dug up. It's not like doing it in the woods where no one goes."

I can't help but think about Jane, though. About the fact that someone went there and found her body. If she was alive, if she walked out, she would have come back for Olive, so that's the only explanation.

"Do you know a good way to get rid of a body and leave very little evidence linking back to us?" Mabel asks. "Or do you want to trust that I know? I'm literally going to school for it."

"That is convenient," Baron muses. "I'll come with you."

"No," she says, holding up a hand. "I'm not going to bring you along and let you see which of my family members know and are therefore complicit. I've trusted you. Now it's your turn to trust me."

She and Baron stare each other down a long minute, and then he pushes his glasses up and picks up a napkin. "Okay. It's all yours."

"Are you serious?" I demand. "She's going to set us up!"

"I'm the one who did it," Baron says. "I'm willing to trust her."

"And I know all about it," I say. "About all of them. Which makes *me* complicit."

"Then I guess you'll have to trust her too," he says. "We're all in this together. We're all a part of it. If anyone gets caught, we all go down together. That's how this works. Everyone plays their part. Everyone does their job. This job is Mabel's."

I jump up and toss my napkin on the table. "I didn't ask to be on a fucking serial killer team," I snap. "I just wanted to get a girlfriend and keep my brother."

"And you did," Baron says evenly. "I'm the one taking the biggest risk. If we get caught, you'll do a little time. You're an accomplice. I'll get the chair. I did the actual killing. I'm willing to do that, for us. If I don't, will you?"

"No, I won't fucking kill people," I say, throwing my hands up. "Listen to yourselves!"

"It sounds like, if anyone is going to break and go to the police, it would be you," Mabel says. "Are you thinking about it? Is that why you're accusing me?"

"I told you to cut back on the Alice," Baron says. "That it's making you paranoid."

"Don't you fucking dare," I snarl, knocking my bowl across the table at him. I wheel around and stomp towards the house.

"Would you rather we hadn't told you?" Mabel calls after me.

I slam the door hard behind me, then lean against it, breathing hard. I'm losing my fucking mind. Baron's right. The Alice is obviously fucking with my head, but they're doing it too. I can't tell if they're doing it on purpose, or if it's the drug making me think so.

Are they trying to cut me out?

They've kept me in the loop, telling me about each thing. Have they been waiting for me to snap, knowing eventually I wouldn't be able to handle it? Now I've proven them right, and they can go on rampaging the town like Bonnie and Clyde in their deliriously happy killing spree without me. Next time, they probably won't even tell me.

Part of the reason I've always wanted Mabel was because Baron did. Because anyone talented and interesting and unique enough to catch my brother's eye, to be worthy of him, has to be special because Baron is special, and he doesn't just give his approval to anyone. So if he loves Mabel, she has to be the most fucking incredible person there is. Naturally, Baron wants the best, so he wanted her, and I didn't want to settle for less than he got, so I wanted her too.

But another reason I wanted to be with her was to make sure she wouldn't come between us. I couldn't bear the thought of losing him. Now, it feels like I am. Like it would have been better if I'd just let him have her to himself and admitted I'm not as good, and I don't deserve a girl as good. But I insisted on being part of it, and now it feels like they're teaming up against me, pushing me out. He'd rather spend time with her, doing whatever they do, and leave me behind, just like I always feared he would from the first time he came home talking about her in a way he'd never talked about a girl before.

I knew right then that I was in danger of losing him.

I can't lose Baron. I won't. I can't live without him. I'd probably be okay without Mabel. She's the perfect fit for Baron, but that doesn't mean she's right me. I could find another girl. She might not be as good as Mabel, but she might be better for me.

But I can't find another twin.

So I swallow a couple pearls for courage. I'll need to be fucked up to stomach what I have to do. Then I turn back around, open the door, and walk back out.

Mabel is already gone. Baron is picking up the dishes.

"Okay," I say. "I'm in. Who's our next victim?"

twenty-two

Mabel Darling

"I still don't get why we had to leave early," Duke grumbles, tossing his stuff in the closet without unpacking. "No one suspects anything. You said you got rid of the body."

"I did," I say. I've come to understand that Duke wants the same things that I do, though, so I go to him. He perches on the edge of the bed, raking a hand through his hair, showing signs of distress. My mind flips through its encyclopedia to find the answer, the reaction that people want in his state. When I find it, I am calm.

"Hey," I say, lifting his arm and pulling it around me. I slide onto his lap and cradle his cheek. "We can go back. Anytime we want, we can go back."

"Then why aren't we there?"

"I understand why you're upset. I know your friends are there. But we'll be back in a month for Labor Day. We just had to leave town until things cooled down. Just in case."

He turns his face away. "You *don't* understand. You don't have friends, and Baron only has friends for show.

He doesn't actually give a fuck about anyone outside our family."

"And you don't think that bothers me?" I ask quietly, his harsh words smarting like a slap.

Duke looks up at me at last. "Does it?"

"Everyone wants to be loved," I say, looking away. "To be accepted into a social group of their peers, even if they're different. Evolutionally, if you were too much of a freak, too crazy, you'd be cast from the safety of the herd, and then you'd die."

"Am I too weak for you and Baron's social group?" he asks. "Are you going to cast me out?"

"No," I say, turning his face to me. "You are the center, the heart."

I lean in and kiss him, and he finally wraps his arms around me.

"But Baron's the leader," he says. "The king. You're the queen. So what am I?"

"You're the duke," I say, smiling.

"Yeah, and what good is that? You don't need me. Baron can do everything I can."

"Not everything."

"What, make you cum?" he asks. "He can do that. He just chooses not to. If he wanted, he could make you think he was me, and you'd never know the difference."

"Eventually, I'd know," I say. "He couldn't keep it up forever."

"I bet he could."

I shake my head slowly. "No. Maybe the opposite. You could play him for longer by turning off your emotion and pretending you're as emotionless as he is. But the one thing he can't do is feel."

"He could pretend to feel."

"He does," I point out. "But something is missing, and without you, he wouldn't really know how to fake it. Not for long. He looks to you for that. For how to be human."

"A king doesn't need to be human," he says. "What's that ever gotten anyone?"

"Belonging," I say. "Membership in the pack."

"That's not enough. A king has to be the best. And everyone else needs to be useful, productive. I'm nothing but extra weight for you and him. What does a duke even do?"

I glance at the door to make sure we're still alone. "He rules once the king is gone."

Duke stares at me a long second. "What are you saying?"

"What are you saying?" I ask carefully.

"I'm not saying anything," he says, scowling at me. "Are you trying to trap me? Because it won't work. I'm not as dumb as you think."

"I know you're not dumb," I say. "I never thought that. I think you're a lot smarter than people give you credit for. Just as smart as Baron. You just use it in a different way than he does."

"What's your angle?" he asks, narrowing his eyes. "No one thinks that."

"I think you know people, and you use that to your advantage."

He scoffs. "And how do you imagine I'm doing that? When have I ever had an advantage?"

"You're sitting here pouting, saying you didn't get your way," I point out. "Except you did. You got us to go back to Faulkner. You got Baron to make amends with Royal, and if I had my guess, you got Royal and Harper to accept whatever meager apology he might have made. You think they did that for him?"

"And you're doing… What? Calling my bluff?"

"No," I say. "I know how important it is for you to be able to go home too. I'm just saying, I never count you out, Duke. I don't think you should, either."

I stand to leave, but he snags my hand. "No," he says. "Get on the bed."

There's something mean in him, a hard glint in his eyes, and I wonder not for the first time if I'll ever really know when they play each other's part.

I swallow hard, then force myself to obey.

"Go on," he says, nodding to my legs. "Take those off."

"I haven't showered," I say, though I know that won't deter him. "We were in the car all day."

He doesn't even answer. I steel myself and obey, quickly shedding my clothes. He smiles, pleased with my compliance. Then he scoots back, unzips, and pulls out his cock. He lays there stroking it, watching me, one arm tucked behind his head.

"What are you waiting for?" he asks, dragging his fist up his shaft to the tip. "Come get me wet. Unless you want me to go in dry. Since I'm so much like Baron."

"I didn't say that," I say faintly. "I said you were just as smart."

"Smart enough to know you hate it more when it doesn't hurt," he says. "So get up here and slobber on my cock until it can slide right in. In fact, you can sit on my face while you do it. That'll guarantee you feel good."

I hesitate, then climb onto the bed. He drags my hips up, turning me around and pulling me down on his face. His mouth is hot and hungry, and a shiver of pleasure rolls through me. I hate it.

I quickly lean over, taking him into my mouth. I hate doing this too. But at least it distracts me from the relentless stroke and thrust of his tongue, so I can almost pretend he's not there, not touching me. I grip his shaft and take him deep into my mouth, sucking at his soft skin, the hard ridges of muscle beneath.

"That's it," he says. "Suck me off just like your brother. He likes to choke on it, so don't be afraid to go a little deeper and gag."

I try to ignore his words, but I can't help but remember hearing that rumor. When I went back for my senior year, I was hooked. They'd made me fall for them, and I was so naïve that when they ghosted me, and I was devastated. I wanted them back. I wanted more.

SELENA

But it was Colt they targeted first. They didn't hide it like my family would have. They had no shame, would go around yelling out that they were going to take him back to the basement, that he looked good on his knees. He was the only one who was shamed for it at school. Laughed at and taunted and ostracized even more than he had been the year before.

And still, I wanted them, sick as it all was. I felt like I'd die if I couldn't impress them, if I couldn't show them that that I was more than nothing, that I wasn't some trash they could use and discard. That I wasn't an unlovable freak.

I almost did die proving it.

They won't forget it again.

They won't, and my grandfather won't, and Mr. Harris won't.

Their father won't, either. He's gone too. I only wish I'd gotten to be there when he went, that I'd gotten to order his execution.

He might have violated me, but I could have kept it secret, and no one would have known, if not for Dixie. She was so infuriated that Colt wouldn't turn his back on me, even when I was too entangled with the Dolces to get out. My brother stood up for me, and they burned his arm while I screamed for them to let him go.

Not until I agreed to be their slave, they said.

He said no. He told me not to agree to that. So they tortured him with a blowtorch until his eyes went glassy with pain, until he went into shock. Until I screamed for them to do anything they wanted to me, until I agreed to it, if they would please just let him go.

Dixie was furious. They had scarred her pretty boyfriend.

So when they did what they wanted, when they took turns with me and left me tied to the bed, when they went off laughing to have a smoke break, it wasn't enough for her. When their father found me there, and I screamed for them to help me, and they didn't come back, and he did what he wanted too, it wasn't enough. When they recorded it to humiliate or blackmail me, because that family loves their cameras, it still wasn't enough. She had to post the video on her blog, so everyone at school knew my shame too. So they loathed me with the loathing reserved for the kind of woman who lets men use her one after another, but never for the men who do the using.

"Get on my dick," Duke says, shoving my hips down.

I slide down the bed and position his slick tip at my entrance, then sink onto him. Ripples of pleasure shiver through me, and I try to ignore them, but I can't anymore. Not when he lifts his hips and pushes all the way in, so deep it hurts. That always snaps me back into my body, where I can't escape.

"Ride me," he commands.

Placing my hands on his knees for balance, I lift up, then sink back down on his shaft. It stretches me, fills me. He grips my hips, massaging my flesh, spreading me so he can see everything. He fucks up into me, and I whimper helplessly. Pain and pleasure twist together, undistinguishable from each other and equally unwelcome.

"Turn around," he says. "I want to watch your face while I make you cum."

I start to climb off, but he stops me. "Spin on it, baby."

I slowly turn my body, clambering awkwardly around his legs, his body, until I'm straddling him. The sensation of his cock pressing against each wall as I turn distracts me from being self-conscious about my clumsiness, my unsexy body, my scars. Then I'm facing him.

"Duchess," he says, smiling up at me.

"Duke."

"Maybe."

I swallow hard. "You're not Duke?"

"I could be Duke."

"You could be Baron."

"Does it matter?"

I hesitate a long moment, then shake my head. "No. I guess not."

"Do you love me?"

"Yes."

"More than you ever loved your grandpa?"

I shiver. "Yes."

"More than you love Colt?"

"Yes."

"More than you love Baron?"

I swallow hard. "Are you Baron?"

"Do you think I am?"

"You could be tricking me, to find out who I love more."

"I could be." He grins. "You'd never know. I know how crazy that makes you."

"I'm not crazy."

"Do you love me more than Baron?"

This time, I don't argue. I nod. "Yes."

"Good girl," he says, running his hands up my thighs. He mashes his thumb over my clit, and the bundle of nerves comes alive. My thighs quake, and he smiles wider, doing it again.

"Are you high?" I whisper.

He shakes his head. "Not this time."

His thumb continues stroking relentlessly, until pulses of pleasure ripple all the way down my legs, up my back. Gooseflesh explodes over my skin, and my inner walks clamp down on him.

He moans, lifting his hips, grinding up into me. "Cum for me, Duchess."

I don't want to, but I do. My body wants it, even as my mind recoils with the same kind of disgust Baron feels for me when I do. Duke watches me, holding me pinned and winding me higher, tormenting my clit until I cry out helplessly. My thighs clench, my back arches, and my hips jerk in spasms as I shatter. My walls grip him, holding him close and bathing him in my release as darkness dots my vision.

SELENA

I scrunch my eyes closed so I don't have to see his smug grin when I'm done.

Duke goes on for a few more minutes before he finishes too. Then he rolls us over so we're facing each other on the bed. He's still inside me, and I have to fight not to show my revulsion at the feeling of him softening inside me, thick and wet.

"Maybe if I keep you plugged up, I'll finally get a baby in you," he says.

My heart tears the way it always does, but I don't say anything, don't tell him there will never be a baby. He blames himself for enough without knowing he took that from me—and from himself.

"You know," I say, stroking his cheek. "You always ask if I love you. But you never tell me you do."

"Of course I love you," he says. "How can you doubt it?"

"I don't know," I say. "You're... Different. Do you still want to be with me? Or are you just doing it for Baron?"

"Of course I want to be with you."

"You never did anything to prove it," I point out, my voice low.

He draws back. "Like what? Kill someone?"

"I mean... You were supposed to kill Jane to begin with. Baron's proven what he'll do for us a few times since we found out he failed. But we knew from the start you did, and no one ever asked you for more."

"I do illegal shit for us all the time," he says. "I ran the operation all year."

"Yeah," I say. "But that's for Baron. You've never did anything to prove you wanted me."

"You're insecure?" he asks.

"I'm human too."

He stares at me a long minute, then draws his hips away. His cock slides out of me in a slippery rush. "Who do you want me to kill?" he asks, frowning up at the ceiling.

"I was thinking about Dixie," I say. "What she did to me in high school."

"Really?" he asks. "She didn't do that much."

"She did a lot," I say. "Not just to me. To my brother too."

"Then have him kill her."

"He doesn't have it in him."

Duke stares at the ceiling another minute, and then he smiles. "He doesn't, does he? Fucking pussy. He's always been soft."

"Will you do it?"

"Someone has to avenge you," he says. "Obviously your family's too weak to do it."

"She's going home for Labor Day," I say. "I thought, maybe we could get her on the way. And then go visit your folks in Faulkner. It's only a month away."

"Really?" he asks. "You'd go back?"

"Of course," I say, planting a soft kiss on his shoulder. "I know how much it means to you."

"Okay. I'll kill Dixie. Since it means so much to you."

"We'll have to make sure she's driving home alone," I say. "I don't want anyone else to get hurt."

"You don't mind killing someone," he points out.

"People who deserve it."

"Why do you get to decide that?" he asks. "You're playing god."

"Well, sometimes god doesn't do a very good job. Someone has to step in and do it for him."

Duke tucks the pillow behind his head and doesn't speak for a long time. Finally, he says, "Am I next?"

"For what?"

"You're getting rid of everyone who wronged you. Didn't we wrong you the most?"

"You're making up for it now."

"You never say you love me unless I ask," he says. "Do you mean it?"

"I mean it as much as you mean it."

"If I do this, will you believe me?" he asks. "Or will you keep asking me to kill more people, like you did Baron?"

"Would you?" I ask, toying with the neck of his t-shirt. "For me?"

"I would try."

"Who would you kill?" I ask. "If you got to pick. Anyone in the world. Who would you kill?"

"I wouldn't kill anyone," he says. "Isn't that the point? To make me do something I wouldn't do, to prove to you how much I love you?"

"Then who would you kill to prove it?" I ask. "Baron got rid of his pet for me. Who would you get rid of? Someone important to you, so I know you love me as much as he does. Or even more."

"You want me to say Olive, don't you?"

"No," I say, appalled. "She's a child." I think about it for a long minute. "I would never ask you to hurt an innocent person. But if I did ask you to, would you do it?"

"You're sick." He tries to take his arm from under my head, but I hold onto him, so he can't.

"I just want to know how far you'd go," I say. "Even Jane's death was meaningless to you. I want to know how much you'd sacrifice for me. Who would you give up, who you love, who's hurt me?"

"Oh," he says flatly. "You want me to kill Baron."

SELENA

twenty-three

Baron Dolce

"There she is," Mabel says, pointing to a pair of headlights coming up the hill, a smile spreading over her face.

"Are you sure this is going to work?" Duke asks.

"There's only one way for her to go," I point out, my gaze moving to the mountain on our right. On our left, the incline is steep, though it's not a sheer drop. Still, her car would tumble a long way, surely crushed as it bounced down the mountain before coming to a stop. If she has any instinct, she'll swerve to the right, where there's no escape.

Duke is supposed to kill her, but came to me and said he couldn't to it, that Dixie didn't deserve to die for posting a video, and even if she did, he wasn't the person to decide that.

I told him I didn't mind doing it. We can make Mabel think it was his kill easily enough.

And in truth, I like my chances with this one. It might be my perfect kill at last.

SELENA

Each time, some unforeseen circumstance prevented me from executing the plan as intended. I don't like admitting weakness, but I have to acknowledge, to myself at least, that each time, the failure was mine.

I almost had Jane, but it was too dark to see her eyes, and I didn't stay long enough because I was distracted by Mabel's escape.

I could have had the Darling patriarch, but I lost control, lost my temper, at the thought of him hurting Mabel.

I could have had Mr. Harris, but if we'd followed the plan, that would have been Black Widow's kill. And since I didn't, it wasn't well planned. The knowledge that he'd hurt Mabel so deeply shook me more than she knows, and though the kill was methodical instead of passionate, he was already unconscious, too feeble to struggle if I'd strangled him the way I've pictured in my mind so many times.

Dixie presents a new opportunity.

She has no control over Mabel, so she can't make me lose control. Mabel has even agreed to stay in the car to minimize potential evidence from being left.

My contact with Dixie was more extensive than either of my companions knows, but I have no loyalty to her. I knew her well in high school, probably better than most. She even thought we were friends, though she downplayed her connection to us to serve her own purposes. I understood that it was all part of her game, and though it wasn't part of mine, I didn't mind the intercept. Sometimes, we had similar ends in mind, and we coordinated efforts.

But she was a means to an end, but she no longer serves us.

With a grim expression, Duke pulls the car out onto the road behind her. We let her get ahead a few minutes, knowing there's nowhere for her to turn for quite some time. We catch up with her soon enough. We pull up close behind her, but she doesn't seem to notice. Our headlights shine through her back window, and we can see her swiveling her neck to a beat, her messy curls knotted on top of her head, bobbing to the rhythm of whatever music she's listening to.

"Why isn't she pulling over?" Duke asks, leaning forward over the wheel and peering at her through his glasses. I would never ask such a thing, but Mabel's too focused on the hunt to notice his slip. I shoot him a warning glance, but he doesn't see it, doesn't look away from the car ahead.

"Maybe she hasn't noticed us," Mabel says, leaning forward between the seats in anticipation.

"We're halfway up her ass," Duke says. "How can she not notice?"

Dixie waves one hand in the air, and though I can't tell if she's waving at us to back off or pass. She can't pull over. There's nowhere to go. The narrow road carved into the side of the mountain barely allows two lanes.

"What is she doing?" Mabel asks, her tone impatient.

"She's dancing," Duke says.

I realize he's right. Dixie returns her hand to the wheel, then swoops it around again, part of a musical performance she's putting on for herself.

We scoot up even closer, hugging a curve and staying on her bumper the whole way. When she doesn't move toward the edge of the road, we creep dangerously close.

"Don't clip her," Mabel says with a grimace. "It'll leave evidence."

"I won't," Duke says, just as Dixie suddenly brake checks us.

Even at the slow speed we're traveling, there's no way to avoid the collision.

"Fuck," I yell, my hand automatically shooting across the space to flatten on Duke's chest, pinning him back against the seat as metal squeals against metal.

Mabel lets out a hysterical giggle.

Duke taps the brake, and Dixie's lighter car swerves from the slight impact, but she corrects quickly.

If there's one thing I should have learned about Dixie in high school, it's that she should never be underestimated.

"It's okay," Mabel says, her eyes sparkling with some feral light when I glance back at her. "We can get a new bumper somewhere."

"What now?" I ask, turning back to the road. It's what Duke would ask.

Dixie starts to speed up, pushing the engine on her car to go faster up the steep incline.

"Now we make her pull over," Duke growls, and he's back in character, intent and focused like I would be.

And then I pull her out of the car and choke the life out of her.

Duke presses down on the accelerator, pushing the big SUV up the mountain after her. We catch up again soon, roaring up close, but she puts on another burst of speed.

"Why doesn't she put on her blinker so you know to pass?" Mabel asks, impatient for the kill.

It's the first time we've planned a murder together, since we were supposed to leave Mr. Harris for the Black Widow. That time, Mabel was calm talking to him online, and once she saw him, her emotions overtook reason. This time, when she knows death is near, she's nearly giddy with excitement. I wasn't expecting that, and it makes me wary. I may be intent on getting a perfect kill, but otherwise, I take no great pleasure in ending someone's life.

Duke slowly eases his foot down on the accelerator, creeping up to within a few inches of Dixie's bumper. Her head is still now, crouched lower, as if she's leaning over the wheel, urging a little more speed from her small SUV. Ours has far more power, though we go hurtling around a curve so fast the momentum threatens to spin us off course and send us crashing down the mountain. Maybe that's her plan, to hurl the bigger vehicle off the road with its greater centrifugal force.

Too bad she's not a match for us in any way—our car is bigger and better, and we're smarter and more skilled. With Mabel cackling encouragement, we roar up and clip Dixie's bumper, sending her swerving toward the rock face on our right. She starts to go off the road, and we brake, ready to pull over when she makes contact. Instead, she jerks her wheel the other direction. The car swerves wildly, turning at a ninety-degree angle to us. Our headlights bathe her face, and for one second, we can see her expression of shocked terror—mouth agape, eyes forced shut against the blinding glare, skin an unnatural pallor cast by the LEDs.

And then the rear or her car fishtails away from us, and her headlights pierce into our car. I throw up a hand, and Duke throws himself back in the seat. Mabel cries out, throwing herself against the back seat.

And then there's only our own lights ahead. I reach over and hit the flashers, and Duke pulls to a stop.

Mabel leans up to see again, letting out a little giggle. "What just happened?"

"Stupid cunt went off the wrong side," I mutter, cursing Dixie for never just making things easy. She was always trying to stir up drama and cause conflict with her posts online. I didn't pay too much attention to it. It was merely obnoxious background noise, of which there was plenty in high school. But now it directly affects me.

Not only has she made things infinitely more complicated, but she's robbed me of the opportunity to get my perfect kill.

"Should we get out?" Mabel asks. "She might be alive. Her car could have gotten stuck on a tree close to the road. We don't want to leave another loose end."

"And she might have seen us," Duke says grimly. "Her lights cut across us before she went over."

"I'll check," I say, reaching automatically to push up my glasses before remembering I'm wearing contacts because I'm Duke today. I brush my messy hair off my forehead instead, then add, "I was supposed to do the deed."

"I'll come with," Duke says.

"I'll stay, as planned," Mabel says. "If anyone comes up behind us, I can pretend we saw an accident."

"We did see an accident," Duke says, climbing out.

We go to the side of the road where Dixie went off. Far below, one headlight shines through the trees before being swallowed by foliage. It's pointing downwards, so it won't draw attention from drivers passing above. It will almost certainly be tomorrow before anyone sees her down there. Unfortunately, her new car is equipped with several safety features, including automatically calling emergency services on impact.

"Think she's dead?" Duke asks.

"Yes."

From below, the eerie strains of a *Mass Hypnosis* song drift up from the wreckage, the speakers still intact.

"Should we go check?"

"No," I say. "We should be gone when emergency vehicles arrive, and it would take longer than you think to climb down there and back up, not to mention all the footprints we'd leave in the dirt. Accidents happen here ever year, and driving at night increases the risk of fatality."

"What if she's not dead?"

"Then we try again," I say. "Sooner than later."

Part of me hopes she isn't, despite the risks. I picture visiting her in the hospital when she's injured, crimping her oxygen while she lays in a coma. But that would deprive me of watching her die. I'm beginning to think I'll never witness the exact moment of someone's death. Each attempt increases the danger, the chances of being caught.

I just need to see it one time. Then I'll stop.

The next day, we have our answer. Back to playing ourselves, we watch the news on the hotel TV.

"The popular influencer was driving through the Smoky Mountains when her car went off the road," the reporter says. "Police have not ruled out foul play in the fatal accident."

"Fuck," Duke says, tossing down the controller. "What do we do now?"

"We follow the plan," I say. "Nothing changes."

"Until it does," he mutters.

In the car, Mabel scrolls on her phone. After a few hours, she says, "There's a conspiracy theorist blowing up a rumor online that could be in our favor. They're saying that band she toured with did it because she left them."

"Unfortunately, I don't think police put much stock in conspiracy theories," I say. "We should probably lay low for a while."

Mabel doesn't say anything. I glance sideways at her, but she's looking out the window, her face hidden from view. Duke said she wouldn't stop, that she'd just keep asking us to kill more people until we got caught. I wanted to kill as much as she did, so I told him he was wrong. Now I wonder.

I still haven't gotten my perfect kill, but I'd rather have my freedom. I've been waiting for years to see that spark of life leave someone's eyes, to feel it enter me. I can wait years longer. I'm a patient man with all the time in the world.

But Mabel is bloodthirsty and reckless. She isn't pulling the trigger, and she's gotten away with it for so long, had Dahlia to clean up her mess each time, that it must have made her think she's invincible. We've been on a killing spree all summer, and I can only guess at who she's thinking about now. We just killed Dixie, and she might already be moving on to her next victim in her mind. But even the most notorious serial killers get caught eventually.

SELENA

I adjust the rearview. Duke is watching Mabel too, a frown on his brow. Our eyes meet in the mirror, and I know it's not only our appearance that's identical in that moment. He's thinking the same thing I am. I need to let him know we're on the same page, that I have the same concerns. I thought it was just the Lady Alice making him paranoid, but now I'm not so sure. This time, maybe he's the smarter one. I know a lot, but he knows people in a way I never will.

I can't say all that with Mabel right here beside us, though. I try to convey it through a look, but I can't be sure that Duke understands. He would have two years ago. But he changed more than I anticipated during that six months I was gone. I assumed he would carry on as he always had, and when I returned for him, he'd remain as unchanged as I had. At the very least, I thought he'd return to his natural state once we were reunited. But without me there to depend on, he seems to have lost himself, and I haven't been able to help him find his way back. Now, he depends more on drugs than on me.

We drive straight through to Faulkner that day. I hope being around the rest of the family will make him happier, like it did earlier in the summer. We've only been gone for a month, but Royal is coming home for Labor Day, and even King agreed to come down for the holiday weekend, so the five of us will be together for a few days. It might be time to bring them in on it, talk over what to do about Duke. If we're all together, he will listen to us. We can listen to him too, help him decide where to go from here.

I have to admit defeat this time. That I don't know what's best for him, though I like to think I do. As much as I don't want it to be true, I have to acknowledge that he might not want the life we've built together. He might want to stay in Arkansas, where he's wanted to return so badly since we left. Or he might be happier in New York, where most of our family is located, including King, our mother, and Royal, though he's not in the city.

They might take care of him in a way I don't know how to, give him whatever it is that I can't, no matter how hard I've tried to determine what that may be. I can't give it to him because I don't know what I'm missing. I know my strengths, and knowing someone's emotional needs without being told is not one of them. I don't share those needs, so they are foreign to me. For most of our lives, I could ask Duke what he needed, and he would tell me. But he's holding back now. Even I can figure that out. What I can't figure out, to my endless frustration, is what he's not telling me.

Pushing up against him over and over isn't getting either of us where we need to go. I always thought we'd be on the same team, that whatever happened, we'd face it together. But now we're becoming the source of each other's ruin. He may show the cracks in his armor more readily, but I've been breaking too. I've made so many mistakes—careless ones, ones that could cost us everything. That's unlike me. I don't ordinarily lose my temper. I don't get sloppy. I don't lose sight of what matters.

Lately, I've done all three.

Between worrying about Duke, watching over Mabel, scaling up distribution of the product that enables us to live the life we've chosen, a grueling class schedule, chasing ghosts online, and now, the bodies stacking up, my tenuous hold is slipping. I can't carry it all anymore. So if Duke wants to break free of my grip, to strike out on his own, I have to let him. No matter what I want, I can't hold onto him any longer. I can't fight for him when he's fighting against me every step of the way.

Even if it destroys me, I have to let him go. I'm beginning to see that if I don't, I'm going to destroy him instead. Watching him struggle, seeing him in pain, is worse than any pain I could feel for myself. It has taught me so many things this year—about him, about myself, about my limitations. I may not need happiness, but he does. I have to let him find that, even if it's not with me. Because if I can't choose us, together, I will always, always choose him.

twenty-four

Duke Dolce

As soon as we're unpacked, Mabel opens Seeley's pet carrier and sets out his food and water dishes. He crouches inside the cage, refusing to come out, glaring at us for forcing him to endure the indignity of another road trip. I don't blame him. I don't see why we ever left Faulkner.

Giving up on getting him to come out, Mabel stands and turns to Baron.

"I need the car," she says. "I have something to take care of."

"What?" I ask, narrowing my eyes at her. "Going to give the damaged bumper to the police as evidence?"

I don't know how Baron can ever trust her. This was my first time killing, and even though she thinks it was Baron driving, Baron who killed her, I still jump at every siren, every flashing light on the way here, even the ones that weren't police. My heart stopped every time I saw a squad car in a town where we stopped for food or gas. I almost pissed myself when a state police drove in the other lane for a full two minutes on the highway.

Mabel frowns. "Why do you still act like I'm the enemy? We're on the same team, Duke. We were all there. We're all accomplices at the very least."

"Because you still act like it," I point out.

"How do I act like it?" she asks, planting her hands on her hips.

I glance at Baron, remembering her words. How tender she was sitting on my lap, lying with me. Asking me to do the impossible. She thinks Baron killed Dixie, so I still owe her. She doesn't even have to ask. I already know what she wants me to do.

"Never mind," I say.

Maybe if she takes the car, if she turns us in, she'll do it in a way that implicates only Baron. No one knows we helped plan it. She could say he rammed Dixie's car off the road while we screamed for him to stop. No one could say otherwise except Baron himself.

I shake the thought away. What has she done to me, that I'm contemplating getting my own brother, my twin, my other half, locked up?

It's better than the alternative, my demon reminds me.

I can't argue. He's right. I can't kill Baron, and if that's what she asks of me, I've already failed. But if he was in prison, I wouldn't have to.

And let's be real, he'd be fine there. He'd thrive. Probably be running the joint in a week's time, running drugs, arranging 'accidents' for the inmates dumb enough to cross him.

I wouldn't survive a day. I'd be turned into some thug's bitch, and then I'd run my mouth and get shanked.

What if that's her plan instead? What if she says the same things to him when they're alone?

He could do it.

Baron can do anything.

He wouldn't like it, but he could kill me.

He'd do that before he'd send me to prison. Baron knows I wouldn't last, and he wouldn't want to let someone else take my life. If someone's going to do it, he'd want it to be him.

"You can go in the morning," Baron tells Mabel, hanging the keys by the door.

"He wants to go by the lawyer's in the morning," she says.

"Tomorrow's Sunday," Baron points out.

"It's Preston," she says with a shrug, like that explains anything.

"We've been driving all day," I argue. "Sit down. Chill. Have a beer."

She sighs. "I can have him bring it here."

"Bring what here?" I ask.

"The paperwork for Grandpa's estate," she says. "I have to sign a bunch of stuff before Summer House is officially mine."

"Is anyone else coming?" I ask, thinking about Colt, his smoky blue eyes, his smoky breath on my lips, the way he always slips through my fingers like smoke.

"Who else would come?" Baron asks, watching me.

"I don't know," Mabel says, pulling out her phone. "I can ask. I don't know if Dolly puts the baby to bed or if the nanny does it."

"Don't bring him here," I say, tossing myself on the couch and pulling out my phone. "I don't want to see your family right now."

"I'll take you over," Baron says, but he's eyeing me. "Want me to drop you by Royal's on the way?"

"No," I say. "I don't feel like seeing anyone right now."

He frowns harder, standing there in a rare moment of indecision before he turns to go with Mabel. I can tell something's up, but I don't know what. Is that suspicion in his eyes? Or regret for what he's about to do to me?

I shouldn't let them leave together, cut me out again. This is their perfect opportunity to get rid of me, for Baron to come clean and tell her I committed a murder. They could go to the police. But I can't bring myself to care.

I swallow a handful of Alice without bothering to hide it. I didn't want to leave Faulkner, but now that I'm back, I don't want to be here. I don't want to be anywhere.

I don't want to see Olive happy with Royal and Harper, and know I'm the reason her sister is gone.

I don't want to see my sister, who is still normal, who still loves me when I don't deserve it, don't deserve her. Why should I get a sister when Olive doesn't?

I don't want to know that Colt is still with Lo, that they're happy now that she's finally out of Cedar Crest and able to be with him.

I just want to be left alone.

Mabel steps outside, but Baron lingers in the door, brow furrowed. "You shouldn't take that many at once."

"Fuck off," I say, not looking up from my phone.

"Duke," he says, glancing out at Mabel and then back. "I want to talk to you. When I get back, can we do that?"

"I'll be high as fuck."

"Tomorrow, then."

I sigh. "You'll do it whether or not I want to. Why even ask?"

"Because you're my brother."

When I shrug, he scowls, then shakes his head and walks out. I lay there for a while, letting Lady Alice creep over me. He said tomorrow, which means he's not getting rid of me tonight, at least. I have one more night. One night to do whatever the fuck I want.

He also said "I."

I want to talk to you. When *I* get back.

Baron never says "I." It's always "we."

He's too evolved for petty feelings like jealousy.

I'm the one who gets mired in feelings. Even Mabel gets jealous. Maybe that's why she picked me. That's what she said he can't give her. I can feel things for her that he never will.

SELENA

He can't give her his heart because he doesn't have one.

He says I am his heart.

What if that's what she asks for, like the Evil Queen asking the Huntsman to bring her Snow White's heart. It makes perfect sense. She will have asked Baron to bring her his own heart, and that is me. He'll deliver me to her.

They'll dump my body wherever it is that they put Mr. Harris, in some secret location where I'll never be found. And who would report me missing?

Like Blue, I have no one. Only a sibling, but mine is the one who will destroy me, like he destroyed her. He wouldn't make me suffer. At least I'm sure of that. He'll make it quick.

When Royal and King ask where I am, Baron will tell them I went my own way. They'll believe him. They would never believe he'd hurt me. They haven't seen how Mabel has changed us, how Alice has, how Blue has. They don't know that when he left me, he tore me out of him, tore out his own heart. Now he studies it with the clinical detachment that he does everything else. He studies himself more than anyone—he is his first subject. He'd be fascinated to know how a man can live without a heart, to study his own reaction like a specimen under a microscope.

That must be where they went. To plan it out.

I thumb open my phone. Wonderland shimmers around me, inside me. It swallows me and pulls me down the rabbit hole, but the rabbit hole is inside me, a sucking vortex that always wants more.

I jerk off for a while, and then I want to move, so I dance until I'm hot, and then I take off my clothes and wander the house, prowling, seeking something new, some novice sensation to feed the beast. Seeley Boots watches me with suspicion from the top of the refrigerator.

"Fuck off, asshole," I mutter to him, grabbing a beer from inside. "You think I'm going to light you on fire? I'm not that evil. Yet."

I grin at him, and he shrinks down, like a fluffy orange turtle trying to retract its head into its shell. I toss the beer cap at him and go back to the living room. I grab my phone and thumb it on.

DukeOfBeavertown: u here?
Dynamo: wsp
DukeOfBeavertown: r u in Faulkner
Dynamo: no
DukeOfBeavertown: wya
Dynamo: at the great lakes w lo
DukeOfBeavertown: y
Dynamo: I told u I was leaving town w her when she got out
DukeOfBeavertown: u dnt come back for labor day?
Dynamo: no lol
Dynamo: not rlly a big holiday 4 2 ppl w/o jobs
DukeOfBeavertown: wb xmas

SELENA

Dynamo: will prob come back 4 that
Dynamo: c u then k? gg
DukeOfBeavertown: I think ur sisters going to kill me
Dynamo: no shes not
DukeOfBeavertown: u don't know her anymore
Dynamo: I know her well enough to know that.
DukeOfBeavertown: u dont
Dynamo: r u hi rn
DukeOfBeavertown: wut does that matter
Dynamo: get help
DukeOfBeavertown: I'm trying
Dynamo: ffs I told u I cant help u. get therapy.
DukeOfBeavertown: I dont need therapy
Dynamo: sorry cant help u
Dynamo: Pls consider it. Srsly. & sobriety. Its hard but so much better here. I know u can get here 2. I believe in u man. Think about it. gg.
[Dynamo has left the chat]
DukeOfBeavertown: I dnt need fcking sboriety
[Dynamo is away]
DukeOfBeavertown: I need u
[Dynamo is away]

"Fuck," I roar, sitting up and hurling my phone across the room. When I go pick it up, cracks have spiderwebbed the screen. I want to smash it into a million pieces, but I don't have a way out of here if I do. They took the car.

I have to get out.

I pace the house, shaking, raging.

How dare he walk away like that? How dare he get better and act all fucking sanctimonious, when he's the one who left me in hell? He was supposed to be here with me, but he crawled out and left me to burn alone.

I'm so fucking hot even without clothes, that my skin feels like it's going to peel off. I stick my head in the freezer, panting in the cool vapors, my eyes stinging.

He doesn't care about you, Duke.

"I don't care about him, either," I mutter, seething as I slam the freezer and pace the kitchen, shaking with cold now.

I thumb open my phone, and I send more, even though I get the away message for him.

DukeOfBeavertown: did u c what happened 2 Dixie
DukeOfBeavertown: I did it 4 u
DukeOfBeavertown: I did what lo couldnt
DukeOfBeavertown: now am I good enough?

I curse myself for that, but I can't unsend messages on the app. He can turn me in if he wants, laugh at me while I'm in prison.

Or he can come back for me.

He did it the last time I saw him. He followed me when I tried to leave.

You're smarter than that, Dad whispers in one ear.

He doesn't want you, Dixie whispers in the other. *Not after what you did to me.*

No one wants you, Dad whispers. *You're weak.*

SELENA

You're a failure, Dixie adds. *You didn't even mean to kill me. Loser.*

I clap my hands over my ears and scream.

They're right though. I can't block out that knowledge, even when the voices recede. Colt doesn't want me, and I shouldn't want him. He's not some hero who's going to come flying back to rescue me from myself. He's a villain like the rest of us.

I hate him.

I asked for help, and he laughed in my face.

He laughed when I told him what Mabel was doing. He probably thinks Baron will protect me. But he doesn't know Mabel, how deep she got into us, infecting us with her toxic Darling blood that poisons everything like Black Widow venom. Everyone thinks Baron is immune, but he's not.

I'm the only one who can stop her.

I stare at my phone, and then I make some calls.

You can stop her.

I don't know who's whispering to me now, if it's me or Baron, the demon or Dad. He always wanted the Darlings gone from this town. My family forgot that. Crystal married one. Even Royal's cozied up with them now. And Baron's too far gone.

But I can do something. I can make Dad proud at last, something I never did in life.

I can make sure Mabel leaves and never comes back. I can make sure there's nothing for her to come back to after she signs those papers.

I can make Baron leave too. I couldn't save anyone from Baron, but I can save him from her.

The kid gets there with his truck filled with five-gallon containers a while later. He asks what they're for, and I tell him to shut his mouth if he knows what's good for him.

"If you're smart, you were never here," I tell him.

He looks at me funny, probably because I'm still fucking naked, but he helps me haul them onto the porch. I hand him all the cash in my wallet.

He looks at it, then back at me. "That's not even enough for the gas!"

I grab my bag and tear it open, pawing through the clothes. I shove a bag of Alice into his hands—hundreds of pearls, maybe more. His eyes widen, and he takes off before I can change my mind. But I don't need it anymore. I'm fucking done with all of it—murder, and Mabel, and Alice. I'm done with everything.

I uncap the first jug and inhale. The fumes feed the demon, wake him. He's happy, thirsty, excited. I stand and slosh it over the floor, my open bag, Mabel's bag by the stairs, Baron's bag with his laptop where he looked for Blue and never found her. He probably never really tried. I hope he didn't. No matter what he says, Baron doesn't make mistakes. If he let her live, it's because he couldn't bear to kill her.

He won't be able to kill me either. And I can't kill him.

But one of us has to go, to make her happy.

SELENA

I back through the room, then the living room. I stop and drink a beer. The fumes are making me sick. I take the next one, open it, and go to the top of the stairs. I watch it flow down like a waterfall. My eyes are watering, but I don't know if it's the fumes or if I got gasoline in them. I take out my contacts and put on my glasses and keep working.

When I'm done, I lie down on the bed. My stomach is churning, and my limbs are buzzing but limp, as if I drained my own lifeblood. In a way, I did.

For them, for all of them, I bled myself dry. It was never enough. But maybe this is.

When people talk about love, they make it sound like this great thing. They say you never forget your first love. That love makes life worth living. That it's better to have loved and lost than never loved at all.

They're right about one thing. I will never forget my first love as long as I live. I won't forget my second love, either—the brother of my beloved, my monster.

I'll never forget the way they became fuel for my nightmares. They dragged me to the depths of hell and made me confront the twin faces of evil. *Their faces.*

Loving them didn't give me a reason to live.

It gave me a reason to die.

I hate them both. Not because they can't give me what I want, but because they won't. They refuse. They will always be there, reminding me of my worst days, my worst self. They will never forgive, never let me forget. I can't undo what I've done. All I can do to make it better for any of them, is to be gone. I have to stop fucking up, to stop hurting people. And there's only one way to guarantee I'll never do that again.

I take out a pack of matches from the drawer beside the bed. I want a cigarette, but I left them downstairs, and it's too much work to go down. I think about how bright I'll burn out. How the last thing I see will be fire, how it will consume me from the outside like the demon has been consuming me from the inside.

Do it, he whispers. *It's the last thing you have to do.*
I believe in you, Colt whispers.
What would you give up for me? Mabel whispers.
"Everything," I whisper, and I open the matchbook.
For a flash, I see it empty.
There's nothing there. No options.
But when I blink, they're back. Half a book still. Plenty of chances, if the first one fails.
"For you, and for Baron," I say. "You always belonged with him."
Colt smirks down at me, all smoke and shadow, and flicks his Bic.
Nothing happens. "Got a light?"
I tear off a match. "And you belong with Lo."
And you belong with me, my demon whispers.
It's the only place I ever belonged. Maybe that's why I made him up, like Mabel thought she made up Dahlia. Because I didn't fit with my family, and he kept me company. He helped me fit with them, helped me belong, like I helped Baron belong to the world. But it

was always just the two of us. Me and my demon. But he's not real, so it's just me.

Colt was right. There is no demon. It was always just me.

I hate him for that. For knowing me better than I knew myself. For calling me 'man' like we're buddies, like that's all we are. For not letting me hate him.

I press the head of the match to the strip. I can smell it, the phantom sulfuric scent through the gasoline. It makes me delirious.

He won't do it, Dad whispers. *He's not man enough.*

I can see them all crowded around the bed now, phantoms in the vapors of gasoline.

They've gathered to watch me go.

Dawson. Dad. The man we killed.

Jane. Dixie. The demon who looks like me.

Is it Baron? Is he my demon?

He doesn't belong to the world. He belongs to me. He is me.

His hand closes around mine, gentle but firm. It crushes my fingers painfully tight.

"Don't. Move."

I stare up at him through my glasses, smudged and splattered with gasoline. He's a mirage, a figment of my imagination like the demon, a drug-fueled hallucination. He's my reflection in the mirror, myself but reversed, the man I want to be. My savior.

"Baron?"

"What. The fuck. Are you doing?" he asks.

"It's really you?" I pull my hand away, and he sucks in a breath through his teeth. I touch his face. I must be dreaming. I must have already done it, and this is what comes after.

"Duke. What are you doing?" he asks, and this time, his voice breaks.

"Are you here to kill me?" I ask, thumbing the slight indent in his square chin, the same one I have. "I knew you'd come. Light the match. It's okay. I'm ready."

"I'm not."

We stare at each other, and he eases the matches from my fingers and pulls them away. Gently, he pulls my glasses off. He sits there, cleaning them on the edge of his shirt, and then slides them back onto my face. They're slightly blurred, but I can see.

"Where is she?" I ask.

"I told her to wait outside. It's not safe in here. Can you stand?"

"She wants me to kill you," I say. "I can't do it, Baron. I'm not a killer. I couldn't live with myself. But you could. You're a killer. You do it."

"Not if we were the last two people on earth and I had to do it to survive." He stares at me, and his eyes are blazing like I've already struck the match. "I would sooner kill myself. I love you, Duke. You are my brother. I would never hurt you."

"Then why did you?" I ask, my throat thick suddenly, aching. I'm a kid again, and I just want to be the Robin to his Batman, and he's saying no. Robin is lame. And I know that means I'm lame, even if I can't articulate it.

He shakes his head. "I'm sorry. I know I didn't make you feel important. I don't understand feelings, so I don't know how to make you feel the way I want you to feel. I failed, Duke. But I want you to know. Whatever you need, I'll do it. Anything you want, it's yours. Anything. If you want space from me, or medication, or therapy... It doesn't matter what I believe in. It only matters that we find what helps you. Just tell me, so I can give it to you. You have to help me too, Duke."

"Are you crying?"

He touches his face, then stares at his fingers like he's never seen them before. "I guess I am." He raises his gaze to mine. His eyes are red, wet. Or maybe that's what I want to see, proof that I matter more than her. More than anyone. That must be why my own eyes sting. I can't remember where I end and he begins anymore.

"I didn't know you could cry."

"I didn't either."

My eyes are burning too, as if I can feel his pain, the depth of it mirrored in our twin hearts.

"I was so focused on setting up the life we planned, getting it all right, at all cost," he says, shaking his head. "I never would have done it if I'd known the cost was you."

"Baron," I say, gripping his fingers. "It's too late. I'm always too late. I don't see it until it's over. But this time

I do. This time, I'm looking ahead. I see what's coming. You don't need me. You'll be fine without me."

"I thought that too, once," he says. "But I was wrong."

"No, you weren't. And she'll keep doing it until one of us is gone. Maybe both. You should be the one to have her. You love her more than I do. You're more like her."

"Then why didn't she ask me to get rid of you?" he says. "It's not because she knew I wouldn't do it. It's because she always wanted you, Duke. She always loved you. Everyone loves you."

I shake my head. "I don't think I can survive her. And I know I can't survive losing you."

"You're not losing me," he says, wiping his nose. "Remember what I said on the way out of Faulkner? I promised I'd never leave you. So get up off this bed and walk out of here, or I'll carry you out."

"I just fuck everything up," I say, sitting up and swiping angrily at my cheeks. "It's better this way. I can show everyone I'm sorry. They don't believe me now, but they will when I'm gone. Will you tell her that for me? That I'm sorry. I wish I could go back in time and undo it all. I can't do that, but I can do this."

"No," he says. "You're going to walk out of here and tell her yourself."

"I made a mess of the life you made—the one I helped plan," I say. "I don't know what's wrong with me. Nothing is ever enough. And if I can't be happy with everything, then I'll never be happy. But you can be happy without me."

"I don't need happiness," Baron says. "I don't even know what that looks like. I need you, Duke. Don't you know that? I need you to help me with all the things I don't have. You're all my missing pieces. I'm only whole when you're with me."

"But you left."

"And I thought I was fine," he says. "I wasn't fine, Duke. Without you, I'm lost, an alien among my own people. I don't belong with them. I belong with you. I don't work without you. Nothing works without you. Now come out of the house. Please, brother. I'm begging you."

"She's out there."

We stare at each other a second, twin eyes behind twin pairs of glasses.

"Yes."

"She could light it," I say. "Get us both at once."

His lips tighten, and I think he'll argue, say that she wouldn't. But he just nods. "Then we'll go out together. I'm not leaving you, Duke. I don't break promises. Not to you. Never to you."

I nod and climb unsteadily from the bed. Baron's eyes are dry again, but mine are still streaming. He wraps an arm around me, throwing my arm over his shoulder and supporting my weight, and we start for the door.

twenty-five

Duke Dolce

"What if we make a spark?" I ask.

"Don't trip, and don't touch anything." He half drags me down the hall, down the stairs.

"I need clothes," I say. "I dumped gas on them."

"It doesn't matter."

Still, he lets me stop at the bottom of the stairs and pull on my wet jeans.

The door is standing open, so we don't have to worry about it making a spark when it opens. He grabs me again anyway, and together, we stumble out onto the porch. The air tastes strange, empty, without the fumes. I trip on the stairs and pitch forward, but Baron grabs onto the railing, holding tight. He doesn't let me go. He walks me out onto the lawn, where Mabel is standing, wringing her hands.

"Seeley's in there," she cries. "I have to go find him."

"Fuck," Baron mutters. "He probably ran out the door. It's been open since we got here."

"He didn't," she says. "I've been watching. I called, but he won't come out when he's scared. He's hiding. I have to find him!"

Baron holds up a hand. "I'll go get your fucking cat. Duke, stay here. Mabel, watch him. Don't let him go back in." He gives me a final look, then shakes his head and starts back for the house. "If I get blown up over a fucking cat..."

When he's inside, we stand in silence a long minute, watching the house.

"We could do it, you know," Mabel says at last.

I look at her. "What?"

"Strike a match. It would all be over. He'd be gone before he ever knew."

"Why didn't you do it when we were both inside?" I ask. "Is this part of your fucked up game? To make me do it, so I have to live with it?"

"He hurt you too," she says. "You can't tell me he hasn't ruined your life. Maybe he didn't force you to do things the way he did to me, but he still forced you. You were his first victim."

"Fuck you, Mabel."

"It might be our only chance," she says, glancing up as a car turns onto the street. She turns her big, luminous eyes back to me. "We could make it on our own. Harley Quinn and the Joker. Just you and me. Forever."

The car slows. I turn that way, distracted for a second.

I hear a series of loud cracks. I see flashes of fire in the car window, starbursts in the darkness. Mabel ducks, throwing her hands up and letting out a shriek of fear. They're so beautiful I can't look away, though, and then the car is speeding off, and heat is spreading through my chest, my stomach.

For a second, I think Mabel punched me. I stumble backwards, my gaze dropping. Mabel is crouched on the grass, covering her head. Baron is running out of the house. And hot, dark blood is throbbing out of a hole in my bare chest.

SELENA

twenty-six

Baron Dolce

I'm almost to the door with the damn cat when I hear three cracks, rapid, loud, like firecrackers.

Like gunshots.

My heartrate spikes.

It must have been kids messing around. A car backfiring. People in the nicest suburb of Faulkner don't shoot guns on the street.

But then I hear an ear-piercing scream.

Mabel.

I race out the door and down the steps, for once not thinking before I act. I drop Seeley as my feet hit the grass, and then I'm across the lawn, to where Mabel is on her knees. That's when I see him. At first, I didn't see him on the ground, in the grass.

Blood is pumping out of a hole in his chest.

I drop to my knees, shoving Mabel aside without awareness, and drag him into my lap, slam my hand over the hole.

"Duke," I cry, the word nothing but breath and panic. "Brother. Look at me."

SELENA

His eyes open, roll up, and then they find their anchor and come back to me. My insides turn to liquid. I gently remove his smeared glasses and stare down into his eyes, my twin, my mirror, my everything. The corner of his mouth trembles, tilts up.

I press down harder. "Duke. Stay with me."

"Baron," he says, his voice rough, fading already. His eyes flutter closed again.

"No," I say. "No, no, no. Don't do that. You said you'd stay with us."

"Baron," he says again, his lids lifting like it takes effort. "I'm scared."

"Me too."

His hand finds mine, and he holds on. "Don't let me go," he says, his eyes searching mine, stronger now, vulnerable, so fucking scared. "I'm not ready."

I turn my top hand over and lace my fingers through his. Under my other palm, I can feel the thuds already slowing, that there's more warmth in my lap now than under my hands.

"I won't let go," I tell him.

"Promise?"

I squeeze his hand, and then I do something I've never done before, something I never do.

"I promise," I say. "You're going to be okay."

His lids flutter again. "You never lie," he whispers faintly.

"Don't go," I tell him. "Not yet. Stay another minute. Please, Duke."

I turn to Mabel. "Light a match."

"What?" she whispers.

"Light a fucking match," I say, my voice shaking so hard I can't yell at her for being so fucking slow.

She backs away, and I think she won't, but I can't do it myself because I can't let go of his hand. I turn back to him, for one horrible second sure it's too late. His face has gone white, his lips colorless. I hear the sirens in the distance, and I'm vaguely aware that she must have called an ambulance, but I know we don't have that much time.

And then there's a crackling behind us, swelling fast, growing louder as golden firelight bathes Duke's face.

"Look, brother," I say, squeezing his hand again. "Open your eyes. We lit a fire for you. Look at the flames. Aren't they dazzling?"

His lids flutter open again, but only halfway. His lip trembles. "Oh," he breathes. "For me?"

"Everything is for you, Duke," I say. "It was always for you."

He stares up at the flames engulfing the house. His fingers twitch and then go still. Slowly, I watch the light fade from his eyes, until all that's left is the refection of the fire behind me.

SELENA

twenty-seven

Mabel Darling

This can't be real.

I'm weightless, floating, a balloon untethered, dropped by a careless child's hand. For once, I want to go back, but I can't find my way, can't seem to return to my body. I can't find the hand that let me go, the one that promised to hold on.

It wasn't supposed to happen this way.

Baron stumbles to his feet, backs away from his brother's lifeless form. His eyes are wild, crazed with pain. For one brief flash, there's hope, and I think, maybe I'm wrong. Maybe that's not Baron at all. Maybe everything will be okay.

Baron never shows that much emotion. Never feels it.

But then his eyes fix on me, and the rage is like nothing I've ever seen, nothing I can withstand. I shrink down, take a single step back. Being invisible, quiet, and harmless as a baby bunny used to save me, and when it didn't, drifting away did. I got greedy. I got tired of being quiet. I wanted to make noise, to strike back. And now I pay.

Baron seizes me by the throat, his fingers digging in.

I am defenseless as a little bunny. I have no poison, no knives, no guns. No window or wine bottle presents itself. There's poison in my pocket, but I don't reach for it.

"What did you do?" he asks, his breath heavy, labored.

"Nothing," I manage.

Baron's fingers tighten, cutting off my air. His eyes blaze hotter than the fire consuming Summer House behind him. Hotter than Baron has ever been.

"Duke?" I mouth, but I have no voice. His fingers are crushing my windpipe. Already, my vision swims, dots of black appearing. Already, my mind is fading.

This is the punishment for my crimes. I always knew the risk. I thought eventually, the police would come for me, no matter how well I hid my tracks, no matter who buried the bodies in my wake. But it's not the courts that will make me pay.

This is a different kind of justice, one as ancient as human sacrifice.

My knees buckle, and Baron does to the ground with me. I'm vaguely aware of the damp, solid earth below, the fire climbing to the sky above.

This is how I pay. With my life.

It's more than fair. I've taken so many.

This is what happens, not when you take a life, but when you get greedy.

No one likes a greedy girl.

The court system wouldn't have been kinder. Probably, they would have been crueler. They would have paraded my traumas out one by one, hanging on every salacious detail, using them for their own titillation later, when they were at home with their wives and husbands and daughters of their own, in bedrooms down the hall.

"Where did he put his fingers?"

"Did it hurt?"

"How old were you the first time it happened?"

"What did he say to you while he was inside you?"

"Why didn't you tell someone?"

"Did you enjoy your grandpa's special kisses?"

"Did you cum?"

They don't like it when ordinary people dole out the justice that they would never have the courage to deliver.

So I don't mind that this is how it ends. I prefer it, even. I stare blindly, sightlessly, up at him, and I feel myself slipping away.

Suddenly Baron jerks his hands back like I'm made of scorching embers and not smooth cardboard. He stumbles halfway to his feet, backing away from me like he did Duke. Then he falls to his knees, and a scream of the deepest, blackest anguish rends the night, his throat, his soul. He slams his fists to the ground, battering the earth, punching it with such ferocity that I listen for the sound of his bones cracking. All I hear is that raw, animal scream, as primal and ancient as the first cry of the first infant being born. It sends shivers down my spine, and some answering part of me pushes me up. I crawl to him, wrap myself around him, even though I'm wrapping myself around the embers that will burn me alive.

We're pulled back from that edge, that dangerous place so deep and dark inside us that it could swallow us and all the world.

Sirens deafen, cut through and silence his screams. Lights blind. Emergency vehicles are speeding down the road.

Baron grabs me, drags me up. "I can't," he says.

Still gripping my hand, he runs for the car.

"What about your brother?" I ask, looking back. "And Seeley?"

"That's not my brother," he says.

"My cat—"

"I got him out," he says, stuffing me into the driver's side of the car. "He's fine. We'll come back for him."

He slides in with me, and I scramble over into the passenger seat as he shoots out of the driveway onto the road, not bothering to look even though it's a busy road. He roars away, away from the house and the fire and the death, as if we can outrun it now that we've been chasing it so long that it finally caught up.

"What happened?" he asks after a minute.

He sounds better, though barely controlled, and his voice is hoarse, raspy.

"I don't know," I say, and without warning, a rush of tears scalds my eyes, pours down my face. I turn to the window so he won't see. "A car drove by, and—"

"What car?" His voice is flat but impatient, hard as stone.

"I don't know," I say again. "A—an Chevy I think."

"You know cars," he says. "What kind of car?"

"It was dark, and it happened so fast," I say. "It slowed down, and the window went down, and in the half-second before it happened, all my brain landed on was that they were going to ask directions. And then they started shooting, and I just threw myself down by instinct, and I covered my head. I didn't see the license plate. It was a sedan, an older model, a mud brown color."

He's silent a minute, his fingers drumming. Then he mutters one word under his breath and rips the car around, sending me crashing into the door.

"Blue."

"Brown," I correct, grabbing the dash when he floors it. The car roars forward, everything outside the windows a blur as he bears down, not letting up. We fly toward down, then onto the road that leads toward my old neighborhood. Baron doesn't speak. I feel sick at the speed, my stomach dropping out when he hits a little dip in the road. And then we're back in the neighborhood where I grew up, where Hickory House and Lilac Place sit side by side, silent sentinels watching over the agony within their walls.

I cut my name into the closet there. I never spoke, but I left my mark. One day, my brother found me sitting in there, and he sat beside me. He carved his name next to mine. Baron's brother lived there after us. The mark he's left will outlast every cut I've made.

As we roar past my mother's house, I remember the night we burned it down. I remember Duke taunting me, mocking me, pushing me past my limits, until I grabbed the gallon of gas and sloshed it along the back wall. I remember him laughing and spinning me around and around as it went up in flames, the sparks dancing in the sky and in his eyes, on a night so much like this one, so different. I remember realizing for the first time that my body was more than a container for my mind, that it mattered too. He brought me to life, made me laugh, taught me the meaning of fun. The realization that I will never again hear him laugh hits me, leaves me reeling.

Baron slams the car into park, throwing us forward. He's out the door and into the house, and I can hear him yelling before I'm even out of the car. By the time I've climbed out, he's in the front, yelling at someone outside.

"Where is she?" he bellows.

I make my way around. Harper and Royal are sitting on the curved staircase, the set to the right, sharing a cigarette.

"She's not here," Harper says, sounding hollow.

"Who's not here?" I ask.

"Where did she go?" Baron shouts. "Where is she?"

"Calm the fuck down," Royal says. "We don't know. Her sister ran in, and grabbed Olive, and said they had to go right now."

"Who?" I ask again.

"Blue," Harper says, tapping the cigarette and frowning. "She was in a panic, talking a mile a minute about getting out of town. I didn't want to let her leave, but she kept saying, 'She's mine,' like I would try to keep her. She was crying and frantic, but fierce too, y'know? I've never seen her like that." She glances at Royal. "Do you think she's in some kind of trouble?"

"Yeah, obviously," he says, scowling.

"Who's Blue?"

"Blue is Jane," Baron says.

"Who is Jane?" Harper asks.

But I'm already putting the pieces together, laying them down like stepping stones in front of me, horror dawning as I go down the path that leads from what I did in that basement a year ago to this moment.

As if he's followed me there, Baron speaks.

"Duke is dead," he says, his voice flat, devoid of any emotion whatsoever. Gone is the madman hammering the earth with his fists like he could open a portal to another world, a world where his brother lived; like he could turn back time if he hit the earth hard enough to spin it backwards on its axis.

Royal gives his head a little shake, blinking at us in shock, uncomprehending. "What?"

"No, he's not," Harper says, like the very thought is ridiculous, like we're playing a joke on her that's so unbelievable she won't even entertain it. "He was just texting earlier today..."

I know how she feels. How impossible it is to picture a world without our messy, chaotic, beautiful boy in it, dancing and laughing and mocking everyone and everything, even death.

Tonight, death gets the last laugh.

"He died a few minutes ago," Baron says.

He once called me a robot, but now he's the automaton, inhuman and methodical.

"It's not possible," Harper whispers, but she must know it is, because she folds in on herself, a slow crumpling. Royal pulls her into his arms, rocking her, his face like marble. The broken boy with the swollen lips and bruised eyes, begging for help, no longer exists. He is a stone statue now, immovable and unbreakable. But inside, I know this will break him. Inside, it will break us all.

I always study them with fascination, this unlikely pair, but tonight, there's no wonder, no curiosity that this spark plug of a girl could disrupt the whole Dolce engine, could bring it to a halt. Tonight, there are too many other thoughts, ideas, feelings I haven't even begun to comprehend. I can't look ahead. Not yet. So I look back.

I replay the moment. The car slowing. The window lowering.

Why didn't he duck?

It was probably the drugs clouding his mind, making him slow. Even then, they might have hit him. A bullet is faster than a person.

Baron hasn't accepted that yet. "I'm going to find her," he swears. "I know where she lives."

He doesn't wait for me, just turns and storms off suddenly, leaving me to face the incomprehensible with these two strangers.

"What happened?" Royal asks me, his gaze unflinching. He always looked at me like that, like he was daring me to tell him that he should look away in shame, like he was forcing me to do it instead.

"He was shot," I whisper.

"By... Blue?" he asks, less certain now.

"I don't know," I say. "Maybe it's a coincidence."

People like to believe things like that.

Harper lifts her head, wipes her cheeks. "Why would Blue shoot Duke?"

"She wouldn't," I say. "But she'd shoot Baron."

She shakes her head. "I don't understand."

"Don't you?" I ask, cutting my eyes at Royal.

I don't know what he knows, but I'm assuming it's enough. He knows what Baron is like, because he's just like him. He knows what Baron does, because he does it too. They all do.

Did.

I swallow hard and look away from them both.

"But when did they even meet?" Harper asks. "And why are you calling her Jane?"

"I thought that was her name," I say. "Tell me what she said. Tell me exactly what she said when she came here."

Harper draws back, and I know I was too intense, too weird.

Instead of telling me I'm a freak, though, she just picks up the pack of cigarettes and takes one out. "I think this calls for an extra smoke," she says, lighting up before speaking to me. "She said... She was ranting, like, all in a rushed panic that didn't make sense. I don't even know everything she said. She said they had to go, and she kept saying, 'right now.' She said someone was waiting in the car, and they had to get out right now."

"A baby," Royal says, taking the cigarette from her. "She said the baby was waiting."

She wasn't lying. She really had it.

"Yes," Harper says, nodding. "She definitely said something about a baby, and something about the forest? And then she grabbed Olive and they ran out. She barely let her say goodbye before she dragged her out the door. Olive wanted to get her stuff, but Blue told her there was no time."

"She gave you that number," Royal says, handing the cigarette back.

"Oh, shit, yeah," Harper says, tucking the filter in the corner of her mouth and digging into her pockets.

She finally comes up with a torn scrap of paper. "She said she couldn't thank us enough, and if we ever needed anything, to call this number and tell them we're a friend of hers."

We all stare at the scrap, weighing its meaning, its significance, its impact on the rest of our lives.

"Should we call it?" she asks, glancing at Royal like she's afraid of his reaction.

He knows Blue killed his brother. He knows Baron will kill her if he finds her.

"Can I see it?" I ask, holding out a hand.

Harper hands it over with all the trust in the world, like she's never considered that I might already know what to do. I crumple the tiny scrap, pull out the pack of matches that Baron gave me when he told me to burn the house, and I light one. I hold the flame to the paper.

"Whoa, what the fuck?" Royal barks, jumping up.

I turn away, so if he grabs me, he won't get the hand with the paper. By the time he could get it, it'll be too late.

But he never reaches me. Harper stops him with a hand on his elbow. In the two seconds of contemplation before he pulls free, the flame has swallowed the paper.

Royal glowers at me, like he's not sure whether to throttle me. There's nothing any of us can do now, though. I've made the choice for all of us. They could beat me up, but it won't bring the number back, and I have a feeling they didn't memorize it, if they even looked at it before Harper shoved it into her pocket in the chaos of Blue rushing in, grabbing Olive, and running out.

"You should have gone with Baron," Royal says to me.

"I don't think he wants company."

"Well, too fucking bad," he says, leaning down to kiss Harper's head. "I'm going to find him."

"You know where he is?"

"I've got his location," he says, striding off toward the garage.

I marvel at that. I didn't think Baron would let anyone know his whereabouts. I didn't even know if his twin had his location. But Duke wasn't his only brother. Baron has two more. They all love each other as well as they can, in their broken ways.

Just like they love us.

I sit down beside Harper.

"Smoke?" she asks.

I shake my head no. "How'd she look?"

"Okay," Harper says, knowing who I mean. She drags on her cigarette. "How do you know her?"

"I don't."

"Doesn't seem like the kind of girl you'd be friends with."

"I'm not friends with any kind of girl," I say. "No one likes me enough to call me a friend."

I wait for her to say that's not true, or that she's my friend. Not because I want her to, but because everyone always does when I say things like that. I'm glad when she doesn't, when I don't have to deal with the discomfort of pretending I don't know she's lying, and her discomfort at knowing I'm pretending.

"Yeah, you're pretty tough to figure out," she says.

"Do you have to figure someone out to be their friend?"

"I guess not," she says. "But it helps to be able to know someone, so you know if you like them. That's kinda the whole basis of friendship."

"I don't think I'm a very likeable person," I point out. "Whether or not someone knows me."

"Well, that makes two of us."

She finishes off her cigarette and sets the butt between her feet on the steps with the other one. "I can't believe he's gone. I mean, I believe it, but I can't believe it at the same time. I want to ask if you're sure. If there's zero chance that he'll just come walking around the side of the house right now, or call and say he got us good."

My throat tightens, and I can't speak. I may be unlikeable, but he found a way. The twins are the only friends I've had in over ten years. And now the one who loved me is gone, and the one who can't will never let me go.

"Are you sure we got the right twin?" Harper asks, apparently having similar thoughts to mine.

I nod, but I'm thinking about how Baron insisted on going in alone to get Duke, how he told me to wait outside. How long it took. Could they have switched? Is this his way of testing me one more time, to see if I want it to be him? To make me prove myself one final time?

But no. I can't think like that. I can't play the game anymore. We played too long, and we all lost. It doesn't matter who's left. It only matters that only one of them remains. I will love him, no matter who he is.

"You know, I always hoped... I hoped you'd pick him," she says. "I was rooting for him. For you."

"Me too," I whisper, and a tear spills down my cheek. I look over at the row of lilacs where we sat that night, when we burned the house. How he held me trapped when the fire trucks came, how I freaked out because I still couldn't stand to be touched. How Baron caught us there, demanded a sacrifice for my betrayal.

"Do you believe in god?" Harper asks after a minute.

"No." I shake my head, wiping away the tears that won't stop coming.

She pauses, like she's waiting for me to elaborate. When I don't, she nods. "I don't either. I always hate when people die, and everyone says, they're in a better place. Like, no, they're just dead. And most people wouldn't go to the 'better place' anyway. When people say, 'they're at peace now,' I always thought it meant they were floating around on a cloud singing kumbaya or whatever. But maybe it just means nothingness. Maybe, for some people, nothingness is better than what they had to endure."

I can't speak. All I can think about is how miserable Duke was, and how we didn't fix it in time, and now it's too late. I should have just let Baron kill Jane. I should never have interfered, should never have gotten involved. I thought I was helping, but all I did was bring the suffering back on us. And it landed on the one who deserved it least of all. I double over, pressing my eye sockets to my knees.

"Royal always says life is suffering," Harper says, absently drawing another cigarette from her pack. "So if peace is the end of suffering, then death is peace."

It's a nice thought, so I don't argue. There's no peace for those left to suffer.

I stand, not wanting to fall to pieces in front of a perfect stranger. As I walk away, Harper calls after me. "You know, if you stick around long enough, we might end up being friends despite our best efforts. I may be a bitch, but I have a habit of seeing the best in people. Even when they don't see it themselves."

That night, after Royal comes back with Baron when they don't find Blue, after they talk to the police, after everything is quiet except for a light, steady rain falling on the roof, Baron crawls into bed with me in my childhood bedroom where Duke once slept. He curls into me, sliding down the bed, hiding his head in my middle, as if he's searching for the softest place to land. He grips my hips, burrowing, seeking, as if he can find his way inside, climb through my navel and into the warmth of a different womb, the one he shared with his brother, and never come out.

"It's my fault," Baron says, his voice raw, shattered. "He was wearing glasses. She meant it for me. He never did anything to her."

"I know," I whisper, threading my fingers through his hair.

"I love you," he says. "I'm sorry."

I don't know if he's apologizing for loving me, or that it's now my burden to bear, his monstrous love. I know he's never said those words to me before—only his brother. My shirt is wet, sticking to my stomach where his face is hidden.

"It's my fault too," I admit. "I should never have interfered."

He doesn't say anything, but his shoulders shake and he holds me tighter, like he's afraid I'll slip away next, like he's the spider and I'm his catch, not the other way around.

"It's just us now," I whisper, cradling his head to my hollow belly, holding all the pieces I have left of this beautiful, terrible boy.

The pillow is wet with my tears, but I still search for his scent in it, bury my face in it the way Baron buries his in me. The pillowcase is clean, though, smelling only of detergent. I wish we'd known, that we could have saved the last one he slept on here, so we could have that tonight.

"I can't," Baron says, pressing his face into my belly. "Mabel, I can't. How can I?"

"I don't know," I whisper, another tear slipping down my cheek. "We just do."

And then he's lower, between my legs, and his mouth is hungry and desperate, and I remember what Harper said. Because Baron never does this—not since one time, in high school, when he pushed a sucker inside me and then licked it out and told me I tasted like cherries.

This is Duke's thing. And when he won't stop, when he refuses until I give in, that's Duke's thing. When he forces me to keep going until my legs are shaking and I'm crying, I hate it even more than usual, because I want it to be him. I wish, and I wonder, and I pretend as I shatter, that it's the right twin who lived.

SELENA

twenty-eight

Baron Dolce

Everyone's crying except me. Everyone thought I was the smart one, but Duke managed something in his short life that I've never been able to accomplish. He figured out how to get everyone to love him despite themselves, despite all the crimes and trespasses he committed, the same evil that they hate me for. They could forgive him, because though he was a monster, he was also human. I'm the inhuman monster, the one they can't love because I don't crave it, because I don't see the point in getting them to love me.

All the tears flowing down the toughest faces in Faulkner can't save him.

They don't bring him back, rising like smoke from the grave, don't make him laugh recklessly or dance wild as a flame.

They don't turn back the clock.

They don't open the eyes I watched close, don't bring the light back into them, the spark, the life.

And what's the point of love if it can't do that?

SELENA

Without him, I will never know. He can't explain it to me, make me see. From this day forward, I will always be an outsider, an observer; this human world with its human emotions an alien land to me.

When I look down at Mabel, she's crying too, her face wet and soft as a baby's. She clings to my chest like one of those damn koalas Duke was always collecting at the end, so I put my arm around her in case she collapses with grief, falls on the coffin and grasps that instead of me, demands to be lowered into the ground because what point is there in a life without him?

Maybe that's what love really is. It's not everything, but it's a reason. A reason to stay up here when the priest closes the book somberly, and later, after we fly the body back to New York, a reason to stay up here when they lower the coffin into the ground next to Dad.

I look down at my brother, but he's not there. It's only a body, like a mannequin. He's flawless in death as he was in life—his hair styled, his cheekbones strong, his chin square. He looks like he could sit up at any moment, laugh at us for believing anything could kill the invincible Duke Dolce. But it wouldn't be him. He's gone.

He always walked on the edge because he knew he'd never fall. That I would always catch him.

But I didn't.

I lost sight of him, lost my grip and let him slip away. I didn't know he'd already let go, that if I released him, even for a moment, he wouldn't hold on. I should have noticed. I knew better than to lose focus. Only one of us could ever be anything at once. That's how it worked. We were two halves of the whole. If he was being stupid, I had to be smart. If he was being reckless, I had to look out for him. If he was being selfish, I couldn't be selfish at the same time.

But I was. I went after what I wanted, apart from him. I wanted this one thing of my own. For years, I dreamed of seeing the light vanish from a man's eyes. Now, it's the moment that will haunt me for the rest of my life.

Everyone is silent for a long moment after Father Salvatore is done. I wonder what secrets he keeps about Duke, if he witnessed his trips to Thorncrown with Dad, if he was there. I wonder who else here keeps secrets about my twin, secrets he never told me, and now he never will.

There are so many faces in the crowd I barely recognize. I don't know how many people attended Judge Darling's funeral earlier this summer, but it couldn't have been many more. And there's no doubt that more tears flow here. Duke touched people in a way that's rare, a way that not many people can. Even Harper is sobbing in Royal's arms beside me, like she doesn't care that it'll ruin her tough-as-nails reputation, like he didn't tie her to a tree and leave her for dead every bit as much as I did.

Even Royal is crying, silent tears carving tracks down his cheeks.

Suddenly, Mabel steps away from me, takes a deep breath, turns her face to the blank white sky, and screams. It's a long, mournful howl that cuts through the silent sobs and muted sniffles, obscene in its power in the somber situation, hideous against the backdrop of assorted flowers that she insisted on, buying out every flower shop in town and then going to Little Rock for more.

Everyone stares at her in shock. Her face goes red, but she takes a deep breath and does it again. She knows she's making a spectacle, which is so unlike quiet, bland little Mabel Darling that no one stops her.

Finally, as she draws a breath for her third scream, which seems more calculated than anguished, I grab her arm. "What are you doing?" I mutter.

This is something my mother would do, wanting people to notice her and her grief. Even now, she's silenced into shock by Mabel's outburst.

Mabel turns to me, her expression determined even with the dark splotches on her cheeks. "Duke once told me that he wanted his funeral to be a big deal. He said he wanted everyone crying, and he wanted wailers. I don't know what that is, exactly, but I'm doing my best. He said we should grieve for the rest of our lives. Why is that so much easier than honoring his other wishes? He didn't want us to mourn quietly, privately. He wanted us to be loud. So I'm being loud."

If I doubted her grief before, I can't now. Being loud, being seen, embarrassing herself—these aren't things

Mabel does. She would rather suffer the worst agony, the worst violation.

But she'll do it for him.

Even though it's too late to show him that she'd do it for him, she's doing it.

I nod, though I don't like it either, and she takes a breath again, deep into her lungs.

This time, when she wails, another voice joins. Surprised, I glance sideways and see Crystal joining in. She steps forward and grips Mabel's hand, and, with tears streaming down her face, lets out a warbling hiccup of a cry.

"If that's what he wanted, then that's what we'll do," Harper says. She grabs Mabel's other hand, throws back her head and lets out a mournful howl. Magnolia takes Harper's other hand and lends her voice, the high, musical note in it adding sweetness to the chorus of voices. Gloria and Colt join in, though I'm not sure if men are supposed to wail for the dead. I don't know when they came back, but they appear from the crowd. More girls join, making a circle around the casket, their heads back, mascara running, voices breaking with grief.

There's Mom, and our grandmother, and Eliza, who came down even though they'll be flying back for the funeral and the burial in New York. There's Dolly and the Walton twins; Mabel's mother and DeShaun's sister; Natalie Fox and Daria Diaz and Lacey Murdock and a dozen other girls whose hearts he broke when he treated them the way he treated everyone.

But they still loved him.

We all still loved him.

Their voices join, twist and twine, rise and fall, the air vibrating with the sound waves, until my ears ring. Dolly's baby starts to cry in her arms, and then Crystal's kids do, and more babies add their distressed shrieks to the din. Somewhere, a dog starts barking, and then another, until the howls seem to spread over the whole town. The grief is too big for Faulkner, too heavy. It mutes the world like the low, featureless white of the clouds that cast the world in a dull gloom, blanketing and swallowing everything in shadow.

It goes on for a long time.

When they're done, the crowd starts to trickle away.

"Two funerals in one week," Crystal says, staring at the casket with bloodshot eyes. "It's too weird. It's like this town is cursed."

"Dixie didn't die in this town," I point out.

"She was just getting famous," says one of the Walton twins. "So sad."

"Not famous enough," Magnolia says, glancing at Colt. "Almost no one went to her funeral. I heard there were only, like, ten people there."

"I can't believe it was just a car accident," says the other twin.

"*La Muerte* says the band killed her," says the first.

"You believe some conspiracy theorist online who won't even show their face?" Gloria asks, looking skeptical. "*Mass Hypnosis* wasn't even in the same state that night."

"Not that *we* know," says her sister. "One of them could have flown to Tennessee."

"Why are we questioning the police?" Mabel asks, frowning. "They ruled it an accident. There were no marks on the road, so she didn't even brake."

The Walton twins give her a funny look. "I know, but it's like, the most boring way to die. She would have wanted something exciting, so she'd be remembered forever. Like a bombing or a mass shooting or—"

Her twin elbows her, and she snaps her mouth closed when she realizes I'm right here. No longer a twin because my brother went out in an 'exciting' way, a random, unexplained drive-by shooting in a nice part of a small town.

"Sorry," they mutter, scampering away.

Harper wraps herself in Royal's arms, pulling them around her. "I'm glad Olive isn't here for this," she says. "I'm glad she never has to know."

"I wouldn't say never," I mutter.

Harper aims a sharp look at me. "He wouldn't want you to hurt her. Or her sister."

"She's right," Royal says. "Killing someone he loved won't avenge him. I know it's not what you'd do, but it's what he'd do. It's what he'd want. That's how you honor his memory. It's all we can do."

That's the part that stops me. That's stopped me from going after them already. I had to be here to honor his wishes, even though he's not. I'm all that's left of him. So I carried on with what he wants. Flowers. Wailers.

Stopping short of vengeance isn't in my nature, though.

"She's right," Mabel says gently. "I think... I think we went too far. I got carried away. Maybe we all did. But we have to stop. If we don't stop now, it will never end."

I said almost those exact words to Duke about her. Now she sees it, when it's too late. When it doesn't matter.

None of it matters. Nothing will bring him back, change the outcome. Nothing short of reversing time could undo what we've done, what we've lost. It can never be found, even if I find her. And what makes me think I could, after I couldn't for the past year, when it mattered? If I'd found her before, this wouldn't have happened. But I didn't find her. I'm not a god, no matter what I want to believe, who I kill, to convince myself. A god could bring him back.

"Just like sending him home to be buried with the family," Royal grumbles. "I wouldn't want to be buried with the bastard for all of eternity, but Duke loved Dad despite everything. He'd want to be laid to rest next to him."

I don't know how they figure out the things he would want. He's not here to want them, so it seems meaningless to me. But I know he loved Dad, so I have to trust them. I know he loved Olive too, though I will never understand why. And I know that he always wanted kids, and she's the closest he will ever come to having one. That's what makes me believe them. They understand the reason behind these things, have some insight into human nature that I don't. And since I can't refute it, I have to trust their judgment on this, because Duke was the human side to us. All that's left now is the demon.

After the crowd disperses, and people have moved inside to eat and share stories, to laugh and cry and take solace in each other in some ritual form of community that only lasts until they leave this place, if the pattern I've observed at other funerals stays consistent, a few people linger.

I pause before making my way over to where Colt and Lo stand near an oversized floral arrangement, their heads bent toward each other, conversing.

Colt looks up first, his eyes hooded and cold, even while they're still red from crying. In them, I see exactly the same impenetrable aloofness that Mabel carries, the one that drew me to her from the start, before she entangled me in her web. Back then, I thought I'd crack her open and lay it bare, solve all her mysteries. Now, I know I never will. There is something in them that's beyond the reach of humanity, or perhaps only beyond the reach of reason. That's all I have to work with now.

I can't imagine going forward with that handicap for the rest of my life. I've always had Duke there to help me, to dumb things down for me so that I could understand. Because when it comes to emotion, to all the subtle, intangible facets of normal people, I was the one who stumbled blindly. I'm only beginning to comprehend all that we've lost. Not just our human side, but the part that *understands* humanity.

"What do you want?" Colt asks.

"It's okay," Gloria says, resting a hand on his arm. "I'm ready."

I look back and forth between them, searching for meaning, for context clues. If I could memorize every word, gesture, and facial expression and bring them home to my twin like I used to, he would tell me what they're saying without words. He would tell me if that look on Gloria's face is pity, or sympathy, or trepidation. But I can't do that now. I am flying blind. I will fly blind for the rest of my life.

"I'll get Mabel," Colt says. "She should be here."

"Okay," Gloria says. "She's over there with your dad and that vampire guy."

Colt chuckles, but when his gaze moves across me, it's as remote as ever. He walks over to get his sister, who's standing with her father, her uncle, and a tall stranger with black hair and pale skin. Whatever made Mabel the way she is, it made her brother the same. There's something in them that none of the other Darlings have, something that cannot be destroyed even when they're crushed to dust beneath our thumbs. Preston reacted with anger, could be tempted to revenge. Devlin ran to protect what was his. Colt and Mabel stayed.

They endured every torture with grim, steadfast perseverance, even a quiet kind of dignity. We broke their bodies and their minds, but they never surrendered. They both show all the signs of human weakness and emotion when it comes to suffering, both their own and that of others, but they never bowed and scraped, never groveled. Maybe that is what drew my brother to Colt—the mystery, the similarity to the girl we loved, the ever-unattainable prey that finally drives the hunter mad.

Gloria clears her throat. "So," she says. "I guess the last time we saw each other, I was threatening to kill you if you ever came back."

"Do you regret not doing it then?"

"No," she says. "I don't think I'm cut out for jail. I enjoy my freedom too much."

"Not even if it would have saved him?" I ask, glancing at the casket, now closed over half my life.

"When you put it that way..." she says. "I won't lie and say everyone here isn't thinking the same thing. We'd all happily make the trade if we could."

"You're as heartless as Mabel."

She smiles. "Just as you made me."

"It's impressive, really," I muse. "You were perfectly formed."

"By your hand."

"And his."

SELENA

She nods, her gaze straying to the casket too. "And his."

"I know it doesn't change anything. You've made up your mind like everyone else. But this one time, for what it's worth, I'm thinking the same as everyone else."

"Actually, that's worth a lot," she says, taking a breath and smoothing her hands down the front of her trim black skirt. "It makes me feel better about this, anyway."

Colt and Mabel join us, Mabel's gaze moving between me and Lo. "Hi, Gloria."

"Hi," Gloria says, licking her lips quickly and glancing at Colt. She smooths her skirt again, then makes a laugh that even I can tell is insincere. "Damn, this is awkward. I guess you don't like me very much."

"I have no feelings about you whatsoever," Mabel says.

"Oh," Gloria says. "I wouldn't blame you if you did. I mean, I bullied you in high school."

"You did what you were told," Mabel says. "I know that."

"Oh," Gloria says again, glancing at me this time. "I figured you hated me."

"People often overestimate the impact they have on others," Mabel says. "I never thought you had any feelings about me one way or the other."

"That's good," Colt says, smiling. "Because she never bore you any ill will, and since we're together, it's nice to see you don't have anything against her either. I want my sister and my lady to get along."

"Okay," Mabel says. "Is that what you wanted to tell me?"

"No," Gloria says, swallowing and glancing around. Finally, her gaze settles on me. "Um, so... Did you check up on me once I went to Cedar Crest?"

"No," I say, scowling at her. "Why would I? You'd served your purpose. Mabel just told you how insignificant you are to us."

"Okay," she says slowly. "Well, I had a baby. I put it up for adoption. It was an open adoption, but I didn't want to know anything about it. I don't even know the sex. I only know... It was probably a Dolce."

"What."

My voice is flat, with no inflection.

Gloria gulps. She isn't like Mabel. She's weak. She groveled and trembled and begged all the time. She has no dignity. No right to do what she's done. "I don't know for sure," she says quickly. "I only saw it once. It's just a guess."

"You had our baby," I say carefully. "And you didn't tell us?"

"Look, you fucking psychopath," Colt cuts in, his brows drawn into a fierce frown, his words a harsh growl. "You raped her. And before you start to spew your bullshit about how she was willing, we all know that's not true. I know it, she knows it, and you know it, even if you won't admit it. Hell, Mabel knows it, and she wasn't even in the state when it happened. Everyone knows what you are, Baron."

He stares me down, his smoky blue eyes dark with a fury so potent even I can identify it. If he thinks he'll intimidate me, though, he should know better.

I don't budge an inch. "What does that have to do with this?"

"It has everything to do with it," Colt says. "Your victim has no obligation to inform you of the consequences of your assault. So if you're going to get all bitchy and act like you had a right to know, save it. You never had a right to anything. You're lucky she's fucking speaking to you, let alone telling you this. So unless you're going to thank her for telling you, don't say another fucking word to her."

I think he might finally lose his temper after all these years and throw the first punch, but before I can make that happen, Ma comes stumbling over, a drink held aloft in one hand.

"Baron," she cries, and then her heel turns in the soft grass, and she lurches sideways, towards the casket. Her body knocks against it, and the hollow sound is like there's nothing inside at all. But I know there is, even if it's not Duke anymore. It starts to tip, and I lunge for it, grabbing the top end with both arms, wrestling for control. Colt darts forward and grabs the foot end, bringing it back into balance. We stare at each other along its length, neither of us speaking. My heart is beating harder than it does on my morning runs.

He could have let it fall.

After all we did, he could have let it fall, let the lid be knocked off and my brother's body roll facedown into the dirt. He could have laughed, said now he's where he belongs.

In his place, it's what I would have done.

But he just blinks those inscrutable eyes at me, a hidden message in their depths that I will never understand. Then he swallows and steps back.

Ma is on the ground, having fallen when the coffin moved. "Baron," she howls. "Look what you did! Threw me on the ground like trash. Your own mother!"

"Ma," I snap, grabbing her under the arms and hauling her to her feet. "Get yourself together. You're making a scene."

She throws herself into my arms, her body a deadweight around my neck as she clings on. "My special boy," she says. "You won't leave me, will you? You're all I have left."

"I can't deal with you right now."

"Don't leave me," she slurs. "He left me, just like your father. You won't do that, will you? Promise me!"

"Ma. I'm in the middle of something. Can you go sit down and wait for me?"

Ma stares up at me, her eyes wide. Then she lets out a loud cry. "You don't have time for your grieving mother?"

Colt is motioning for our grandmother, who comes hurrying over.

"Nonna," I say. "Can you get her inside?"

"But I need you," Ma wails. "I need my baby boy!"

I disentangle myself and shift her into Nonna's arms. "You got her?"

"I got her," she assures me, even as Mom clings to her neck, sagging toward the ground.

"Fine," Mom snaps. "Abandon me, just like your brother. You always put him first. As if I didn't give you both life! I gave you everything, and this is all the thanks I get?"

"No one has the strength to carry the burden of your grief," Nonna says to Ma. "We're all collapsing under the weight of our own. Now put some starch in those legs and stop acting like a baby, or I'll let you lie on the ground and throw a fit like one."

They stumble off together, Ma berating her mother-in-law now.

I turn back to the others. "When did this happen?"

"Damn," Colt says, shaking his head and watching my family depart. "So that's your mom. Explains a few things."

"Yeah, and yours is braindead, which explains you. So let's get back to business."

"It was a year ago," Gloria says, having collected herself in the few minutes since she spoke last. She looks like the cool queen we made her, hard as diamond and just as implacable. "I put the date of conception around Thanksgiving. Maybe that day in the library. It was before Colt, and after Rylan. Not long after, so he's an option too, if the pregnancy wasn't exactly 40 weeks."

"Five guys fucked you in the library."

She swallows, and something flickers across her face, but she lifts her chin and holds my gaze. "Cotton wore a condom. Gideon didn't cum. And DeShaun is Black, so unless it has none of his features at all, it's not his. Which leaves you and Duke."

A heavy silence stretches.

Finally, Mabel speaks for the first time. She's standing motionless, having not moved an inch since she came over. Her face is a mystery, her expression one that Duke might have solved, but I can't.

"Why are you telling us this?"

Gloria shrugs. "I just thought you might want to know. Now that he's gone... Of course I can't be sure it's his. There's no way to know, really. But... I don't how. I just do. Maybe you don't believe in intuition, but I know."

She can't know, though. No one can. That baby is mine as much as it is Duke's. Because biologically, we are the same person. One person.

I open my mouth to correct her, but then I see Colt's frown, the way he's glaring at me, like the close call with the casket never happened.

But it did happen.

He didn't have to do that, to save Duke's body its dignity. But he did.

SELENA

I give him a curt nod, then a deeper one to Gloria. "Thank you."

twenty-nine

Mabel Darling

Baron's busy making calls and searching things on his computer, so I wander the hallway of my old house like a ghost, with Seeley at my heels. Summer House is gone, so we have nowhere else to go but here, with the other broken pieces of our broken families.

I pause before stepping into his room, as if someone will stop me. As if I'll turn and see Royal and King watching, like they always watched in high school. Waiting.

But the wait is over. I've done the worst thing. They know what I'm capable of now.

I remember when King called me harmless, and I want to laugh and cry at the same time.

We both made mistakes.

I open his door, the door to the room that used to be mine. For one painful, half-second, I remember it as it was the first time I saw Duke's room, with his huge shoes kicked off haphazardly, a hoodie hanging on the back of a chair, a couple silk ties draped over the arms.

SELENA

But his room is neat, not a thing out of place, just like it is every day. The maid put anything he left back in order a long time ago. They didn't repurpose his room, though, and we've been sleeping here instead of in Baron's room. It's still his, with framed posters of football players and professional boxers on the wall, a championship ring in a shadow box from when they won the state championship one year. A crucifix hangs over the bed, his rosary hanging from Jesus's hand.

Seeley jumps onto the bed and lies down at the foot, like he's adopted the bed as his own already, and starts to clean himself.

Since I'm alone and Baron won't tell me I'm odd, I go to his closet, remembering how I hid in there for hours when my parents were fighting. I cut my name into the wall beside the door, before I ever cut myself just to feel, to make sure I was still alive, when I'd been floating out of my body for so long. Since Olive knew my name, I know they didn't replace that section of the wall before selling the house. Probably, they didn't even notice. Most people don't turn around inside a closet and look at the inside of the door or the wall beside it, especially not at the bottom.

I hit the light switch and step inside. My breath catches, and I slide down the back of the closet, just like I did all those years ago. In my mind, Colt was sitting with me, his back to the wall beside mine. Now that I see it, though, I remember how many times I lay in here alone, staring at the names, tracing my fingers over them.

I know I didn't imagine it, that he was here when I wrote my name, because he wrote his right beside it. We didn't put a plus sign between. Even as kids, we knew that's what you did for boyfriend-girlfriend. For a brother and sister, we didn't add anything between, just a space.

"MABEL" And a foot away, *"COLT."*

Except someone did see our names. They didn't replace the panel. They replaced my brother, scratched out Colt's name, carving a deep, angry X into the wall over the letters. And underneath, he replaced it with, *"+ DUKE."*

Tears sting my eyes, and I squeeze my lids closed so I won't see the wish he so fervently made for us to end up together.

After a minute, the closet feels claustrophobic, and I crawl out and stand again, my legs wobbly now. I think about leaving, about finding Baron and taking comfort in what remains of Duke. Instead, I find myself staring at his desk that sits directly across from the closet. Three photos sit there—a graduation photo, another of him and one of the Walton twins at prom, a third of their whole group crammed into the frame at Homecoming—all official, matted in the school frames they came in. A black leather folder with the Willow Heights crest embossed in gold on the front lies on his desk, his diploma behind the plastic window inside. His proud father is no longer here to frame it and hang it on the wall.

SELENA

That death is not on my hands, but I wonder, when Duke stood back and watched him burn, did he think of me? Is that why he didn't try to talk the others out of it, even though he loved his father and had a tender heart?

I pull open the drawers on the desk. The top one is full of condoms, along with two vibrators and a bottle of lube. I quickly shut it, but not before I glimpse the edge of a magazine under all of it.

The middle drawer is full of stuffed animals, all of them new, with the tags still on.

I'm not sure why I pause then. Maybe because I suspect he bought these for Olive, and Olive is the only thing that stopped Baron from avenging his brother. Even a man with no heart can understand that Duke's love makes her sacred.

I sink onto my knees, and it becomes something more than aimless wandering.

I lift each animal from the drawer carefully and set them on the edge of the desk in a row. Most are sloths, but there are two stuffed koala bears too. When the last one is arranged, I look into the bottom of the drawer, where only an old, faded and threadbare blanket remains. I lift it out reverently, spreading it out on the floor. In the corner, his initials are monogrammed in silk thread—DAD.

Tears blur my vision, and I snatch up the blanket and hold it to my hammering heart. If Baron finds the baby, I will wrap it in Duke's baby blanket, let it know his smell before it's gone. But because I'm selfish, I lift it to my face, inhaling it first, trying to find a trace of the boy I loved and hated so much. I can't find it, though. There's only the slightly musty odor of clothes left for several years in the bottom of a drawer.

I start to replace the animals, until we know. If there's really a baby, they can have them. For now, they belong to Duke. But I'm keeping the blanket either way.

I'm settling one into the back corner when I feel a lump under the velvet lining of the drawer. I press down on it, and it gives slightly, then rises when I let go. I take the animals out again and pull up the corner of the lining. It's been pressed tight around the edges, but underneath, a plain manilla folder is concealed. I peel back the lining and pull it out, my heart skipping and faltering. For a second, I just stand there with it unopened in my hands. I'm not sure I want to know what's inside, not sure if I have a right to know what he wanted to keep hidden.

But my curiosity wins, and I flip it open. The first picture is Colt's graduation picture, his cap tilted slightly, a cool look in his eyes like he's staring down the camera.

Odd.

I turn it over, and find a hundred more—not the posed graduation portrait, but everything else. Pictures cut from the yearbook, senior pictures in color, the other classes in black and white. Activity photos from the pages of the yearbook featuring clubs and sports.

A dozen photos of Colt on the field, stretching to make a catch or with a football tucked under one arm, during the two seasons he played before the Dolces ruined his football dreams.

At first, I think they're just high school friends of Duke's, but after a half dozen, the pattern becomes clear. My heart starts beating erratically as I flip through them faster.

My brother is in every single picture.

There are local newspaper clippings of the beating that took his memory and almost his life; printouts of the online school newspaper articles about it.

A handful of Polaroids of Colt showing off tattoos inside the tattoo parlor or in the parking lot outside. I quickly flip past one of my brother smiling into the camera with a look on his face I never wanted to see, showing off a piercing I never needed to know he has.

There are several dozen candid shots that must have been taken on phones and printed out—photos of Colt and Dixie, one of Colt and Gloria dancing at prom, another of Colt and Harper with their arms thrown around each other's shoulders, cheesing for the camera while Royal watches from the sidelines with a scowl on his face.

The photos span all five years that Colt spent in high school, even his freshman year, before the Dolces moved here. I could tell myself that they have a folder like this on all the Darlings, that he was stalking my brother to destroy him. But why is only Colt's folder here, and why is it hidden? Why is Dixie marked out with a permanent marker in some of the photos? Why not just keep an encrypted folder on a computer, like Baron would do?

I sink onto the edge of his desk, my head spinning. My mind goes back to the deep, angry cuts he made over my brother's name on the wall.

It didn't say MABEL + DUKE. His name was written under Colt's, before or after he carved away my brother's name, as if he could remove him from the equation.

I was never even part of the equation.

I stood alone on the left: MABEL.

A foot away,

COLT

+ DUKE

I clench my fists, dropping my head, my breaths hitching as I try to fit it all into place, rearrange the pieces to form a picture I didn't know existed. All along, I was trying to piece together the wrong puzzle.

What was real? What was my imagination, my desire—no, my *need*—to be special?

To be loved by someone who was capable of real love.

Now I'll never know. I'll be forever left wondering if, in the end, Duke won the final round. Because here I am, questioning my entire world, my reality, just like I did the first time.

I'm not crazy.

Maybe it wasn't about me at all. I picture Duke the first time he came to my house, trading barbs with my brother. I remember him wanting to go to my house later, saying it was to rub it in Colt's face. Now I'm not sure if he meant it the way I thought at the time. Now I see a million moments I missed. And I picture moments I didn't see at all—Duke sitting in the dark where I did so many times, not much more than a kid himself. I see him now as he must have been then, a fourteen-year-old boy filled with rage and confusion and guilt for feelings he couldn't understand or change, feelings that would never be acceptable in his family. I picture him cutting his name into the wall the way I did, the way Colt did, because it was the only way he could express what he wanted, what he wasn't allowed to want.

I'm still sitting there when the door opens, and my brother sticks his head in. "You okay?" he asks. "I think we're going to take off in the morning. Get back on the road where we belong. Should I say goodbye now?"

I stuff the photos into the folder before he can see. But after a second, I motion him over, and I shove it into his hands. "Did you know about this?"

He swallows and looks down at it, but he doesn't open it.

"Did you?" I press, my heart somehow breaking again, though it's already in smithereens.

He opens the folder slowly, as if he's reluctant to see what's inside. His thumb skims over the first picture, and he stares down at it, not looking up to answer.

"Colt?" I whisper, my throat tight.

"Yes, I fucking knew."

He slams the folder shut without looking at anything else and hurls it across the room. It crashes into the wall, and the pictures scatter, tumbling down across the floor.

"How?" I ask.

Colt rakes a hand through his hair. "I didn't know about... That," he says, gesturing to the mess before turning away, like he can't bear to see more than he already has.

"How'd you know?" I press.

He paces in front of the door a moment, one hand over the bottom of his face, the other planted on his hip. At last, he turns to me, his eyes steely and unflinching. "We fucked."

I nod slowly. "For how long?"

"What?" He blinks at me, then gives a quick shake of his head. "No. It was one time. Christ, Mabel. We fucked *once*."

"And then?"

"What do you mean, *and then?*" he demands, resuming his pacing, like he wants to run but won't let himself.

Colt didn't fail me like the others, but he thinks he did. To atone for his part in it, Dad covered up a murder for me, became an accomplice after the fact when he got rid of the body. Colt stays to face my questions, though I hold him blameless. He did what he could, and what he had to do, just like I did for him.

SELENA

"You like men too," I point out after a moment's silence.

He never told me that, but I don't watch men for nothing. I never brought it up because it didn't matter to me. But I noticed it the first time he brought Maverick over to hang out. The way they touched each other, as familiar as he was with our cousins, though he'd only known Maverick a few months. The different nature of those touches, almost possessive, strangely intimate—Maverick giving Colt's hip a little squeeze when he left the room, Colt's fingers ghosting over the back of Maverick's neck when he walked behind the couch. That made me remember just how many nights he spent away when things got bad, and how he talked about Maverick in a way he'd never talked about his friends before.

"It wasn't like that," Colt says, holding up a hand and stopping me from going too far down that path. "Duke was straight. He just wanted... Something extreme."

I swallow hard, my pulse hammering as I stare at the evidence strewn across the floor. "He loved you."

"What do you want me to say?" Colt asks, stopping and dropping his hands to his sides, his shoulders slumping in defeat. "That it's my fault? That he'd be alive if I could've loved him back and gotten him away from Baron? Maybe you're right. But I couldn't. Or wouldn't. I don't even fucking know anymore. Does it really even matter? He's gone, and yes, I fucking failed him. After what he did to me, and to you… Mom, Dad, our whole goddamn family was destroyed. I'm sorry I couldn't forgive him. I'm not a fucking saint like everyone else in this town."

"He tried to protect you," I whisper.

"Bullshit," Colt says flatly. "Don't try to rewrite history now that he's dead. He was there for all of it, just like his brothers. He enjoyed it. He doesn't get to be romanticized now."

"Do you want to tell Baron?"

Colt scowls. "Why would I do that?"

"To be honest about who he was, like you said. He didn't get to live his truth. Shouldn't he get to die in it?"

Colt thinks a minute. "If he wanted Baron to know, he would have told him," he says at last. "I think we should honor what he chose in life. I think that's how he'd want to be remembered. But none of us can really know. He was your boyfriend. You should do what you think is right for his memory."

I go to the mess and start picking up the pictures. Tears drip down my face, but I ignore them. I need to get this cleaned up before anyone sees. Colt's right. He left Baron with the image of him that he wanted him to have.

After a minute, Colt joins me, crouching to sweep the pictures back into a pile. When we're done, we stand facing each other in my childhood bedroom, the room where he came to find me hiding when our parents fought, where he sat with me in the closet, our backs pressed to the wall, both of us knowing he was the reason for all of it, blameless or not.

"Do you think that's why he was with me?" I ask. "I'm the closest he could get to you?"

"Maybe I was the closest he could get to you," Colt says. "He loved you first."

My throat tightens, and I think about what it must have been like for him after I left. Did he really love me that much? I didn't know he was capable. Colt says he was straight. Would he look for pieces of me in everyone, even a man, just to feel close to me for a moment?

"I think you're right," I say at last. "I don't think Baron needs to know."

He loved you first.

The grief hits me all at once, not like a tsunami but like a lightning strike. I go to my knees on Duke's bedroom floor, and Colt sinks to his knees beside me. He wraps his arms around me, and I fold into him. I let my tears drip onto his shirt, and I pretend I don't see his falling with mine, soaking the fabric in our mingled Darling guilt and grief.

When we're done, I tell Colt I'll burn the folder, and we go downstairs together. Everyone is still up, lingering after the memorial, though the guests have gone home. When I see Baron there, guilt twists inside me. He looks at us like he knows. Or maybe, like he knows that we know.

Not for the first time, I'm reminded of the way he insisted on burning himself to match his brother, and before that, of all the times they switched places on me, until I didn't know one from the other, right from wrong. Until I thought I was losing my mind.

They did that on purpose.

Like Colt said, Duke participated equally, reveled in our destruction, laughed as we screamed in agony. He wasn't innocent. Now he's paid.

And Baron has lost the only thing he ever truly loved.

I was always trying to figure out what it was, the way to hurt him, and now I know. There's no way to hurt him anymore.

In a sick way, one I never would have chosen, I've won the game.

It's over.

As I look around at the stricken faces left, though, there's no joy to be found in victory. Crystal sits on the floor between Devlin's feet, looking exhausted and puffy, while he rubs her shoulders. Beside his cousin, Preston sits on the couch, while Dolly sits on the floor next to Crystal, patting her leg and offering comforting words. At the end of the sectional, Eliza sits draped over King's lap next, murmuring to him and stroking his cheek. Harper is squeezed into the loveseat with Royal, both of them glassy-eyed with grief and alcohol but secure in each other. Baron sits alone in an armchair, an untouched drink in one hand.

In my pocket, I curl my fingers around the bottle I found at Christmas. I'll never use it, but I keep it as a reminder. Dahlia is real. I'm not crazy. Someone loved me, and not just the boy I bewitched, ensnared in my web, and wrapped up like a precious gift. It's what I wanted from the very first day he spoke to me, when I knew he truly saw me, saw that I was different and came closer instead of running away. That was when I knew that he was special. And now he's mine forever.

I shiver at the thought.

Gloria pats the sofa next to her, scooting down so Colt can join her. I watch my boyfriend watching her boyfriend move across the room to her. I watch him set his drink down with a little more force than necessary. He grabs me and drags me down on his lap, his grip on my hips bruising, as if he's punishing me for the crimes I haven't committed instead of the ones I have. The crime of being who I am instead of what he wants.

I promise myself that I will never punish him for doing the same.

I know that ultimately it doesn't matter. I will never really know. I can only trust his word as much as he trusts mine. Which is to say, not at all.

But I am not crazy. I will not let him make me think so. Even when I don't know what's real, I know that much.

And I know three things for sure.

We are both liars. We both have secrets. And neither of us will ever tell.

epilogue

Ten Years Later

"We got something special for you," I say, setting down our daughter's bags at the foot of the stairs. "Do you want to see now, or wait until your party this weekend?"

"Now, obviously," she says, rolling her eyes.

She's just started doing that, and every time it reminds me that she's growing up, that time is passing, each day another day without him in the world, each as impossible as the last. Next week will be the ten year anniversary, each year even more inconceivable than the days, that there can be life without him. That there can be even one person living under our roof who doesn't know the hollowness this world holds, who doesn't feel his absence.

"Since today's your actual birthday, we thought we'd have a celebration here at home," Mabel says, closing the door behind us. "Just us."

She pauses, a wistful look crossing her face, and I know she's remembering him too.

There should be one more person in our family, one more plate at the table when we cut the birthday cake.

SELENA

"Well, what's the big surprise?" the kid asks, impatient as ever.

I wonder who she got that from. I know there's no way to know for sure who her father is. We're both her father. That's what the DNA says. There's no difference between us. We're the same person. Sometimes I think about that. How I'm just as much him as I am myself. That makes me feel a little better somehow. To know he's as alive as I am.

A long time ago, though, before I saw her face the first time, I decided to believe that he was her father. We get to have our daughter now, the one he always wanted. I have this piece of him here with me, someone to take care of outside of myself, a way to honor him. I have her, and me.

And I have Mabel, the girl of my dreams and sometimes my nightmares, the only woman who never bores me, forever my addiction. She's an equation without a solution, a riddle with no answer. Even after ten years, there are parts of her I've never seen, doors in her mind that I can't access. But I will die trying.

"It's out back," Mabel says, leading the way. "We had it done while you were at camp."

The girl skips ahead, eager to see. For a second, she's all long limbs and long hair, and I see someone else, the ghost of another little girl, in our hallway.

Outside, she pulls up short, gaping in shock.

"You built a castle?" she shrieks, all childlike wonder now. "*For me?*"

Her words knock the breath out of me, and I'm glad she's too overcome with her own emotion to notice her parents. She launches herself off the back porch and hurtles towards it, diving inside. I hear doors opening and slamming, and then she's on the second floor, throwing open a window and waving, grinning ear to ear.

"I think she likes it," Mabel says. "Maybe it'll help her stay a kid a little longer."

It's not easy to impress a kid who has everything she's ever asked for, but we seem to have managed. I could never say no to her. Saying no to her is saying no to him, and I couldn't do that. Not after I failed him in life.

In all likelihood, we'd never have known about our daughter if he were here. They never would have told us. That thought always fills me with fury, but not as much as the fury at myself every time I catch myself thinking that if I had to choose, I would have chosen him instead. She would have been happy with her adoptive family, and we would have been happy with ours. I love her more than I thought myself capable, but if it came down to never knowing she existed and having my brother back, I would still always choose him.

In every lifetime, in every timeline, I would choose him. I hope he knew that at the end.

"I'm glad you're home for her birthday," Mabel says, taking a seat on the top step.

I join her. "I wouldn't miss it."

In truth, I've missed a lot of days. Never a birthday, but a lot of others. Becoming one of the world's youngest neurosurgeons doesn't happen without sacrifice. But family is the most important thing. It always comes first. So when they need me, I've made it happen, no matter the cost. Mabel has done the same, determined to give our kids the family she needed growing up.

We watch the girl find one of the doors and traipse along the suspension bridge.

"Careful," I call.

She finally finds the way out to the swings and drops down into one. The other one sways beside her, empty.

"Do you see it?" Mabel asks.

"What?"

"The other swing is moving," Mabel says. "It must be her imaginary friend."

I don't tell her that it's not imaginary. It's him. His ghost is always there beside her. He hovers, never far away. I know that even though I can't see him on the swing when it moves in the breeze, he's here. He's never really gone. He's beside us in the bed, making sure I never go too far when I wrap my fingers around Mabel's throat. He's in our son's eyes. And he's in me. He will always be in me, a part of me, maybe the biggest part. It doesn't really matter which one of us died, because we are both still here.

For two decades, we were lived apart, one person torn in two, split in half, forced to live in separate bodies. Now we live in one. Because I am him as much as I'm me, and he's me as much as I am. Like I promised Mabel all those years ago, the earth can't hold us. Nothing can separate us, not even death.

"Mom," Hemlock yells, leaning back and forward to make herself go higher with each pump of her legs. "Come swing with me!"

Mabel climbs to her feet and ambles over. I watch them swing together. I wonder if she's thinking about him, or about her own ghosts, her own childhood companion. As far as I know, she's never seen Dahlia again. But there's a lot I don't know.

I used to think I knew everything, had all the answers, could fix everything.

I used to want to see that light go out, the one that haunts me now, that's never far from my mind, whether I'm watching my family or standing over the operating table. Life is not something trivial, not something to be toyed and trifled with. It's not a game.

Watching a man die didn't make me powerful. It made me humble.

It took losing the game we were all playing to see that.

But sometimes I suspect Mabel played a little longer, a little smarter. That she was still playing when we thought it was over. I will probably always wonder. Because no matter what she says, I can never know what's inside her mind, can never open up her brain the way I do my patients and find the answers in black and white.

Did she plan it all?

She always played the long game. Was that her final move, her checkmate? Her final revenge, to take what I loved most in the world, the one thing that could break me more completely than I could ever break her? Is that why she didn't light the match when we were both inside—because she wanted me to live, to suffer, like Royal forced her to do?

I remember his words in that room so often.

"One of us is going to be next."

He knew. He foresaw it, even when I didn't.

He knew she'd win, even before she made her final move.

When she went to the basement that day and talked to Jane without us knowing, did they come up with it then? Can I trust her, even now, a decade after everything went wrong? Is she still playing, even now? Or did her plan go sideways, and it was always supposed to be me on the lawn that night? When she sent me back into the house for her cat, did she plan for me to never come out? All these years later, when I've given her a house and a family, every material possession she could want and the child she never thought she'd have, does she still wish it had been?

Those are the questions that keep me up at night, ones that can't be researched online. These days, she's the one more likely to be found online, slipping unknown into someone's server, extracting information like she extracts a carpet fiber from a crime scene to tie back to a criminal who thought they got away with it. She searches the way I used to, endlessly, fruitlessly. The network around the Black Widow Killer simply vanished one day, though, blown away like a spiderweb in the wind.

They never found her. As far as I know, no one has. But I wonder.

Even though Mabel is not the Black Widow Killer, they're linked in some mysterious way that transcends years of silence, like it did the first time. Sometimes I think it was a mistake to let her go out there alone with her. To trust her. I still wonder what they really said, if they hatched a plan that day, two spiders spinning an invisible web, an hourglass of venom measuring out the lives of their victims in drops of blood.

One day, Mabel could signal for her to return. She could decide that I've suffered enough, and it's time to let me join my brother at last.

I think, when it happens, I'll be ready. I hope I've made him proud.

Sometimes I wonder too, if Mabel is just waiting until our kids are grown, until it's just the two of us, before she'll unearth that body she disposed of and tie me to it. There's no statute of limitations on murder. Or on her memory. And if anyone can find forensic evidence a decade later, it's Dr. Mabel Dolce.

SELENA

It does no good to wonder, but I still do.

My phone buzzes in my pocket. I pull it out and read the text. Then I stand and call to the girls. "The nanny's almost back. Want to go in and have cake with Max?"

"Not yet," protests the little girl. "Please?"

"Don't you want to see your brother?" Mabel coaxes. "You haven't seen him in a week. He missed you."

"Ugh, boys ruin everything," Hemlock says, jumping out of the swing before it stops. "I wish I didn't have a brother."

"Don't ever say that again," I snap.

"Sorry," she mutters, stomping past me into the house.

"She's just overstimulated from camp," Mabel says, resting a hand on my arm. "She doesn't mean it."

"I know."

She gives me a sympathetic smile, then stands on tiptoes to plant a kiss on my chin. I wrap my arms around her, turning her so we can look at the castle in our backyard, under the sprawling oak.

"Look at us," she says. "Great kids, a beautiful home, our dream jobs. We really did it."

I squeeze her to me and rest my chin on top of her head. "Are you happy?"

Her body twitches, but then she relaxes back into me. "Yes. Are you?"

"As happy as I have any right to be."

"Good." She draws away and squeezes my hand before stepping past me into the house. "I'll set the table."

I stand for another moment, watching the swings slow to a stop. The late afternoon sun streams between the leaves of the oak overhead, forming visible rays. They land on the suspension bridge of the wooden castle, and for just one second, I think I see a shadow moving. But it's just the hot August breeze rustling the trees, and the old orange cat sunning himself on the wooden planks. No matter how hard I look, my brother is never there.

I stay another minute anyway, hoping for the impossible.

I know we can't go back, but part of me doesn't have to. It never left. Part of me died that summer, and part of me still lives there, trapped in the crumbling remains of our wonderland. When we went home, I sold off all the product, enough to fund several lifetimes of luxury. I never made another pearl, and eventually, newer, trendier street drugs popped up to replace it. But Alice is never too far, her opalescent hands reaching across the years, her ghostly voice whispering a reminder in my ear. Not everyone who goes down the rabbit hole finds their way out.

While one of us wandered alone in the wonderland we created together, the other was lost in the one Mabel did. One where we were gods, where we decided who lived and who died.

SELENA

Except we were never gods. We may have played god that summer, but we were always mortal. That's why we forgot the one rule you can never forget. When you play with fire, someone's going to get burned.

Inside, Max runs down the hall in his socks and launches himself into my arms. "Can I light the birthday candles?" he asks, wrapping his arms around my neck.

"When you're older," I tell him. "Let your mom do it this year."

He pouts and hops off me and into a chair, leaning up on one leg, scouting for the best piece even before the cake is cut. After we sing and eat cake, Hemlock is all smiles, her earlier outburst forgotten.

"Thanks for the castle," she says, wrapping her arms around me. "You're the best Daddy there ever was. I love you, Mom." She turns and hugs Mabel.

Mabel's eyes meet mine over our daughter's head, and she smiles her Mona Lisa smile, the one I still can't read after all these years. Again it reminds me of all that I don't know, all I will never know.

Most days, I think she's done, that she put away the board the same day I did, when I finally witnessed the moment I'd always wanted and realized the truth.

All that time, I thought I was the puppeteer pulling the strings, even for my brothers. That I was the mastermind behind the game. But even the king falls in chess.

Some days, I wonder if she's still on that board, the final piece standing alone—the queen.

Thank you so much for finishing the journey with me. I know it was a hard road, but I hope you found closure in the closure. If you can't quite let go of these characters yet, you can join my Enemy Readers group to get a second epilogue here:

https://landing.mailerlite.com/webforms/landing/j7n0a8

acknowledgments

A huge thanks to every reader who read all 17 books in this series, who stuck with me through all the ups and downs, breakups and makeups, and final, happy ending for each couple. I can't thank you enough!

A special shout-out to my patrons who help make this possible every month: Seren, Kat, Doreen, Courtney, Audriana, Ashley B, Haley, Jessica, Valarie, Dawn, Sarah, Marbelys, Crystal, Melissa, Tabitha, Nikki T, Samantha, Kelly, Rebecca, Shaz, Hayley, Ana, Mindy, Meredith, Kim, Michelle, Jasmine, Amy, Megan, Annalisse, LeAnna L, LeAnna V, Nicole, Breanne, Kellie, Terra, Ashley, Amanda, Susan, Nineette, Jessi, Deani, Mea, Livia, and Julie.

Made in the USA
Coppell, TX
19 January 2026